WITHDRAWN

ONE SUMMER IN ITALY

LILLY MIRREN

Black Lab Press

Copyright © 2019 by Lilly Mirren

All rights reserved.

No part of this book may be reproduced in any form or by any electronic or mechanical means, including information storage and retrieval systems, without written permission from the author, except for the use of brief quotations in a book review.

To my Dad. My rock.

❧ 1 ❧

APRIL 1996

SYDNEY

A kookaburra called in the distance, but the sound was soon replaced by the murmur of traffic. The bedroom was a study in browns and tans, with a king-sized bed, brown satin sheets, and a tan doona the centrepiece. An assortment of throw pillows formed a neat pile at the end of the bed beside a white blanket box, and a pair of long, black stiletto boots leaned lopsidedly on a plush, cream-coloured shag rug.

Sunlight peeked beneath the light brown blackout blinds and Nyreeda Houston's eyes blinked open as a slice of that light drifted across her face. She yawned and stretched both arms over her head, then swung her feet to the floor. Cold, white tiles met the soles of her feet and sent a shiver up her spine. She fished around beneath the bed for her Ugg boots, eyes still half-lidded, and slipped her feet into the cosy woollen slippers.

In the kitchen, Reeda cinched the belt of her dressing gown more tightly around her thin waist before standing on tiptoe to retrieve a large coffee mug from an overhead cupboard.

"Good morning," said Duncan.

She turned to him, the empty mug clasped between her hands. "'Morning."

"Did you sleep well?"

She nodded. "You?"

He grimaced. "The guest bed is a little hard...might see the physiotherapist today."

Reeda waited for the jug to boil, then filled the coffee plunger with scalding hot water. It made her uncomfortable, talking about her husband's sleeping habits. He was in the guest room, she in the master bedroom. She wasn't even sure when he'd begun to sleep there full-time, since he'd done it every now and then for at least two years. Ten months? Twelve?

It was hard to keep track. Especially given the fact that she'd spent the past eight months in Cabarita Beach renovating the inn she and her sisters inherited when Nan died.

"I'm sorry to hear that..." What else could she say? She didn't want him to move back into their bedroom. Space was what she needed. Though sometimes she thought perhaps he gave her too much space.

It was complicated.

Duncan poured himself a cup of coffee, then disappeared. He returned a minute later with the morning newspaper folded in one hand and sat at the dining table. Spreading the newspaper open in front of him, he sipped his coffee, one leg crossed over the other.

"Surgery today?" she asked. The tension between them

gave her a headache. Words helped to break the silence, but they didn't assuage the anguish she felt over everything unspoken between them.

He nodded with a grunt.

"Yes. I'd better get ready for work. I'll see you later."

Another nod, no eye contact. She exhaled a long breath as she padded back along the hallway. A large photograph of the two of them on their wedding day stared back at her from the end of the hall. She glared at it as she turned into the master bedroom.

What had become of their marriage?

They'd been so much in love. Two people with everything in common. They'd been sickening, according to everyone who knew them. Sickeningly, head over heels, in love.

And now, all that remained between them was awkward tension, polite silences, and avoidance pockmarked by yelling matches.

After showering and dressing in a grey skirt and matching suit jacket, Reeda ran a brush through her long, dark hair until it crackled. She grimaced at her reflection then turned to one side then the other as she smoothed her skirt with one hand. She couldn't hear any noise in the house and assumed her husband had already left for the hospital.

Duncan was a general surgeon; they'd met at the University of Technology Sydney. He was in his fourth year of a degree in medicine, she was in her first, studying interior design. He was handsome, sophisticated, and mysterious. The air of intrigue around the handsome surgeon continued throughout their relationship, which she now knew was simply a reluctance to talk. About anything.

Duncan preferred to keep things civil. To ignore conflict in the hopes it would dissolve of its own accord. He hated confrontations and would do whatever he could to avoid them.

She'd found his reticence more and more frustrating with every year of their marriage. Now, after ten years as husband and wife, she wanted to shake the words out of him. But even provoking him hadn't helped.

Halfway down the long hallway she stood in front of the guest bedroom doorway. It was ajar, so she tapped it with her fingertips. When it creaked open, she saw Duncan wasn't there. His bed was neatly made, as always, and his briefcase was gone from the place it generally occupied at the foot of the bed.

She inhaled a long slow breath, squeezing her eyes shut.

The door across from the guest room was shut. She turned the handle, leaned on its cool, white surface a moment, then pushed it open.

Yellow paint greeted her, along with the faint scent of plastic.

In one corner, a white cot stood alone, a sheet draped over the mobile that hung above the teddy bear sheets, giving it a haunted look. A yellow bean bag beside the cot was over-shadowed by an enormous teddy bear. Next to the bear, her rocking chair sat still, unmoving, a brown cushion in the place where she should be.

Both hands clenched together as one fist in front of her chest, her brow furrowed as her gaze swept the room. Everything was in its place. Each item ready for the baby that had never come.

She spun on her heel and marched away from the room, pain clenching in her gut.

GUM TREES RUSTLED WITH THE COOL BREATH OF WIND that sent dried, brown leaves scurrying along the footpath. A double-story red-brick building squatted, sturdy and bold beside a black square of bitumen. Cars dotted the parking lot, blocking the path of the leaves forcing them to cluster against the tyres, a smudge of autumn on cold rubber.

The double glass doors pushed open and Reeda hurried out. She tightened a red scarf around her neck, flicked her long, brown hair free, straightened her thin, black coat and stepped off the curb. Her black stockinged legs strode forward in a military rhythm.

A black folder beneath her arm shifted, almost dropped to the tarmac below, and she caught it at the last moment, shuffling the papers back into place. She was meeting a client and had put together a pitch she thought would pique his interest based on her initial research.

Summer had beat a quiet retreat a few days earlier and already the crisp morning air announced a new season. Autumn in Sydney swept in on a biting wind. Something her sisters wouldn't have to deal with at The Waratah Inn.

The inn stood on the shores of Cabarita Beach, along the state's northernmost coastline. No doubt they'd already been out for a surf before Kate threw together a gourmet breakfast for their guests and Bindi got to work on guest services and whatever administration needed doing. Still, Reeda loved winter in Sydney, the whistle of a slicing wind, pink cheeks and tightly wrapped coats and scarves.

Even so, she missed being there with them. Missed the warmth, the beachside lifestyle, the casual conversations with all three of them seated around a table in the breakfast nook, or over a hand of cards in the sitting room. Mima would serve them all mugs of hot chocolate, and Jack would snore in an armchair close by, a newspaper open in his lap.

She sighed as she unlocked her BMW sedan, frowned as she slid a fingertip over a new scratch along its sleek black door, then slipped into the leather seat.

Five fingers tapped out a rhythm on the leather steering wheel while she watched the building's entrance. Finally, the doors flew open and Karen Nguyen, her VP of Design, scurried from the building to the waiting car.

She opened the passenger door and dropped into the bucket seat with a huff.

"Phew, it's getting cold out there."

"Finally," replied Reeda, turning a key in the ignition.

"I hate the cold."

"It's my favourite time of year." Reeda grinned as the engine sprang to life.

"That's because you're a weirdo." Karen's nose wrinkled and she shivered, then reached for the heat controls on Reeda's dashboard.

Hot air blasted from the vents and Karen leaned back with a sigh. "Ready for the pitch?"

Reeda turned out of the parking lot and into traffic with a nod. "I think we've got a good chance of landing this contract. Tomoko Restaurants are a big client, if we can get them to sign up with us for this fit-out, we might be able to encourage them to do an update in all of their restaurants. It could be huge for us. I know we haven't really branched out into restaurants before now, but if it works out, we might have a new division on our hands."

Karen stared silently out the window for a few moments before responding. "It's good to have you back."

Reeda smiled her way, refocusing on the road as she pulled up at a set of stop lights. "Thanks, it's good to be back. And thank you again for taking care of everything while I was gone. You did an amazing job; it was almost as though I wasn't gone at all."

Karen smiled. "I'm glad. Happy to do it any time. It was great to get the chance to try out some leadership skills..."

"You might get another chance sooner than you think," murmured Reeda.

Karen arched an eyebrow. "Oh?"

"I've been thinking of taking a few days off. No big deal. Maybe longer...if you think you can handle it." She glanced at Karen, awaiting a response. If Karen could take on the responsibility of running the design firm, it would give Reeda the opportunity she needed to take care of some things.

To investigate something that'd been lingering in her thoughts lately more than anything else.

"Do you want to tell me what's going on?" asked Karen.

Reeda hesitated. She hadn't told anyone what she'd been planning. Should she say something now? It almost seemed as though if she spoke the words out loud, the whole thing would disappear like mist hit by the hot rays of a rising sun.

"I found out my grandfather wasn't my biological grandfather." She kept her eyes on the road, her knuckles whitening against the black steering wheel.

"Really? Wow."

"My biological grandfather died during the second world war; he was shot down somewhere over the ocean or something like that. Anyway, he was from Bathurst, and I think I'm going to take some time off to drive out there—see if I can find any family members still living."

"I get it, that makes sense. What if there's no one there?"

Reeda shook her head. "I don't know...I guess I'll drop it. But I have to try...I can't stop thinking about it. About him. Nan loved him, but he never came home from the war. So, she and Pop raised my dad together, even though he wasn't Pop's child."

"That's a lot to take in..."

Reeda laughed. "You're not kidding."

"How have your sisters taken it?"

Reeda shrugged. "They're fine, I guess. We're all in a bit of shock, still mourning Nan, trying to figure out how much Dad knew about it all...It's hard for me to believe Nan had this secret all her life and didn't tell anyone."

Skyscrapers loomed on both sides. The streets narrowed and traffic thickened. They pulled into an underground parking lot. Reeda's stiletto heels clacked across the concrete as they made their way to the lifts.

"So, I'll take the lead, but you jump in with anything you want to add to the discussion," she said.

Karen nodded. "Okay, will do."

On the twelfth floor, they stepped out of the lift and into a spacious reception area. A long, dark timber desk took up one wall, art covered another, and dark leather couches were dotted over a colourful floor rug.

The meeting went well. Mr. Ito, who'd named the restaurant chain after his wife, listened with interest to their pitch, asking questions every now and then. His wife, glossy, black hair swept over one shoulder, perfectly red lips, and sporting a svelte black suit, sat quietly, nodding every now and then in agreement.

Mr. Ito loved their ideas and offered them the contract before the meeting was over. Reeda was happy but couldn't muster the same level of excitement she felt emanating from Karen. Her employee fairly bounced across the room to talk over the details with their new client, and Reeda was glad to see Karen's confidence. She was a different woman from the graduate Reeda had hired five years earlier—strong, self-assured, and experienced. It warmed her heart.

"You gave a wonderful presentation," murmured Tomoko, leaning towards Reeda with a smile, hands clasped together on the table between them.

"Thank you. I'm so glad you like our ideas. I think it'll come together beautifully."

"I do too." Tomoko's voice was like velvet.

"Will you be overseeing the work?" asked Reeda.

Tomoko dipped her head. "I will. I believe you said that Karen will be my contact. Is that correct?"

Reeda nodded. "Yes, she's very good. I'm sure the two of you will get along great."

"Wonderful." Tomoko smoothed her already perfect hair away from her face. "I see you are married." She nodded in the direction of Reeda's ring finger.

Reeda twirled her ring with a twinge of sadness. She was, but for how much longer? "Yes, I'm married."

"Children?" asked Tomoko.

Karen joined them, gathering together the papers that had been spread across the table and pushing them into her briefcase.

The stab of pain to her gut didn't surprise her anymore. It was as familiar as breathing. "No, no children."

Karen glanced at Reeda, a flush in her cheeks, and her eyes filled with understanding and sympathy.

Tomoko continued, seeming oblivious to Reeda's discomfort. "They will come soon. Children are such a blessing."

Reeda pursed her lips. "Yes, they are. Do you have any?"

Tomoko's smile widened. "Yes, I have two. I can't imagine my life without them, it would be so empty."

Reeda's stomach twisted into a knot. She forced a curve to her lips. "I suppose we should be going. Thank you so much for meeting with us."

Karen hurried after her out of the room. Reeda glanced up and down the length of the hallway. Her stomach roiled.

"Bathroom...where's the bathroom?" she hissed.

Karen pointed. "I think I saw one down there."

By the time Reeda had stumbled into a stall, her stomach was in full revolt. She threw up until there was nothing left, then slumped against the sink to wash her face and rinse her mouth. Karen stood close by, her back to the wall, arms crossed.

"I'm sorry, Reeda," she said. "People can be really insensitive."

9

"She couldn't know," whispered Reeda, dabbing at her lips with a paper towel.

Her face in the mirror was pale with a yellow tinge. Her brown eyes were like coals in the snow. The contact lenses she wore suddenly made the whites of her eyes look irritated and red.

"Still...people don't realise what they're saying sometimes. I don't have kids and my life isn't empty. It's a ridiculous thing to say." Karen's voice wobbled with emotion. She reached out to pat Reeda's back. "Do you feel better?"

Reeda inhaled a slow breath. "I think so. There's been a lot going on lately, I haven't been myself."

"Maybe you need a bit more time off..." suggested Karen.

Reeda grinned as she tossed the napkin into the rubbish. "You'd like that, wouldn't you?"

She pushed out through the bathroom door with Karen close behind.

"No, it's not like that—I want you to feel better. You're stressed...and yes, I'm happy to take over and run things like I did while you were in Cabarita."

Reeda faced Karen and rested her hands on Karen's shoulders, looking her in the eye. "I'm really glad you were able to do that. You did an amazing job. You proved you're more than capable of running things, and I'm grateful for you."

Karen beamed. "So, does this mean I'm getting a raise?"

Reeda chuckled, turned on her heel and strode down the hallway.

"No, really...that sounded like the kind of thing a boss would say to an employee who's about to get a raise."

"We'll see," replied Reeda.

Karen trotted after her. "So, when you say we'll see...do you mean soon? Can I get an approximate number of weeks, months?"

THE ENGINE TICKED QUIETLY AS REEDA PULLED THE KEY out of the ignition. She sat a moment in her car, one hand pressed to her flat stomach.

She hadn't wanted to say anything—she didn't want to think about it at all—but why had she thrown up earlier? Did she have a stomach bug, or was it the poached egg she'd had for breakfast?

Or was it possible...?

Things between her and Duncan had been tense since she'd returned from Cabarita. She'd barely seen him, but they had spent some time together, gone out for dinner and returned home afterward for a romantic, candlelit drink together out on the patio. They'd spent the night together. Most of the time these days he slept in the guest room, but he hadn't that night. She'd hoped it might help things, but he'd barely been home since. That had been three weeks ago. Could she be pregnant?

It might be too much to hope for, but maybe a baby would fix things. They'd been so close once, before all the fertility issues. They'd loved each other, had fun together, laughed more than she'd thought possible. Perhaps they could get all of it back...if she was pregnant.

Or maybe it was already too late.

With a sigh she pushed the car door open and stepped out. A chill wind rushed through the parking lot and lifted the hair from the back of her neck, sending goosebumps over her skin.

She shivered and pushed both hands deep into her coat pockets, then hurried across the bitumen. Shoulders hunched, she walked the aisles in the chemist's. A helpful woman dressed in a white uniform kept glancing in her direction with a smile, but Reeda studiously avoided eye contact.

The last thing she wanted was to discuss her purchase or ask where to find what she was looking for. All she needed was to be left alone.

By the time she'd driven home and rushed into the master bathroom, she'd worked up such a sweat that she had to peel the coat from her back with a grimace. She tossed it out the door in the direction of the bed and it landed on the floor with a soft huff.

Reeda eyed the box in her hand. She didn't want to do this. Knew what the outcome would be, what it had been for years. Why did she think anything would be different this time?

She tugged the pregnancy test free and sat on the loo with resignation.

When she was done, she set the test on the sink to watch it. It was taking what seemed like an eternity, but gradually a blue line appeared. Her breath stuck in her throat and her eyes refused to blink.

No second line.

She wasn't pregnant.

Perhaps if she waited...

She stood there an interminably long time. No. She wasn't pregnant.

She swallowed the lump that'd formed in her throat and tossed the test into the rubbish bin. Then, flopped onto her bed with a groan.

Why did she continue to hope? It only ended in pain. This time the pain began in her gut and worked its way up to her chest as though it had fingers that clutched at her heart and squeezed until she couldn't breathe.

She blinked away the dampness from her eyes, refusing to cry. There had been so many tears shed over the emptiness inside her, she wouldn't spill more. Not today.

How did she keep going? How could she continue to care,

to move forward, to strive? What purpose was there to her career, her marriage, her life? The emptiness inside wanted to consume her and she let it as grief washed over her.

After a few minutes, she sucked in a deep breath, then padded down the hall to the empty nursery. She lowered herself into the bean bag, hunched over, and hugged her legs to her chest. Time passed as she sat there, still, waiting for something to happen. Anything. Her life was empty, she knew that now. She had everything most people wanted and spent their lives working for—a handsome husband, a big house, a successful business. But what if that husband didn't love her anymore, and the big house was empty? What then? She squeezed her eyes shut and pushed the thoughts from her mind.

When her eyes blinked open again hours later the house was bathed in gloom. As her eyes adjusted to the darkness, she found her body shaking with cold, her limbs stiff. Her neck was bent at an odd angle, and when she straightened it, she gasped with pain then massaged it with her fingertips.

She padded out to the postbox to check for mail. A dozen black shadows fluttered by, the cries of the bats slicing through the still night air. There were only a few bills in the postbox, along with a large brown envelope, one edge curved and squashed. Curiosity piqued, she held it up in the dim light and recognised her sister Kate's handwriting. She tore it open as she returned to the house.

Inside, she sat at the dining table and poured the contents of the envelope out onto the table. Three envelopes, flaps carefully slit open, lay on the table. Each was yellowed with age, and an unfamiliar neat script showed they were addressed to Edith Watson—Nan!

In contrast, a single piece of paper, brilliantly white, lay half folded on top of the pile. She opened it and read.

· · ·

Dear Reeda,

I found these letters in some of Nan's things up in the attic. I'd shoved the box in the storage space under the staircase during renovations and forgot about it.

They were written by Charlie, to Nan, when he was a kid and while he was away at war. I thought you might find them interesting. I certainly did.

Hope you are going well. Everything here is good, apart from a small issue with Cocoa the possum and her newly discovered motherhood that may have resulted in a rather nasty scratch to my arm.

Never mind, we've made up and are as good friends as ever. Still, I will be more astute regarding the way I touch her for at least a few months and be sure to give her the personal space she needs.

With love,

Kate xo

Reeda smiled, imagining Cocoa with Kate. That possum had Kate wrapped around her little paw. Her eyes narrowed and she tugged a letter, with care, from within one of the aged envelopes.

It began with:

My dearest Edie...

And finished with:

All my love, Charlie.

Reeda shook her head, her eyes wide. Perhaps the letters would answer some of her questions. She carried the letters to her room and lowered herself onto the neatly made bed.

Nan's small, timber box perched on the bedside table. Its etched sides, darkened by age and in need of a coat of oil, gleamed in the dim light. She tugged it into her lap and stared at the outline of a horse's head on the lid. When she opened it, she ran a fingertip over the ragged, green fabric cover of a book. A journal. Nan's journal.

When Nan died, Reeda's sister, Kate, had discovered this box of journals beneath Nan's bed while looking for photographs to use at the funeral service. She'd told Reeda about Charlie Jackson, Nan's first love, then gave the box of journals to Reeda when she left Cabarita Beach to fly back to Sydney after they finished renovating Nan's Waratah Inn— the legacy she'd left her three granddaughters.

Reeda had been reading the first journal the previous night before bed and hadn't put it away. She fingered its tattered cover.

The sound of the garage door whirring shut caught her ear. Duncan was home. She shuffled the envelopes into a neat pile and pushed them between the last page of Nan's journal and the hard cover. Still tipping her head slowly from one side to the other, working out the stiffness in her neck, she glanced at her watch. Midnight. Duncan was getting home later and later all the time. What was he doing so late at night? He was a surgeon, so there were times he was called in for emergency surgery. But these days he was staying late at the office every night. She knew there weren't that many emergencies he couldn't share with the rest of his team.

Was he having an affair?

Even as the thought crossed her mind, she pushed it aside. It was something she'd never believed possible, but now she didn't know. Didn't feel like she knew him at all anymore. Still, she didn't have the strength to care, to be angry or ask questions. Not anymore.

What did it matter? She'd already lost him.

The sound of the guest shower echoed down the hall. With slow movements she stood to her feet and shuffled across the room. One glance revealed light sneaking out from beneath the guest bedroom door. She studied it a moment, her cheeks drawn, lips pursed. She wanted to tell him about the pregnancy test, about throwing up, and the things her client had said. Then again, she didn't want to see the look in his eyes when she spoke the words, "not pregnant".

They'd end up arguing, they always did. He didn't understand why she couldn't move on, couldn't let go of her dream for a child of her own. They could build a life together, just the two of them, couldn't they? Then he'd throw his hands up in the air and switch off, tell her he was tired and didn't have the energy. He never had the energy anymore. Didn't seem to want to speak to her about anything at all. He gave everything he had, his strength, compassion, smiles, all of it to his patients. He saved none of it for her.

Reeda turned away and headed for the master suite. She slumped onto the bed, reached for Nan's journal, and opened it to the last page, then pulled out the letter she'd began to read from Charlie. It was dated August 1939, and was written in a stilted, childish hand. Nan must have been only fourteen years old at the time. From Nan's journal, she'd guessed Charlie must've been at least two years older than her grandmother.

The letter opened with a single line: *The first time I knew I loved you was at your house. You'd been out horse riding, as usual. I was going shooting with Bobby. You wore a pink ribbon in your hair.*

2

JULY 1935

BATHURST

Grey gloom filtered through the square front window. The view to the street through the panes was frosted thick with ice on the inside of the glass. It was like looking through the bottom of a soda bottle. Charlie Jackson stepped closer, leaning against the three-seater couch and tapped the glass with one finger, exhaling a long, warm breath. A puff of white ballooned in the air.

He shivered.

"Don't forget to bring tea back with you tomorrow," called Mum from the kitchen.

He nodded. "I won't forget."

Why would he forget? She'd only asked him three times already that morning.

Rabbit again for tea tomorrow night.

Would it be rabbit stew, or some other concoction with

whatever his mother could find in the cupboard? She loved to make meals from the game he and Dad shot; it saved her spending more at the butcher and Mum was always one to save where she could. She said a penny saved was a penny earned, that she'd grown up poor and knew what it was to go hungry. She didn't want that for him or his sister.

Not that Dad went shooting much these days. It was usually Charlie and his best friend Bobby who rode their bicycles out past Bobby's farm, or to their favourite camp near Peel, while Dad worked at the office. His father spent so much time at the office these days, Charlie barely saw him. He missed their times together. Though he knew how important it was for Dad to do his work, how much people around Bathurst appreciated and respected him.

He pressed the bottom of his fist to the glass pane, feeling the ice melt slowly beneath his hand then rubbed a circle with the sleeve of his coat on the window, letting the morning light shine through. It was a dull, watery kind of light, the kind that didn't warm the body or soul. He peered out and spied the milko's cart in the distance. The old Clydesdale, its eyes shielded by blinkers, plodded along the side of the road, pulling the cart slowly and steadily behind it.

The milko was nowhere in sight. Then Charlie spotted him, standing on the back step of the cart, shielded by a dozen tall, shining cream cans. One of the neighbour's children emerged through a rickety front gate and onto the street.

"Mum! Milko's here," called Charlie over his shoulder, without taking his eyes off the horse.

Clydesdales were a thing of beauty. He couldn't help admiring the way they always did as they were asked, never shied away from a loud noise or unexpected sight, their large hooves moving forward in a steady rhythm, feathered and round.

A tap on his shoulder made him spin and Mum was there, holding a quart billy between her hands, a dish cloth slung over her shoulder and a floral print apron tied neatly around her slim waist. Her shining, brown hair was pulled back into a neat chignon at the base of her neck and her cheeks were ruddy from the cold.

She smiled. "Here you go."

He grinned, grabbed the billy, and headed for the front door. A few long strides and he was at the gate, just as the cart reached the house. The horse stopped without prompting, then stood waiting patiently.

"Mornin' Charlie, how ya going on this fine morning?" asked Sam Jones with a sparkle in his eye. He wiped a hand on his worn trousers and tugged his collar a little higher under his pale chin.

"Good thanks, Mr. Jones."

"Bit of a chill in the air today."

Charlie nodded and passed Sam his billy. Sam held a long-handled steel dipper in one hand. He sank the dipper into the nearest cream can and pulled it out, filled and dripping with the creamy liquid. Each time he pulled the dipper from the can, the level in Charlie's billy rose.

His stomach growled and he ran his tongue over his lips as he eyed the yellow cream that lingered around the top of the can.

"Ah the cream's the best part, don't you reckon?" Sam's eyes twinkled. "Was a time no one drank the milk, that was given to the pigs. All anyone wanted was the cream."

Sam handed it back to him. "Tell your mum I said hello," he said. "And your dad as well, of course."

Everyone knew Sam had a thing for Charlie's mum when they were both young. Charlie had heard Mrs. Miller next door say as much when he was playing with Danny Miller and wasn't supposed to be listening in on her conversation. That was when Monique Jackson had been the most beautiful woman in Bathurst, at least that was what they'd said, and Dad said it often enough as well so it must be true.

He nodded. "Thanks, Mr. Jones."

The walk back to the house was much more sedate, as he worked hard to stop any spills. Fresh, creamy milk in his porridge was his favourite breakfast, and a small cup to drink in greedy gulps if he was lucky.

He split wood in the back yard while Mum made the porridge with lashings of milk and brown sugar. Inside, the house smelled warm and good, and he sat at the table, his nose red with the cold. He could see his nose, if he crossed his eyes just a little and squinted hard enough, and the end of it looked like a cherry. He touched it with his fingers and found them to be as cold as his nose.

Mum pushed a bowl of porridge in front of him, and he grinned, then steepled his hands together over the bowl, feeling the heat of it warm them. He studied it with half-shut hungry eyes as Dad said grace, then pushed a spoon into its creamy centre.

"Charles is going shooting with Bobby today. He promised me rabbit for tea tomorrow night," said Mum.

Dad's eyebrows arched for a moment, then pushed back low again like caterpillars on their way down the garden path. He slurped up a mouthful of porridge, then washed it down with hot tea.

"And I've got that Bible study meeting with the other women from the Baptist church this evening. Will you be home?" His mother waited, her spoon lying beside her bowl.

Dad nodded. He was a man of few words. But when he spoke, he chose those words carefully and everyone made sure to listen. Charlie wished he'd say more sometimes, but Mum told him Dad had a lot of thoughts swirling around in his head, and responsibilities that Charlie couldn't understand yet.

He reckoned she was right, but still, he ached for a connection with his father. An exchange of words that were his, and no one else's. A shared understanding, a joke, a nickname. Bobby didn't have a nickname either, though his Dad called him Bob. Charlie told Bobby that counted, since his real name was Robert.

With breakfast done, Charlie rolled his bicycle out of the garden shed. He tugged a wool cap over his blond curls and slung a Lithgow .22 calibre rifle over one shoulder, the strap across his chest. When he patted his pocket, the cold metal of the bullets scraped against one another.

On the back of the bike sat an old canvas tarp and a sleeping bag, tied down with a thin rope, along with a billy and a thick slice of bread he'd cut himself and wrapped in waxed paper. With a satisfied smile, he climbed onto the bicycle and pushed down hard on one pedal, propelling the bike forward.

The chill wind bit at his cheeks, creeping down his collar and slicing into his bare hands as they gripped hard on the handlebars. On his head, the woollen balaclava Mum had knitted him the previous winter didn't stop the frigid air from numbing his skin. His legs pumped up and down, faster and faster as he made his way along the street, then turned the corner to head into the centre of Bathurst.

Cheshire Creek at Peel was a twelve-mile ride. He'd have to stop every now and then to blow on his hands before they made it that far. But he and Bobby had done it plenty of times before, and at twelve years of age they could do it alone now. He felt like a man, rifle over his shoulder, setting out to bring home meat for tea. Dad told him he was a man the day he shot his first roo. But roos were hard to come by and too heavy to carry home. Besides, fox and rabbit skins brought in more from the skin merchant. He was almost salivating over what he and Bobby could buy once they turned in those skins.

Fruit tingles, Marella Jubes, or maybe a packet of Fantales, and of course the latest dime mystery. He and Bobby had been dying to buy one, but Mum said they were a waste of money. They'd sit under the peach trees over by the creek at Bobby's house, read the mysteries and guess over whodunnit. They'd unwrap each Fantale, one by one, scan the wrappings to find out all about some movie star or other, and then eat the delicious treats together while they stared at the sky and talked about all the things they'd do when summer finally came; when it would be so hot they'd have to wipe the sweat from the hard timber seats at school so they didn't stick to them.

His breath marked his trail like smoke from a chimney as he breathed deep and blew it out in puffs. He passed the Acropol Café, then stood up on the pedals to make his way down William Street. The centre of the road was paved with tar, but on each side, there was a wide swathe of dirt and gravel. Horses pulled carts or parked in the gravel, and a smattering of cars puttered along the paved centre.

He ducked around a lamp standard at the intersection and glanced at the Cobb and Co Coach Depot before turning down Keppel Street. There was one place on Bentinck Street he always liked to stop (his father had taken him there once), and he pulled up his bike to stare into the farrier's yard through the large open gateway.

Outside, Clydesdales were lined up, ropes tied to posts, necks slack and one hind hoof tipped forward. Relaxed, they chewed on mouthfuls of hay or oats. Inside, a large cast-iron forge glowered with heat.

A bay horse with a long black mane was tied close to the forge. A farrier filed down one of the horse's hooves, the leg held tight between his thighs. He used a pair of long, steel tongs to pull a half circle of steel from the hot bed of coals. He set it on an anvil and lightly tapped it a minute, filing rough edges with deft swipes. Then, with the horse's hoof again between his knees, he pushed the hot shoe into place, smoke curling into the air. He removed it a moment and plunged it into a bucket of water, then returned it to the upturned hoof and nailed it into place.

Charlie watched with wide eyes. He never could get enough of those horses. This one didn't move. It stood, quiet and patient, waiting for the farrier to finish. A long forelock obscured its vision, and soft feathery hair covered each hoof.

The farrier let the foot down and reached for the tongs to begin work on the next shoe.

Wishing he could stay and watch the farrier work, Charlie inhaled a deep breath then set off again on his bike. He headed out of town to where the Watson family peach orchard perched on the banks of a small, winding creek. He and Bobby had been firm friends ever since Charlie left a large frog in their teacher's desk in year two at the local school.

Bobby followed up Charlie's prank with a sheep's tail shoved beneath the staff room floorboards in the middle of summer until, much to the boys' delight, all the teachers abandoned the room, handkerchiefs pressed to their noses, and spent their lunch break out beneath the single wattle tree that shaded the school yard from the scorching sun. Sensing kindred spirits, Charlie and Bobby had joined forces from then on.

He pedalled past a horse and cart that was stopped still on the side of the road in the dust and dirt. Two men stood behind the cart holding long-handled, square-mouth shovels. They scooped up horse manure in one swift movement and deposited it into the back of the cart. He offered the men a wave and one of them nodded in his direction.

People in Bathurst knew who he was. They knew his father, and that was as good as knowing him to anyone that mattered. He was the Jackson boy, the son of Clive Jackson— the solicitor, whom everyone admired so much. His chest swelled at the thought of the way the men tipped their hats to his father whenever the two of them walked through town together.

Before long, he saw the Watsons' orchard to his left. The flat grasslands surrounding the orchard were bleached pale by the sun. Peach trees stood bare, like scarecrows guarding a wasteland, their thin, reddish-brown branches reaching skyward.

He turned the bike onto the long driveway, then stood again in the pedals to push hard up the gentle incline to where the house sat, serene and dark, with shuttered eyes atop the small rise.

A pack of dogs ran out at him, barking and yapping, as their tails wagged his way in recognition. He reached down to pet the head of a black and white one, then slid from his bike seat to push it the rest of the way to the house.

Before he reached it, the screen door flapped open, then clanged shut behind Bobby, who stood with his hands on his hips, a wide grin splitting his face.

"Took you long enough."

Charlie laughed. "Get over it."

The pounding of hooves made them both swing their heads. Bobby's sister, Edie, rode into view on her bay whaler. The horse's coat was dark with sweat around the saddle rug. Edie reined the animal to a stop.

"Hi, Edie," said Charlie, his throat suddenly tight.

She smiled, revealing straight white teeth with a gap

where one eye tooth was still growing in. Her blue eyes fixed on his and a little shiver ran down his spine.

"Hi Charlie, where are you two going?" She slid from the horse's back and threaded the reins over his head.

While she and Bobby argued about whether he was allowed to go shooting or not, and what their mum would have to say about it, Charlie studied her through half-lidded eyes. He didn't want her to see him watching, but he couldn't stop looking.

Charlie swallowed. "See you tomorrow."

Edie nodded. "See you then, Charlie."

He pushed a smile onto his face. Then he swung a leg over his bike seat and pushed, willing himself not to fall and land on his rear end in the dirt in front of Edie Watson.

The two boys pedalled down the driveway together.

"Why are your cheeks so red?" asked Bobby, his brows knitting together.

"Because it's cold, you simpleton." Charlie's cheeks blazed hotter.

Satisfied with his response, Bobby turned his attention to the road. "Bet I can beat you to Peel," he cried.

Charlie grinned and stood tall on his pedals to push down as hard as he could with each pump of his legs. "You can try!"

❧

THE SOUND OF THE WHISTLE ECHOED ALONG THE GULLY and when he tugged it from his mouth, Charlie grinned at Bobby. They sat at the base of some gum trees on one side of the gully, facing down to where the water would've trickled by in summer. It was dry now and a pea-soup fog hung low over the hills on either side. Only the lowest point of the valley was clear, and Charlie watched it with eager eyes, waiting.

He'd blown the whistle, the sound like the call of a distressed rabbit. Now all they had to do was wait.

He got a thrill from whistling up foxes. The animals were as quiet as they were crafty and fooling them wasn't something just anyone could do. He'd figured it out pretty well. Though the last time he did it the fox had run along the bottom of the gully behind a fallen log, circled around behind him and surprised him. He'd seen it at the last moment and swung his rifle around to take aim, but the movement sent the fox running and he didn't shoot anything other than a scrawny rabbit that day.

He blew the whistle again, then shoved it into his pocket, took aim at the bottom of the gully with his rifle and let his eyes rove up and down its length.

After a while he caught sight of movement down amongst the sticks and debris left behind in the last rainfall.

A fox poked its head up, both front paws resting on the top of one old, grey log. He didn't dare move other than to pan the scope as he followed the fox pattering along the top of the log.

When the shot rang out, the fox fell before the sound of it reverberated through the valley. Bobby issued a quiet whoop, and the two boys hustled down the gully to claim their prize.

On the way back to camp, they stopped by a rabbit warren they'd found earlier to check their traps. Blackberry briars hung low over the entrances to the warren, and the traps shone dull in the foggy light. They found two rabbits there, unhitched them from the traps, slung them over their shoulders along with the four others they'd shot as well as the fox, and continued on.

When they reached camp, the first thing Bobby did was build a fire. Charlie cleared the ground of sticks and rocks for them to sleep on. Then he tied the rabbits and the fox together with a rope.

He squinted up at a young snow gum beside their camp, its branches stretching out through the wisps of smoke that curled from the fire. Then he strung the rabbits together and threw the rope holding them over one stout branch, pulling until the carcasses all hung high in the air.

"Hungry?" asked Bobby.

Charlie grunted. "Starving."

"I've got a can of beans."

"I brought bread," replied Charlie, tying the rope into place.

"Perfect."

They sat on a hollowed-out log together and ate. Charlie scanned the hills, always on the lookout for rabbits, though they'd scored themselves a half dozen already.

He remembered the way he'd felt when Edie Watson looked at him with those big blue eyes. His stomach squirmed. He should've thought of something better to say than, "See you tomorrow". Something that would've made her smile. He loved to see her smile; it gave him a warm feeling in his chest.

When they were finished eating, he built up the fire and they sat together, staring into the popping and crackling flames until late. Bobby set up their sleeping bags on a piece of canvas on the hard ground, and the two of them silently added more wood to the fire before climbing into their bags.

"You're my best friend," Bobby told him as the dark night settled over them.

"You're mine too."

"Do you ever think about what you want to do when you grow up?" asked Bobby.

Charlie stared into the fog, wishing he could see the stars. It sucked all the joy out of camping, this cold gloom.

"I don't know. Maybe I'll be a farrier. Although Dad says I can't do that. He wants me to go to University in Sydney."

"Lucky you." Bobby's words were followed by silence.

"You can come with me," suggested Charlie. "It'll be great. I won't mind going so much if you're there too."

Bobby huffed. "I can't. Dad wants me to stay on the property—take care of things. Besides, we don't have the kind of money..."

That you have, Charlie thought. The unfinished sentence hung between them.

"I don't see why we can't just do what we want to do with our lives." Irritation buzzed in Charlie's chest. "Why do parents always want to tell us what to do?"

"Just the way it is, I reckon."

Charlie didn't like things being the way they were. Maybe he'd want to go to University when the time came, maybe he wouldn't. But he should be able to make the choice himself. He couldn't imagine going so far away without Mum or Dad, or Bobby. And the thought of not seeing Edie whenever he wanted put an ache in his gut. Though, he couldn't tell that to Bobby. His friend wouldn't understand.

"I don't want to go without you, that's all," he said.

Bobby inhaled a deep breath. "Yeah. Me neither."

Charlie shivered. It'd be cold that night. Cold enough to freeze the strung-up game solid. He hated the cold. One day he was going to live somewhere hot. Somewhere there was a beach, with sand that could tickle his toes, and waves he could ride to shore on his stomach. He'd never been to a beach, but Mum had told him about the ones she'd visited in Sydney, and how those waves could lift you up and carry you. She'd promised to take him there one day.

"And after uni, let's move north," murmured Charlie.

"North?" asked Bobby, with a wide yawn.

"Somewhere with a nice beach and sunshine all year long."

"Mmmm. I'd like to swim in the ocean."

"What do you think it's like?" asked Charlie, leaning on one elbow to face his friend.

Bobby's nose wrinkled. "I think it's warm."

"Too right."

Charlie wriggled down into his sleeping bag, pulled the other half of the canvas over the top of him and Bobby, and linked his hands together behind his head.

Before long, he knew the fire would die down, his head would crackle whenever he moved on his frozen pillow in the middle of the frost-bitten night, and the clothes he'd shoved down into the waterproof sack he was sleeping in wouldn't be enough to keep the cold at bay.

When he was grown and could do what he liked, he'd live somewhere he could camp under the stars without shivering. But he couldn't leave Mum or Dad, they'd have to come too. He knew Mum wouldn't mind. She'd told him she loved the beach, loved walking through the sand and dipping her toes in the warm water.

That was what he'd do—he'd find somewhere warm with beautiful, golden beaches that reached from one end of the world to the other, and he'd pack up Mum, Dad, and his sister Sylvia, and they'd all move to paradise together. He could work hard to provide for the family, maybe as a bricky or a carpenter, and they'd have a happy life together. And Bobby could come too, if he wanted; maybe Edie as well.

3

APRIL 1996

SYDNEY

Leaves scuttled past along the footpath. Overhead, a magpie called a lullaby as the sun dipped beyond the horizon of tall, dark buildings. The noise of traffic, stopping, starting, and humming homeward sifted through the cool air and Reeda tugged her coat tighter around her body.

A young woman strode towards her, head down, a labrador trotting at her side. Reeda watched the dog, its tongue lolling, as it approached. Her lips pulled into a smile and she met the woman's gaze.

"Beautiful dog."

The woman grinned. "Thank you." She stopped and commanded the animal to sit.

The labrador sat obediently in front of Reeda and she reached out a hand to stroke its soft, chocolate coloured fur.

"Wow, that was impressive." Reeda chuckled. "We had a dog when I was a kid, and it never sat on command like that. I had to be holding a dog treat in my hand before it would listen."

The woman laughed. "We've been practicing."

As the woman and her dog disappeared down the footpath Reeda glanced away from them, her gaze sweeping over the looming hospital, now dark in the fading light. She inhaled a sharp breath then hurried towards it, slipping between the glass doors as they swished open.

Duncan's office was on the third floor. She'd been there enough times that most of the staff knew who she was, but she didn't want to see them tonight. Nerves fluttered in her stomach. Would he be happy or irritated that she'd chosen to call on him without warning? How had it come to this? Five years ago, she could've stopped in at any time to see him and if he was at his desk, he'd look up over the top of his glasses as she walked in, flashing that grin of his that lit up his blue eyes and pushed dimples into his cheeks.

At his office door she hesitated, drew a deep breath, and squeezed her eyes shut. She had to try to fight for her marriage. Likely it was already beyond repair, but if she didn't try, she'd never know.

She raised a fist and knocked.

"Come in."

As she pushed the door open, Duncan's eyes narrowed. He slid the glasses from his face and set them on the desk.

"Reeda?"

She smiled. "I thought I'd surprise you."

He leaned back in his chair and linked his hands behind his head. "You did."

"Can I come in?"

He waved a hand towards an empty chair. "Please."

He used to greet her with a kiss. Her stomach tightened into a knot.

She sat, fidgeting with her hair. "Have you had a good day?"

His eyebrows shot upward, then pushed back down again. "It was okay, I suppose. Four surgeries, all successful."

"That's good," she replied. "Do you think you'd have time to grab some tea?"

His eyes narrowed, and he shot a quick glance at his watch. "It's still early...I have a lot of paperwork to get through."

The knot in her gut twisted tighter still. "Of course."

"But I suppose it can wait until tomorrow."

She smiled. "Wonderful."

ॐ

THE RESTAURANT WAS DIMLY LIT. TEA CANDLES MARKED each small, square table. Couples leaned towards each other, some hands linked, each involved in hushed conversations interrupted by quiet bursts of laughter. Stone-washed jeans were folded beneath tables and crossed feet sported Doc Marten boots in various shades. Reeda smoothed the skirt of her grey dress and tapped one stiletto heel against the hardwood floor. Across from her, Duncan studiously avoided her gaze, clad in blue scrubs, every-which-way curls piled on his head.

Reeda stared at the menu in her hands. It was awkward, this silence between them, but they had to face it, had to work through whatever it was between them.

And if things ended, what then? She'd never considered her life as a single woman again, not since he'd proposed to her all those years ago. That was it, she'd thought, she was finished with the dating scene and would never be alone again.

And now this. This quiet loneliness. It singed her nerves like a flame held to a square of paper.

"I think I'll order the crumbed shark bites," said Duncan, suddenly setting his menu on the table between them. He crossed his arms over his chest.

She smiled. "That sounds delicious. I'm going to get the chicken skewers." Less calories, and she'd eaten the dish before. It was tasty and light. If she was going to rock the off-the-shoulder dress she'd been eying at Debbie Dunston's, a boutique store in Newtown, she'd have to watch what she ate.

He nodded, still not smiling.

She sighed. "I thought I might take a little trip..."

His brows pressed low over narrowed eyes. "Another trip?"

"Just a few days, not long. I want to look into something."

She hadn't told him about her grandfather and the things she and her sisters had discovered during her time at The Waratah Inn with them. He'd been so morose, so curt with her. Maybe he was upset she'd already been gone so long, or it could've simply been the ongoing tension between them. Bringing up the subject seemed too much. Especially when they were hardly able to hold a civil conversation on any subject.

"I see..." He stared at the menu, fidgeting with the edge of it.

It was impossible to talk to him without him getting upset these days. Why couldn't he listen and hear what she was trying to say? "I won't go if you don't want me to."

He shrugged. "Do what you like."

She resisted the urge to roll her eyes. He could be such a child.

"We have Jennifer and David's baby shower tomorrow," she said.

His gaze fixed on hers, eyes dark. "What?"

"You remember...we talked about it a few days ago."

He ran one hand through his hair, sending curls flying. "I've got too much to do."

"It's Saturday."

"I've got to catch up on paperwork."

Her throat ached. "Fine, I'll give them your apologies."

"No, don't worry about it, I'll come." He shook his head and muttered, "Though why we torture ourselves this way is beyond my comprehension."

A waitress interrupted their conversation, her young face brightened by a wide smile. "Are you ready to order?"

She took their orders and hurried away, the noise of the packed restaurant easily filling the space between them.

"You don't have to go," Reeda murmured.

"Neither do you," snapped Duncan, eyes flashing.

"Yes, I do. Jennifer has been a good friend to me for almost fifteen years. We were at high school together. I can't simply skip her baby shower. You know how much this baby means to her and David."

His face softened. "Don't you ever feel...angry about it?"

Reeda's gut twisted and she fought back tears. "Of course. But what will that achieve?"

"Do you *want* to go?"

She pursed her lips. "No, I don't."

"Then let's do something else."

"I can't."

He laughed, a forced, ugly sound. "Of course we can't. You never do anything irresponsible. Always the right thing, even when it hurts."

She shrank from his words. "That's not true. Only...she's my friend."

"And what about me, your husband?" Pain skipped over his tanned face, and she caught a glimpse of dark smudges beneath his eyes she hadn't noticed earlier.

She reached for his hand across the table and squeezed it gently. "I'm sorry. I care about you as well, but we can't hide from our lives. We can't hide from our friends and the world around us. We have to face it, face facts. I'm not pregnant, she is. It's the way things are and hiding won't change that."

She could choke on the lump in her throat. It wouldn't budge, she had to talk around it. Her voice sounded broken.

He sighed. "I know, but we don't have to make it harder on ourselves."

"Will you come with me?"

He nodded. "Okay."

"Thanks."

"Can I ask you something, without you getting mad?" he questioned.

She steeled herself, nodded. Sometimes she wasn't sure she could take his pain on top of her own. It was too much to bear, especially knowing she was the source of it. The cause of so much of his grief, turmoil. Why he spent hours longer than necessary in his office each day. If only she'd been able to fall pregnant. Why was it called falling? As though it was as easy as tripping over a stone in your path.

"I'd like us to stop."

"Stop?"

"Stop trying for a baby."

His voice echoed in her ears. "Stop trying?"

He pushed at the rebellious curls on his forehead with a grunt. "It's too much. Too hard on you, your body, on us...I can't even remember why I wanted a baby in the first place now. I've lost sight of what we set out to do. Everything is about getting pregnant—our conversations, friendships, sex life...I want it to stop."

She inhaled a sharp breath. "Okay..." Grief welled, but she pushed it down again, willing herself to hold everything together. She'd known this day was coming, it was obvious he'd grown tired of the fertility treatments, her mood swings, the constant reminder of an empty nursery.

"I'm sorry, Reeda. I want us to...to find each other again. I don't want to live this way. We've been happy for a decade without a child, well, almost. I know we could be happy again."

"It's only been five years. Five years and six months since the first doctor told me there was a problem." Her voice was monotone, her eyes fixed on the table.

She felt his sigh rather than heard it.

"It's fine, we can stop," she relented. "No worries at all."

He cupped her hand with both of his. "I know it hurts, and it's hard for you to let go. But I think this will be for the best for both of us. There's too much pressure."

What did he know about what was best? He'd abandoned her years earlier. He'd left her to deal with her grief alone and buried himself in his work.

She pushed a smile onto her lips, met his gaze. "Yes, of course."

4

AUGUST 1945

SYDNEY

Edie slipped through the open office door and into the hallway with a grin. At the end of the hall, Mima's head peeked around the corner. She caught Edie's eye, and Edie dipped her head in a brief nod.

Mima squealed, threw a hand over her mouth to silence herself, then danced a jig in place, arms waving over her head.

Edie laughed silently as she strode towards her friend. When she reached her, Mima embraced Edie with a strength that knocked the breath from her lungs.

"Ugh. You're squeezing me to death!" whispered Edie.

"What did she say?" asked Mima, releasing Edie with a laugh.

"She said we can have two days off for the celebrations, but not to go around telling people since everyone's asking her for time off, and we've got patients who need care. Then she said, for Heaven's sakes could I get out of her office since some people still had work to do even if everyone else in the country was at a street party." Edie paused to catch her breath. "So, we're free!" Edie tucked a strand of blonde hair back into her white nurse's cap with a grin. "What do you want to do?"

Mima looped an arm through Edie's and steered them both in the direction of the dormitory. She pursed her lips. "Hmmm...where to start. There are so many options, I'm not sure what we should do first. How about, we get changed then head down to see a news reel? I want to hear the Prime Minister announce the war is over, but we don't have a lot of time, so we've got to hurry. Then, we can kick up our heels!"

Edie changed into a pair of navy pants with thin white pinstripes, and a white wool top with long sleeves, covered by a navy coat, and accentuated with a red scarf knotted around her neck. It was the most patriotic costume she had in her closet, using all three colours of the flag.

In typical Mima fashion, her friend wore a tight, knee length skirt with a ruffle in the back, seamed nylons, red leather Oxfords, a tight knit shirt, no jacket, and a small, knotted scarf.

"You'll freeze," Edie said when she found her in the shared bathroom applying bright red lipstick to her full lips.

Mima laughed. "Some of us have to suffer to be beautiful. We can't all be natural stunners like you."

Edie rolled her eyes. "I'm nothing of the kind, and you are beautiful, with or without all that makeup."

Mima squeezed her with one arm around Edie's waist, then, worked on her false eyelashes. "You're a doll, but I don't believe a word you say."

Edie huffed. "You sound like the American patients. Speaking of Americans, have you heard from Ollie lately? Do you know if he's headed back to America?"

Mima's smile faded and the light in her eyes dimmed. "Uh...no. I haven't heard from him. I'm sure they're too busy, with everything that's going on. The Japanese have surrendered, but no doubt they still have a lot to do. And when he gets to port, he'll send me a letter or a telegram or something." She sighed, finished with the eyelashes, and stared at her reflection in the mirror. "It's hard waiting though."

Edie patted Mima's back. "I know."

After they were ready, the two of them hurried to a newsreel a few streets away from the hospital. They watched with the rest of the crowd in the packed room as the new Prime Minister of Australia, Ben Chifley, announced via a radio broadcast the end of the war.

FELLOW CITIZENS, THE WAR IS OVER.

THE JAPANESE GOVERNMENT HAS ACCEPTED THE TERMS OF surrender imposed by the Allied Nations and hostilities will now cease. The reply by the Japanese Government to the note sent by Britain, the United States, the USSR, and China, has been received and accepted by the Allied Nations.

AT THIS MOMENT LET US OFFER THANKS TO GOD.

LET US REMEMBER THOSE WHOSE LIVES WERE GIVEN THAT WE may enjoy this glorious moment and may look forward to a peace which they have won for us.

WHEN THE LAST WORD WAS SAID, THE ENTIRE CROWD

erupted into shouting, applause, and laughter. A young man in uniform beside Edie grabbed her and planted a wet kiss on her lips before turning and kissing Mima next.

Edie tugged a handkerchief from her pocket and wiped her mouth dry again. A smile pulled at the corner of her lips, but something in her heart ached. The war was over. But it had taken something from her that could never be replaced. Charlie was most likely dead. She still had hope that he'd show up, but what if he didn't? Her brother Bobby was gone too. The pain of it was almost more than she could bear. She couldn't think about that. It was time to celebrate. There was no chance Mima would let her sit out this party.

Mima reached for her, threw her arms around Edie, and squeezed her hard until she coughed. She laughed and squeezed Mima back.

"It's over," she whispered against Mima's hair.

The two women looked at each other, tears glimmering in their eyes. Mima's red lips pulled back to reveal white teeth in a wide smile. "It's over. Let's go. I'm thirsty."

Mima grabbed Edie's hand and pulled her, winding through the crowd. She ducked beneath an arm here, circled around a couple there, and finally they were free. The cool air soothed Edie's hot face after the stuffiness of the crowded theatre.

They trotted through the streets, caught a tram part of the way, and finally made it to Martin Place. Thousands of people packed the city centre, with celebrations already well underway. Edie had never seen anything like it. People had come from everywhere and were jammed into Martin Place and the surrounding streets like beans in a tin.

People sang, swaying in groups with arms wrapped around each other's waists. Others danced, drank, or sat alone staring into the distance with tears pouring down pale cheeks. Most were smiling, laughing, shouting, hooting, and whistling.

One man had made an Adolf Hitler-shaped dummy with a swastika on the front of it and hoisted it to the top of a building then lowered it to hang by the neck ignominiously in front of the building's facade. A man stood on the building's roof, dressed in overalls. He tugged on the rope that was looped around the dummy's neck, pulling Hitler back to the top of the building. Then, to the delight of the watching crowd, he set about kicking Hitler's nether region. The man punched Hitler under the chin, knocking the hat off his head. People watching doubled over with laughter, pointing up at the man in overalls as he continued his assault on the dummy.

Edie studied the scene in silence, walking backward, her hand still threaded with Mima's who was jolting her through the thick crowd. She ran into someone with a sudden bump, apologising as she turned around and found herself on the edge of a circle. The man she'd run into tipped his hat with a smile. Thirty or forty young women stood about in front of him, watching another young man, dressed in grey slacks, a shirt with the sleeves rolled up, as he performed the highland fling.

Toes pointed, one hand raised over his head, he jigged and danced. The women cheered, whistled, and shouted encouragement. Edie couldn't help joining in. She clapped her hands together in time to his kicking feet, laughing at the joy on his face and the way he leapt through the air.

Mima yanked hard on her hand and Edie stumbled after her. "Come on!"

Mima lead her to a large group of Australian soldiers, Marines and young women, all in a circle and all doing the hokey-cokey as someone accompanied them on a piano-accordion. Mima joined in, waiving for Edie to follow her. With a nod of her head and a bubble of laughter on her lips, Edie stepped into the circle beside Mima and danced.

When she couldn't dance any longer, Edie drifted off to

one side and sat on the ground, panting for air. A military cenotaph was nearby, a large, rectangular block with soldiers in bronze standing guard on either end. Its base was plied with wreathes and bunches of fresh flowers. Some people stood in silence, peering blankly at the statue, hats in hand or with teardrops marking their cheeks.

Edie's own smile faded. She pushed up onto her feet and walked slowly to the cenotaph, her heart thudding. Along one side of the concrete memorial were emblazoned the words, "To our glorious dead". She choked back a sob. Bobby was dead. Charlie might be. They hadn't heard from Mima's fiancé, Ollie, in months. The war might be over, but it had taken so much from so many.

Mima ran over to Edie, laughing. Her hair disheveled, her lipstick smeared across her lips, she grabbed Edie by both cheeks.

"What are you doing?" asked Edie.

Mima poked her tongue out of the corner of her mouth in concentration. "Stay still."

She drew something on Edie's cheeks with her lipstick.

"Now do me?" she said, handing the lipstick to Edie.

Edie arched an eyebrow. "What? I don't know what you did."

"Write a V on each of my cheeks."

"Oh, okay." Edie did as Mima asked, then her friend ran off to join a group of revellers, all dancing and singing together.

Edie watched them a moment, then wandered over to join them. Mima slid an arm around her waist and hugged her close. Someone passed Edie a cup of beer. She chugged it down fast; it was warm and bitter. Mima drank one too, then one of the men in a Marines uniform refilled their cups from a bottle. Mima faced Edie with a look filled with intense emotions. A mixture of hope, pain, and sorrow. "Let's drink to Bobby," she said.

Edie nodded, a lump forming in her throat. "And to Charlie and Ollie."

Mima pursed her lips. "Yes, to Bobby, Charlie and Ollie."

They smiled, clinked their cups together and drank.

5

APRIL 1996

SYDNEY

Reeda's fingernails tapped the outside of her champagne glass. She studied the crowd of friends, all gathered around the expectant mother. The men had congregated on one side of David and Jennifer's back yard. They stood around the BBQ, laughing, and talking. She couldn't hear what they were saying, but she imagined their conversation revolved around surgery, golf, and an upcoming medical conference. Those were the topics Duncan and his friends usually stuck to, not that she minded.

Jennifer waved her over to the gift table. She steeled herself, then meandered in that direction.

The women would want to talk about babies, pregnancy, how they'd planned on a natural labour but in the end had opted for drugs. It was how all these things ended up going.

Then everyone would laugh together, each commiserating or congratulating over their shared experiences. All but her.

It wasn't as though she blamed them. None of it was their fault. She didn't fit in, which was something new for her. All throughout her childhood and teenage years, she'd been the girl that easily found her place. Unlike her sisters, Kate and Bindi, she'd slipped into high school as though she was made for it. As a dancer, it'd been easy to be part of the group of girls who attended dance lessons with her. They'd done everything together, shared every part of their lives: developed crushes, had their hearts broken, sneaked out of their homes to go to the movies and occasionally skipped school together. They'd shared every season of life.

Until now.

"You made out like a bandit," said Reeda with a chuckle. She adjusted the neckline of her new off-the-shoulder dress.

Jennifer's face glowed. "I know, everyone's so generous. Thank you for your gift. I think they baby's going to love the Jolly Jumper. It looks like a lot of fun."

"You're so welcome." She embraced her friend, kissing her ruddy cheek. Reeda couldn't wait to see Jennifer's little one bouncing away in the contraption. She was excited to meet the baby, whether boy or girl, they'd decided not to find out ahead of time what they were having.

Jennifer moved away to talk to other guests and Reeda watched her go, holding the champagne glass tight in one hand.

"She's a beautiful pregnant lady," said Penny.

"Yes she is."

"I'm not. I hate being pregnant, all the bloating, swelling, pain...and don't even get me started on the sleepless nights."

Reeda offered her a polite smile. Penny had been part of their friendship circle since university. She wasn't one of the original schoolgirls, or a dancer, but they'd welcomed her into their group when she'd joined Jennifer in a teaching degree.

Her stomach bulged beneath a blue tunic and she shoved a crostini covered in avocado and smoked salmon into her mouth, chewing loudly.

"Well, it doesn't last forever, thank goodness." Reeda's lips pulled into a tight line.

"No, it just feels like it does. And now, here I go, number four. Can you believe it? I didn't even want two. One was plenty, I told Ed, but it just keeps happening."

Reeda's eyebrows arched, but she kept quiet.

"I feel like my body is going to fall into pieces right here on the spot. Like, if I don't hold my legs together, this baby's going to drop onto the grass." She laughed and reached for another crostini.

"You're very blessed to have such a large family." Reeda worked hard to keep her irritation from showing. Penny didn't know when to stop. She'd always been oblivious to the effect her words had on people, but Reeda wasn't sure she could remain civil today. Not after her conversation with Duncan last night.

"I guess...I mean I love them, don't get me wrong, but I'm ready to get some rest. I'm just so tired." Penny rubbed her eyes with her fingertips.

"That's understandable."

"You have no idea..." continued Penny. "It's not only the getting up at all hours of the day and night, it's the whining, the fighting, the constant need to be held. Why can't I get some time to myself? I mean, I can't even go to the toilet without at least two of them under my feet."

Reeda's head felt light. She blinked. How many times had she sat through a mother's complaints about her children, all the while wishing she could be in their shoes? They didn't know how she felt. Jennifer was the only friend she'd told

49

about her issues with infertility. It wasn't their fault if they didn't know, she couldn't expect them to be sensitive to her pain if she wasn't willing to talk about it. She knew that, in her head, but her heart squeezed.

"That must be really hard," she replied.

"And look at you," said Penny, her reddened eyes wandering up and down Reeda's frame. "You're so thin, fit, in shape. You look young, for heaven's sakes. I think I've aged a decade with each pregnancy, at least it seems that way whenever I get a chance to glance in the mirror. It must be so great to still be living it up at our age...I can't even imagine. You probably go out to dinner with Duncan, go dancing, sleep in on the weekends...Lucky thing!"

Reeda's teeth ground together. Penny watched her expectantly, waiting for a response. She could see Duncan making his way towards her through the crowd, a plate piled with steaks and salads held high in each hand.

She inhaled a quick breath then spun to face Penny. "You should be grateful every day that you have those beautiful babies. You don't deserve them, but they're yours so you better take good care of them and love them with every breath you have, because there are plenty of people out there who wish they had what you have!"

Penny's eyes widened and she gaped. "What...? I'm sorry...I..."

Reeda turned away from her and found herself face-to-face with her husband. Duncan's eyes narrowed and he studied her as though she were an insect beneath a magnifying glass.

"Reeda? What's going on?"

Reeda's cheeks flamed. "Nothing, it's fine."

"I brought you some lunch..."

She reached for the plate. "Thanks."

"Do you want to leave?" he asked.

She shook her head. "No, we should at least eat first. Then, let's get out of here. I don't want to stay any longer than we have to."

With a quick nod of his head, he led the way to a pair of chairs on the porch. Reeda lowered herself into one and rested the white, paper plate on her lap. Her hands trembled as she retrieved her fork from a pile of potato salad.

It wasn't like her to lose her cool that way. She'd heard Penny complain a thousand times about motherhood, and usually she kept her retorts bottled up inside until she could cry them into a pillow at home. But she hadn't been able to hold in her emotions today, not after Duncan had dashed any sliver of hope she'd been holding onto by saying he wanted to stop trying for a baby.

"You can't talk to people that way, Reeda." Duncan's voice was low, but she heard the anger bubbling below the surface.

Her heart skipped a beat. "I know, I'm sorry. She was just..."

"She was being herself. It's how Penny is, you know that. She's not happy unless she's complaining, I'm sure it doesn't mean anything."

"I know..."

Duncan chewed a piece of steak, swallowed. "We can't keep living like this. It's destroying us."

Her eyes smarted. "I'm sorry."

"It's not your fault, it's both of us."

"You were right, we shouldn't have come." Reeda's throat tightened. She scooped some potato salad into her mouth, forcing herself to chew. She almost choked on it.

"No...it's not that. We have to accept things...as they are. Or..." His words hung in the air between them. All the things unsaid, the future unknown.

Or what?

She didn't want to ask the question; she didn't have to.

She could see it on his face. He couldn't keep going the way they had been, it was eating him from the inside out. It was eating her too.

Reeda tried to remember what it'd been like before they had the first conversation about having a baby.

Duncan had come home from work and she'd been in the pool swimming laps. It was summer and she often cooled off after work with a few laps as the sun set. She hung from the side of the pool, watching him as he grunted into a pool chair, crossing his ankles.

"I love you," she said.

He'd rubbed his eyes with one hand and pushed a smile onto his tired face. "I love you too."

"Long day?"

He'd nodded. He'd looked so handsome, so vulnerable and yet strong at the same time. His chestnut curls mussed, his dimples faint, strong arms folded over his thick chest.

She'd smiled at him until he laughed.

"What?"

She'd chuckled too. "Nothing, I'm a lucky girl."

"We should have a baby," he'd said, leaning forward to rest his forearms on his knees.

Her heart had thunked in her chest. Yes. Yes!

But even as the memories swirled and her eyes misted, she couldn't push past the fact that there'd been another feeling in her gut at the same time. A feeling that something was wrong with her, wrong enough that it could mean disaster for their family, for any children they had.

She'd been the cause of her parents' death.

There it was. That was the thing that was curled like a stone in her stomach, that'd set her heart racing with fear at his words.

She couldn't get past the fact that she'd lost her own mother and father as a teenager and it'd been her fault. She'd pushed to get what she wanted, and they'd died because of it.

How could she become a mother?

That was what she'd thought for a split second still...

Maybe all of this was for the best after all.

She set her plate down on the ground. "Let's go," she whispered.

Back at the house, Reeda stepped from the shower and pulled on a dressing gown, cinching the belt tightly around her waist. She climbed into her bed, the sound of the television set blaring out a sports broadcast hummed down the hallway and through the open door.

They'd barely spoken on the drive home. She couldn't tell if Duncan was angry with her, or just angry.

Reeda reached for Nan's timber box. She pulled a journal out of the box, returned the box to the bedside table, then slid beneath the covers with the diary in her hands. She opened the cover and ran a fingertip over the words on the first yellowed page. She'd already read a few of Nan's entries but wanted to linger over the words. To ruminate over what Nan must've been like.

1935-1950

IT WAS SO DIFFICULT TO IMAGINE NAN, AS A YOUNG GIRL, holding that same book in her hands, hunching over it to write about all her thoughts, dreams, and fears.

She turned another page and let her gaze wander over the lines of sloping, black script. Nan's handwriting had changed over the years but was still recognisable. It was a little neater and less jagged in the journal, but still Nan.

An ache built in her chest, and she ignored the push of

tears that threatened to fill her eyes. She missed Nan. Missed calling her at the end of a long day, missed knowing she was there if Reeda needed her.

With a grunt she pushed down deeper beneath her covers and held the journal close to her face to read.

6

DECEMBER 1945

SYDNEY

The New Year's Eve party was at a friend's house a few blocks away from the hospital. In fact, several of the hospital's doctors shared the house and one of them was married to a nurse who'd worked with Edie and Mima for a year. They'd invited all the nurses who weren't working to the party, and the house was crammed to the brim with hospital staff, along with their family and friends.

Edie and Mima were in the lounge room, dancing to a record blasting from the speakers of a record player in the corner. The lights had been dimmed and the crowd were separated into pairs, moving in time with the music. Mima had her arms around Edie's neck and Edie held onto Mima's waist. Champagne made her head light and gave her stomach a feeling of warmth. She didn't usually drink, but Mima had convinced her that the first New Year's Eve since the end of the war was cause for celebration, so Edie had buckled and drank two whole glasses of champagne before pulling Mima onto the dance floor.

Neither of them had a date, she'd said, so they'd be each other's. Mima laughed and said that she wasn't about to be the man, so if Edie wanted to dance, she'd have to lead. Edie had agreed and they'd spent the last five songs talking about the past, while the music drowned out every other noise around them.

"And do you remember the time Barry pushed you into the river in the middle of winter?" asked Edie. She almost had to shout to be heard.

Mima laughed. "Of course. How can I forget? I got him back though, put a frog in his trousers during maths."

Edie threw her head back and guffawed. It'd been one of the funniest things she'd ever seen in her life: Barry Holstead dancing around maths class with a frog in his pants. The look on his face had been priceless.

The two women giggled together as the memory of it filled their minds' eyes.

"Ah...those days were such fun," said Edie with a sigh. "Who knew they wouldn't last?"

When the countdown began, both women stopped dancing to join in. As the crowd shouted, "Happy New Year," Mima hugged Edie. They watched the couples around them kiss and Edie's champagne buzz faded.

"Let's go home," she said.

Mima nodded. "Okay."

Outside, the quiet of the night buzzed in their ears after the loud music. They walked back to the hospital dormitory arm in arm. Overhead, stars sparkled in the black sky and cicadas hummed, interrupted only by the honk of a horn, or the growl of a distant car's engine.

In the dormitory, Edie's vision had begun to spin. She

splashed water on her face, kicked off her shoes and fell into bed with a grunt.

When Mima's cry split the night's silence she jumped to her feet, heart in her throat. She found her friend in the dim light and grasped her by the arm. Mima held a crumpled piece of paper aloft in one hand. The limb hung there, as though suspended, unable to move. A torn envelope sat on the floor, a smudge of white in the gloom.

"Mima, what is it? What's wrong?" she said.

Mima looked at her, tears streaming down her face. Mascara sluiced into puddles beneath her eyes. "Ollie's dead," she said.

Edie's stomach dropped. "Oh no. Oh darling Mima..."

Mima's face crumpled. "What's the point, Edie? What's the point of winning the war if they don't come home? If none of them come home?"

☙ 7 ❧

SYDNEY

The sound of the alarm clock jolted Reeda from a fitful sleep. She rolled onto her side, heart pounding, and slapped the clock radio. It fell silent and she covered her eyes with the palms of both hands.

Outside, a kookaburra announced the morning, and the twitter of swallows filled the quiet when it ended. Pale, weak rays of sunlight slid beneath the curtains, drawing a dappled pattern on the Turkish rug that covered most of the bedroom floor.

Reeda groaned. It'd taken her so long to fall to sleep and just as she'd gotten into a dream state the alarm had sounded. At least, that was how it felt.

The phone on the bedside table jangled to life.

Reeda grabbed the handpiece, heart racing, before realising Duncan had probably already left for work and wouldn't be woken by the sound.

"Hello?" she croaked, cleared her throat, and tried again. "Hello?"

"Reeda, it's Karen, good morning."

"Hi Karen." Reeda rolled onto her back and squeezed her eyes shut. Her chief designer had a habit of calling her before she'd even had a chance to down her first cup of coffee.

"I'm sorry to call you at home..."

"It's fine, what's up?"

"Tomoko's not happy with the wallpaper choice. We're on a deadline and the manufacturer might not be able to make the switch in time..."

"Right, well she might have to accept that we'll need to push back the finish date."

Karen chuckled. "Yes, I tried telling her that. How long do you think it will take you to get here? I need to get your approval on some swatches."

Reeda swung her feet over the side of the bed, felt around for the slippers she kept handy and slid her feet into them. "I don't know. I've barely opened my eyes."

"Rough night?" asked Karen.

Reeda grunted. "You could say that."

"I can take this myself, if you'd prefer. I'm happy to meet with Tomoko and keep things rolling." Karen's efficiency was astounding, even after all these years.

In the past, Reeda had often found the designer pushy and difficult, but today, it was just what she needed.

"That would be wonderful," Reeda said. "In fact, I'm handing you the account."

"Really?" Karen's voice betrayed her excitement. "It's a big account, are you sure?"

"Yes, I'm sure. I'm taking some more time off. You're in

charge again, I know I can count on you." She hadn't made the decision until that moment, but the idea of facing a design dilemma after the weekend she'd had seemed impossible.

She'd spent most of Sunday in bed reading Nan's journals or watching a *Golden Girls* marathon on the television set in her bedroom. She hadn't even changed out of her pyjamas. It wasn't like her to lounge in bed all day long, but something inside her had changed, broken.

Duncan had poked his head through the doorway once or twice to see if she needed anything but seemed to sense what she needed most was time to herself to mourn the thing they'd never had so couldn't have lost. Still, it felt like a loss. And a huge, heavy knot sat in the pit of her stomach, even as Monday dawned.

She hung up the phone and sat on the edge of the bed a moment, then reached for her dressing gown. As she tied it in place, she padded down the long hallway to their home office.

On the bookshelf she located the New South Wales Street Directory and pulled it free, opening it on the desk and folding herself into a chair. She flipped the pages open until she located the city of Bathurst.

Only about a three-hour drive away. She could go there today and be back in time for dinner. Or perhaps she could stay a few days. It was where Charlie and Nan had grown up, surely someone there must remember them? Maybe she'd find out what'd happened to Charlie, other than what they'd already discovered through Nan's journals—that he'd been listed as missing in action over Crete or the Gulf of Tunis.

Had his body ever been found? Did he have a family still in Bathurst? Who was he?

From Nan's journal entries it was clear he was Reeda's biological grandfather, but Nan had never mentioned him.

Reeda knew nothing more about him other than that he'd been the boy Nan loved as a teenage girl before the war pulled them apart, that he fathered the baby who'd grown up to be her own Dad. Nan had married Pop later and she still wasn't sure if they'd ever told Dad about his true heritage. He'd certainly never mentioned anything to her or her sisters.

She tucked the street directory under one arm and headed for the kitchen.

Coffee. She needed coffee if she was going on a road trip.

❦

THE DRIVE TO BATHURST WAS UNEVENTFUL. AS SOON AS she'd broken free of Sydney's gridlocked traffic, the road opened up and she made good time.

When she pulled into the edge of Bathurst's city limits three hours later, she stopped for petrol and grabbed a bag of potato chips at the same time, munching as she pulled the car back out onto the road.

Now that she was here, she had no idea where to start. How did you go back in time to find someone who no longer existed?

Perhaps a phone book would be a good place to start, although it was likely more than one family of Jacksons lived in a city of this size. Bathurst had grown in recent years and wasn't the same town described in Nan's journals, where everyone knew everyone else and what was going on in their lives.

It wasn't long before Reeda spied a phone booth in a Woolworth's parking lot. She pulled into the lot and parked the car on the edge of the bitumen, away from the crowds. The phone booth was empty and listed to one side as though it was losing its balance.

She searched the cup holder for spare change. She kept it stocked for the times she drove through one of the many toll booths around Sydney's maze of highways. A fifty-cent coin would do the trick. She tucked it into the pocket of her jeans and climbed out of the car.

Squinting into the midday sun, she tented a hand over her face and scanned the parking lot. A few cars were parked up near the supermarket entrance, several others crawled around looking for the best space. Overhead, a crow cawed on a power line with the hum of traffic as a backdrop.

The air seemed dry. Drier than it'd been in Sydney. Yellowed grass lined the edge of the parking lot, the tarmac looked as though it'd crack apart if she stepped on it. The air was frigid; she reached back into the car for her red puffy jacket and shrugged into it with a shiver.

She strode to the payphone while zipping her jacket, and tugged open the door, pulling it shut behind her. A dog-eared White Pages with half the cover torn free sat on a metal shelf beside the phone on top of a Yellow Pages. She flicked through it until she found the J's.

Jackson.
C.A. Jackson.
B. & M. Jackson
J. Jackson

How was she supposed to know which of these names might have anything to do with the Charlie Jackson she was searching for? She'd have to go through every single one of them. This was going to take a while, and she'd need more change.

AFTER TEN PHONE CALLS THAT LED NOWHERE AND A TRIP

across the lot to the Woolworths grocery shop for more change, Reeda was ready to give up for the day. She'd make one more phone call and then go looking for a motel to spend the night. Returning to Sydney with no leads at all wasn't an option. She'd stay until she found something, anything—even if what she discovered was that every one of Charlie's relatives were dead and gone.

She pushed her last fifty-cent piece into the slot and dialled.

"Yello," said a man's voice.

"Hi, my name is Reeda Summer, and I'm looking for someone who lived in Bathurst before World War Two called Charlie Jackson." She'd learned from the previous phone conversations it was best to get all the information out as quickly as she could. It meant fewer questions, and less chance she'd be mistaken for a telemarketer or debt collector.

At some stage in the process she'd reverted to using her maiden name. Not Reeda Houston, but the name she'd grown up using, Reeda Summer. She tried not to think too hard about why she'd done that, since it made her heart hurt.

"Charlie Jackson? Hang on a minute, Grandad's over for a bit of lunch. I'll ask him, he might remember."

Before she could reply, there was a clunk on the other end of the line, and it went quiet. She waited, drumming fingernails against the metal shelf and watching as her breath formed white clouds in front of her mouth.

"Hello? You still there?" The man was back.

She drew in a deep breath. "Yes, I'm here."

"Grandad says he reckons he knew a Charlie Jackson; he was his cousin."

Her heart skipped a beat. "Really?"

"Yep. He died in the war, apparently."

She pursed her lips. "Yes, I know. I was hoping I might find some of his family, someone I could talk to about him."

"You doing an article for the paper or something?" His voice was laced with suspicion.

She chuckled. "No, I'm his granddaughter." She hadn't said the words out loud before, they felt strange on her tongue.

He laughed. "Well, that's different then. Grandad says Charlie had a sister. What was her name Grandad?" The last was shouted. Reeda pulled her ear away from the phone with a grimace.

"He says her name is Sylvia. She's over at the Rosebud Retirement Community."

"She's alive?" Reeda's eyes widened and she patted down her pockets looking for the pen she'd shoved there earlier in dejection when none of the phone calls seemed to be going anywhere. She pulled it free, along with a small notepad.

"Yeah, she's alive. Not for much longer, he says, but he sees her every now and then."

"Does your grandfather remember much about Charlie?"

"Hey, Grandad, what do you remember about Charlie?" the man shouted. Then, "He says he didn't really know him, was too young when Charlie went off to war. He mostly only remembers hearing about him, how he died a hero...that kind of thing."

"Thank you. I'm sorry, what is your name?"

"No worries, I'm Daniel Jackson. Grandad's name is Daniel too, so that's pretty easy to remember." He laughed, though it soon turned into a hacking cough, as though he'd smoked one too many Winfields.

"Sorry, I've got a lurgy."

"I hope you feel better soon. Look, I'm going to write down your number and keep it. Do you mind if I give you another call sometime? You know, if I have questions?"

"No worries, fine by me."

"Thank you again. I really appreciate it."

"Hey, I guess that means we're related, since your grandfather and mine were cousins," he said.

She arched an eyebrow. "I guess it does. Nice to meet you, cuz."

He laughed. "Yeah, you too Reeda."

8

MAY 1996

BATHURST

The Rosebud Retirement Community was more of a nursing home than a true retirement community. Reeda waited at the reception desk as a nurse padded her way in white Reeboks.

"Yes, can I help you?" she asked, hands shoved into the pockets of her grey slacks. The aqua T-shirt she wore was emblazoned with the Rosebud logo above the pocket, and half-covered by a beige cardigan.

Reeda peeled off her coat, already beginning to sweat in the quiet building's oppressive heat. Nerves fluttered in Reeda's gut and her breathing quickened. Perhaps Sylvia would be happy to find a relative she hadn't known about. Or maybe she wouldn't believe her. Reeda had no idea what to expect, only that she was excited to finally meet Charlie Jackson's sister.

Would she find out more about her grandfather? Who he was? How he looked? Maybe even discover things about herself in the process.

"Hi, my name is Reeda Summer and I'm hoping to visit my grand-aunt, her name is Sylvia Jackson."

The nurse smiled, her eyes narrowing. "Sylvia? I didn't realise she had a grand-niece. Have we seen you before? You're not from around here, are you?"

She turned and beckoned Reeda to follow her down a long white-tiled hallway.

Reeda shook her head and fell into step beside the woman. A name tag pinned to her cardigan read "Sharon".

"No, I'm from Sydney. Honestly, I didn't realise I had a great-aunt until very recently, so I've never met her before. I hope that won't be an issue…"

"Not with Sylvia, it won't." The nurse smiled again, then fell silent. "I'm afraid she has dementia. So, she wouldn't recognise you even if she knew you. Sometimes she can remember things from years ago, but her recent memories are vague or completely non-existent. It's good you came in the morning, she's better then."

Reeda's heart fell. What if Sylvia couldn't tell her anything about Charlie? She'd be back to square one.

They entered a large sitting room. Elderly patients were scattered around the place. Two men sat playing cards by a window in armchairs, a small round table between them. Another woman rested in a chair close by, staring into the distance, a colourful crocheted blanket covering her lap.

Sharon lead Reeda to a group of three women who all hunched side by side, staring at a large television set in the corner of the room.

"Sylvia?"

One woman turned to face them with a warm smile, her blue eyes twinkling.

"Sylvia, this is Reeda Summer. She says she's your great-niece."

"Really?" The woman's smile widened. She tried to stand but struggled with the slope of the chair.

Reeda reached for her hand and helped her to her feet. She plodded forward, grasped Reeda's cheeks between her strong fingers and studied her.

"What did you say your name was?"

"Reeda," she replied.

The woman grinned. "That's a pretty name."

"Do you mind if we go somewhere where we can sit and talk?" asked Reeda.

She glanced at Sharon, who nodded towards a window on the opposite side of the room where two chairs stood empty. Reeda led Sylvia to the chairs and helped her to sit. Sharon watched them for a moment, then turned on her heel and left the room.

"Sylvia, I was hoping you might tell me about your brother, Charlie. You see, he's my grandfather."

"Charlie? Oh, yes, Charlie was my brother." Sylvia's eyes misted over.

Reeda pulled a packet of tissues from her cardigan pocket and handed one to Sylvia.

"Here you go."

The older woman wiped tears from the corners of her eyes with the tissue.

"He was a wonderful brother. He teased me of course, all brothers do that, but I miss him so much."

"What did he look like?" She wasn't sure where to start. There were so many questions burning her tongue.

"He had blue eyes, bright blue, and full of mischief. He was always planning something, that boy." Sylvia laughed and scrunched the tissue into the palm of her hand. "Blond hair, of course, just like me." Sylvia tugged at her grey curls as though to smooth them. Reeda imagined the younger woman regarding herself in a mirror, blond curls bouncing with each bob of her head.

She smiled. "Sounds like you had a good relationship with him."

"With who, dear?" asked Sylvia, eyes vacant.

"With your brother, Charlie..."

"Oh yes, Charlie and I were very close. Of course, all that ended when he went off to war. He was a hero, you know? Shot down over the ocean...horrible thing. Horrible. I can't imagine what it must've been like for him."

Reeda leaned back in her chair, squeezing her eyes shut. She didn't want to imagine it either, the black ocean swallowing him whole. It was no way to die.

She sighed. "Do you know if he loved someone, a girl here in Bathurst?"

Sylvia's eyes squinted as she rifled through memories. Reeda could tell it was difficult; the look on her face showed the strain. "He did have a girl. Yes, someone here in Bathurst. What was her name? Edie, I think. Edith...that's right. I'm trying to recall. Oh drat, my memory's not what it used to be. Getting old is no fun at all, young woman. No fun."

Reeda pursed her lips. "It's okay, Sylvia. You're right about the name. Edie was my grandmother."

"Oh, that's nice dear."

Reeda could tell she'd lost Sylvia all over again. Her blank stare panned the room.

"And what about your parents. Do you remember them?"

Sylvia hesitated. "My parents? Oh yes, of course I do. Mother was beautiful. Long, black hair—nothing like mine of course. Charlie and I took after our father. He was the blond one. We lived in town; Daddy was a solicitor. Very well respected around town. We were one of the first families to own a car. It was a beautiful, sleek black thing.

Everyone was jealous. Of course, Daddy had to swerve it to miss the piles of horse manure. Can you imagine?" She laughed then, a musical sound that brought a smile to Reeda's face.

She wished she'd known Sylvia before, when her mind hadn't yet been addled by disease. They would've gotten along.

"No, I can't imagine. There are so many cars on the road these days, it's strange to think it wasn't always that way."

"Oh no, it certainly wasn't. Things were different back then. But it was another time, before the war, everything was different." Her lined face took on a wistful look and she stared at the hands clenched around the tissue in her lap.

"I'm staying in town for a few days. Do you mind if I visit again?" asked Reeda, standing to her feet.

Sylvia looked up at her with still misty eyes. "That would be nice, dear."

Reeda kissed her cheek and headed for the door. What had she hoped to learn about Charlie? It made sense that the only people who knew him barely remembered anything at all. It was so long ago. Seeing his sister had given her some insight into who he might've been though. She was jovial, kind, Reeda could tell by her voice and her eyes. Perhaps he had been as well.

"You're heading out?" asked the nurse, as Reeda passed the reception desk.

"Yes, but I might visit again. I'll be hanging around for a little longer."

"We'll see you then." Sharon smiled and offered a wave.

Outside, Reeda stopped and stared up into the sky. What now? She could visit Daniel Jackson, ask him about his cousin, though he'd already said he didn't remember much. Perhaps she could find a motel first, have a rest and something to eat. Food made everything seem better, every complicated situation simpler, every hurt, less biting. She missed her sister Kate's cooking at The Waratah Inn.

She stepped off the curb, jogging towards her car. Then she slid into the seat and leaned her head back on the cushion with a sigh. A lump formed in her throat and she pushed out thoughts of what Charlie had been through, what he must've faced and experienced, and the fact that Nan had lost him all those years ago. The way Nan wrote about it in her journal made it clear—losing Charlie had torn out her heart and left her bereft. She swallowed around the lump, drew a quick breath, and turned the key in the ignition.

❧

"CHARLIE WAS GREAT WITH A GUN," croaked DANIEL Jackson. "That's all I remember really. That and his blue eyes. Bright blue they were. Just like a Jackson."

Mr. Jackson's own blue eyes were rimmed with red. He sat in a floral print chair. A cigarette butt in an ashtray on the side table next to him leaked a curl of smoke that crept slowly towards the ceiling. The room was dark. Mr. Jackson sat by the window and the dim light of a cold day lit him up from behind like a halo.

His grandson set a cup of tea in front of Reeda, then lowered himself onto the couch across from her. He looked to be about thirty years old, his nose was red, and he tugged a jacket a little tighter around his body. Blond hair hung around his neck, brushing his shoulders. He pushed it behind both ears with a fingertip.

"Sorry about the cold," he said, reaching for a tissue and blowing his nose into it with gusto.

He tossed the tissue into a growing pile at the foot of the couch. She made a mental note to wash her hands thoroughly as soon as she got back to the motel room.

She sipped the tea, hoping he hadn't touched the cup where her lips pressed against it.

"So, Mr. Jackson, is there anything else you can tell me about Charlie or his family?"

"His parents were devastated when they heard he was shot down. I can tell you that for sure." He shook his head. "But then, they didn't talk about it. At least, not in my hearing. It was an unspoken thing in the family, from what I remember. But of course, I was just a kid, so I didn't pay too much attention."

She nodded, wondering what else she should ask. "Is anyone else left—from the family, I mean?"

His old eyes narrowed. "Nope. Not that I know of. Charlie's parents died years ago. My own followed a decade or so later. I was an only child, and of course you met Sylvia. So... that's about it. I'm sure we have other relatives, just none I know."

When she headed back to the motel, Reeda had learned little more than that Charlie had loved horses and had taken a particular interest in the Clydesdales that used to pull carts around town to do various things like deliver bread and milk.

Nothing important. Nothing more that might give her any indication about how he'd died, whether his body had been found, what kind of a man he'd been and how Nan had coped without him.

Back in her room, she called Duncan but wasn't able to reach him at the office or at home. She left a message for him on the home answering-machine, then switched on the television and flicked through the four channels over and over, hoping to find something interesting to watch but knowing the selection would be the same every time she ran through it.

The motel room was neat but tired. Two single beds ran parallel at either end of the room. On one wall a heater emitted a blast of hot, dry air beside a tiny bathroom. Finally, she switched off the television set and slipped beneath the covers. She reached for her purse and took out Nan's journal. She'd carried it to Bathurst with her wrapped in brown paper and inside a linen bag. She took it out carefully and opened it up to where she'd last finished reading.

She was curious to see whether Nan wrote any more about Pop. From what she'd read so far, he'd asked Nan to marry him at the Army hospital where she worked, and Nan had turned him down since she was still hoping Charlie would come back from the war.

But it seemed Charlie never returned. Which meant that sometime after the proposal Pop had come back to Australia and Nan had changed her mind. Part of her didn't want to read about what had driven Nan to that point. She wanted to believe Nan had loved Pop. It'd certainly seemed so during her own lifetime. She'd never doubted it before now.

Still, Nan must've suffered, losing her fiancé in the war, and having to raise a son on her own. A single mother in post-war Australia would've had plenty of obstacles to face, not to mention social ostracism.

The phone beside the bed pierced the silence with a tinny ringing that startled Reeda.

"Hello, this is Reeda."

"Reeda, it's Duncan."

"Oh hi, honey. How are you?"

He hesitated. "I'm fine. I didn't realise you were going to Bathurst today." Frustration edged his voice.

"Sorry, I should've told you. It was a last-minute decision."

He sighed. "Find what you're looking for?"

"Yes, I suppose I did."

"I'm glad. When are you coming home?"

She squeezed her eyes shut. She wanted to visit Sylvia one more time, but other than that, there wasn't much more for her to do. Any other research, she could do over the telephone. And she could always come back to Bathurst if she needed to. Even with all these arguments running through her mind, something was pulling at her soul, urging her to stay. But she knew she couldn't, that she had to get back to her home, her husband, her life. Only she didn't want to. It was easier to stay away.

"I'll head home tomorrow after lunch, I should be there when you get back from work."

He sighed. "Good, because we need to talk."

⚜

ALL THE NEXT DAY, REEDA THOUGHT ABOUT DUNCAN'S words on the telephone the previous night.

We need to talk.

She knew what was coming, but that didn't make it any easier to face. In fact, what she wanted to do was run. Run to somewhere far away where he couldn't say what he was going to say. That their marriage was over.

If she didn't hear him, it didn't count.

She knew he was right. They'd barely spoken to each other for two years. When they did talk, it was to snap or shout. He wilfully misunderstood everything she said, and she took offence at every utterance from his mouth. They'd passed the point of no return months earlier. Where else could they go from here but in separate directions?

Still, her heart ached at the thought.

As she drove down the long highway towards Sydney, her mind wandered over the possibilities even as fear sent tremors through her gut.

She'd be single again for the first time in over a decade. If she didn't want to stay single for the rest of her life, she'd have to date. The thought made her shudder.

And what would everyone say?

Their friends would be shocked. Somehow, she and Duncan had both managed to shield their problems from everyone they cared about. Looking back now, she wished she'd had someone she could talk to about what they'd both been going through, but that wasn't her way. Whenever she faced a pain this great, she tucked it inside herself, wrapped her arms around it, and held it in that dark place alone. She didn't share it, didn't talk about it, instead pretending to all the world that everything was right, just as it should be, nothing to see here.

She talked about other things, anything else that bothered her, but not the most painful, the hurt that ran the deepest. That she kept hidden away.

She pulled the car into the garage, glad to see she had a little more time before she should expect to see Duncan. His space in the garage was empty, and the clock on the dashboard read five p.m.

She lugged her suitcase into the master bedroom, set it on the bed, then headed for the shower. Hot water beat against her shoulders, her neck, working out the tension she'd been storing up for so long.

When she was dressed, she sat on the back porch, legs tucked up in front of her while she ate two-minute noodles from a large bowl and looked out over the tree-lined valley. Each nook and cranny was fitted with a large house, roofs jutting at different angles, the azure waters of backyard swimming pools sparkling beneath the waning sunlight.

The glass door slid open. "There you are," said Duncan.

She smiled and slid one hand over her still wet hair.

He lowered himself into a seat next to her with a grunt. "How was work?"

He shrugged. "It was fine."

The look on his face said he was as uncomfortable as she

felt over the conversation they were about to have. Still, she wasn't going to make it any easier on him. If he wanted to end ten years of commitment, love, and struggle, he wouldn't get her help in doing it.

He sighed and leaned forward so that his elbows rested on his knees.

"Reeda...things aren't working between us."

She'd been waiting for it, knew it was coming, but it still hit her like a mallet to the gut. She didn't reply, instead she kept watching the view. It was so peaceful out on the porch; she'd always loved it there. Almost felt as though they weren't squashed into the heart of a bustling metropolitan city with traffic jammed along spiderwebbed roads all around them.

"Say something..." he continued, irritation edging his voice.

She glanced at him. "What do you want me to say?"

"That you agree, that you see what I do...that you understand what I'm saying."

"I understand," she replied.

He huffed. "It's been falling apart between us for a long time, and it's made me very unhappy. I'm stressed all the time, not just from work, but when I come home all we do is fight. I can't live this way, and you shouldn't want to either."

"So you're giving up?" she asked.

He ran both hands through his hair, propping them on top of his head. Emotions teased his features, anger, pain, resignation...

"I'm not giving up; I'm opening a dialogue between us."

"Ah, because it sounds like you're giving up on us."

"Don't you see?" he asked, throwing his hands up as though in surrender.

She nodded, throat thick. "I do, I see it. I just don't want to say it's over."

He pursed his lips. "Okay, we won't say it yet. But, I'm not sure we can get through this. It's too hard..."

The pain, the uncertainty, never knowing what each month would bring but trying all the same for hope, for love, for life. She understood. Only, what had she been fighting for all this time if not for them? And now...Was it over? "I know."

9

OCTOBER 1945

SYDNEY

The hospital dormitory had fallen silent a half hour earlier when most of the women either began their shifts or headed downtown. Ever since the war ended, people had been living it in up Sydney, although the mood had begun to change a little in some quarters. People kept expecting soldiers to return home from the Pacific theatre, and they didn't come. The war had ended, families wanted to see their sons, brothers, and husbands, but many were stranded in places like New Guinea, waiting for the ships that would take them home.

Edie stared at the off-white wall. It was covered in chipped paint, scuff marks and stains. In the centre of it, a small, square window stood open, white curtains undulating in the gentle breeze.

She rolled onto her back with a sigh and held the letter above her head to read again.

Keith had celebrated his third birthday a week earlier. Edie hadn't seen him in a year and a half. Was he completely different? Would he even recognise her if she saw him?

She missed his chubby, smiling face, his blond curls, the feel of his little hands around her neck, squeezing tight as she kissed his soft cheek.

Edie sighed and let the letter fall to her side. Mother said he'd received a tin truck for his birthday from her and Father. They'd moved back to the farm already, since Father received his discharge papers as soon as the war was ended. He'd already begun working in the orchard, according to Mother. Everything was back to normal.

There was a forced cheerfulness in Mother's letters these days, ever since the one about Bobby's death.

Mother had adored Bobby. He'd meant everything to her, though she didn't express it in the ways some people might. Edie could tell how she felt by the way she looked at him, smiled at his jokes, and rested a hand on his shoulder at the table before they ate.

"What are you doing? It's after nine o'clock," said Mima, coming in from the bathroom. She blew her nose into a handkerchief. "Ugh. I feel horrible. The matron says I can't work today, I'll make people sick. So, I'm stuck in the dormitory. But you could go out, have some fun. Or are you sick as well?"

Edie squeezed her eyes shut. "No, I'm fine. I don't want to go out. I want to lie here."

"Okay."

Mima sidled onto Edie's bed, squashing against her legs.

"Ouch. Mima," complained Edie, eyelids flinging open. She frowned at Mima. "Leave me alone."

Mima shrugged. "I can't. If something's wrong with my best friend, I've got to find out what it is. I know you're not sick, so you must be sad. What's going on in that beautiful head of yours?" She lay a hand on Edie's blanket-covered legs.

Edie's throat tightened. It was very simple. She was sad. She didn't know what to do with her life now that the war was over. The fighting was done, she could relax, let down her guard. Only she couldn't, because nothing made sense anymore. Everyone was returning to their old lives, as best they could. But Edie didn't know where to go or what to do. She only knew she didn't want to stay where she was.

Mima waited in silence. It wasn't like her, to be quiet. Usually Edie could count on Mima's incessant chatter, could hide behind it.

She sat up in bed, plumping the pillow behind her back, as the lump in her throat grew until it ached. "There's something I have to tell you."

Mima nodded.

A tear trailed down Edie's cheek. "You know Keith?"

"Your brother?" asked Mima.

Edie inhaled a sharp breath. "He's not my brother, he's my son. Mine and Charlie's."

Mima's brow furrowed. "Is that it?"

Edie's eyes narrowed. "What do you mean is that it? Yes, that's it." It wasn't the response she'd been expecting from her closest friend.

Mima smiled. "Oh, well, I knew that. I'm not an idiot you know. You disappeared for months and then there were all those rumours...Plus, I actually snuck out to the farm once to check on you."

"What? You did?" Edie's eyes widened in surprise.

"I was worried about you." Mima shook her head. "I hadn't heard from you, and people were starting to whisper. Anyway, I saw you outside feeding some lambs or something. You were pregnant."

"Why didn't you say anything?" asked Edie.

Mima cocked her head to one side. "You didn't seem to want to talk about it. So, is that why you're sad today?"

Edie nodded. "I miss him. I'm missing out on all the important stuff. He turned three on the first of October."

"Three? Wow." Mima beamed. "I'll bet he's gorgeous."

"Yes. I'll bet he is."

THE TRAIN SAT IDLE AT THE STATION, DOORS OPEN. EDIE studied it, then looked back up the stairs, anxiety filling her chest. Where was Mima? She'd promised to send Edie off, but the train would be leaving in a few minutes. If she didn't get on board now, she'd miss it.

She tapped an Oxford-clad toe against the timber platform, her gloved hands gripping tight to the handle of her suitcase. She was going home. Finally. Anxiety sent a twinge through her stomach.

A shout at the top of the stairs revealed Mima, arms high in the air. "Edie! There you are. I couldn't find the platform, and I was running late because the Matron made me scrub bed pans if you can believe it."

Mima skipped down the stairs, her heels clacking with each footstep.

Edie grinned and embraced her friend before taking a step back, nerves twisting a knot in her gut. "I'm going to miss you."

Mima laughed. "You too. Guess where I'm going?"

Edie shook her head.

"Newcastle. A group of nurses are going to share a house there, right by the beach. Can you believe it? Me, at the beach. I can't wait."

"What will you do there?"

Mima pursed her lips. "I don't know. But I'll figure it out.

The future is filled with possibility. Besides, with Ollie gone, I have nothing stopping me from doing anything I choose." Her eyes glistened and she poked out her trembling chin.

Edie nodded. "Well, take care of yourself." She embraced her friend, stroking the back of her head with one hand. "You'll get through this," she whispered.

Mima wiped her eyes with one sleeve. "You should come with us," she pouted, crossing her arms over her chest.

"No, I can't. I want to see Keith. It's been too long since I saw him, I'm fairly itching with it."

Mima shrugged. "Okay. But if you change your mind..."

"If I change my mind, I'll write you a letter and let you know. Just make sure to send me your new address please."

"Of course." Mima hugged her again, squeezing hard. "Stay in touch. Okay?"

Edie gave a quick nod. "You too."

As she climbed on the train, Edie glanced back over her shoulder. Her friend stood in the middle of the platform, one gloved hand raised in farewell. Her caramel hair was perfectly curled to frame her face, a stylish jacket with belt cinched around her waist accentuated her curves. Tall red heels contrasted with the grey of the surrounding train station.

Edie waved through the window until Mima was no longer visible, then slumped into a seat. She'd left behind a good job, friends who cared about her, and the only life she'd known for almost two years. What was she returning to? She'd left Bathurst a girl and was returning a woman. She'd left broken-hearted, glad to get as far away from the town as she could, not thinking about the son she was leaving behind. She was returning to rebuild her relationship with that son, if she could.

When the train pulled into the station in Bathurst three hours later, her heart was in her throat. It hadn't changed at all. Everything was just the same as it had been before she left. Memories washed over her and she found herself eager to get home.

Father was waiting outside with the truck. He embraced her quickly, then took her suitcase from her. She watched him load it into the back of the truck. He looked older, thinner than she remembered. She'd always thought of him as impossibly strong, unbreakable even. Yet now he looked somehow fragile. There was grey in his moustache and peppered through the dark hair that peeked out from beneath his hat. His jacket swam on him, and his Sunday-best shoes were scuffed.

She caught his gaze as he opened the passenger door for her. "It's good to see you, Daddy."

He smiled, eyes glistening. "You too, love."

As they drove home, she chattered about Sydney, working as a nurse, what it was like to be in the centre of things when the war ended. He listened in silence as the old vehicle bounced over potholes and dodged piles of horse manure.

The farmhouse stood as it always had, on top of a small rise as though standing guard over the valley. The driveway curved up through waving grass to meet it. A pack of dogs ran out to greet them, sniffing and licking at Edie's legs when she climbed from the truck. She laughed and patted each head until they dispersed, one by one.

As she was walking towards the house, the front door banged open and a little boy ran out. He stopped by Mother's waratah tree when he saw her, smiling shyly.

"Hi Keith," Edie said, stooping to crouch in front of him.

His eyes widened. "Do you like horses?" he asked. "Mother says you like horses."

Her eyes filled with tears and she nodded. "Yes, I love horses."

"Me too." He wiggled in place. He'd no doubt been

instructed to use company manners, just the way she had when she was his age.

"Can I have a hug?" she asked.

His eyes narrowed. "I guess."

"Only if you want to," she replied.

He shook his head. "Maybe later."

She pushed down her disappointment. It'd take time. He didn't remember her, or if he did, his memories would've been vague at best. She had to be patient.

She stood and saw Mother in the doorway, smiling at her. "Mother!" She ran into her mother's arms.

"You look older, wiser," said Mother with a laugh, as she stroked Edie's hair away from her face.

Edie smiled. "I am...much."

Mother laughed again, but her laugh sounded tired. "Come inside, you must be exhausted. I'll make us some tea."

10

JUNE 1996

CABARITA BEACH

A light breeze blew down the narrow highway and into a short drive that bent in a circular shape in front of the Inn. A sign swayed gently, outlined in yellow, the white lettering announcing: *The Waratah Inn: Beachside Bed and Breakfast.*

Off to one side, a blacktop car lot, pockmarked by an assortment of vehicles, cut a rectangular swathe in the midst of a stand of coastal gum trees, ragged sea grasses, and squat Pandanus.

The inn rose majestically against an ocean backdrop. Two full stories of pale yellow, with an attic hidden by tall eaves, it was accented by white verandahs, window frames and shutters. Wide white steps led to a large timber door.

Kate stood on the bottom step before the entrance to the inn, a sprig of fresh rosemary pinched between two fingertips. A large white apron was fitted around her waist and a bandana held a head of straight, brown hair back from her face.

She smiled and climbed the stairs just as the front door flung open. Jack stood in the doorway, a cup of coffee held between his hands. A tan Akubra hat sat on his head and he smiled beneath the scruff of a new grey moustache. One set of fingers reached for the moustache, stroking it as though practicing for the day it would reach its full potential.

"Wait here, Jack," said Kate, hurrying past him.

She soon returned with a spoon held in one hand. "Try this," she said.

She held up the spoon. He eyed it as though he needed a moment to focus on its contents, then leaned forward to sip.

"Gravy?" he asked.

She sighed with exasperation. "Yes, it's gravy. Is it good?"

He chuckled. "Delicious. Your food is always amazing, Kate. You don't need me to tell you that, although I'm always happy to do it."

He sipped the coffee, watching her expression shift towards a smile.

"Tea will be ready soon."

Jack nodded. "I'm going to enjoy the sunset a minute. See you soon."

The scent of roast beef wafted around Kate and she inhaled it with a slow breath. The meal was coming together nicely, the inn was clean and quiet, and the horses had been stabled for the night. Everything was as it should be before the bedlam of the dinner crowd.

She headed for the kitchen and found Mima there, bent over the stove, stirring the same gravy she'd just offered to Jack to taste test. Jemima Everest was a large woman. Grey curls framed her face, her skirts billowed out around full hips, and a buxom chest pushed at the confines of a red, rose-print apron.

"I believe the gravy is ready. The beef is done to perfection, it's just resting on the bench."

"I'll check the potatoes," replied Kate, deftly tugging open the oven and studying the crisp, golden mounds. "Looking good, I think we're ready."

"Just in time."

Kate was looking forward to the day when she could open the inn up to the public for meals. The restaurant idea played on her mind regularly, but there was a lot to be done before they could get to that point. They'd only just finished a complete renovation of the inn and she and her sister Bindi were learning how to run it, with Mima and Jack's help. The two older members of the team had worked with her grandmother for years managing the place, and so far, they had been patient, attentive and kind with Kate and Bindi as they stumbled through their learning curve.

Just as she set the large saucepan of gravy on the bench, Mima clutched the edge of it with both hands until her knuckles whitened. She gasped.

Kate rushed to her side and threw her arms around Mima for support. "Mima, are you okay?"

Mima grunted. "I don't know. I felt a bit faint all of a sudden."

Kate helped the older woman to the kitchen table and pulled out a chair for her. Mima lowered herself to sit, her face pale.

"Are you feeling bad? What's wrong?" asked Kate, fussing around Mima like a bee on a lavender bush.

Mima pressed a hand to her forehead. "I think I overdid it. I'm dizzy, can't seem to focus."

Kate hurried to wet a cloth and pressed it to Mima's forehead, her heart racing. "I'm going to call an ambulance." She'd just lost Nan, she wasn't sure she could take losing Mima so close to Nan's funeral. What if Mima was really sick? How could they manage without her?

"No, don't bother. I'll be fine in a moment." Mima shushed her with a wave of her hand.

"What's going on?" Jack asked, having just wandered into the kitchen.

"Mima's not feeling well," replied Kate.

Jack's eyes narrowed and he sat in a chair beside Mima, reaching for her hand to squeeze it. "You sick, Mima?"

She nodded, a smile pressed to her pale lips. "I'll be all right, I think I needed to sit down."

"Might be a good time for a check-up," he replied.

Mima shrugged. "I suppose so. I've been putting it off for long enough, maybe I should take the plunge." She chuckled.

Some colour was returning to her face and Kate's heart rate slowed to a normal pace.

"Jack, do you think you could take Mima to the doctor? I've got to get tea on the table, the guests will be down any moment to eat..."

"Happy to," he replied. "I think there's a twenty-four-hour surgery in Tweed Heads."

❧

KATE SUMMER CUPPED THE MUG OF TEA BETWEEN HER hands and blew on the surface of it sending a thin stream of steam into the cool night air. Her feet rested on the verandah rail and she leaned back in the rocking chair, a blanket covering her lap.

She'd taken to sitting outside after the evening meal was finished and the staff had been sent home. It gave her a chance to gather her thoughts, to run over the day in her mind, and to enjoy the sounds of the waves crashing against the sandy shore close by.

An owl hooted somewhere near, and cicadas hummed a deafening chorus from the nearby grove of gums. A rustle in the garden bed caught her ear and she turned to see a black and brown possum climbing up the railing and walking trapeze towards her, tail curling softly around the timber.

"Cocoa, there you are. I was waiting for you."

The animal climbed from the railing onto Kate's jean-clad legs and then scrambled onto her lap. She nosed about, looking for apple slices.

Kate laughed and retrieved a slice from the bowl on the table beside her. "Here you go. Is this what you're looking for? By the way, you really need a pedicure, those toenails of yours are sharp."

Cocoa carried the apple slice back to the verandah railing, sat on her haunches and munched happily, watching Kate as she ate. Her baby hadn't made an appearance yet, was still growing in her pouch, but Kate had seen it move beneath Cocoa's soft fur more than once.

The back door slapped open and Bindi stepped outside, a mug in one hand, a book in the other.

"Do you mind if I join you?" Her sandy-blonde hair was pulled into a messy ponytail and she'd changed from her plain skirt and button-down shirt into a pair of pyjama bottoms and a hooded jumper.

Kate nodded and patted the base of the seat beside her.

Bindi slumped into it with a sigh, crossing her legs in front of her. "My feet hurt."

"It's been a long day."

Bindi nodded. "Thanks for your help with that customer today."

"No worries."

As the Inn's manager, Bindi had to deal with every grievance, concern or gripe from their guests. Today, she'd had to face a particularly difficult situation and she'd handled it with maturity. Kate had stepped in for support, but even she could see Bindi didn't really need it. Her little sister was all grown up.

"You were great, by the way. Very calm and professional."

"Thanks," replied Bindi with a grin. She gulped a mouthful of tea, then studied Cocoa. "Is your possum bigger?"

"I don't know. Possibly...it happens."

"Is Mima okay?" asked Bindi. "I heard she wasn't feeling well."

"I don't know. Jack took her to the doctor and they haven't gotten back yet. I'm waiting for them."

"What will we do if Mima can't keep up with the work needed in the kitchen?" asked Bindi, chewing on her lower lip.

"I guess it's probably time for me to take over completely. I've got enough staff now to manage without her. I like having her around, but if it's a choice between her cooking and her health, I choose her health."

Bindi nodded. "I agree. I'm glad you're here."

Kate grinned. "Me too." She could say that now, in all honesty. A year ago she would've been horrified by the idea of throwing away her career as a high-profile chef in the city to cook at The Waratah Inn. But now, she couldn't imagine living and working anywhere else.

The glint of a diamond on her ring finger caught her eye. She moved her finger to one side, then the other, studying the ring. She also couldn't have imagined she'd be engaged to marry a man she hadn't even known existed a year ago. A high school maths teacher who worked part-time at the Inn, taking care of the horses they kept for guests to ride.

Alex was everything she never knew she'd always wanted

in a man, a partner. He was strong, caring, kind and yet quiet at the same time. He wasn't interested in pursuing an executive career like her previous fiancé had been, at the expense of everything else, including her. He was content to live in a small coastal town, teach kids how to do equations, and help tourists learn to ride horses on the beach on weekends.

In other words, he was perfect for her.

Tyres crackled on the driveway and headlights flashed at the side of the house.

"That must be Jack and Mima," said Kate, pushing to her feet and setting her mug down on the small, round table.

She jogged across the yard and around to the front of the inn where she saw Jack's truck parked, headlights still brightly illuminating the inn in a swathe of golden light. He turned them off and Kate was thrown into darkness. She blinked, hesitated until her sight returned, then moved forward.

By the time she reached them, Jack was already helping Mima from the passenger side.

"Mima, how did it go?" asked Kate, embracing her.

Mima laughed. "I'm fine, fine. Don't you worry about me. I'm not as old as Jack here, he's the one you should be sending to the doctor."

Jack huffed. "I'm as fit as a fiddle."

"Yeah, yeah, we all know just how fit you are, but you're still older than me," Mima grumbled, as Jack supported her arm.

They made it into the inn before Mima collapsed with a sigh into an armchair. The sitting room had been redecorated. Each piece, every colour lovingly selected by her sister, Reeda. She missed Reeda now that she'd moved back to Sydney. Something she never thought she'd feel, given the tensions that'd defined their relationship ever since they lost their parents.

Pale yellows, light blues, ocean art, shell wall hangings,

leather sofas and neutral rugs filled the space with warmth. Kate found a chair across from Mima, her eyes narrowed with worry.

"So, tell me what the doctor said."

Mima sighed. "We have to do this now?"

"Yes, now. Why not now?" Kate's stomach curled into a knot. She knew Mima well enough to know when she was drawing things out, buying time. Something wasn't right.

Bindi hovered behind her, hands clenched together.

Mima's gaze went from Kate's face, to Bindi's and back again. She shook her head. "Okay, I guess we're doing this now. The doctor says I have diabetes."

"What?"

"I know, I can't imagine how that happened," quipped Mima, patting her hips. "It's a mystery." She chuckled. "I guess I like my own cooking just a bit too much. Anyway, it's not bad yet, but the doctor says I need to rest more and watch what I eat. Can it get any worse than that?" Her brow furrowed and she slapped a palm on the arm of the chair.

Kate sat back, eyebrows arched. "Wow, I'm sorry Mima."

"Well, sugar and I had a good run." Mima laughed.

Jack chuckled along with her. "You'll be fine, Mima. It's not the end of the world. I'm sure there are plenty of sugar-free things for you to enjoy."

Mima rolled her eyes. "I'm sure there are, Mister Disciplined. But I'll bet they taste better than your homemade bread does. Ugh!"

Kate hid a laugh behind her hand. The two of them always griped at each other. She couldn't remember a time when they didn't tease and poke, but the love behind their banter was impossible to miss.

"My bread is delicious," retorted Jack, his brow furrowed.

"If you enjoy chomping on tree bark," replied Mima.

"Tree bark?"

"Now, come on you two," soothed Bindi. "Let's all get along. Mima's had some bad news. Would you like a cup of tea, Mima?"

Mima nodded, and Bindi trotted off to the kitchen to get it. A few guests milled about the sitting room. Some sat in front of the television set at the other end of the room, two played a game of chess, and two more occupied either end of a sofa, open books in their hands, heads bent.

Kate took Mima's hands between her own, leaning forward to give them some privacy. "Mima, I think we should talk about you retiring."

Mima's eyes widened. "But..."

"I know, we need you here, we love having you work here, but it's probably too much. Now with this diagnosis..."

Mima smiled. "I was going to bring it up, I thought you'd be upset."

"Of course I'm upset." Tears filled Kate's eyes and she swallowed down a sob. "But that doesn't mean it's not the right thing to do."

Mima nodded and patted her arm. "You're ready to do this on your own?"

Kate sniffled. "I'm ready."

"Good. You'll be fantastic, love. And I can't wait to see how it plays out. Of course, I'll be watching from my lounge chair by the swimming pool."

"Swimming pool?" queried Kate, eyebrows drawn low.

"Oh yes, well that's the other thing. I've decided to move out. I'm going to live in a retirement community in Banora Point with my friend Betty."

11

SYDNEY

Reeda fidgeted with the zipper on her jacket. The line to board the plane was moving forward at an agonisingly slow pace. Only one attendant was checking people in, and a family ahead of her seemed confused over what would be allowable as checked luggage.

She sighed and glanced at her watch. Kate had called with news that Mima was sick but hadn't called back with a promised update. Instead of waiting, Reeda had booked a last-minute flight to the Gold Coast.

It gave her an excuse to get out of town. And after her conversation with Duncan, she needed one. Even thinking about what he'd said put an ache in her chest.

She inhaled a sharp breath. She wouldn't think about it. Not today, not with Mima sick and her sisters needing her. That was what she should focus on.

The line moved forward and she boarded the plane. Grateful for a window seat, she hugged the wall, staring out at the runway below as rugged-up baggage personnel tugged luggage from a trailer and onto a conveyor belt. The bags slid into a space hidden from view.

"I guess I'm your neighbour for the next hour or so," said a gruff voice.

Reeda glanced up to see an elderly man sliding into the seat beside her. A woman followed, taking the aisle seat. The woman smiled, hazel eyes twinkling.

"Are you going on holiday, love?"

Reeda shook her head. "No, visiting family."

"Oh that's nice. We're moving to the Gold Coast." The woman's eyes widened briefly. She clutched her seatbelt, working hard to fasten it.

"Moving, huh? That's a big decision."

"Oh, I know. We're not moving yet, flying up to take a look around, see what we like. We haven't decided exactly where we want to land." The woman pushed out a hand in Reeda's direction. "I'm Eve, and this is John."

"Pleased to meet you, Eve and John, I'm Reeda." She shook the proffered hand.

They settled into their seats and Reeda clenched the arm rest as the plane lurched into the air. She wasn't exactly afraid of flying, but the takeoff and landing set loose a flurry of wings in her stomach. Still, she generally enjoyed the exhilarating feeling of adventure, travelling somewhere new, hurtling through the air above people going about their daily lives.

"Peanut?" asked John, offering Reeda an open bag.

"No, thank you."

He pulled a magazine from a satchel and opened it on his lap. Pictures of Tuscany, the Amalfi Coast, and Venice adorned each page and Reeda couldn't help looking over his shoulder. She'd never been to Italy, and it'd been a dream of hers since she was a girl. Europe in general held an appeal, especially after studying European history in high school. Something about a place with hundreds of years' worth of written history and buildings older than anything in Australia opened a door of curiosity and intrigue in her mind that had never closed.

"Beautiful, isn't it?" asked Eve.

"Yes, it really is."

"Ever been?" questioned John.

Reeda pursed her lips. "No, but I've always wanted to."

"You've got plenty of time yet," replied Eve. "We've had it on our bucket list forever and we're finally going next month."

"I'm sure you'll have a wonderful time." A twinge of envy stirred in Reeda's gut. It was crazy to be envious of a retired couple who had all the time in the world to do the things they'd dreamed of. A thriving business and a successful husband were hardly worthy of complaint. Still, she couldn't help wishing she had the freedom to follow her own dreams.

Maybe everything was different now though.

If Duncan wanted to end their marriage, what was keeping her in Sydney? She could go anywhere, do anything she wanted. Her business didn't mean so much to her that she'd keep hold of it at the expense of following her heart. Only Duncan could do that, and he was ready to let her go.

Her throat ached.

Was it her fault that she hadn't been able to fall pregnant? Anger pulsed through her veins.

She sighed. In fairness, that wasn't the reason for him pulling away. It was the stress that'd caused her to lash out at him in ways she'd never thought she would. She'd accused him of things, called him names, blamed him for the empty nursery—all while blaming herself in private.

It wasn't his fault. She'd brought this on herself. Though he hadn't fought to keep their marriage together either. He'd hidden himself away, refusing to face their problems head on. He'd buried himself in his work rather than deal with the fact that his wife was desperately unhappy and there wasn't a thing he could do about it.

And he'd grieved too. She'd seen it, though he did his best to hide it. Seen him emerge from the nursery wiping his eyes with the back of one hand. Seen his vacant looks, the downward turn of his lips, the way he studied her sometimes as though he didn't understand her at all.

The plane's engine hummed steadily. Reeda gazed out the window at the pale green bushland below, the long curve of beach and the stormy blue ocean as it appeared in bursts between fluffy clouds.

She reached beneath the seat to retrieve her purse and pulled out Nan's journal. Nan would know just what to say to ease her mind, only Nan wasn't here. Reeda would have to learn how to comfort herself, since now she had no one left in the world to do it for her.

12

JUNE 1946

BATHURST

Eddie skipped down the two front steps at the Migrant Centre. The chill winter wind whipped at her hair. She smoothed flyaway strands back against her head and tucked them into a wool cap, pulling it low over her forehead. Then, she tugged on a pair of gloves over dry, cracked hands. A pale blue sky stretched above her while thin white clouds hung high.

She'd gotten a job teaching English lessons after it changed from an Army recruitment centre to an Infantry Training Centre and finally a migrant camp.

"Goodbye Miss Watson," called one of the young girls she'd taught earlier that day.

The girl waved to her from the doorway of one of the many simple timber barracks that were stacked in rows throughout the camps to house the many European migrants and refugees flooding into the area after the war.

She waved to the girl with a smile, tugged her bicycle from the place where she'd laid it against the fence when she arrived that morning, threw her leg over the seat and set off peddling down the short, dusty drive to the main road.

It wasn't far to ride home, only a few miles, and she loved the ride. It gave her time to think about her day, what she'd done, whom she'd spoken with, what'd happened and to mull over what Keith may have done with his day.

Edie had come to terms with the fact that Charlie wasn't coming home. At first it was a hunch, a cramping in her gut whenever she thought about him. Then, as the months after the war passed by and there was no sign of him, no letter, no telegrams, she'd been in denial. There were plenty of men still stranded in different parts of the world who hadn't made it home yet. He might've been one of them.

But it was almost a year since the victory celebrations in Martin Place, and she still hadn't heard from him. Neither had his family. The official governmental line was that he was missing in action, MIA. They'd held a memorial service six months earlier, and Edie had cried until she had no tears left to cry. Then, she'd risen the next morning determined to start her life again.

Keith needed her to be well, happy, and healthy. She couldn't afford to stay buried in grief. Life must go on, and so must she.

So, that's what she did. She got a job and began saving for the time when she and Keith could be a family, just the two of them.

When she pulled her bicycle into the shed, she heard Keith squealing in the back yard. She put the bike away, tugged her jumper down over her slacks and set off to find him. He was playing with his tin truck in a pile of dirt near the clothesline. Mother was hanging out wet laundry to dry, even though Edie knew it wouldn't take long to freeze in this weather.

"It's a bit late to be hanging laundry, isn't it?" she asked with a chuckle, ducking down to kiss Keith's dirty cheek.

Mother grimaced. "It is, but this is the first opportunity I've had all day to hang it out, so it will have to do. How was your day, dear?" She offered Edie a cheek and Edie kissed it before reaching for a pair of pants to peg on the line.

"It was fine. I think I'm getting better at teaching people. At least I hope so."

"I'm sure you are." Mother was nothing if not encouraging, a trait Edie was learning to appreciate more the older she got.

"Where's Father?" asked Edie.

"He's in the orchard, pruning I believe. He's outside so much these days. I think he doesn't want to stop to..." Mother hesitated. She hadn't been the kind of woman to share personal information or make judgements of others. Still, lately she'd opened up to Edie more than ever before. Creases lined the corners of her eyes and mouth, her hair had begun to turn silver, almost as though a switch had been flicked to make the change. And her waist was thicker than it'd been the year before when Edie first returned to Bathurst.

"He doesn't want to stop and think about Bobby, you mean," Edie finished for her.

Mother bit her lower lip, then gave a curt nod. "Yes."

"I know." She looped an arm around Mother's shoulder and squeezed. "I know."

"Mummy, look at my truck! Look!" cried Keith, pointing his truck in the air, then smashing it into a pile of dirt by his feet.

Every time he called Mother that, it hurt Edie's heart a

little. She'd been wanting to bring it up for a while but was afraid it would be one more thing to grieve her parents. She didn't want that, but she hoped to take Keith with her one day when she left the farm, and she couldn't do that if he thought of her as a sister. It was time for everyone to learn the truth. It'd be difficult to face the community, in post-war Bathurst, most people frowned on women who had children out of wedlock. Still, she couldn't let things stay the way they were now. It was too hard for her to bear.

"Mother, I've been wanting to talk to you about something. Something that's been on my mind for a while..."

Mother glanced her way, a peg stuck between her teeth. "Uh huh."

"Keith calls you Mummy and thinks of me as his sister."

Mother's eyes narrowed.

Edie couldn't stop now. "I'd like to tell him. You know, that I'm his mother."

Mother pegged a handkerchief to the clothesline, then faced Edie with a frown. "Edith, we've talked about this. It's for the best that everyone, including Keith, thinks of you as his sister. I don't know what people would say..."

"I don't care. I'm ready to face them. I'm ready to deal with it."

"I don't think you are," countered Mother, looking suddenly older.

Edie rested a hand on Mother's arm. "He's my son, and I want to raise him as my son. I'm so grateful for what you and Father have done, I'll be forever in your debt. But I want him to know that I'm his mother. I can't..." Her voice broke and she couldn't go on.

Mother patted her hand. "I understand. You should tell him." She sighed. "I'm going inside."

"What about Father?" asked Edie, panic gnawing at her gut.

"I'll deal with your father." Mother offered her a pinched smile. "You're growing up, my darling girl." She patted Edie's hand again, wiped her hands on her apron and wandered back to the house.

Keith was making growling engine noises as he pushed his truck back and forth in the dirt. Edie watched him for a few moments, heart thundering against her ribcage. What should she say? How could she tell a three-year-old boy she was his mother?

She walked slowly towards him, then sat on the grass beside him.

"Wanna turn?" he asked, squinting up at her.

She nodded. "Yes, please."

She pushed the truck around in the dirt, making the best truck sounds she could, while watching him out of the corner of her eye. He laughed with delight at her efforts, then snatched back the truck.

Instead of admonishing him, she inhaled a deep breath. "Keith, I want to talk to you about something important."

He stopped *vrooming* and looked at her with curiosity. "Okay."

She didn't know how to say it. How to begin. Would he understand? "I...I'm your mother."

He studied her eyes narrowed but not saying anything.

"I'm your mother. Not your sister. Mummy isn't your mother, and Daddy isn't your father..."

"But Mummy and Daddy are here." His brow furrowed.

"Yes, I know..." She exhaled. "We told you they were your parents because..." What could she say? Because people can be cruel? Because she was too young to care for him? "Because your granny thought it would be for the best."

"Granny?" Confusion twisted his face.

"Um..." It wasn't going well, but how could it? He was three years old; it was too much for him to understand.

"Keith, do you think you could call Mummy, Granny, and call me Mummy?"

He shrugged. "I dunno."

"You don't have to right away. When you're ready."

"Okay." He went back to driving the truck through the dirt, this time quietly.

She stood and brushed the grass from her pants, watching him for a while longer. Then she finished hanging the clothes on the line. Maybe one day she'd tell him about Charlie, but he was already so confused. It was clear he hadn't understood what she'd said, it'd take time and more conversations to help him comprehend the truth. When he was ready, she'd talk to him about Charlie as well. Tell him all about the father who'd died a hero in the war.

She sighed, watching her son as he threw the truck into the air and laughed as it smashed to the ground. She should never have left him, should never have put him in this situation. She'd confused things between them and wasn't certain that they could ever be made right again.

❧ 13 ❧

JUNE 1996

CABARITA BEACH

The yellow taxi pulled up in front of The Waratah Inn and Reeda climbed out with a smile on her face. It hadn't been long since she was last there, only a few weeks, but it felt like an age. She'd missed it, missed her family, and the quiet calm of the beach.

Kate and Bindi hadn't known she was coming, so no one greeted her. She'd wanted it that way, liked showing up to surprise them and not making a fuss.

She couldn't stop thinking about Mima. With no updates other than Kate telling her Mima seemed fine when she left for her doctor's appointment, she had to believe her friend would be okay. Still, nerves gathered in the pit of her stomach as she eyed the inn's solid front door.

She'd taken an early morning flight, so it was likely they were serving breakfast.

A flock of cockatoos passed by overhead, their chorus of screeches drowning out the rush and sigh of waves against the shore. Sunshine beat down on her head, warming her hair, and she marvelled at the difference in temperature. She paid the taxi driver, then shucked her coat, laying it over the top of her bag.

Reeda climbed the white stairs one at a time, the small, round wheels of her bag thunking on each step. She turned the doorknob and it opened with the low squeak of new hinges. The sound of voices and aroma of frying bacon met her immediately, and she grinned as she stepped over the threshold.

"Hello?" she called towards the kitchen.

Kate peered around the corner with eyes narrowed. Her face erupted into a grin and she rushed toward Reeda, laughing.

"Reeda! I didn't know you were coming. You didn't say anything. I tried calling you first thing but couldn't reach you. Now I know why."

They embraced and Reeda felt the tension leave her shoulders with her sister's arms around her. The two of them had been through a lot together and had their differences, but the last few months had drawn them closer than they'd been since childhood.

Reeda chuckled. "I know, I'm sorry. As soon as I hung up the phone, I knew I wanted to come. So, I booked a ticket for a ridiculous hour of the morning, and here I am."

Kate took Reeda's bag and led her towards the kitchen. "Bindi is going to be so thrilled you're here. I know she's missed you. We both have." Kate's cheeks flushed red and Reeda's heart warmed.

Her sisters had come to mean more to her than she'd thought possible only a year ago. During her twenties, she'd pushed ahead with her career, met Duncan, and spent all her time with him, built friendships with other strong women, and all but ignored her family. Her parents were gone, Nan lived so far away, and her sisters irritated her to no end. They didn't understand her, didn't really know her. She'd changed, become a different person, a better person, than she had been when they knew her.

That was what she'd believed. That she didn't need them.

Now that she'd moved into her thirties, all that was changing. Family mattered more to her and career seemed less important than it had been. She still loved her job, but it didn't consume her the way it had. And with Duncan ready to break ties with her, perhaps family was all she had left.

Them and an old inn.

Her throat thickened and tears threatened. She cleared her throat with a cough and shook her head as Bindi bounded out of the office.

"Reeda! It's so good to see you." They embraced and, as Bindi chatted her ear off, she smiled and took in the sights, sounds, and smells of the busy bed and breakfast.

"Looks like everything is going well," she said. "Do you have a full house?"

Kate nodded, returning to the stove where a pan of eggs was scrambling. She pushed the mixture around with a spoon. "Yep. Full house every week since opening. It's been crazy. But in a good way, of course."

"That's great to hear. Although, I'm really dying to know how Mima is going. That's why I flew up here..."

Bindi and Kate exchanged a glance. Kate motioned for one of the staff to take over with the eggs. Bindi poured three cups of tea and Kate led Reeda out onto the porch. They sat in rocking chairs, side by side, the ocean a rhythmic undercurrent, a magpie's call the melody.

Sweat beads formed on Reeda's brow. Why didn't they say something? Tell her what was going on? "So, come on, spill."

Kate sighed. "She has diabetes."

"Oh no, that's not good." Reeda's brow furrowed. "But it's not the end of the world, either."

"And she's resigned from the inn," continued Bindi.

It wasn't completely unexpected. Mima was getting older and Reeda had hinted more than once that perhaps she should slow down. She never expected that Mima would do it, though. Mima and the Waratah had seemed inseparable. She'd been there almost as long as Nan had.

"I suppose that's not the end of the world either," mumbled Reeda. "We knew it was coming. Maybe not so suddenly, but we knew..."

"I'm glad you're taking it so well," encouraged Bindi with a hand on Reeda's back.

"Yeah, it's going to be fine. I'm taking over for Mima, so nothing will change. The inn will continue as it has done, Mima will get her swimming pool and jacuzzi, and everyone will be fine," Kate said.

"What?" Reeda asked.

"She's moving in with a friend, Betty. Apparently, there's a jacuzzi involved," replied Kate with a chuckle.

"Mima has a friend?"

All three of the women laughed together.

"I'm glad it's nothing more serious. You had me worried... by the way, where is Mima, I'd like to talk to her."

Kate stood and smoothed her apron with one hand. "She's looking at units in the retirement community with Betty."

"Well, good for her."

IT WAS STRANGE TO BE AT THE INN WITHOUT HAVING A JOB to do. The entire place ran like clockwork, and all without her help. When she'd stayed there before she'd been managing the renovation. It'd kept her busy and made her feel needed.

Now, Bindi and Kate ran everything, and apparently didn't require anything from her. Kate had given her strict instructions to relax and enjoy herself. So, she'd spent the day reading Nan's journals, walking around the inn's grounds, visiting the horses, feeding the chooks, and now was seated on the verandah in a rocking chair staring at the horizon.

She wasn't used to relaxing. It didn't seem to come naturally to her.

Itching to do something, she jumped up and strode inside. In the office, she dialled her home phone number, expecting to get the answering machine. Instead, Duncan's gruff voice answered.

"Hi, Duncan. I wasn't expecting to reach you. Are you okay?"

"I think I have a cold, it's nothing. Did you make it there?"

"Yep, I'm here. It's much warmer than Sydney." She issued an awkward laugh. It was strange not having the usual comfortable conversation with her husband. Things between them had shifted, she didn't know where she stood.

"Say hi to everyone for me," he said, as though to round off the conversation.

"Wait, Duncan, I'm thinking of staying a while longer. I need some time...time to think things through. I brought everything with me I might need in case."

He hesitated. "That's probably a good idea, Reeda."

"You don't mind?"

"No, we both know we need some time apart."

Her heart dropped and a lump built in her throat. "I guess that's true."

"Take all the time you need."

Anger stirred in her gut. He was pushing her away, and it

seemed to cost him nothing. How could he do it so easily? All those years, the commitment they'd made, and he could let go as though it was the easiest thing in the world to do. Why fight it?

She was tired. Tired of fighting—for a baby, for her husband. Tired of fighting the burden of guilt she'd carried around all these years over the way her own parents had died, depriving her sisters of their mother and father. It was too much. All of it.

Tears welled in her eyes and this time she didn't push them down. She needed to get away. To find a place where she could rest, be herself, not think. Where could she go? Charlie went to Italy. She'd always wanted to see Italy, the paintings, the cathedrals, the cobblestone streets. It was everything Australia wasn't. It was old, ripe with history, brimming with culture and tradition, simultaneously embracing and balking at modernity. Australia was young, still finding its path, a hodgepodge of cultures and traditions mashed up into one, careening into the modern age with barely a backwards glance.

"I might travel to Italy, just in case you can't get hold of me here."

Silence at the other end of the line gave her a brief flash of satisfaction. He hadn't been expecting that. In truth, neither had she. The starkness of her words, their simplicity, and the impact they brought, had a deliciousness that curled her lips just a little.

"Okay..."

He was so cool, so collected. Didn't he care, even a bit?

"I'll talk to you later." A stone formed in her gut.

"Italy, Reeda? Where did this come from? You've never said anything about going to Italy."

Sometimes it felt as though he didn't know her at all. She'd talked to him about it several times over the years.

Didn't he ever listen to her? "Yes, I have, I always wanted to go. Don't you remember me discussing Florence, Venice, Rome?"

He huffed. "Years ago."

"Well, now I'm going." She was. She'd decided. At first, she'd only wanted to provoke him into saying something, anything to show he still cared. That he wanted her to stay. But even as she said the words, the idea took hold in her mind like moss growing on a rock. She was going to Italy. He obviously didn't care, so what did it matter? She'd go to Italy and get fat on gelato, and he could do whatever it was that made him happy when he wasn't with her.

"Fine," he growled.

"Fine!"

"Call me when you get back," his voice brimmed with hostility.

"I will!"

She slammed the earpiece back into the cradle, tears trailing down her cheeks. She stared at her ring finger, then tugged the wedding band free. The engagement ring was harder to dislodge. She grimaced and pulled until it sat beside the plain gold band on top of the desk. Then, she shoved the rings into her jeans pocket, her vision blurring.

Reeda jumped to her feet and rushed through the kitchen and past the staff all working hard to prepare dinner for the guests. Kate glanced at her but Reeda wasn't about to stop, didn't want her sister to see how upset she was. If she noticed Reeda's tears she'd want to talk about it, and Reeda wasn't ready to do that yet. It still hurt too much. Words would make it real, and she couldn't face the fact that Duncan was slipping away and there wasn't anything she could do about it.

She broke into a jog at the bottom of the stairs. She ran along the garden path, past the chook shed, the garden shed, then the stables where the horses were milling around after an afternoon of trotting along the beach, guests bouncing around on their backs.

If he couldn't be trusted with her heart, to be there through the good and the bad, maybe it was best she found out now. She'd already wasted ten years of her life with him, she'd rather not waste another ten before she discovered his disdain.

Angry clouds gathered overhead, blue, black, and heavy with rain. Reeda barely noticed them as she slowed her pace on the trail down to the cove. She tugged the collar of her shirt up around her neck and paused on the makeshift stairs to look out over the length of the curved beach and kick off her shoes.

Castle Rock stood black and foreboding about twenty metres from the shore. Fierce waves crashed against it sending salt spray skyward, then rushing the shore. Foam gathered along the sand where the waves reached their limit before sighing back into the sea.

She inhaled a deep breath, then skipped down the stairs and across the sand, her bare toes digging deep into the cool, dry sand. When she reached the hard-packed wet sand, the cold bit into the soles of her feet. She shivered and hunched her shoulders against the gathering wind, shoving her hands deep into her jeans pockets. She fingered the top of the rings buried in one pocket, turning them slowly, feeling the sharp edges of the diamond and the smooth worn gold.

She'd reached the end of the cove before she realised where she was. Deep in thought, she'd hardly noticed her surroundings. When she met the outcropping of rocks that reached into the ocean, she paused in confusion. Then, hands pressed to hips, turned back to survey the landscape.

A fat raindrop landed on her cheek. She peered up into the sky as three more took its place.

She should've thought to grab a jacket.

❧ 14 ❧

JUNE 1981

CABARITA BEACH

The cave was dark. So dark, Reeda couldn't see the back of it. She stood on a large, black rock with edges so sharp they cut into the soles of her feet and peeked around the rock-face. The sounds of water lapping at the edges of something was welcoming and a little spooky all at the same time. Still, she was the eldest and if she showed fear to Kate and Bindi, there was no way they'd follow her into the cave, and she wanted to explore it.

They didn't have anything like this at home in Sydney. Spending the winter holidays at the inn with Nan was the best. Well, maybe not quite as good as summer at the Inn, but pretty close. In summer her teeth didn't chatter when she surfed the waves in the cove, and she could wear her new bikini without freezing to death, the one with the red stripes and the thin straps.

They'd never been to this end of the cove without Nan before. When Nan came with them, she didn't let them go into the cave. Said the tide could come up too fast, but Reeda was sixteen years old. She wasn't a baby anymore. She could watch for the tide and get out in time.

"Kate, Bindi, come here!" she called.

Her sisters, clad in swimsuits and shorts, came running over the wet sand. The sky was dark with clouds that hung low over the beach, obscuring the sunlight, and throwing everything into shadow. A rumble in the distance was barely audible but made Reeda glance skyward a moment before returning her attention to her sisters. Bindi's hands were cupped together, overflowing with seashells of all shapes and colours.

"Look what I got," Bindi said, excitement tinging her cheeks pink.

Reeda rolled her eyes. She wasn't interested in seashells.

Kate frowned. "What? What do you want?"

"Let's explore this cave," Reeda said.

"Nan says we shouldn't go in there..." Bindi's brow furrowed.

Reeda huffed. "Are you going to do everything Nan says your whole life?"

Reeda jumped down from the rock and strode into the cave, her heart pounding. It was black in the cave. So dark she couldn't see the way forward. She slowed her pace until her eyes adjusted to the dim light, then moved on with cautious steps. The cave walls were built of hard, black rock, pockmarked with indentations where the water had worn the rock away. Up ahead that sound of water lapping against rock continued and she headed towards it.

Sea water rose up around her feet and ankles as the cave's floor sloped downward. Sand squelched between her toes. Bindi slipped her hand into Reeda's. She was thirteen years old but sometimes she seemed younger. She'd always been the baby of the family, but Reeda didn't say anything about it since secretly she loved the way Bindi looked up to her and followed her lead.

Kate hovered close behind the two of them, her deep breathing loud in the enclosed space.

"You're so loud," complained Reeda, her own heart still pounding noisily in her chest.

"I ran up the beach, I'm puffed," pouted Kate.

At the back of the cave a rock pool was filled with water from a narrow trickle that ran from the sea along one side of the cave, ending in the pool. The pool looked black, and the water slapped soft and wet against the cave's wall almost in time with the motion of the waves outside.

"Wow," whispered Kate, kneeling beside the pool.

Reeda dropped to her knees as well and released Bindi's hand to plunge both her own into the frigid water. It sent a shiver up her arms and down her spine.

"It's cold!"

"No duh!" retorted Kate with what Reeda imagined was a smirk.

She stood to run her palm over the wall's surface, feeling sharp edges and smooth, round hollows beneath it. A splash in the pool made her jump, Bindi squealed and leapt away from the water. Kate fell on her rear end in the sand.

"What was that?" cried Reeda, eyes wide.

"I don't know," replied Bindi.

"A fish?" suggested Kate, then burst out laughing.

All three of the girls laughed together, a nervous, giggling sound, as though they weren't entirely in control of their reactions. When the sound died away, the shadow of it echoed around the cavernous space.

In the silence, they heard the first crack of thunder.

"It's storming," said Kate.

"No duh!" replied Reeda with her own smirk in her sister's general direction.

"Shut up."

They spent the next ten minutes exploring the rest of the cave as the sounds of rain on water, breaking waves, and the crash of thunder filled the cave around them. It was a marvellous place and Reeda couldn't believe they'd never been inside it before during one of their visits to the Waratah. Nan was too cautious. The water level had risen a little since they entered it, but not enough to be dangerous.

When the tide did rise, it came quickly and Reeda was so busy poking a stick at a crayfish she found in one of the small crevices of the rock pool that she didn't notice at first.

"Um, Reeda, I think we should go," said Bindi, a tremor in her voice.

When Reeda looked up towards the cave's entrance, her heart sank. The water level was chest height at least. She climbed down from her vantage point, gasping as the cold water climbed up the length of her. Kate had been higher still up the far wall; she climbed down as well and all three of them waded as quickly as they could back to the entrance. The driving waves were impacting against the front of the cave now, and each one sent them back off their feet and deeper into the hollow.

"I'm scared," mumbled Bindi, teeth chattering against the cold.

Reeda took her hand, and Kate's as well. Kate didn't complain but squeezed tight, not letting go. They surged forward together, fighting against every wave that tried to sink or bury them in that cave.

At the entrance, they climbed one at a time up a rocky outcropping, holding tight every time a wave lashed at them. Reeda went last, and by the time she began to climb her feet were no longer touching the sandy floor of the cave. Finally, gasping for breath, Reeda flung herself down on the rock beside her sisters who were laid out on their backs staring up into the rain, breathing hard as water sluiced down the sides of their faces.

She rolled onto her stomach, grimaced at the pain of the rock cutting into her flesh and peaked a hand over her eyes to shelter them from the rain.

Her stomach clenched into a knot when she saw the tide had risen so high, they were now cut off from the beach. The rock they were laying on was effectively an island, surrounded on all sides by swirling water and pounding waves.

"Oh no," she said.

"What?" questioned Kate, sitting up with a frown.

"We're cut off."

Bindi joined them, still breathing hard, her nose red. "What will we do?"

"I don't know, but we're safe here for now," said Reeda.

She didn't feel as safe as she let them believe, since the tide was still rising and she'd seen the cove during high tide, the rock they were seated on was usually the place the salt spray went the highest as the waves crashed over it. It wouldn't protrude above the waterline for long.

A wave hit the rock face now, splashing the three of them. Reeda shivered, hugging herself tight. They huddled together, peering helplessly back towards the trail that would lead them to the safety of the inn. Only now they couldn't reach it, and shouting for help wouldn't do much, given how loud the rain and waves were, not to mention the volume of the regular cracks of thunder as lightning streaked across the menacing sky.

Just then, Reeda saw a dark figure on the beach. She stood to her feet and waved her hands over her head.

"Hey! Hey! Help!"

The other two girls joined her when they saw the person

striding down the beach towards them. It was Jack, Nan's new handyman. He'd spotted them. He waved, then turned back to the trail and broke into a run.

"Where's he going?" wailed Bindi, her lips trembling. "Wait!"

"He's probably going to get help or something. Don't worry, he saw us," replied Reeda.

He returned before long with a rope and two life vests. They watched, shivering as he tied one end of the rope to a nearby Pandanus trunk. The tree leaned over the rocky outcropping, lower branches almost touching the water's surface. Then, he tied the other end of the rope around himself. He donned a life jacket, and with the other jacket in one hand waded into the water where it was sheltered from the brunt of the waves by the rocks.

He had to swim to reach the rocks they squatted on, and climbed it slowly, ducking as each wave pummelled him. When he reached the girls, they all threw their arms around his waist. Relief flooded through Reeda. If he could get to them, they could make it back, surely.

He patted their heads, one by one. "It's okay, girls. I'm here now. We'll be back on shore before you know it."

His blue eyes were warm, his hands strong, his grey-streaked reddish beard soaked through with salt water, his hair caked against his head.

He pushed the spare life vest over Bindi's head and helped her to the edge of the rock. When he climbed down, Bindi looked back over her shoulder with a weak smile, then turned to follow him.

By the time it was Reeda's turn, she'd watched her sisters make their way to the beach without incident and felt much more confident about how to do it.

Jack helped her down. He protected her with his body when each wave came. The water made its way down her throat and buffeted her body. She fell to her knees twice and was grasping for something to cling to before she was washed out to sea. Then Jack's hands grasped her by the arm and pulled her to her feet. Finally, she made it on the beach, hacking and coughing up sea water as she stumbled across the sand. She collapsed beside her sisters, weak with exhaustion and cold.

Muted shouts behind her sounded but she was too tired to turn her head. Then Mum, Dad, and Nan were there. They collapsed in the sand beside the girls. Mum peppered them with kisses as rain dripped from her nose. Dad sighed and held each hand tightly one by one.

"Where have you been? We've been looking everywhere for you," cried Mum, raindrops mingling with tears on her cheeks.

Then, they helped the girls to their feet and half-carried them back to the inn.

Nan trotted beside Reeda, one arm looped through Reeda's. She turned her head to look back with a wave, her brow furrowed. When Reeda glanced over her shoulder, Jack stood in the rain, lungs heaving as he watched them walk away. He nodded and sent her a wide smile. Then he turned and trudged away through the pouring rain.

❧ 15 ❧

CABARITA BEACH

Reeda stood staring at the cave's entrance. The tide was low, the waves lolled, deceptively safe, some distance from the gaping opening. Overhead, thunder cracked as lightning tracked across the stormy sky.

Rain pitter-pattered over the sand, wetting Reeda's hair, shoulders, cheeks. She grimaced with an upward glance as another trail of lightning snaked its path through the sky, then jumped as the thunder boomed in its wake.

She'd been so scared the day she and her sisters were caught in that cave. Certain she'd die, that they'd all die. Dashed against the rocks or carried out to see on a riptide. Either way, she didn't think she'd see her parents ever again. But then she had. Jack came to the rescue.

She'd barely known him then. He was new to the inn's staff, and mostly kept to himself. He was kind, quiet, and good at his job. That was all she'd known about him. But that day he'd become part of the family, at least in her mind. She'd be forever grateful for what he'd done for them.

Whenever there was a storm at the beach, she recalled that day. The memories of her fear never seemed to fade.

But what she'd forgotten until that moment was the closeness she'd felt to her sisters back then. Before the accident tore their family apart, they'd loved each other in a confident, careless kind of way. As if they each knew how the other felt and didn't believe it could ever change. They didn't doubt they were loved, didn't doubt their love for each other. How could they know that one day it would be shaken so badly they'd pull apart for over a decade?

If Nan hadn't died and left them the inn to renovate, they'd still be distant, still wouldn't be the sisters they were today. The sisters they should always have been.

She sighed and ran a hand over her wet hair as the rain grew heavier, then wiped the water from her eyes. Nan had known what they needed and had done her best to help them find each other all over again.

It wasn't the way it had been then, even now. But they'd come a long way. She couldn't change the past and the way she'd drifted from her sisters over the years, but she could find out the truth about Charlie Jackson—for all of them.

She was going to Italy. It was something she'd always wanted to do, and while she was there, she could find out if the Italian government had information on allied soldiers who were shot down in the gulf. Maybe it'd be a dead end, but maybe she'd find something. It was worth a try. Besides, she had nothing better to do. She had no desire to return to her business and preferred to avoid going home for now. Time to herself was what she needed, even if it meant facing her fear of being left alone. If she was going to be single, she might as well get started by taking a holiday on her own. And besides, she'd already told Duncan she was going. She had no intention of backing down now.

She squared her shoulders and marched to the inn as rain trickled down her back and matted her hair to her head.

After a hot shower and change of clothes, she headed to the office to make a phone call. Her assistant, Kay, answered on the second ring.

"Good afternoon, this is Nyreeda Summer Designs. How may I help you?"

"Hi Kay, it's Reeda."

"Oh hi, Reeda. How are you? How's the north coast?"

"It's great. Wet. Listen, Kay, I need you to do something for me."

"Shoot," replied Kay, in a businesslike tone.

"Can you please book me a return ticket to Rome, leaving as soon as possible? And I'll probably need a visa as well. I've got my passport here with me, but there's a photocopy of it in the filing cabinet in my office if you need it."

"Rome? Really? What's going on in Rome?" asked Kay.

"I'm taking a holiday."

"Oh wow, that's so great. Good for you," replied Kay. "Is Duncan going with you?"

"Not this time. It's just me. I thought it would be nice to spend some time alone." That would get the office gossips talking, it sounded pathetic even to her own ears. How could it possibly matter, though, given that soon enough everyone would know the truth. When Duncan asked for a divorce, she wouldn't be able to hide their troubles any longer.

"Oh wow. Okay. Well, good for you. I'll give you a call at the inn when I've got it sorted, shall I?"

"Yes, please," replied Reeda.

When she hung up the phone she leaned back in her chair and linked her fingers behind her head. She was going to Italy. Her heart fluttered. Was she crazy to travel to Europe on her own? She'd never done anything like it before. She and Duncan had married so soon after she finished her studies, and neither one of them had any money. He'd travelled a little in Asia with his parents, but she'd never been anywhere outside Australia.

They'd taken trips together, of course, throughout their decade of marriage. But for most of that ten-year period, Duncan had his head in books studying for his medical degree and then for his surgical qualifications. Since then they'd had one holiday in New Zealand, and a luxurious week in Fiji, but Europe hadn't been on the agenda. Mostly because Duncan didn't want to take so much time off work. And then, when her business took off and the fertility treatments began, it didn't make sense to travel so far away.

Now she was going, and she'd be doing it alone. Butterflies turned somersaults in her stomach, and she swallowed hard, then smiled. She'd soon be headed to Italy.

WHEN SHE GOT BACK FROM AN HOUR LONG WALK ALONG the beach to clear her head, Reeda found Kate trying out a new sponge cake recipe in the kitchen.

"Kate, where did you find those letters from Charlie to Nan?"

Kate pursed her lips. "Uh, there's a box under the staircase, in that storage cupboard. I think I labeled it, "*Nan's correspondence*". There are hundreds of letters in there, from family and friends, over the years. I found those few from Charlie, but there might be more. I didn't go through the whole lot."

Reeda found the cupboard and spent a good five minutes trying to tug it open. The new white paint stuck together, making it hard to get the door to budge. Finally it opened and she landed on her rear end against the wall as it flew wide.

With a grunt, she brushed herself off and crawled into the narrow, dark space. She'd brought a torch with her and didn't take long to locate the box.

She pulled it out of the cupboard, then sat on the floor to go through the contents. After a while, she found another letter with Charlie's distinctive handwriting on it. She looked for a postmark. There wasn't one.

The paper was aged and stained, just like the other letters. Only this one hadn't been posted.

Her eyes narrowed as she took the letter from the envelope and unfolded it. There was no date on the letter, but it was obvious from the condition of the paper, it'd been written many years earlier.

She began to read.

❧ 16 ❧

9 JULY 1943

THE GULF OF TUNIS

"A re you ready?" asked Scotty Morris, smacking on a piece of gum with his tongue.

Charlie ran a cloth over his rifle, shining the wood until it gleamed. He leaned it against his bunk and stared at it a moment. "Yep. Heading out in a few minutes."

He glanced at his watch. It was difficult to read in the late-night gloom. He held it closer to the lantern that swung from the low ceiling.

"Let's go then," replied Scotty, as he slipped into his jacket.

"Time to harass some Nazis," replied Charlie as he extinguished the lamp and followed the small group of pilots outside.

They marched together out to the field. Tent barracks

stretched out on both sides of them, door flaps popping and snapping in the breeze. Ahead of the men, rows of olive, drab-coloured P-40 Kittyhawks, Gloster Gladiator biplanes, and Bristol Blenheim light bombers stretched into the distance under the dim light of a half moon. Clouds hung low in the sky, moving swiftly before the warm gusting wind. Charlie tugged his jacket collar up around the scarf that was looped around his neck. He was overdressed for a summer's evening in north Africa, but it would be cold soon enough when they reached altitude.

Light footsteps behind them were followed by a slap on Charlie's back. He spun to face Cobber, who grinned. Cobber slung an arm around Charlie's neck as they walked.

"Let's get 'em mate," he said. "We'll see who'll be the ace pilot after tonight, eh Cap?"

Charlie laughed. "That's Squadron Leader to you, Pilot Officer Cobman. And you know it'll be me. You've only got two kills. You're never gonna catch up."

Cobber blurted. "What? Strewth! I've taken down at least three of Fritz's flyers."

"I don't think it counts if you ram them," replied Scotty with a chuckle. He rubbed his fist back and forth over the top of Cobber's head until Cobber's leather hat fell off.

"Hey, stop it." Cobber reached for his hat and pushed it back onto his head, then grinned. "I guess we'll have to wait and see who comes out on top tonight. And ramming definitely counts. That's why I love me Polly, she'll take a beating, and keep on flying."

They each climbed into their own planes. Charlie checked his instruments, fitted his harness, leather cap with ear cups for radio communication, goggles, and oxygen mask with microphone, and waited for the ground crew to direct him for take off. His heart pumped a steady rhythm, his mind stayed clear and focused. He'd done similar runs enough times to know the drill. Get in the air, lead the squadron out over The Bay of Tunis, locate the fleet cutting through that deep, dark stretch of ocean bound for Italy, and hold off the German fighters. The bombers, troop carriers, and battleships would do the rest. Simple enough.

It was day one of the offensive to take back Italy from the Axis, and the small group of Australian flyers with the RAAF Squadron 454 had been stationed with the British RAF as part of the Desert Air Force for several months. The base in Tunisia gave them ready access to the bay where they could provide air support for the anti-submarine, anti-mine Bathurst Class Corvettes that were to escort a convoy of ships as part of the Husky offensive to invade Sicily, under the direction of General Dwight D. Eisenhower, Commander-in-Chief of the Allied forces in North Africa.

Charlie stretched out his neck, rocking his head to one side, then the other. His thick leather jacket with knit-wool jumper beneath made him sweat. Still, he knew his legs would get cold up there; they always did. No doubt the adrenaline would do its part to keep him warm. He barely noticed the cold when he was up there, it usually wasn't until he was flying back to the base that his teeth began to chatter, but he couldn't blame the temperature for that entirely. When the adrenaline surge slowed, he didn't seem to be able to help it.

He glanced over each wing to where he knew the Browning machine guns were nestled. Then he did a mental run through of the tactics he'd use, his targets, the goals of the mission and why he did what he did—whom he was fighting for. It was a ritual he performed before each flight and it helped him stay focused. They'd enjoyed a string of successes in North Africa over the past two years and this was the final push. He had to keep going, stay on task, and it'd all be over soon.

The war had lasted much longer than he'd ever believed

possible. He'd promised Edie he'd be back almost a year ago. But there wasn't anything more he could do about it than he was already doing. The battle had extended into the Pacific now and the German and Italian troops had held off a formidable force of Allies, but now they were losing ground every day. It wouldn't be long, and this would all be over, and he could go home to Edie and Keith. They'd finally be able to start their lives together, be a family.

He pulled a photograph of Edie and Keith from his pocket and stared at it. The image had a crease mark down the centre where she'd folded it into an envelope to send him. Her pretty blonde hair, blue eyes, and peaches and cream skin all sported different shades of grey in the simple image. But he didn't care. She was the most beautiful creature he'd ever seen, and he couldn't wait to get back to her. Keith held still in her arms, a frown leaving a crease between his eyebrows, chubby legs were covered by a cotton suit, and one fist hovered close to the baby's mouth. He wondered whom she'd asked to take the picture, since it wasn't likely her parents would've agreed to it.

He kissed the photograph once, then tucked it back into his pocket.

The take-off was smooth, but as soon as he was in the air, he felt the buffeting wind sweep the Kittyhawk to one side. He adjusted direction and shifted back on course, but his brow furrowed with concern. How would they manage a massive troop landing and aerial attack in weather like this?

A quick glance over his shoulder showed the rest of the squadron had fallen into formation behind him. He smiled and steered in the direction of the bay; his hand steady on the shuddering yoke.

THE GROUND BELOW LIT UP LIKE A FIREWORKS DISPLAY. IT was just after midnight and the sky was dark, apart from the sliver of moon and a few winking stars. The clouds had been swept away by the fierce wind, and the entire armada below were clearly being buffeted and shaken by it, just as Charlie was.

The bombing had started a few minutes earlier and seemed to take the Axis troops stationed in Sicily by surprise. There was no response at first. From where he flew, Charlie couldn't see much. He and the rest of his squadron were waiting for the enemy fighters to arrive, and adrenaline pumped in anticipation. He knew from experience they'd be difficult to see until they were almost upon his squadron, so staying alert was his main priority. That and keeping track of what was going on below via a few crackled radio messages from base and the occasional dip of wings to peer down in that direction.

He tipped the plane to one side again to study the long string of beaches below. Troop carriers were pushed up close to the shoreline and he could just make out the dark shadows of men rushing up the beaches in clusters. Beyond the beach was darkness, probably bushes or trees. He couldn't tell. It was as if the troops were rushing into darkness itself.

Aircrafts dropped paratroopers like dandelions in the spring. White silk parachutes sailed beneath him, driven off course by the relentless wind. Bright blobs floated in the black ocean below. Men already lost in the dark heaving waters, with more on their way to join them.

He inhaled a sharp breath, then righted his plane as a spray of bullets thudded into its tail. He dove the plane and looked over his shoulder to see the squadron disperse. German fighters chased the Allied planes in every direction.

They couldn't outrun them, he knew that. As much as he

loved his Polly, the all-metal P40 Kittyhawk he'd flown since he arrived in north Africa wasn't fast enough to beat Jerry when it came to aerial combat. They had their nicknames for the enemy, Jerry, Fritz, it didn't make any difference but lightened the mood a little, and they could do with some of that. But even though Jerry was faster, his Polly could pull high-G turns and took tremendous punishment without complaint. She'd survived several bouts of heavy fire, and Cobber had come through midair collisions in his plane almost entirely unharmed. Still, they wouldn't win a dogfight if it came down to speed, so he had to make sure it didn't.

After a tight turn, he was ready to give chase. He followed a Luftwaffe Messerschmitt Bf 109 in pursuit of one of his men, its tail in his sights. It ducked to the left and he followed. It fired on the allied craft ahead of it, closing the gap with each moment that passed. He had to act soon, or his man would be shot down. When the enemy was within range, he aimed the dorsal machine guns attached to the Kittyhawk's nose. He sprayed the plane with bullets and it hesitated mid-air, then fell from the sky, smoke billowing from its belly.

The air was full of the wail of plane engines and the thunder of machine-gun fire. He jerked his head this way and that, trying to catch a glimpse of his squadron, and to see who needed his help. He'd lost sight of the Luftwaffer on his tail but knew the enemy fighter wouldn't give up so easily.

Charlie turned again, the G-forces punishing his body as the Kittyhawk cornered hard. A pair of planes screamed by, noses aimed downward, Jerry on the tail of one of his own.

Scotty.

He dove in pursuit.

The entire plane shuddered and shook as he took the almost vertical dive. He caught them in moments and fired, still in free fall. The German plane broke up with a flash of orange midair, then plunged towards the dark, formless landscape, lit only by tracer bullets and flak.

Charlie grinned with victory as he pulled hard on the yoke to right his plane. Just as he levelled out, the rat-a-tat of machine-gun fire filled his ears. He was hit, again, and this time it was bad. He saw a hole in the control panel in front of him, and several more in the metal plates surrounding the forward engine.

The plane stalled, the sound of the engine fading to silence, then its nose tipped forward and he fell towards the earth. Charlie unbuckled his harness, ear cups, and mask, watching and waiting for the right moment. He'd flown several miles away from the battle lines when he followed Scotty, and all he could see through the plane's one window was dark, formless land. Tracer bullets pierced the air close by, followed by a round of flak. They came close, whistling through the air around him, thudding into the plane's metal frame.

With a quick pull of a lever, he was catapulted into the air. Then, he tugged on a line and his parachute exploded from the pack on his back. When the chute filled with air, he jerked like a just hooked trout, then settled into the fall as machine-gun fire whistled by his ears and thwacked into the ballooning fabric overhead.

He watched as the wind pulled his parachute away from the plummeting plane. The aircraft landed in the ocean, just off the coast, disappearing beneath the surging water within moments. His chute carried him inland, over the beach and out of the line of anti-aircraft fire that continued to pierce the night with its staccato rhythm and bright tracers.

When the bullet hit him, it pierced through his calf. The pain didn't come at first, then the heat of it stabbed up his leg, making him shout. He groaned and grabbed for the leg where the bullet had lodged. He was close to the ground now and able to confirm that the black smudges he'd seen from the sky were trees. He crashed into one of them, its branches ripping through his clothing and tearing at his flesh.

Then everything went black.

❧ 17 ❧

JUNE 1996

BRISBANE

The car crept through traffic, turned into another lane, moved forward again. Reeda stared at the street directory in her lap.

"Uh...turn left at the next intersection. I think...that should be Edward Street."

"What? You think? Are you sure? I can't get back over if I merge...drat all these one-way streets." Kate glanced over her shoulder, back to the rearview mirror, ahead and repeated the movements over again.

Reeda smiled to herself. "Left, yes turn left up here. I'll get out around the corner."

When they turned the corner, Kate drew the car to a stop, Reeda climbed out and Kate waved goodbye as she pulled back into traffic. Reeda stepped onto the footpath and stared up at the towering building in front of her. Skyscrapers surrounded her on all sides. She pushed her hands into her jeans pockets and scanned the street.

Opposite her was the building she was looking for. Inside, she hoped to find the Brisbane branch of the *Department of Veteran Affairs*. She hoped she might be able to discover more information about Charlie and what'd happened to him before her trip to Italy. If they didn't have any information on him here, she supposed it wasn't likely there would be anything in the archives in Italy.

She rode the elevator up to the fifth floor and stepped out into a simple reception area. The receptionist asked her to take a seat, and soon someone came out to meet her.

The woman asked her a few questions as she led her to a computer, then typed in some information based on Reeda's responses.

Within a few moments, she looked up and met Reeda's gaze. "Charles Jackson of Bathurst?"

"Yes, that's right."

"I have information here on a Charles Jackson from Bathurst. It says he was shot down over Sicily, Italy, on July 23rd, 1943."

"Sicily? Are you sure? The family was told it was Crete, or possibly the Gulf of Tunis."

The woman squinted at the screen, large glasses obscuring most of her pretty face. She pushed them up the bridge of her nose. "Yes, it says Sicily."

"Wow, okay, thanks."

"There's more...let's see. He was listed as a Prisoner of War in a place called Sulmona, Italy."

"Really?" Reeda's heart skipped a beat, goosebumps prickling up her spine. Charlie hadn't died in 1943?

"Yes, he was a POW in Sulmona. I know a little bit about

that camp. There were a number of Australian soldiers interned there, along with mostly British troops."

Reeda's eyes widened. What if he'd lived? No, he must've died, otherwise he would've come home to Nan and Dad.

"Does it say he died in the camp?" She tried to peer over the desk that stood between them.

The woman eyed her with suspicion, then focused on the computer screen again. "No, there's no record of his death, but it also says he wasn't with the troops recorded at liberation."

"What does that mean?" asked Reeda, her spine still tingling.

"It means, when the Allies made it to the camp, he wasn't there."

"But he didn't die, either?"

The woman frowned. "No, not according to our records. But that doesn't make much sense..."

"No, it doesn't." Reeda frowned. There were a couple of possibilities: maybe the records were incomplete, or perhaps he escaped. "So, you don't have any other information?"

The woman shook her head. "Sorry, love. That's all we've got."

When she left the office, only a half hour had passed. She still had three hours to fill before Kate was due to pick her up. Her sister was visiting friends in Brisbane and had agreed to let Reeda come along for the ride. She hadn't expected to be finished at the Veterans Affairs office so quickly. After all, she was dealing with a government department. She inhaled a slow breath. Well, she'd simply have to find a way to kill the time.

She wandered down the street, letting the pedestrian traffic carry her along Edward Street. If Charlie didn't die in a plane crash, and he didn't die in the POW camp, and wasn't there when it was liberated...where was he? What'd happened to him? Was it possible he'd escaped? Did anyone successfully escape POW camps? She'd never read much about it and didn't even know if it was possible.

She'd seen the show *Hogan's Heroes* of course when she was a kid, but that hardly counted as historical evidence. Besides, Hogan and his friends were always recaptured and returned to the camp.

She shook her head. Now her trip to Italy had even more purpose than before. She'd have to find this place, Sulmona, and see if there was any evidence of her grandfather's existence. Maybe someone would be able to tell her what had happened to him.

She reached a cross street and stopped. A sign told her it was Queen Street. The street was bricked and closed to traffic. Shoppers milled about, and a busker played guitar to one side, a black guitar case lined with red velvet open in front of him.

There was an ice cream shop, something selling soaps and lotions, a Chinese restaurant, a Hungry Jacks, and a chemist ahead of her. The street stretched away to her right and left, shops filling both sides as far as she could see.

Her attention returned to the chemist's. If she bought another pregnancy test, would that technically be considered neurotic? After all, she'd already taken a test and it'd been negative. She and Duncan had barely spoken to each other since, so the chances of her being pregnant were slim to none. Still, she hadn't gotten her period yet. It could be the stress, or maybe...No. It was time to break the habit of this obsessive behaviour. She'd been doing the same thing every month for years now. Take a test, throw it out, take another, always living in hope. Always disappointed.

She headed for a café. Instead, she'd get a coffee and

people watch. Maybe she could even locate a book shop and buy something to read. She'd need a book for her flight anyway, and it would give her something to do that would distract her from the urge to walk into the chemist's.

✣ 18 ✣

JULY 1943

ITALY

Charlie groaned and tried to move, but something was stopping him. Pain reverberated up his leg. He felt down the length of it with one gloved hand, thought better of it, tugged the glove off with his teeth and groaned again. This time, glove hanging between his lips, he felt the wound and found it was wet with blood.

The feeling had begun to return to his body and pain came with it, shooting agonising blasts down his back, along his arms and up his legs. Everything hurt. It was dark, but his vision had returned enough for him to tell he was stuck in the branches of a tree. The parachute had settled all around him, torn in places by the tree's sharp shoots.

Gunfire blasted in the distance. The rat-a-tat of machine guns, anti-aircraft weapons. In the sky, tracers arced through the air, searching for planes. The drone of their engines faded as the battle line progressed, moving away from where Charlie had landed.

What about his squadron? Had they made it? He had no way of knowing. The last he'd seen was Scotty being chased by Jerry, but he'd managed to take out Scotty's pursuer. Still, one of the wowsers had shot him out of the sky. They might have gone after the rest of his squadron next.

Frustration burned in his gut at having been downed. There wasn't anything he could do now to help them. They were on their own. And so was he.

He took the glove from his mouth and shoved it back onto his hand. The climb down the tree would be rough on his hands. Still, it was hot in his flight suit and he was already beginning to sweat.

He found the pocketknife he always kept handy and used it to cut himself free of the parachute. He'd gotten tangled and in the dark, confined space, couldn't see how to get loose. It wasn't long before the pocketknife released him from the last of the chute's cords and he slumped against the branch that was holding him up with a gasp, heart hammering against his rib cage.

No doubt the troops on the ground had seen him fall. Someone had shot him while he drifted towards the earth. If they saw where he landed, they'd be on their way to find him and Charlie didn't know how long he had. He'd do his best to move quickly, but his leg was pulsing with pain, he'd lost blood, and he couldn't say yet whether he had any other serious injuries from the crash landing.

Now free of the chute, he found he could move. He stretched out each leg; they seemed to function well enough to hold his weight. He started out slowly at first, taking cautious steps down the tree from branch to branch. Sliding, scraping flesh against rough bark, knocking the wind out of himself when he landed after an unexpectedly long drop, gut first onto another branch.

He grunted with the effort, then finally found himself eying the ground below. In the distance, voices shouted. He didn't recognise the language, possibly Italian. It was faint, and hard to make out. He'd never heard Italian before in his life, but he'd remembered some German from high school and figured he'd be able to identify it if he had to. The sound of the voices moving closer set his heart racing again and sent a blast of goose pimples up his spine.

There wasn't much time before they'd stumble across him if they continued in the same direction.

Charlie grabbed hold of the lowest branch, swung his legs down and dropped to the ground. It was a long fall and he landed on both feet, then fell to one side as the injured leg crumpled beneath him. He bit down on his tongue to keep from crying out with pain, clutching at his leg. Head light, he squeezed his eyes shut and lay still a moment waiting for the dizziness to subside.

Several more shouts and what sounded like clipped instructions echoed through the night air. This time closer still to where he lay on his side, hands clasped around his buckled leg. He couldn't stay where he was, they'd be on him soon.

With a grimace, he pushed himself into a squat, then forced himself to stand. The pain radiated out from his calf in a way that pushed stars before his vision. Still, he had to keep going. He stumbled forward through the grove of trees that'd stalled his plummet to earth. If he remembered right, beyond the trees had been a large, lighter looking area that might've been a field. If he could reach it, skirt around the edge of it, he might be able to stay out of sight long enough to make an escape. Although, where he'd go after that was something he'd have to figure out later.

The pain in his leg didn't seem so bad now he was moving. He found a kind of rhythm with loping steps that propelled him forward, without making too much noise in the leaf litter. Although, he couldn't help the rustling that followed his every step. His only hope was to make it to the field where the grass would muffle his movements and maybe even hide his tracks.

The trees thinned ahead, and Charlie could make out the faint glow of moonlight between them. His heart rose at the sight and he hurried his movements to shuffle towards the clearing he'd seen from his vantage point in the sky.

Gunfire rang out through the darkness and Charlie ducked for cover, though the shots weren't close. It was an instinct, a reaction. He glanced back over his shoulder, then up to the sky. He seemed to have lost his sense of direction. Where were the guns? How close was his enemy? Had they found his abandoned chute?

Moving again, he lurched forward to the edge of the clearing. Just as he'd suspected, fields of grass, vineyards, and other crops he didn't recognise in the gloom stretched out ahead of him. He smiled at the sight, took another look back over his shoulder and proceeded onto the grass, away from the noisy leaf litter that'd plagued every step since he'd fallen from the tree. The silence gave him an opportunity to listen for a pursuit.

Nothing.

He heard only the distant smatter of guns and the faint croon of an aircraft, followed by the muffled sound of a dog barking, a burst of yaps followed by quiet.

He hurried as best he could around the edge of the field, retaining some shelter from the tree branches but letting the grass hide his footprints. A house on the rise ahead lay in silent darkness. One of the things that'd struck him the first time he flew over enemy territory was the lack of lights. Everything was dark, the landscape from above seemed to be devoid of life. Though he could see the buildings now, farmhouses dotted here and there on rises and sloping hills. No light glowed from within. Were the occupants at home and cowering in their beds, or had they fled to somewhere safer?

One thing he'd learned since he left Bathurst: nowhere was safe.

A light pierced the darkness up ahead. The blinkered headlights of a vehicle as it bumped and waved along a road on the other side of the field. He hadn't seen the road before, the vineyard had hidden it from view. But it was close, and the car was headed in his direction with two motorbikes trailing it, the high-pitched buzzing of their engines like a warning bell.

Charlie ducked down where he stood, knees jutting upward beneath his armpits, eyes narrowed. Where were they going? Which direction should he take?

His thoughts swirled as his heart thundered. The dampness of his bloody calf seeped through his pants and was cold against his thigh.

Behind him, the sound of voices again. Barked commands, a yelp from a dog, closer now.

He gasped for breath; sweat trickled down the sides of his face. Where was Edie? Was she thinking of him? He should never have left her. If he'd known Keith would result from their time on the creek bank together, he would've stayed, wouldn't have gone anywhere without them. They'd have been a family. He missed the touch of her hand, the feel of her lips on his, the way she looked into his eyes with strength and certainty in her love for him, and his for her.

She was home to him. How he wished he was home with her now.

A quick dash towards the road. The car and motorbikes had passed where he was, if he could make it to the farmhouse maybe they'd take pity on him. Maybe they wouldn't be home and he could break in, find a place to hide until the Allies took back Italy from Fritz.

The noise of his pursuers rustled in his ears as he stumbled forward. Feet hustling through leaves and undergrowth. Another dog's yelp followed by a shouted command.

He was moving, running. His lungs cried out for air. Every step was painful, impossible, and yet still he kept going. The road was up ahead, he had only to climb through a fence. Or over? Would over be better, or through? He wasn't sure he could make it over the fence, so pushed his way through the narrow space between sturdy, weathered, timber fence rails. In his hurry, his knee knocked against the railing, but he barely registered the pain.

The sound of the engine behind him startled him with its suddenness. Where had it come from? The car had turned around. Motorcycles converged on him, overtook the car, and passed him by, then skidded to a halt.

He stopped, spun in place, and blinked in the glare of the headlights. A man in uniform ran up to him, a dog strained at his leash, barking incessantly at Charlie. It lurched towards him, almost reaching him, teeth bared.

He raised his hands, still half-blinded by the headlights as another man grabbed his arm and pushed him forward. He stumbled towards the car and climbed into the back seat. The man settled in beside him, a handgun pointed at Charlie's head. He said something Charlie didn't understand, glared at Charlie as though waiting for a response. Charlie blinked.

As the car sputtered forward, a motorcycle in front and one following behind, Charlie stared back at the field. The line of trees where he'd been hidden briefly faded into the distance. A stone formed in his gut. He'd been captured. He'd heard the rumours of what happened to downed pilots. And now he was one of them. He swallowed the fear and inhaled a deep breath. Whatever came next, he'd have to face it, since there was no going back no matter how much he wished for it.

❧ 19 ❧

JUNE 1996

CABARITA BEACH

It was her last day in Cabarita before she flew to Italy. Reeda was anxious about travelling internationally on her own, but excited as well. Focusing on finding out more about Charlie helped keep the nerves at bay.

She'd found another dozen or so letters from Charlie to Nan in the box under the stairs, most had been filled with declarations of love and regret, reminiscences of times past. Nothing to provide her with more details than they already had about what had happened to him after the war ended. Only that he'd spent a considerable amount of time as a prisoner of war.

She'd spent the day in the kitchen with Kate and Bindi. They'd cooked together, talked about their childhood, laughed over their antics, and discussed plans for the future. She was thrilled to hear about Kate's ideas for a restaurant at the Inn. It was bound to be a success, and no doubt would be popular with the locals as well as the tourists, given how few eating options there were in Cabarita and Kingscliff.

Now, she sat on the beach in the cove. Her arms linked around her legs, and her knees tucked beneath her chin. She watched the waves rush to the shore, bubble, froth, and thin as they ran, then drew back towards the ocean as though afraid to come closer.

The cold wetness from the sand leeched through her jeans and soaked her skin. She shivered, and pulled her legs closer to her body, resting her chin on her knees with a sigh.

Part of her wished she weren't travelling alone. The other part of her was proud. She could do this. She was a strong, independent, modern woman. Nothing could hold her back, not even the threat of loneliness.

She'd never really been alone before.

She'd had her parents, then Nan, and her sisters. Moving away to University had been the closest she'd come to feeling totally alone, but she'd discovered Jennifer and some of her other friends from high school were there. She hadn't seen them in over a year and their reunion was full of hugs, tears, and laughter.

She smiled at the memory.

Jennifer had never let her feel alone after that.

It wasn't long before she met Duncan. He'd been quiet, serious, and kind. She'd felt immediately at home with him, comfortable enough to share with him what'd happened to her parents. How their deaths had severed her family into pieces and broken her relationships with her sisters in a way that she thought was irreparable at that time.

And now, ten years later, she was here with them again, and about to embark on an adventure all alone.

Laughter caught her ear. The delicious tinkle of a child's giggle coasted over the cold sand. She turned her head to see a family playing at the water's edge at the other end of the cove.

She frowned. That was strange. They didn't have a family staying at the inn at the moment, at least not that she was aware of. And this beach rarely saw anyone other than guests of the inn. It wasn't a private beach, just out of the way enough to discourage most from making the trek.

Still, sometimes people stumbled across it on their way to somewhere else.

She ran a hand through her hair, watching them play. A mother, father, and two girls—maybe eight and ten years old. The girls ran at the waves laughing, then squealed and beat a hasty retreat as the waves nipped at their heels.

Long, dark brown hair flipped and whispered in the breeze. Long, tanned legs above pumping feet. The man grabbed one of the girls, eliciting a louder squeal than before, and whirled her around in an arc. Her sister jumped up and down in place shouting that it was her turn next. He laughed, set the first one down and grabbed the other one, prompting the same happy squeal.

Reeda smiled at their antics as their mother looked on, her hands pressed into her pockets. Tears filled Reeda's eyes and she dabbed them away with the back of her hand.

They were the kind of family she'd always wanted for herself, and now knew with certainty she'd never have. She'd never let herself admit that before now. She'd never have it, the dream she'd kept hidden behind career goals, a big house, and a host of social engagements. The dream of a happy family, a simple life, people to share her days with, laughter to fill her heart.

A memory of a similar moment flashed through her mind and she jolted.

The car.

She was in the car with Mum and Dad. The dance

eisteddfod had gone well. She'd performed probably the best routine she'd ever done. It was crazy that she'd begged Mum and Dad to let her enter to the competition. In the end, it'd been a small affair, with few real competitors compared to the Sydney dance scene. Still, it'd given her a chance to shine, to stand out from the crowd, and she had. She hadn't been able to wipe the smile from her face. She'd received the largest ovation of all the performers, and when they handed her the trophy, she'd felt her heart might burst. She couldn't wait to tell Nan all about it.

Mum turned around in her seat to grin and congratulate Reeda all over again on the drive back.

"Sweetie, you were amazing. I was so proud of you. I've never seen you dance so beautifully. You deserve that trophy." She reached back and squeezed Reeda's hand in hers.

"You're becoming a beautiful and accomplished young woman, Reeda," added Dad, a glance in the rear vision mirror. "We're both proud of you."

She'd blinked back the tears as happiness filled her soul. When she looked out the window, only darkness peered back at her. It was late. She yawned, her reflection in the window mirroring her fatigue. Shadows of shrubbery flashed by the window, but otherwise it was dark. Only the car's headlights provided an illumination on the country road, and a faint glow from the moon overhead.

When the accident happened, she'd been looking out that window. She didn't see what it was that caused the other car to swerve into their path. Didn't know what'd happened until later, since she was knocked unconscious as the car rolled down the road.

Reeda ducked her head so her face was hidden as tears streaked her cheeks over the memory. She'd lost so much that day. The only family she'd known, and now she couldn't have one of her own. Nothing was working out the way she'd thought it would. It wasn't fair, to her, or to Duncan, Kate or Bindi.

"Reeda?" a voice jolted her to attention.

She looked up to see Jack standing in front of her, a concerned expression on his lined face. "Are you okay?"

She nodded and wiped the tears from her cheeks with her jacket sleeve. "I'm okay. Thanks Jack."

He lowered himself onto the sand beside her with a grunt. "That's not as easy as it used to be." He grinned.

She laughed, sniffled.

"What's up buttercup?" he asked.

Her throat constricted. "I was thinking about Mum and Dad, and the accident."

He nodded, his smile fading. "Ah. I see."

"Sometimes it feels like so long ago, and sometimes..."

"Like yesterday?" he asked. "I know what you mean."

He placed an arm around her shoulders and kissed the crown of her head. "Pain is a part of life, it's what lets us know we've loved well, my dear."

"Really?" she asked. "Then, I'm not sure I want to love that well again. It hurts too much."

He patted her back. "If you don't, you'll be missing out. Trust me, you can handle the pain of losing those you love, but not ever having someone to love—that's much worse."

The lump in her throat grew. That was the direction she was headed, though Jack didn't know it.

"You've always got us, you know," he added, as though reading her thoughts. "Your sisters, me, Mima. We're here for you."

She smiled, unable to reply.

"You can't change the past, my dear. Oh, how I wish you could. But you can choose to make the most of now and tell people you love them when the chance comes along."

She gazed into his blue eyes, crinkled around the edges.

His grey hair blustered back and forth on his head with the wind.

"I love you, Jack," she whispered.

He grinned. "Love you too, Reeda." He kissed her head again, then pushed himself to his feet with another groan. "Harder on the way up, I'm afraid."

She chuckled through her tears.

He glanced over at the family on the beach.

"Who are they, do you think?" she asked.

His head cocked to one side. "Just a local family. I'll introduce them to you sometime when you're feeling more like it."

She nodded. "Okay."

He waved goodbye and headed in the direction of the family. The girls were seated in the sand, building a sandcastle, the man and woman close by, wrapped in each other's arms.

He waved a greeting to them, and they released their hold on each other to embrace him one at a time.

Reeda frowned. He seemed to know the family well. She supposed it made sense. He'd lived in the area for long enough to know everyone local.

She watched them together for a while. Jack helped the girls with their sandcastle, then chased them up the beach and away from where she was sitting. The parents walked after them at a leisurely pace, hand in hand.

Reeda sighed and stood to her feet, brushed the sand from her jeans, and trudged back towards the inn.

✿ 20 ✿

JUNE 1996

BRISBANE

Reeda shifted in her seat, searching for the other end of the seat belt. The captain's voice droned through the overhead speakers, and travellers shuffled along the aeroplane's narrow aisle, looking for their seat.

She was wedged between a man in a grey suit and a young woman with a Walkman held possessively in her lap, her eyes fixed on something beyond the small, round window. Her entire body language screamed, don't talk to me. Reeda leaned her head back against the seat and looked at the distant, rectangular television screen, fixed to the wall at the far end of the cabin. It wasn't likely she'd be able to watch a movie from this seat, so she'd have to find other ways to pass the twenty-two-hour flight.

The seatbelt light dinged on, and as the plane taxied to

the runway, flight attendants smiled their way through the safety procedures. Reeda watched them, her mind elsewhere. What would she find in Italy? She'd made the decision to go without thinking it through. Kate was worried about her, she could tell. Still, something inside of her buzzed with excitement, a small cry welling up from deep within her. She needed this. Needed time to herself, time to turn off her brain, stop dwelling on all the pain. She smiled as the plane roared into the air, leaving Brisbane behind her. This was her chance for a new beginning.

DECEMBER 1983

CABARITA BEACH

Kingscliff State High School had never truly been Reeda's high school. She'd hated almost every single moment of her single year there. Almost. The exception being that she could take surfing for sport, and the boys in her year at school were exceptionally cute.

Too bad they didn't feel the same way about her.

She walked away from the school for the last time, with Kate and Bindi flanking her on either side. The bus stop was close by and would take them all the way to The Waratah Inn.

She knew Nan, Mima, and Jack would be waiting with a cake at the very least. And, knowing Nan, there might be streamers and gifts as well. Nan loved to celebrate, though Reeda wasn't sure what there was worth celebrating after the year they'd had.

She couldn't wait to put this hick town behind her and get as far away as she could from the tragedy and pain that made everyone in Cabarita look at her with pity written on their faces.

Here, she'd always be the girl who didn't die when both her parents did. Small towns like Cabarita and Kingscliff didn't see much tragedy of any kind, not even car accidents. In Sydney, it'd be just another day in the city, but not here. Here, everyone knew her story, and they all felt sorry for her. People whispered about what she'd been through behind her back, as if she couldn't hear them.

Bindi and Kate were talking and laughing together over something, leaving her out as usual. They never seemed to include her in their secret club these days. She'd been the outsider, ever since the accident. No doubt they blamed her for it, heck, she blamed herself. If she hadn't insisted on going to that stupid dance competition...if they'd stayed in Sydney, kept living their normal day to day lives, Mum and Dad would still be here.

Her stomach roiled and she scowled as the bus pulled into the stop. Kids climbed on board and she paused to watch, thinking. Her last time on this ridiculous bus. Last time at school, with these kids who couldn't care less about her.

She'd hoped this day would be so different. She'd had plans for a massive celebration in Sydney at their house. Mum and Dad would be excited, but teary, her friends would all be there. Only now, she hardly spoke to Jennifer anymore, and the rest of the group had stopped calling entirely after about two months.

She was on her own.

Kate and Bindi were already on the bus. They waved through the window to her, beckoning her to climb aboard before the driver shut the door and the bus lurched away from the curb. She didn't much like the idea of walking all the way to the inn on foot, so ran to catch the bus just as the door whirred shut. She thudded one palm on the glass, and the door slid open again.

"Cutting it a little close today, Reeda?" asked the bus driver with a huff.

"Sorry," she murmured as she climbed the steps and flung herself into an empty seat.

The bus rumbled away from the stop and Reeda glanced back over her shoulder at the red brick buildings of the school she was happily leaving behind.

What now?

She'd applied to study at several different universities but hadn't heard yet which she'd be attending. She had good enough marks to get accepted, her concern was where. She wanted to go to the University of Technology in Sydney, it was her number one choice. But it was competitive, and she wasn't sure she'd get a spot. Still, if she went there, she'd be close to home, her real home. She might even be able to catch up with some of her old friends, if they hadn't already forgotten her entirely.

The farther away she could get from Cabarita, the better.

The bus pulled to a stop in front of the inn. Dark pink paint peeked between silver gums and Pandanus trees. A sign swung by the front gate, announcing the inn had vacancies. Nan's truck was parked at an angle in front of the building.

Reeda followed her sisters inside, dragging her feet as she went. She threw her school bag down on the hardwood floor inside the front door, glanced around and noticed the telltale sign of a curled ribbon peeking out from the breakfast nook.

"Surprise!" shouted Nan and Mima as they leapt through the doorway.

She couldn't help smiling.

"Congratulations to our new graduate," continued Nan, dancing over to kiss Reeda on the cheek. "I'm so happy for you, love. On to new adventures, eh?"

She squeezed Reeda until her lungs were empty. Reeda gasped for breath. "Nan you're squashing me!"

"Oops, sorry about that." Nan winked. "Come in here and have some cake with us, my love. We're celebrating!"

It warmed Reeda's heart to see Nan dance and smile that way. She'd been bedridden for months after the accident and still hadn't smiled long after she'd finally emerged from the bedroom. Losing Mum and Dad had been hard on all of them. Reeda didn't think it'd been fair of Nan to disappear into her grief that way. She was grieving too, and she couldn't disappear. She had to take care of her sisters. Had to step up if Nan wasn't going to. Someone had to be the adult. Responsibility. Yet another thing she was ready to leave in her wake.

❧

SALT WATER DRIPPED DOWN HER CHEEKS AND BETWEEN HER parted lips. Reeda licked it with a smile, her feet dangling in the water on either side of her board. She watched as waves rolled to shore, looked back over her shoulder for the swell of the next set.

The heat of the day was fading as the sun drifted towards the horizon. The water was cool on her skin. After an entire day of sweating it was a relief. What were her Sydney school friends doing today? Had they attended their all-girls school on the last day? Or had they skipped and gone to a café, followed by a club for some late afternoon dancing? Or maybe they'd gone back to Jennifer's house to swim in her enormous pool.

The Kingscliff graduates had headed directly for the pub

after lunch. Hadn't stuck around for afternoon classes. She'd been invited, of course, but hadn't wanted to go. There was something about today that set an ache in her throat and made her want to hide away from the world.

The sea moved beneath her and she slid onto her stomach, grinning across at Kate a few metres away from her.

"First in..." said Kate with a wink.

"Best dressed..." replied Reeda, already paddling.

The wave carried her almost to shore. She'd had enough, so she jogged through the last of the water and up the sand, her board under one arm.

She slumped onto the sand beside Bindi, who'd given up surfing a half hour earlier and was laid out beside her board, one arm flung over her eyes to keep out the sun's blinding rays.

Bindi glanced at her with a squint. "Finished?"

Reeda grunted, linking her arms around her knees to stare out at the ocean, rising, falling, sighing, and heaving, the sun glinting off its surface like a light shone on so many jewels.

"I'm gonna miss you," whispered Bindi.

Reeda almost didn't hear her. "I'll miss you too." She pushed Bindi's shoulder with the palm of her hand.

"It won't be the same...with just Kate."

Reeda chuckled. "That is true."

"Did you decide what you're going to study yet? Interior Design or Architecture?"

"Design, definitely design."

"Good, I think that'll suit you," replied Bindi.

"Yeah." The truth was, Reeda wasn't so certain. She had no idea what to study, but she'd always loved colours and decor. She'd never had a chance to do anything with it, since Nan's idea of decorating was to find something secondhand at a garage sale and then shove it into a corner at the inn, wherever it would fit.

Kate joined them, puffing as she set down her board then sat in the sand. "That was great."

Reeda nodded.

"Why didn't you go out with everyone else? I heard they were going to the pub..." Kate studied her, one eye squeezed shut against the glare.

"I didn't feel like it. They're not..."

"Not what?" asked Kate.

Reeda sighed. "Not my class."

"Yes they are." Kate was always so literal. Why couldn't she understand without Reeda having to spell it out? She didn't want to talk about it. Her throat tightened.

"No, Saint Arden's, that's my class. Those are my friends. Not here..."

"Ah, I see. You know, you're going to miss out on life if you don't let that go."

Reeda turned on her, heat rising in her chest. "Let that go? What exactly do you mean by that?"

"You know, move on," Kate said. "Kingscliff High is your school, this is your graduation day, and you're pining after our old school, and your old friends. You're missing out. You should be celebrating."

Reeda frowned. "I *am* celebrating."

Kate huffed.

"And I don't know how you moved on so quickly. Mum and Dad..." Reeda couldn't finish the sentence.

Bindi shifted in place, but didn't speak, instead fixing her eyes on the horizon.

Kate's eyes narrowed. "You think I moved on quickly? I can't believe you'd say that. I miss them just as much as you do."

"Do you really? Because it doesn't seem that way," hissed Reeda.

Bindi's head swivelled in an instant, her eyes gleaming

with moisture, her cheeks red. "Stop it, stop it! It's all your fault anyway, Reeda. If you hadn't wanted to go to that stupid dance competition, they'd still be here. Stop yelling at Kate, it isn't her fault they're gone!"

Bindi leapt to her feet and ran down the beach in the direction of Castle Rock. Sand kicked up from each footstep, damp hair swayed from side to side down the length of her back.

Reeda gaped, her heart seemed to tear in two, it hurt so bad. "You can't...you can't say that."

"Why not, it's true," whispered Kate, staring at her feet. "It's all your fault and I hate you for it."

JUNE 1996

BRISBANE

Reeda gasped for breath. She lurched up straight in her seat, eyes flying open as a moan built deep in the depths of her gut.

"You okay?" asked the man sitting two seats over.

She glanced wildly at him, closed her mouth, leaned back against the seat with a nod. "Yes, thank you. Just a bad dream."

Tears dripped down her cheeks and she stared straight ahead over the seats in front of her. A movie played soundlessly on the small, square screen in the distance. The plane's engine was a dull but constant roar, under which the murmur of conversation, the clink of knives and forks and the occasional burst of laughter played a melody.

She squeezed her eyes shut, the memory of her sisters' words still ringing in her head. They'd blamed her for their parents' deaths all those years ago. She'd almost forgotten it, buried it deep down beneath other memories, better memories. The dream had brought the pain of their accusations to the surface again and her chest ached as though something heavy was pressing down on it.

21

JULY 1943

ITALY

The rattle of the train on the tracks jostled Charlie awake. He'd dozed for a few minutes. But after days of getting no sleep, he needed more than that. His eyes flitted open and he balled his jacket a little tighter, using it against the wall as a pillow for his head. Wind whistled through the open car doors, giving them some respite from the heat. Around him, men lounged, sat in groups, or stood staring out at the landscape as it flashed by.

He'd been questioned by the Italian military for three days during which time they'd also treated his wounded leg. The bullet had passed through his calf muscle, so apart from a loss of blood, the doctor assured him in broken English that it would heal in time.

Since he wouldn't give his interrogators anything but his name and rank, they'd put him on a train to Rome. From there, he'd boarded this train. He couldn't say where it was headed, since he didn't understand anything said to him, nor did he recognise the signs at the train station, or at any of the stations they passed by along the way.

Two armed guards stood at either end of the carriage, watching the men. There were more in the other carriages, and plenty more Allied prisoners as well.

"Where were you taken?" asked a voice by his elbow.

He glanced at the man, red haired, green eyed with a freckled face. He looked to be about the same age as Charlie was, his accent sounded British to Charlie's ear. "I was shot down over Sicily."

The man nodded. "Oh yes? They shipped me here from North Africa. Nearly got blown clean out of the boat by our own on the way over here. Can you believe it?" He made a huffing sound. "Last thing you expect, machine-gun fire from one of your own jockeys barreling towards the leaky tub you're clinging to."

The man shook his head. "Name's Henry Dunmore." He pushed out a hand. The insignia on his uniform showed he was a second lieutenant with the British Army.

Charlie shook his hand. "Sorry to hear that, but glad you made it. I'm Charlie Jackson."

"Pleasure to meet you," replied Henry with a flash of white teeth. "Though, not entirely sure I've made it yet." He tipped his head in the direction of the nearest guard.

Charlie's stomach churned. "Yeah, I know what you mean. Where do you think they're taking us?"

"Beats me," replied Henry with a shrug. "But I'd rather stay here than be shipped off to the fatherland."

Charlie nodded. He wasn't keen on the idea of being sent to Germany either. Not that there was anything they could do about it now.

The train slowed its pace and the carriage jerked as the brakes squeezed the rails.

"Looks like we're stopping," said Henry, pushing himself to his feet.

Charlie and others who'd been seated stood as well, all anxious to find out their fate. If it was a firing squad, Charlie would face it without hesitation. He wouldn't give Jerry the satisfaction of seeing him flinch. Although so far, the Italians who'd captured and questioned him hadn't treated him too badly. They'd seemed almost disinterested in what he'd had to say or the fact that he refused to give them what they wanted.

When the train stopped, the guards shepherded the group out of the carriage and onto the platform. A sign hung nearby, old and stained by weather, it read: Sulmona.

Regal, arched windows ran the length of the station house. A second story jutted out above it, with a wide porch roof reaching out towards the tracks. With shouts and prods the guards moved the group down the length of the platform and onto the street. They shuffled in twos and threes along the dusty road, through the small town with the guards flanking them, pushing them forward. Locals peered silently at them through curious eyes but kept their distance. Charlie's bandaged leg throbbed a little, but he managed to walk by putting most of his weight on his healthy leg and hobbling as he went.

Mountains surrounded the village, and along the ridge of one foothill, the town's buildings crouched, rising higher and higher. Stucco painted in dirty whites and pale pastels, with orange and brown tiled roofs. The residences were pushed together, piled on top of each other, as they climbed the ridge towards the mountaintop. A church spire stuck up from within the cluster of buildings, with a fortified lookout not far beyond it. The medieval village was like nothing Charlie had ever seen before. It was beautiful and bold, no doubt it'd weathered more wars than this one.

They weren't headed that way though. The guards were ushering them out of the town and into the countryside. One man made a run for it at the front of the group, the nearest guard shouted, chased him, then hit him with the butt of his rifle in the back of the head. The man slid to the ground with a cry. The guard pulled him back onto his feet, and he stuttered forward, stumbling and weaving with one hand held to his head.

Henry sidled up to Charlie, eyes down. "I believe we travelled about an hour from Rome, but I traded my watch to a local back in Palermo for a cup of water so I couldn't say for sure."

Charlie nodded. "They took mine during a search."

"Ah, too bad old chap. I'd say we're still in the south, or halfway up the boot. Not in Germany, and if we were going there, they'd have put us on another train or something. Don't you think?"

Charlie pursed his lips. He'd studied the map of Italy enough before his mission to have some idea of where they were, somewhere east of Rome. Still, he had no way of guessing what their captors had planned for them. Perhaps they were taking the group of fifty men out into the countryside to shoot. Although they could've done that where they were captured rather than transporting them by train to this small village in central Italy.

"Don't know," he said.

One of the guards shot them a dirty look.

"We'd better keep quiet for now," Charlie whispered.

Henry nodded and ambled away.

The heat was intense, and Charlie hadn't drunk water in at least a day. His throat was parched, and the last gulp of fluid the soldiers had given him wasn't enough to march for hours in the Italian summer. He swallowed, but his throat was dry, and his tongue seemed to stick to the roof of his mouth.

He wasn't sure how long they'd marched when they passed through a small village. A sign on the side of the road announced its name: *Fonte d'Amore*. It was barely a hamlet, walled in by majestic mountains with sharp, snow-capped peaks with rolling green foothills that stretched to fields and crops.

They hadn't walked far from the hamlet when they came to a long, white fence topped with curls of barbed wire. Some of the men whispered about it, but Charlie kept to himself. He wanted to stay alert, to make sure he was ready for whatever came next.

The fence line stopped abruptly, and they found themselves in front of a fortified gate. More guards, these in different uniforms, stepped forward to converse with the ones transporting the men. Charlie watched with interest. This must be where they were staying; it seemed to be some kind of prison camp. The top of the gates were dressed with barbed wire as well. There was a watch tower in the distance. He could see the end of a machine gun butting out of a rectangular cavity near the top of the tower.

After a heated conversation, the new guards rolled open a metal gate and ushered the hodgepodge group of Allied soldiers through. The old guards remained outside, and Charlie wasn't sorry to see the last of them. These new guards lumbered around, laughing, and joking with one another. One had a cigarette shoved behind his ear. They didn't seem the type who'd shoot unarmed prisoners. The tightness in his gut began to unwind.

He looked around, waiting for further orders. From what he could tell, by studying their uniforms, the group of prisoners he'd travelled aboard the train with were mostly British, some Australians dressed in shorts and long socks, and a few from other places like Greece, Canada, and New Zealand.

As they pushed deeper into the camp, Charlie noticed there were rows of white buildings, all the same, all perfectly aligned. Men milled about, smoking, sitting. Some played a kind of ball game, still others seemed to be digging in a garden. They all stopped what they were doing to stare at the newcomers. Then, one by one they came forward, shaking hands and smiling as they went. The guards watched with bored expressions, then wandered off.

"Hi there, Squadron Leader. I'm Sergeant John Crook, with the British Army Rifles, originally from Hackney, pleased to meet you," said one of the men, shaking Charlie's hands.

Charlie nodded. "Thank you, Sergeant. I'm Charlie Jackson, with the RAAF, from Bathurst, Australia."

He introduced himself the same way to several of the other men. Some slapped him on the back, others smiled, still others promised to show him around. Some were fit and strong, some thin, pallid with concave cheeks and skin stretched tight across bony chests. Others hobbled or shuffled. The rest watched from the paltry shade of the narrow, guttered overhangs on the white huts, which were probably bunk houses, based on the layout of the place.

It didn't look too different to the military training camp at Bathurst, aside from the armed sentries in the watchtower and dotted around the walls of the camp and the towering rock face that loomed mountainous behind the camp.

"Looks like we're staying here." Henry had found Charlie again. He smiled with his arms crossed over his chest.

"Looks like it."

"Hey, you two, come with me. We'll find you a bunk," shouted one of the men who'd greeted them.

Charlie and Henry followed the man into one of the white

buildings. It was a bunkhouse, basic, sterile, and open to the elements. The barracks were built of concrete with bunks pressed along their length. The man introduced himself as Colin Statham, an Australian soldier. He was a cheery chap, with knobbly knees poking out of his shorts, and a handlebar moustache.

"This is the officer's section. We've got five compounds—one for the officers, one for the sergeants, and three for everyone else, like me." Colin grinned, waving a hand beneath his Australian Army Corporal insignia.

He found them a set of bunks. Henry took the top, leaving Charlie the one underneath. Charlie sat on the bed, hands resting on his thighs. He had no belongings, nothing to unpack. Just the clothes on his back. His pocketknife and watch had been taken by the Italians who captured him, but he still had Edie's photograph. And he was grateful for it.

He tugged the picture from his pocket and traced the outline of her face and Keith's with a fingertip. It was hard to believe she existed in this world. This cruel, dark world. She was kind and good. How could the two things exist at the same time? He inhaled a deep breath.

Around the barracks, men lounged on bunks, sat with backs pressed to the walls smoking cigarettes or playing games. They seemed to be in good spirits given the circumstances.

Henry's face appeared next to him, hung over the edge of the top bunk. "This isn't too bad, not bad at all. I was talking to the guy in the next bunk and he says the guards are nice enough. There's not much in the way of food, but otherwise they're generally left alone."

Charlie nodded. "That's something, I suppose."

Colin returned then and leaned against the wall with his arms crossed over his chest. "Where you from, Squadron

Leader?" he asked Charlie, eying the rank insignia on Charlie's chest.

"Bathurst," replied Charlie. Charlie was young to be a Squadron Leader, he knew it and saw the fact reflected in people's eyes, Colin was no exception. But Charlie's first three Squadron Leaders had all been shot down and he'd been handed the job. It wasn't so much an honour as a responsibility in his eyes. The weight of it had rested heavy on his shoulders ever since.

"Oh yeah? I'm from Grafton myself."

"I haven't heard of Grafton," replied Charlie.

"Northern New South Wales," replied Colin.

"Ah, right. Where were you captured?"

"Libya. Shipped here two years ago. What about you?"

Charlie nodded. "Shot down over Sicily last week."

"So, we're moving on Sicily? That's good. Very good." Colin's eyes narrowed. "I want to hear everything, but for now food's on. If we line up first, we might even get a bit of canned meat. I doubt it, but we can live in hope. We get one meal a day and usually it's some kind of watered-down rice they call soup, or *la minestra*. Still, can't complain. At least we have that and the fortnightly packages from the Red Cross."

"I'd kill for some water," replied Charlie, pushing tiredly to his feet, wincing at the pain in his leg. He pressed a hand to the bandage gently; he'd have to check later to make sure it hadn't begun to bleed again on the journey.

Colin patted Charlie's shoulder. "Well, sir, stick with me and I'll make sure you have all the water you need. Now, food...that's another matter."

22

JUNE 1996

ROME

The balcony outside her room at the Palazzo Manfredi had an unobstructed view of the Colosseum. Reeda stood with her hands resting on the railing to look out over the magnificent ruins of a place so steeped in history and horror it made her head spin.

How was it possible the structure had been standing for almost two thousand years? It was staggering to think of all the things the building had seen, the number of feet that had trampled the ground beneath its curved archways and climbed the steps beside those brick walls.

Australian architecture was infant-like in comparison. At most, anything built in her home country was two hundred years old, the Colosseum was ten times that. The contrast between the newness of her hometown and the ancientness of Rome was exhilarating. Even with the jet lag, Reeda felt a surge of excitement at the thought of what lay ahead. For the first time, she knew she'd done the right thing in coming, even if she was alone. She was in Rome. Something she'd dreamed of since she was a girl.

There was a knock at the door, and she hurried to let in the room service waiter. He sported a head of thick, black hair. His lively brown eyes met hers with a spark, and he smiled, revealing a set of straight white teeth. He set down a tray on the balcony for her, with a bottle of Chianti and a plate of cheese, olives, and slices of crusty bread.

"*Buongiorno, signora*, I am Lorenzo."

"Pleased to meet you, Lorenzo," replied Reeda. Her cheeks flushed with warmth at the bold way he looked at her. He must have been ten years younger than she was, and yet she could have sworn he was flirting with her.

When he'd finished setting the table, he stood back, hands linked together. "Can I get you anything else, signora?"

She adjusted her glasses. "No, this is perfect. Thank you."

"*Prego*." He turned to leave.

"Actually, there is one thing I wanted to ask..." Reeda took a step in his direction, then stopped.

"*Si?*"

"I want to visit Sulmona. What would be the best way to travel there?"

He smiled. "I am happy to book you passage on a bus, signora. If this would be good for you."

She nodded. "That sounds perfect. Thank you."

"Can I ask, what you want to do in Sulmona, signora? It is not the usual tourist destination." He cocked his head to one side, studying her as dimples danced in his tanned cheeks.

She swallowed. "Well, I'm looking for information about my grandfather. He was a prisoner of war there, and I never met him. I'm hoping to find out what happened to him."

His smile widened. "*Si*, that is a good thing you do. I have a cousin in Sulmona, she runs a *locanda*, ah how you say? Bed and breakfast, I think. I am going to see her in a few days, with some supplies she needs from Rome. If you like, I can take you with me. She might have a room for you."

He seemed like a nice young man. She was hesitant to take up his offer, but perhaps she could ask about him at the front desk. She'd do that after morning tea, then take a stroll around Rome.

"I would love that. If it's not too much trouble, Lorenzo. I'm happy to take the bus..."

He grinned. "No trouble at all. I'm honoured to take you."

After Lorenzo was gone, Reeda sat on the balcony and sipped a glass of Chianti while she ate the snack provided and looked through a guidebook she'd picked up at the airport.

The wine warmed her body, and the view, her soul. It was surreal to be there, and so quiet to be all alone. Her days were generally spent surrounded by needy staff and ringing telephones, not to mention meetings with clients and evenings out with friends. She was only ever alone when she was back in her house. Then, even when Duncan was there with her, she felt alone. It was why each of them spent so little time there these days, she supposed.

Below the balcony, tourists strode past or wandered by holding cones filled with colourful scoops of gelato. She itched to get moving. There was so much to see and do, she hated to waste a single moment. But the deliciousness of wasting time was something she wanted to savour as well.

She took her time showering and changing, unpacked her bags, then headed downstairs and out into the hot sunshine. It was summer in Rome and the heat was oppressive even in her shorts and singlet top. She pushed her hands into her pockets and aimed in the direction of the Colosseum.

By lunchtime she'd visited the Pantheon as well and located a cute pizzeria close to the Trevi fountain. She sat at a small round table, ordered a margherita pizza for one and a mineral water and watched the crowd drifting by.

Several local men winked in her direction or met her gaze with a knowing smile. She wasn't used to the attention, but it felt good to be noticed. It seemed as though Duncan hadn't noticed her in years. He hadn't understood her or given her much attention other than the minimum anyway. Perhaps she was being unfair, but the more time he spent away from her, away from their home, the more it seemed he saw her as a frustration, an irritation in his otherwise perfect life. She'd withdrawn deeper into herself, as he'd pulled away. It was no wonder things were falling apart between them. She didn't know how to stop the inevitable. Even if she had the energy to try.

23

AUGUST 1943

CAMPO 78

The stink of fifty men squashed into a stifling hut grew more oppressive as the morning progressed. Charlie lay on his bunk, staring at the wall. He'd bartered with one of the other prisoners for a stub of a pencil and used it now to put the finishing touches on the RAAF's roundel on the wall beside his bunk. He was having trouble getting the bird's wings just right. He smudged one edge with a fingertip, then set about finalising it with as much concentration as he could muster given his stomach had been rumbling and complaining non-stop for the entire month since his capture, making his head light.

The hut's door groaned and squealed as it slid open. Sunlight flooded into the hut and several men murmured things along the lines of, "about time". The men took their time wandering out into the daylight. Fresh air blew in on an insipid breeze.

Charlie pushed the pencil stub into a pocket and out of sight, then joined the queue to exit the hut. Outside, he tipped back his hat and peered around, waiting for his eyes to adjust to the blazing sunlight. Henry, as usual, was by his side.

"Another day with nothing whatsoever to do," murmured Henry, shoving his hands deep into his pockets and leaning against the hut's wall.

Charlie grunted in response.

"Shall we try for it again today?" asked Henry, glancing at Charlie with a quirked eyebrow.

Charlie shrugged. "Nothing else to do."

They'd dug a tunnel from one of the huts closest to the fence over the past few months and had used it to escape the week before. They almost made it to Fonte d'Amore, where they planned on begging for help from the locals, before they were rounded up by the Italian military.

"Starting all over again?" asked Colin, sidling up to Charlie. He had a habit of showing up in the officer's compound.

"Yep."

Colin's shoulders slouched. His bones protruded more than they had when Charlie arrived, which wasn't surprising to anyone in the camp, given the fact that the food rations had gotten worse, not better in that time. Every prisoner at Campo 78 was slowly starving to death and would've done so already if it weren't for the Red Cross packages that arrived with decent regularity.

The worst things about being taken prisoner by the Nazi collaborators in Italy were starvation and boredom. Charlie's mood shifted between optimism that they'd escape, or the Allies would break through and set them free, and complete hopelessness that the war would never end.

Some of the men had tried gardening, but the lack of

seeds or seedlings, fertiliser or water meant that much of their efforts were in vain. For the most part they'd given up trying, instead preferring to preserve their strength. Any unneeded exertion would mean they'd starve sooner, and most believed the Allies would prevail, if only they could survive until that time.

There would be no breakfast, the single meal they were served each day wouldn't come until much later. Guards languished on the outskirts of the camp. The prisoners had learned the hard way that sentries in watchtowers and lining the rocky cliff behind the camp, had a bird's eye view of activity and any attempts at escape were quickly thwarted. The remote location of the camp, along with the towering rock face behind it and elevated sentry points, made escape virtually impossible.

Charlie sauntered across the yard. Colin and Henry followed at a distance, each careful not to appear as though they had any kind of purpose to their movements. They'd already agreed with the men in another of the huts that theirs would be the next entry point for a tunnel. The men had promised to prepare a place behind the hut, in the shade of a small bush, for them to dig. Though they didn't want to be part of the digging or the escape themselves.

Charlie, Henry, and Colin took turns digging with their hands, and sharp rocks they'd hidden nearby. They didn't get far, since they were reluctant to draw attention to themselves and had to take regular breaks to rest. The heat of the day bore down on them and Charlie found his head swimming with dizziness after a few hours of the back-breaking work.

"Cabbage Hat's coming," hissed their lookout, before disappearing back around the corner of the hut.

Charlie, Henry, and Colin hurried to disperse, all headed in different directions. Charlie almost ran smack into Cabbage Hat's chest. The Italian guard puffed out his uniform, tilted his head in what appeared to be an attempt to look taller, and pushed his thumbs into his waist band.

"What you doing back here, eh?"

Charlie shook his head, smiled. "Getting some exercise. There's more shade behind the huts, too hot out here in the yard."

Cabbage Hat, whose actual name was Andrea Mattel, but whose face the men had decided looked similar to a cabbage, had no idea that was what they called him. He was the worst of the guards, always looking for a reason to punish the prisoners for the slightest of infractions. His beady brown eyes were fixed on Charlie's face, watching him closely.

"Nice seeing you again...sir." He had to stop himself from using the guard's moniker. He touched fingertips to his cap and kept walking.

"I'm watching you, Jackson," Cabbage Hat shouted after him.

Charlie spun around to face him, walking backwards, performed a faux bow, then continued on his way. Several of the men standing around and watching the exchange laughed in response, nodding their heads at Charlie. His heart thudded against his ribcage. A few seconds later and Cabbage Hat would've stumbled on their tunnel. The guard had vowed to punish the next crew who attempted an escape. So far, the punishments had been mild—a rifle butt to the head or skipping the daily meal. But Charlie had no desire to push the man to see what he'd do next.

As the afternoon's shadows lengthened across the yard, the men sought refuge in them, sipping water from the single dripping tap that protruded from a stone wall near the camp's entrance. When the meal came, Charlie guzzled it down, his stomach still pining for more even as he swallowed the last mouthful of watery rice.

The rest of the afternoon stretched ahead of him.

Nothing to do but talk, wander, think. Many of the men had bouts of depression that kept them in bed, sweat dripping from their overheated bodies. Others would gather around them, listening, attempting to reason them out of their lethargy. Charlie had vowed to himself not to fall into the trap of self-pity. He had to get out of there. Escape or victory were the only options. He couldn't think about anything else. Edie and Keith needed him; they were waiting for him to return to Bathurst.

He recalled every last word in the final letter he'd received from Edie before he set out in the Kittyhawk that night in July. She'd begged him to come home in one piece, to stay safe because they needed him whole. He'd written her a response but hadn't had the chance to send it. Perhaps his commander might've found the letter in his things and forwarded it onto her. He hoped so. He hated to think of what would go through her mind when she discovered he'd been captured by the enemy. His parents would be devastated as well. They'd think the worst. Perhaps even now, all his loved ones believed him to be dead. He had to get through this, had to escape so they'd know he was still alive, and he would be home soon. Then, they could start their lives together as a family.

❧ 24 ❧

JUNE 1996

ROME

When Reeda woke the next morning, it took her several disoriented moments to remember where she was. She'd slept so soundly the ear on the left side of her head was numb. She must not have moved for hours.

She rubbed her ear as her feet hit the floor, yawned then wandered to the curtains. When she pulled them aside, sunlight streamed into the room. It was late morning. She'd slept longer than she'd planned to sleep, but she felt fantastic. Better than she had in a long time. She reached for her eyeglasses, pushed them up the bridge of her nose and blinked as her sight focused.

She ordered an espresso from room service, sipped it on the balcony, wrapped in a thin, silk dressing gown and then dressed for a day of walking. Thick soled Doc Martens, jeans, a cotton shirt, wide-brimmed hat, and contact lenses replaced her black-rimmed glasses.

She was starving. She'd slept until ten am, local time, and hadn't eaten much over the past two days. A café across the street served her a second espresso, and she couldn't resist ordering a serving of *ciambella*—fried donuts rolled in granulated sugar and some fresh fruit. It might take her body a while to adjust to the strength of the coffee, but the food was delicious. Satisfied she sipped a glass of water as the sun rose higher still in the sky overhead.

She spent the day walking around Rome. Her backpack contained a novel, a block of Italian chocolate, mineral water, a camera, and the guidebook. She sat on the Spanish steps and read for a while, breaking off pieces of chocolate to eat, and looking up to watch pigeons fighting over bread crumbs thrown by a group of children, tourists climbing up and down the steps, and the water spurting from a fountain nearby.

Next stop was the Vatican, Saint Peter's Square, and St. Peter's Basilica. Reeda took dozens of photographs. There was so much to see, she couldn't resist capturing it all. Thankfully there was plenty of film available in a small convenience shop across the street from her hotel. She was amazed by the sight of remains, hundreds of years old, that'd been kept for their healing properties. Not being a Catholic herself, most of the things on display didn't mean much to her, but she couldn't ignore the beauty and serenity of the buildings, paintings, sculptures, and gardens.

Everywhere she went, Italians bustled about dressed in suits, gowns, the latest fashions. The men had hair combed just so, dark and slick against their scalps, tanned faces, dark eyes, all with somewhere to go. And in their midst, tourists milled about, in shorts and T-shirts, maps unfolded between clutching hands, hats perched on top of heads and wearing comfortable walking shoes. It was easy to spot the difference, and Reeda felt under dressed. Not something she was accustomed to.

She'd been hoping to see the Galleria Colonna, but it was only open to the public on Saturdays, and she'd planned to leave for Sulmona on Thursday. Still, by the time she made it back to the hotel in the afternoon, she was exhausted, hands clutching bags of shopping. She hadn't been able to resist a few souvenirs and some local fashions. The leather jacket she bought fit like a glove, and she'd found a few cashmere pashminas in various shades as well that she was dying to try out when the weather cooled.

She stopped at the reception desk to ask if there were any messages. Duncan hadn't called, but Karen had. She was certain whatever the issue was, Karen could manage it by herself, but she'd call her when she returned to her room. Lorenzo passed by, pushing a trolley filled with luggage of various shapes and sizes towards an elevator. She'd asked at the front desk about him earlier, and had been satisfied by the concierge's response—Lorenzo could be relied upon to get her to Sulmona.

"Lorenzo!" called Reeda, hurrying after him.

He faced her with a smile. "Signora Summer."

"Hi," she muttered, breathless after the short jog from the reception desk. She must look a complete mess, after a day of walking around Rome bathed in sweat, and with hat hair.

"What can I do for you, signora?"

"I wanted to check that it's still okay for me to go to Sulmona with you on Thursday? Does your aunt have a room I can rent?"

He nodded. "*Si, bueno, bueno.* She has a room booked for you. I will be leaving here around ten in the morning. Is that too early for you?"

"No, ten is fine."

"Where have you been today, signora?" he asked, eyes twinkling. "I see you found some things to purchase."

"I've been sightseeing. Rome is very beautiful...and so are its fashions."

He laughed. "*Si*, that is true. I love my city, and my fashion. What will you do tonight? You are alone, yes?"

Her cheeks flushed. Was he flirting again? It seemed like he was flirting, although she was out of practice enough to doubt her instincts. "Yes, I thought I might eat at the hotel restaurant. Or, possibly venture out and find somewhere else to dine. I hadn't decided yet. What I really need right now is a shower and to sit down for a little while."

He shook his head. "No, no such a beautiful young woman cannot dine alone in Rome. It is not allowed."

"Not allowed?" she arched an eyebrow.

"No, certainly not. You will eat with me tonight. Yes?"

Surely a meal with a man ten years her junior was harmless. He wasn't really flirting with her; it was how Italian men communicated with women. He was being nice, considerate, that was all it was. "That would be lovely, Lorenzo."

"Wonderful. Meet me in the lobby at eight."

"Eight?" she asked.

She usually dined at seven at the latest, she'd be starving by then. Perhaps she'd have a late afternoon tea to compensate.

"*Si*, eight o'clock."

"Fine, I'll see you then."

He dipped his head and pushed the trolley on its way. She watched him go, then headed for her own elevator.

Upstairs, her room had been tidied, the bed made, and fresh flowers adorned a crystal glass on the small, round table near the wall. It was nice to be pampered. A pang of nostalgia swept through her body, remembering her honeymoon with Duncan.

They'd honeymooned just outside of Gosford, on the central coast. A little bed and breakfast with a view of the ocean. It hadn't been as luxurious as this suite was, since they'd been poor as church mice back then, but it'd been just as beautiful to her. Someone had left fresh cut flowers in a vase on the bedside table as a welcome when they arrived, along with a chocolate each and a note of congratulations on their marriage. It was the happiest time she could remember having, just the two of them, hidden away from the world, from work, study, families, friends. They'd explored each other, their love, talked about hopes, dreams, and plans. It'd been wonderful in every way.

And now it was all over.

She'd assumed they would raise a family together, had built everything around that assumption. Her business, her life, her very self-worth, hinged on the family they'd planned to grow together. She hadn't realised that of course. It was an assumption, not something she'd ever articulated even to herself. But when it didn't happen, her world began to fall apart piece by piece until she knew nothing would ever be the way they'd dreamed it would in that little bed and breakfast.

She showered and changed, then ordered another cheese and olive tray with Chianti from room service and sat on the bed. The phone was on the bedside table and she lay back on the pillows and dialled The Waratah Inn.

Bindi answered and seemed excited to hear from her. She told her all the news, that Mima was doing well and had already moved out of the inn. Kate was thriving in the kitchen. And Jack had a fall while fixing a leaking gutter on the garden shed, but Bindi assured her he was fine, and they were making him rest while Kate force fed him plenty of his favourite meals.

Reeda was laughing when she hung up the phone. It did her soul good to talk to her sisters. She hesitated with the handpiece held high in one hand. She should call Duncan; he'd be wondering how she was doing. Or should she?

He'd told her they needed time away from each other, and space. She'd agreed, but only because she didn't want to fight with him anymore. It was strange to be away from him. Even though he'd been distant for so long, he was always there, always close by. Now he was on the other side of the world. She had no idea where he was, what he was doing, who he was talking to. The ache in her heart grew.

She dialled then, and her breath caught in her throat.

"Hello?"

"Hi, Duncan, it's Reeda."

"Reeda, I was hoping you'd call."

Her eyes widened. "Oh, good, I wasn't sure if you'd want to hear from me or not..."

"Yes, of course I do. I don't want to interrupt your holiday, but I'm glad you've arrived safely."

She swallowed. "Yes, here safe and sound. The hotel is beautiful. I miss...I miss home of course, but there's so much to see and do here, I think I'll be fine." She laughed and an uncomfortable silence descended between them.

"Uh, yeah, well, have a great time."

"Everything okay with you?" she asked around the lump forming in her throat.

"Yes, I'm working a lot."

"Good."

"Thanks for calling, Reeda. I'm glad you're having a nice time."

"Yes, of course. I'll let you know how I go."

"Good, thanks. Talk later."

When he hung up, Reeda held the phone to her ear listening to the dial tone for another full minute. She called Karen and talked through some of the issues in the office, then hung up the phone again with a sigh.

The knock at the door startled her. She wiped her eyes dry with the back of her hand and hurried to meet room service with her tray of food and drinks. Seated on the balcony again, she cradled a wine glass in one hand and stared out over the busy streets below and the wall of the ruined Colosseum ahead of her. Dark shadows angled down the length of the broken wall, lending it a sinister look.

By the time eight o'clock arrived, Reeda had changed into a sleeveless black pant suit with flowing, charcoal pashmina and stiletto heels. She'd straightened her freshly washed hair and applied her standard evening makeup—smoky eyes with pale lips and plenty of blush.

She strode with confidence through the lobby and found Lorenzo waiting in a pair of dark blue jeans and a suit jacket by the front doors. He whistled when he saw her, his gaze raking up and down her body.

"Wow," he said.

Her cheeks flamed. "Thank you."

"*Bellissimo*! Let's go."

He reached for her hand and slid his over hers, pulling her along beside him. He walked quickly outside, forcing her to practically jog to keep up with him, which was quite a task in high-heeled shoes.

"Where are we going?" she asked, breathless with the effort.

"There is a little restaurant down this alley." He pointed one hand to a side street up ahead. "It has the best ravioli in the city, and live music."

"That sounds perfect," she replied.

When they reached the restaurant, he still held her hand firmly in his. Her skin tingled and she wondered if she should pull away. He spoke a few words in Italian to the host, who seated them inside by a window that looked out onto the small, dimly lit alley. Some people were dining outside at round tables with red and white checked tablecloths with tea candles. Laughter filtered in through the doorway every time it was pushed open.

Inside, the restaurant was dotted with patrons here and there. Huddled over tables, deep in discussion, some holding hands, others clearly seated with groups of friends. All appeared to be locals—there were no gaudy tourist clothes, only the blacks, charcoals, and other dark, fashionable coloured clothing worn by the Italians Reeda had seen since she arrived in Rome.

In one corner of the room, a four-piece folk band was setting up with a vocalist, accordion, flute, and bag pipes.

When they sat, Lorenzo released his hold of her hand and laced his fingers together over the table.

He grinned. "Nice, eh?"

She nodded. "It's perfect. I would've thought it might be busier..."

"It is only now getting started, the people will come."

She wasn't sure she'd ever get used to the way the Italian people ate so late at night and stayed up until all hours of the morning. She needed her sleep, or she didn't function well the next day.

"How do you do it?" she asked. "How do you stay up so late, when you have work tomorrow?"

He laughed. "Why sleep when you can live?"

A waiter stopped at their table. He glanced at her with interest, then gave his attention to Lorenzo, who barked a few words at him in Italian. The waiter dipped his head in assent and moved on.

The band struck up the first notes of a song, and Lorenzo reached for her hand, tugging her to her feet. "Come, let us dance."

She resisted. "Dance? No one is dancing. There's no dance floor...I'm not sure..."

He laughed, pulling her after him. "We will make a dance floor."

When they reached the space where the band played, he stopped, spun towards her, and pulled her to his chest. Then, expertly led her around the dance floor, his feet moving in time to the music. Her head felt light, giddy with the heady scents, the music, the feel of a strange man's arms around her body.

He smiled with his eyes fixed on hers. "You are a wonderful dancer," he said.

She threw her head back and laughed. "Now, I know you're flattering me."

He laughed along with her, then spun her out in a turn, and back into his arms. Was he real, or something conjured by her imagination?

It wasn't long before the restaurant filled. Lorenzo wanted to keep dancing, and soon Reeda had caught his infectious enthusiasm for it. She let herself relax, moved with the music, threw her hands in the air over her head and released her inhibitions. Sweat trickled down her forehead, her breath came in gasps, but she was having fun. She laughed, ran her fingers through her lank hair. Other couples joined them on the tiny dance floor and the entire place seemed to heat up like they'd added coals to a hearth.

Finally exhausted, they both collapsed into their chairs, laughing. A plate of olives, cheeses, crackers, breads, dips, prosciutto, and a few things she didn't recognise awaited them, along with a bottle of red wine.

"That was amazing," she gasped, wiping the sweat from her brow with her napkin.

He laughed. "You dance well, signora."

"No, you dance well, Lorenzo. You made me look much better than I am. Thank you."

Something had settled between them while they danced.

She felt relaxed. The tension that'd crackled between them earlier was gone, and into its place had drifted a comfortable familiarity.

They ate with gusto then, and every morsel was like heaven on her tongue. The food was full of flavour, exciting and teasing her tastebuds: eggplant dip of some kind on crostini with vegetables marinated in olive oil. Several different types of olives, some stuffed with cheese, others whole. Pastrami, salami, and an aged cheddar that melted in her mouth, along with long, thin crackers that crumbled as soon as she bit into them.

They talked and laughed while they ate, and she found she enjoyed Lorenzo's company more than she'd expected she would. The restaurant was full now, people squashed around tables, speaking in loud voices to be heard over the band. Animated, they waved their hands as they spoke, eyes flashing, punctuated always with bouts of raucous laughter.

"So, signora, will you tell me why you have come to Rome alone?" asked Lorenzo, holding a glass of wine between both hands, eyes fixed on hers.

She pursed her lips. "I'm...I suppose I'm taking some time to think about my marriage."

"Uh, I see. And what do you have to think about?"

"My husband thinks we should go our separate ways." Saying it out loud felt like a punch to her gut. She inhaled a sharp breath.

"I'm sorry to hear that. He must be a fool." Lorenzo's eyes smiled to soften his words.

She sighed. "He's not. We've had a few hard years...And I have another purpose for my trip. As I told you, I'm trying to track down my grandfather."

"Yes, of course, in Sulmona. I hope you will find everything you came to Italy in search of."

"Thank you."

"I know what it is like to have trouble in love," he continued, one hand pressed to his heart.

"You do?"

"Yes, *mio amore* is separated from me even now."

"Oh, I'm so sorry."

"Thank you. She lives in Milan, studying the finance. And here I am, in Rome. We have been apart now for almost one full year, and I feel as though my heart is not within my body any longer."

Reeda patted his arm. "You love her."

"*Si*, I love her, and she loves me. It is hard, but we will make it work. I am saving money while she is studying and in three more years we will marry."

"That sounds like a very good plan," replied Reeda, her eyes misting.

"You and your husband will work things out also, no?"

She shook her head. "I don't think so but thank you for your kind words."

How could they work things out? Nothing had changed. She still wasn't pregnant, and it wasn't likely she ever would be. He was a workaholic who neglected their relationship and avoided dealing with anything difficult they had to face. Between them, they were a disaster.

Besides, he'd already told her he couldn't see things working out between them. And if there was one thing she knew about her husband, it was that when he made a decision, he'd thought everything through rationally and thoroughly to get to that point, which meant it was almost impossible to get him to change his mind. That resolve made him a good surgeon, but difficult to live with.

And besides, she wasn't sure she'd ever learn to fully come to terms with her own infertility. It wasn't fair to keep him committed to someone who couldn't face reality. Bitterness flooded through her soul, tainting the happiness she'd felt moments earlier. How could she move forward with her life if she couldn't let go of a dream that would never happen?

❦ 25 ❦

SEPTEMBER 1946

BATHURST

Three rows of Italian migrants watched Edie closely. Brown eyes fixed on her mouth as she spoke.

"One, two, three, four..." She counted all the way through to twenty, pointing at each number drawn in chalk on the blackboard behind her as she did.

When she stopped, she nodded her head in encouragement, and the group repeated the numbers along with her in concert. Her legs were tired, and a headache had begun at the base of her neck and worked its way up until it pounded across her scalp. She'd been teaching for almost eight hours, with only a short break for lunch. It was time to go home.

"That's all for today. Well done everyone. I'll see you tomorrow."

Muttering thanks and dipping their heads in acknowledgement, the students, of all ages, filed out of the small, square school room. Edie slumped into her hard, timber chair and squeezed her eyes shut.

What she really needed was a cup of tea and a rest. She hadn't been getting as much sleep lately what with the hours she was working at the migrant camp and taking care of Keith. She'd insisted on taking over as much of the mothering duties as she could, whenever she was home. And now her after-work hours were consumed by food preparation, cleaning, laundry, playing trucks, and reading stories.

Charlie's mother, Monique Jackson, had become more involved in Keith's life as well. She often drove out to the farm during the day while Edie was at work to help Mother with Keith, bringing baked goods or treats for the little boy with her. He adored her as much as she did him, and it brought Edie some satisfaction to see the way he bonded with Charlie's mother. Charlie would've liked to see them get along so well. They hadn't spoken of it, not in so many words. But it was obvious Mrs. Jackson knew Charlie was Keith's father in the way she treated him, and Edie played along. She knew how uncomfortable it would make Charlie's parents to admit their son had a child out of wedlock and she had no desire to do that to them. She was simply glad Keith had them in his life.

Thoughts of Charlie no longer sucked the air from her lungs the way they used to. She could imagine him now, laughing, riding his bike, pushing her into the river, without the pang of pain, the tears, the aching deep inside. Instead, she felt a dull sadness and sometimes even managed a smile when remembering the happiest moments.

With a sigh, she set about straightening up the classroom, preparing for the next day's lessons. Then she reached for her cardigan and purse and headed out the door, pulling it shut behind her.

"Goodbye, Miss Watson," called one of the students, waving across the dusty yard.

She waved back, slipping an arm into her cardigan.

Bunk houses were laid out in straight lines, children raced about in bare feet, shouting, laughing, and playing. Men sat on rough-hewn chairs and smoked, talking over the activities of the day. The women, by this time, were mostly inside making the evening meal. Smoke curled from narrow chimneys.

Two of the other teachers walked by, deep in conversation, arms wrapped around textbooks, hair curled perfectly to accentuate powdered cheekbones.

"Bye Helen, bye Sue," called Edie, waving to them. She'd attended school with both girls for years. Now, they were grown, Helen worked a few days per week as a secretary for Charlie's father, and Sue was engaged to be married to one of the local boys who'd returned from the war with one leg.

Sue glanced her way, nostrils flared. Helen didn't lift her head but kept walking to where they'd each parked their bicycles. Edie's eyes narrowed. Ever since she'd come out with the truth about Keith, there were some in the small community who no longer spoke to her. Some didn't even make eye contact. She shook her head, tightened the grip on her purse and strode towards her own bicycle. Let them shun her, what did she care?

Tears blinded her vision and she dashed them away with the back of her hand. She had to be stronger than that; she couldn't let other people's petty judgements get to her. Keith needed her, he loved her, that was all that mattered now.

"Edie?"

She spun on her heel, her eyes still half-blurred. A tall figure loomed before her.

"Paul Summer? Is that really you?"

Green eyes sparkled at her. He was dapper in a charcoal suit with black tie and shiny patent leather shoes.

Paul plucked a charcoal fedora from his head and pressed it to his chest. Thick hair spilled free. "It's me. I can't believe I found you. You're as beautiful as I remembered."

❧

PAUL LED HER TO FATHER'S TRUCK. SHE CLIMBED IN, HER thoughts in a jumble. Paul started the truck, then managed to drive them back in the direction of the farm on the left side of the road with her bike in the back, and only a few ground gears in the process.

"What are you doing here?" she asked.

He was taller than she remembered, strong, and smelled of cigars and aftershave. Her mind was working overtime to understand what was going on. He was supposed to be in America. She thought she'd never see him again. When he'd walked out that day, after proposing to her in the hospital, she'd been heartbroken over losing her brother, and pining for Charlie to return. She'd been a different woman. Looking back, it was as though she was seeing someone else's life. She no longer felt like the woman he'd asked to be his wife. She was a mother, a country woman, a teacher. Not the Edith Watson he remembered, the vibrant, fun-loving nurse from Sydney.

"I came to find you," he said.

She studied his profile, her brow furrowed. He came to find her?

"How did you get Father's truck?" she asked, focusing her gaze on the road ahead as the truck jounced over potholes.

"I caught a ride from Bathurst out to your farm. Your father was there, I told him why I'd come, and he said you were at the migrant camp, gave me directions, and let me borrow the truck."

Her eyes narrowed. It wasn't like father to be so cavalier, or generous with his beloved truck. "I still don't understand..." Her heart thudded, her head spun, and the headache began to pound in her temples.

Paul pulled the truck over to the side of the road at the entrance to the Watson family driveway. He set the hand brake, turned to her, and leaned his arm along the back of the seat. "After you turned me down..."

"I'm sorry about that," she interrupted, her cheeks flushing with heat.

"No, don't apologise." He waved a hand. "You were absolutely right. We hardly knew each other, I was from the other side of the world, it made no sense for us to be married. You turned me down, when I made a half-hearted attempt to win you over with an impromptu proposal. I get it."

"It was a nice proposal," she whispered.

He chuckled, his gaze meeting hers and sending a spark of electricity down her spine. "It was nothing like you deserved."

She smiled.

"After that, I went back to the ship and when the war ended, we returned home to the States. I thought that was it. I'd go to college, back to my family, my old life. That everything would be normal again. Only, I couldn't get you out of my head. Everywhere I went, everyone I talked to, I'd see your face, I'd remember your voice."

Edie clutched her hands together in her lap. They were shaking. Her throat ached and she didn't know what to say, how to respond.

Paul slid towards her across the bench seat, took her hand in his and pressed it to his lips. His eyes were full of compassion; the warmth of his skin on hers set her heart racing.

"Things are different now, between us. I'm not the patient

anymore, and you're not the nurse in charge of when I eat, drink, or get dressed." He laughed. "Instead, I'm a man who's travelled to the other side of the globe to ask you on a date. You can say no, and I'll leave you be. But I'm hoping you'll give me a second chance."

She met his gaze, her eyes misting over. "Yes, I'll go on a date with you. But there's something I have to tell you first."

When she told Paul about Charlie, he nodded with understanding. Then, she shared the truth about Keith, and he sat back against the seat, his eyes on the road ahead.

"When you asked me to marry you, I'd only just lost my brother, I was waiting for Charlie to come home so we could be a family...It was a difficult time for me. I couldn't tell you all of that, because I kept it to myself. I had to, if I was going to be able to function, to do the things I needed to do for my job, to take care of you and the other men in the hospital. I hope you can understand that."

He nodded. "Of course I understand. We all lost people we loved." His voice was low, it trembled over the words.

"And Keith...I know that's a lot to take in...but he's mine, I love him and we're a family, the two of us. If you still want to go on that date, then that would be fine with me. If you don't, I understand, and I won't hold it against you."

He smiled, eyes crinkling around the edges. "You're not getting out of our date that easily Miss Watson."

❧ 26 ❧

JUNE 1996

ROME

When Lorenzo pulled up in front of the Palazzo Manfredi on Thursday morning, Reeda's eyebrows arched over widened eyes at the sight of his scooter towing a small trailer.

He pushed the visor up on his helmet and grinned at her, the engine still idling in the valet turning circle.

"Good morning signora. I hope you are ready to go to Sulmona, climb on board."

She gaped, unable to speak. Her luggage sat neatly packed beside her. She wore wide-legged trousers, a blouse and scarf knotted around her neck. Her hair was pulled into a ponytail. She'd put on makeup, made an effort to look nice. And now here he was, seated on what looked almost like a toy motorbike, asking if she was ready to ride more than one hundred and sixty kilometres over a mountain range with him.

Had he lost his mind?

"Um...on that?" she stuttered.

He set down the kickstand and tugged off his helmet, fitting it over one handlebar. "Don't worry, signora, your luggage will fit nicely in the trailer."

She wasn't convinced. "Are you sure?"

He opened the trailer's sleek, hard lid. "Yes, I am certain," he said as he lifted her luggage into the trailer. It fit, much to her amazement. While he manoeuvred it into place beside what looked to be bags of groceries, she studied the bike. So much for her hairstyle.

Lorenzo handed her a spare helmet and climbed back on, winking at her. "Let's go," he said.

She studied the bike a moment longer. Perhaps she'd die on a scooter in southern Italy, but at least she'd seen Rome first. She threw one leg over the seat behind Lorenzo, then slid her hands around his waist.

He knocked the kickstand back into place with one heel, and revved the engine, then pulled out of the circular drive and into traffic. Reeda clung tight to Lorenzo's strong waist; her breath stuck in her throat.

This was crazy. What was she doing? She barely knew the man and now he was going to get her killed. This wasn't the kind of thing Reeda Summer did. She was responsible, the CEO of a successful company in Sydney. People looked up to her, respected her and she never did anything spontaneous or potentially life-threatening. Not like this. And yet here she was on the back of a virtual stranger's scooter, motoring in and out of four scattered lanes of traffic in a city on the other side of the world from everyone she knew and loved.

Lorenzo drove as though he had no concept of road rules or safety. He didn't bother much with lanes, simply weaved and ducked between the lines of vehicles that stopped, started, and honked their way through the city.

She squeezed her eyes shut as he flanked a large truck, then slid in front of it, eliciting a loud beep. She couldn't look anymore. Her heart thudded, sweat beaded across her forehead, and her breath was shallow.

After a while, the sounds of traffic diminished and the ducking and weaving slowed, then stopped entirely as the scooter accelerated forward in a mostly straight line.

Reeda's eyes flickered open and she saw they'd left the city behind and were on a highway, surrounded by rolling, almost bare, pale green hills on both sides. The slopes' only embellishment: tight-knit, dark shrubbery that hugged the hills as though afraid to tumble down their steep banks. In the distance, jagged peaks almost blended seamlessly with the white-washed light blue sky. White stucco villages with orange roofs dotted the hillsides here and there.

She smiled and let out a shout of delight. "Woohoo!"

She felt rather than heard Lorenzo's laughter.

Both sides of the road were flanked by rolling green hills, clutches of dark bushes and the occasional tree. Every now and then, they zipped past an olive grove or vineyard.

They stopped to eat lunch at a petrol station and restaurant that spanned the highway. It stood like a spider, its legs meeting the ground on either side of the eight-lane road. They rode an elevator up one of the legs and ate at a busy restaurant hanging over the speeding traffic.

When they pulled into Sulmona, Lorenzo tapped the back of her hand, where it rested around his waist, then pointed to the sign that announced the town's limits.

The streets were narrower than the main roads in Rome. Buildings made of stone or pale orange and yellow stucco loomed up on all sides. People strode along footpaths, wearing simple jeans, T-shirts, or dresses. Graffiti marred the side of a stone bridge. A snow-capped mountain range rose majestic just beyond the town's border.

Lorenzo pulled into the driveway of a tall, grey stone building, set close to other tall stone buildings on either side of it. A small sign in Italian hung from a front gate. The bike sputtered to a stop. Reeda climbed off, her legs so stiff it was difficult to walk for several moments. She stood still to stretch each leg and her back, while Lorenzo dismounted and took off his helmet. Then, she handed her helmet to him as well.

"This is my aunt's place," he said. "Her name is Estelle Cancio. Just as I am Lorenzo Cancio."

Reeda nodded. "It's beautiful here."

Ivy climbed the front wall of the house. Square, shuttered windows sleepily eyed the street. Green bushes and shrubs filled a neat garden bed that ran the length of the fence line.

"Yes, she keeps it well," he replied, already walking down the driveway to a side entrance.

He raised a fist to knock on the door. It opened within moments, and a buxom woman pulled him into her arms, kissing both his cheeks one by one.

"Lorenzo," she cried, kissing him again.

They spoke together in hushed Italian for a few moments, before Estelle gave Reeda her attention.

"You must be Reeda," she said, her accent softening the words. "Please, won't you come inside."

Reeda smiled. "Yes, it's so nice to meet you, signora. Lorenzo speaks very highly of you."

"He's a good boy," replied Estelle, leading them down a short, dark hallway and into an open living room.

"I will bring your luggage upstairs," said Lorenzo. "Enjoy your stay." He smiled and ducked back outside.

Reeda's room was tidy and quaint with a patchwork quilt on a double bed and a sloped ceiling overhead. It contained a single window that looked out across the local neighbourhood, yards split by fences, trees, bushes, and colourful laundry hung on lines.

She settled into the room, unpacked a few things when Lorenzo brought them up, then lay on the bed until she fell asleep. An hour later, she woke to the sound of a horn blaring on the street outside. The cooler air made her shiver and she hobbled to the window to pull it shut, arms wrapping around herself. The sun had dipped in the sky and clouds hung low, full of rain.

Wrapped up in a pashmina, and with one of Nan's diaries tucked beneath her arm, Reeda trundled down the narrow, winding staircase. She found Estelle in the living room, going over some account books in an armchair with a small cup of steaming espresso on the table beside her.

"There you are," exclaimed Estelle.

"I wonder if you could tell me, is there a café nearby?" asked Reeda.

Estelle stood to her feet, straightening her skirts with a squint. "*Si*, there is a café. Just follow this side of the street for one hundred metres. You cannot miss it."

"Thank you. And I wanted to ask as well, I was hoping to go to the prisoner of war camp tomorrow, can you tell me how to get there?"

Estelle wasn't surprised, or if she was, she didn't show it. She simply nodded. "Yes, of course. My nephew will take you, if you like. Lorenzo will be heading back to Rome the day after, but he will be here tomorrow."

"I don't want to be a nuisance..." began Reeda.

Estelle interrupted her. "Never, never, he is happy to do it. He's a good boy."

"Okay, well, thank you."

Reeda waved goodbye and stepped out onto the street, grateful for her warm shoulder wrap. It was cooler in Sulmona than it had been in stifling Rome. She'd have to hurry if she didn't want to get caught in the rainstorm threatening in the rolling clouds overhead.

The Marchetti Café was where Estelle had promised it would be. Reeda ordered an espresso and a croissant, then sat at one of the tables on the footpath outside the café. She watched people walk by, studied the threatening sky, and sipped her espresso. Thoughts competed in her mind on the state of her marriage, the children she'd never have, the successful business that awaited her return in Sydney which she wasn't sure she wanted anymore, the dream she'd had on the plane, reminding her of the fight with her sisters years earlier, and the pain it'd reignited inside her. It also reminded her of a conversation they'd had before Nan's funeral where Kate and Bindi had assured her they didn't hold her accountable for the accident. Could she accept that? Perhaps they'd forgiven her, but could she forgive herself?

She finished the espresso and dessert, then set Nan's journal on the table in front of her. It was hard to believe she'd done it. She was in Sulmona, Italy, where Charlie Jackson had been held prisoner. Tomorrow, she'd visit whatever remained of that prison camp. It was all so surreal. Maybe she'd discover what'd become of him, maybe she wouldn't. Either way, she couldn't believe she'd come this far, to the other side of the world, to follow the cold trail he'd left behind.

Would Nan be proud of her? She hoped she would. She hoped Nan would've blessed what she was doing, if she'd lived to know about it. If only Nan had thought to tell them, to tell someone, the truth about their family, about who Charlie was, it might've made this whole thing a lot easier. Still, she was enjoying the journey, the discovery. And it'd prompted her to travel to a place she'd always wanted to see.

She turned the pages of the journal until she found her bookmark, then settled down to keep reading.

❧ 27 ❧

NOVEMBER 1946

BATHURST

K eith lay in her arms, sound asleep. A curl rested on his forehead and Edie leaned forward to kiss it. A smile tickled the corners of her mouth. As hard as it was to manage single motherhood, his angelic face made it all worth it. Especially when he was sleeping. There was something so precious about his drowsing face, with its button nose, pink cheeks, and dark eyelashes resting on white cheeks like half-moons.

"Goodbye Mrs. Jackson," she said, nodding her head.

Monique Jackson sat in the driver's seat of her black Ford Prefect sedan. She waved a gloved hand, ground the car into reverse, and backed up to turn the vehicle so she could head back to town. She often came to visit on a Saturday, and sometimes convinced Edie and Keith to drive to town with her for an ice cream. That way, she could arrange a meet up with Mr. Jackson, who'd never agreed to come out to the farm to see his grandson and in fact had yet to admit Keith was his grandson. Still, after a pleasant morning spent at their home, Edie could see Keith was breaking through his grandfather's cool reserve.

Mr. and Mrs. Jackson had aged since the outbreak of the war. Both had streaks of grey through their hair. Mrs. Jackson had developed a paunch, in place of her svelte pre-war figure. And Mr. Jackson had bags beneath his eyes and lines on his face that gave him a haggard look. Their daughter, Sylvia, had moved to Sydney during the war, married a carpenter there and hadn't returned. They still mourned Charlie, while always living with the hope that one day he'd come home. And it showed on their faces.

Edie carried Keith up the farmhouse steps. The scent of baking bread wafted over her as she pushed through the front door. Mother peeped around the corner, a dash of flour on her cheek and coating the apron tied around her waist.

She smiled. "Ah, there you are. Did you have a nice time?"

"Keith's sleeping," whispered Edie. "I'll put him in bed and come down for a cuppa."

Mother nodded, wiping her hands on the soiled apron.

Edie carried Keith up the creaking stairs and laid him on the narrow bed that had been slotted into her room against the wall opposite her own bed. She hadn't wanted to broach the subject of him moving into Bobby's room. It was exactly the way Bobby had left it when he went off to war, and Edie often caught Mother sitting on Bobby's bed, staring blankly at the wall. She'd prefer to share a room with Keith than disturb her parents' grief that way.

She covered Keith with a thin, white sheet, kissed his forehead one last time and crept from the room. He didn't often nap these days, and when he did, she knew he'd be up late that night. But he'd had such a busy morning, playing tea parties, and digging in the garden at the Jackson's house, he needed a rest.

Downstairs, Mother had made a pot of tea and was pouring two cups. She smiled at Edie. "Did he go down okay?"

Edie nodded. "He was worn out."

"It's good he can spend time with the Jacksons." Mother pursed her lips as she finished pouring the tea.

Edie hid a smile. Mother had fought against the idea of introducing a second set of grandparents. She didn't want the Jacksons to have any claim over Keith, or to interrupt his life, she'd said. Edie figured it was simple jealousy. Mother had already had to deal with Edie changing her role in Keith's life, it was hard for her to let go further still and give the Jacksons a place. But so far, she'd been gracious about it. Mother was nothing if not gracious.

Edie slid into a chair at the small, round dining table the family shared. She sipped her tea, as Mother sat across from her, straight-backed and head high, as always.

"Have you seen Paul this week?" asked Mother suddenly.

Edie set down her tea. It'd been two months since Paul showed up in Bathurst unexpectedly. Since then, they'd seen each other several times a week. Usually he'd call on her at the farmhouse, though on weekends he'd take her out in the car he'd bought from a local dealership. He'd rented a room in town and had put out feelers for a job within the first two weeks. He'd started work at the Ford dealership as a salesperson soon after and had bought his first car right away. When she'd asked him where he got the money for such a big purchase, he'd mumbled something about his parents and a trust fund that he'd inherited when he turned twenty-one.

"I saw him here on Wednesday evening. Remember?"

Mother nodded. "Yes, of course. You went for a walk through the orchard. He's been coming around a lot. Do you think things are progressing between the two of you?"

Edie studied Mother through narrowed eyes. She loved her mother but sometimes it was difficult to know what she thought about things. She kept her views so close to her chest. Did she like Paul? Was she concerned about them moving too fast?

"I think so. He loves me, and he's told me as much."

"And?" asked Mother, cradling her tea between her hands.

"And...I'm taking my time. I want to be sure before I commit myself to him."

Mother nodded. "That's wise. Marriage is serious business. When you're young it can be easy to be cavalier about the heart, love, and romance. But marriage is a lifelong commitment, and one of the most tragic things a woman can do is commit herself to the wrong kind of man for the rest of her life."

Edie's eyes widened. "Do you think Paul is the wrong kind of man?"

Mother smiled and rested one hand on top of Edie's. "No, no darling of course not. I'm saying I'm proud of you for taking the time to think it through. I don't know him well, but from what I know of him he seems like a nice, young man. He's treated you with respect, he's liked around town... Your father and I have no objections, except that..." Mother hesitated.

"What? Except what?"

"He's American."

"And what's wrong with being American?" asked Edie, her temper flaring.

"Nothing's wrong with it. But what will happen if he

decides it's time for the family to return to his home country? We might never see you again." Mother's voice broke and she stared at the top of her teacup, her lower lip trembling.

Edie inhaled a sharp breath. She hadn't considered that. Since Paul had come all the way to Australia to court her, she'd assumed he would stay there if they were married. But what if he didn't want to? Would she and Keith have to move to the other side of the world? She'd never had the desire to travel that Mima had. She was a homebody more than anything else. She couldn't imagine living so far from her homeland.

"I don't know..." she whispered.

Mother smiled, patting her hand gently. "Never mind, darling. These are the kinds of things you should talk about, the two of you, before you make any decisions."

A car growled up the drive and pulled to a stop in front of the house. Edie sighed. Mrs. Jackson must've forgotten something. She hurried out the front and found Paul with his fist raised about to knock on the door frame.

He smiled, slipped the cowboy hat from his head, and winked. "Howdy ma'am."

She laughed. He leaned down to kiss her cheek and sparks raced through her skin sending goosebumps down her neck.

"What are you doing here?" she asked.

"I realised we hadn't made any plans for tonight, so I finished my shift at work and thought I'd ride out here to sweep you away for the evening."

She leaned back against the door frame to look up at his handsome face, cheeks burning. "Really? What should we do?"

"I don't know. How about we drive around, enjoy each other's company, and see what happens?"

She giggled. "I suppose we could do that. I put Keith

down for a nap a few minutes ago, but I'm sure Mother wouldn't mind watching him."

"Great."

Mother appeared in the entry. "Paul, how lovely to see you."

He nodded. "You too ma'am."

"Why don't you come in and have a cup of tea with me?"

"I'd love to, thank you." Paul wiped his boots on the door mat and stepped inside. The room seemed small when he was in it.

"We're going out, Mother. Would it be okay if you watched Keith for me tonight?"

Mother nodded, linking her hands together in front of her apron. "That's fine."

"I'm going upstairs to change. I'll be back in a few minutes." Edie glanced up at Paul. His eyes crinkled at the corners, full of a love that made her head spin.

She raced up the stairs, hearing the murmur of conversation in the kitchen as she looked through the meagre offerings in her cupboard. She had so few pretty dresses, it made dating more difficult. She'd have to wear the same navy cotton dress she'd worn the last time they went out. She sighed. She supposed it would just have to do.

As she dressed, she pondered how much things had changed. The way she'd felt about Charlie was different to her relationship with Paul. With Charlie, things had been passionate, heady, desperate. They had to be together, if they couldn't be, she'd felt as though she might die. When he left, a part of her left with him. She was empty inside, lonely, dark, couldn't live without him.

But he was gone. And she had gone on living with the gap in her heart he'd left behind.

When she was with Paul, she felt safe, loved, happy. The

desperation, the cloying need was gone, instead there was affection, respect, and love. She'd admitted it to herself a few days earlier. She loved him. She hadn't recognised the feeling at first since it was so removed from how she'd felt for Charlie, but it was there. A stable, strong kind of love, with a foundation she didn't think would be easily moved.

She'd marry him, it was only a matter of time. As Mother said, there were things they had to discuss first. But she was certain, given how well they'd come to know one another, that he wouldn't expect more of her than she was willing to give. She felt as though he was the kind of man she could rely on not to break her heart, pull her apart or leave her desperate and alone. And that was something to hold onto.

❦

THE DRIVE UP TO MOUNT PANORAMA WAS PICTURESQUE. IT was almost summer, so even though it was seven o'clock, the sun had only just dipped beyond the horizon. A glow lit up the western sky, and long shafts of orange light fingered the hood of the car.

Edie slid closer to Paul on the wide, plush seat. He raised his arm and she snuggled beneath it, resting a hand on his chest. His hand fell onto her shoulder and he massaged her sleeve.

"This is nice," she said.

He nodded. "It is."

"Can I ask you something?" she said.

"Sure, shoot."

"What did your family think about you coming out here, to Australia?"

He shrugged. "They were okay with it."

"Really?"

He chuckled. "Fine, they weren't happy about me travelling to the other side of the world. It's a long way to go by ship, expensive too. They knew I might not come back. Mom cried...a lot." He pursed his lips. "Why do you ask?"

Edie's heart fell. She hated to think of his parents going through the pain of separating from their son that way. He had siblings, but being a mother, she knew she'd never be able to let go of Keith without experiencing heartache.

"I'm curious, I guess. I wasn't sure if you were planning on staying in Australia forever, or returning home. You haven't mentioned anything about it."

"I guess that depends."

"On what?" she asked.

He glanced at her, eyes sparkling. "On whether or not you agree to marry me."

She laughed. "Oh. So, you're saying, if we get married, you'll stay here forever?"

He nodded. "I will."

"And if we don't, you'll leave?"

Another nod.

"So, when are you going to ask me?"

Paul's eyebrows arched high. He pulled the car to the side of the road with a squeal of tires. Gravel shot in every direction as they rolled to a halt overlooking the township of Bathurst. Lights dappled the metropolis as the twilight rolled over it.

Paul spun in his seat to face her; his eyes wide. "What are you saying?"

She laughed, her eyes filling with tears. "Ask me again?"

He grinned, a wide, happy smile. Swallowed. "Edith Watson, I didn't think I'd ever see you again. When I walked away in that hospital, I thought my heart would tear in two. It didn't, but it also never forgot you. I came here because you're the love of my life. I know you have a history, that you and Keith are a family, but I'm the missing piece. Will you do me the honour of becoming my wife?"

Tears spilled down her cheeks and her heart thundered in her chest. She reached her arms around his neck and kissed his lips, her own wet with tears. "Yes, I'll marry you. I'll marry you Paul Summer."

❧ 28 ❧

JUNE 1996

SULMONA

The scent of donuts filled the small room. Reeda slapped Nan's journal shut, her eyes misting with tears. She reached for her morning coffee and sipped it.

Birds twittered nearby. After her trip to the café the previous afternoon, she'd run home in the rain. The downpour had continued for the rest of the evening and all night long. With morning, the sky cleared, and blue peeked out from between fluffy white clouds. Reeda sat on her private balcony and stared out over the Sulmona neighbourhood as it wakened, and people hustled out of doors to start their days.

The bed and breakfast didn't serve dinner, and since it was bucketing down with rain the night before, she'd ordered a pizza to be delivered to her room. The empty box sat on top of the small rubbish bin by the door, still pungent with the aroma of tomato sauce and cheese.

That scent mingled with the smell of Reeda's breakfast, gave the place a pleasant feeling. Cool air drifted in through the open balcony door bringing relief in the stuffy room. Reeda pushed the balcony door wider to breath deep, then cinched her dressing gown more tightly around her body.

She could've eaten indoors, but it was too beautiful a day to ignore. She'd spent the previous evening reading Nan's journals, then fell asleep in front of an Italian program about sports that she didn't understand. This morning, she'd ordered breakfast in her room, then started again where she'd left off.

After breakfast, Reeda dressed quickly in cool, sensible clothing. The day was already warming and would be hot soon enough. She wasn't sure how much walking she'd be doing at the camp, but she knew she was getting there on the back of Lorenzo's scooter and didn't intend to be caught out wearing inappropriate clothing.

"Ready to go?" asked Lorenzo, in the living room. He was waiting with an espresso, one long jean-clad leg crossed over the other, a newspaper open in his lap.

She nodded. "Ready. Where are we going exactly?"

"A place called Fonte d'Amore, just outside Sulmona."

"Great, I'm excited...well, a little nervous too. This could be the end of something...or the beginning. I'm not sure what I'll find."

He laughed. "I guess we better get going then."

As they zoomed through Sulmona, more modern buildings, likely offices or apartments, flanked the road. Fir trees planted at even intervals dotted the roadside, and a few cars puttered through the quiet streets.

Within minutes, they'd left the town behind. The buzz of

the scooter's engine and the wind in her ears was the only noise. The landscape opened up along the narrow road lined by bare-limbed trees. Green fields stretched out until they met the foothills of a majestic mountain range that travelled and grew until it pressed against the horizon, snowy peaks stark against an azure sky.

Within ten minutes they'd reached Fonte d'Amore, a squat village surrounded by fields and bare hillsides. The ancient stucco buildings were built together, as if to defend themselves. A few of the structures sheltered kitchen gardens surrounded by rusted or weathered fencing. A tall grey water tower loomed above it all, like a sentinel, watching over the towns, fields, and leafless trees that sprang up throughout.

The village passed by in a flash and they came to a sign on its outskirts. Hung on a wire fence, the sign looked official and Lorenzo pulled over to the side of the road and killed the engine.

"Here we are, signora," he said.

She tugged off her helmet and studied the sign. It was in Italian, and she couldn't make out many of the words, other than *Campo 78*.

Reeda waved goodbye to Lorenzo, who promised to return for her in a few hours' time and checked in at the reception counter in a mobile office behind the fence. There were a few other people there for the tour, and she waited outside for the group to be ready. The tour guide, a woman named Rosa, stamped out a cigarette on the gravel road, then waved them all over. She led them throughout the camp, her voice monotone in broken English. The rest of the tourists spoke English as well, half were from England, a few from Australia and one man from France.

She led the group to a stout, stained iron gate that slid slowly open with a rattle. Tall fences stretched away from the gate on either side, now overgrown with vines and weeds, a stark reminder of what it had once been—a place from which there was no escape. To one side, a grove of olive trees with gnarled branches dotted the landscape.

"The prisoners arrived in Sulmona by train and marched here to Fonte d'Amore on foot. The camp housed three thousand prisoners during the years of operation, mostly British, with a large contingent of Australians and some from other countries as well..."

Reeda listened as the group walked through the neatly aligned rows of barracks, where weeds pushed up through cracked pavement and overgrown bushes brushed against the buildings. Her heart pounded, thinking of Charlie locked up in this place.

The sight of empty watch towers and dilapidated sentry boxes chilled her. She shivered and pulled her jacket more tightly around her frame.

After the tour was over, she approached the tour guide, a woman wearing a pair of Nikes, jeans, and a button-down khaki top. A name tag was pinned to her shirt. She was flipping through pages pegged to a clipboard.

"Excuse me, Rosa, I was wondering if I could ask you a few questions?"

Rosa offered her a quick smile above half-moon spectacles. "Of course."

"My grandfather was a prisoner here..."

"British, or Australian?"

"Australian."

"Ah yes, what would you like to know?" asked Rosa, giving Reeda her full attention.

"I was told that there is no record of him dying here..."

"There were only two deaths in this camp for the duration of the war, both from disease. The Abruzzo people are proud of our record for the humane treatment of prisoners in Campo 78."

Reeda nodded. "Yes, of course. But the thing is, he wasn't listed as a resident when the camp was liberated, either. And he didn't come back home to Australia. So, we have no idea what happened to him."

"Ah...interesting." Rosa's smile widened; her eyes sparked. "This is a very interesting case. There is another possibility, you know?"

Reeda's eyes widened. "There is?"

"Yes, in 1943 when Italy surrendered to the Allies, the prisoners awoke one morning to find that all the guards had left. They simply abandoned their posts. Many of the prisoners escaped at this time. When the Germans arrived to re-establish order, after the surrender was overturned, they caught a number of the escaped prisoners, but not all of them. Perhaps your grandfather was one of the prisoners who wasn't recovered?"

"Wow, maybe..."

"In which case," Rosa went on, "he might've been injured or died in his attempts to escape. He would not have known his way, and if he went into the Apennine Mountains...as you can imagine, it would have been cold."

Reeda's gaze drifted to the nearby mountain range, jagged peaks covered in white snow.

"What happened to the prisoners who didn't escape? And the ones recaptured?" asked Reeda.

"They were sent to concentration camps in Germany."

A shudder ran through Reeda's body. "Is it possible that happened to him?"

"I can't be sure, but if you say there was no record of his name...perhaps you will look there next?"

The enormity of the task overwhelmed Reeda and her

heart fell. She might never discover what'd happened to Charlie Jackson.

"And if he escaped, where would he have gone?"

Rosa pursed her lips. She tugged a sheet of paper from her clipboard and handed it to Reeda. It was a map of the Abruzzo region.

"See here, this is Campo 78," she began, tracing a line with her pencil. "And here, is the route some of the prisoners took through the mountains. You see it passes through this village, Pacentro, and then on to Casoli. Some headed the other direction, towards Rome, they were most likely captured. Others went over the mountains to the north..." She pointed at the distant snowy peaks. "It was a hard trek. A lot of them were recaptured and returned to the camp before they reached freedom."

⁂

THE CAFÉ WAS BUSIER THIS AFTERNOON THAN IT HAD BEEN the day before. Reeda had to wait ten minutes for a table, but she didn't mind. She listened to conversations in Italian around her, enjoyed the view, and studied the map Rosa had given her.

If Charlie had escaped and followed the trail through the mountains, what had become of him?

She might never know. If he'd been recaptured and sent to Dachau or Auschwitz, would there be a record of his fate?

So much time had passed, uncovering the truth seemed too mammoth a task to undertake. She'd been so full of hope when she arrived, so certain she'd find something, she couldn't help feeling disappointed now.

She ached for the grandfather she'd never know. He'd been separated from his loved ones, didn't get to hold his son in his arms, longed for the baby he'd never know. She understood what longing felt like. It sapped your strength and stole your hope if it dragged on for too long, the way it had for Charlie, the way it was doing for her.

A waiter dressed in black and white, with a white apron tied neatly around his thin waist led her to a small table in a corner of the café. She ordered an espresso—she was a little concerned she might be forming an addiction, but not worried enough to change her order—and a panini, then settled down to read more of Nan's journal.

She read a few paragraphs, then gazed into the distance, lost in thought.

It seemed Nan had experienced infertility as well. Not in the same way as Reeda, she had a son, after all. But she hadn't fallen pregnant with Pop. Had the two of them had struggled to build their family together? Reeda wished she'd known, wished she'd had a chance to talk to Nan about her own struggle.

Reeda had been too proud, hadn't wanted her family to know what she was going through. Was it pride, or fear? She couldn't say for certain, but either way, she'd never discussed her desire to have a baby with Nan, and the pain of waiting, month after month, for a dream that never came true.

How had Nan and Pop kept going? How had they stayed strong in their marriage?

She and Duncan had let infertility tear them apart. If only she could ask Nan about it.

Now her marriage was over. Duncan wanted to move on with his life, to put their pain behind him. She couldn't blame him, not entirely. If she were honest with herself, she'd probably been depressed for at least two years, though she'd never admitted it. It wasn't easy living with a depressed spouse. Only distance had given her the perspective to see that. Maybe time would help her understand why he was ready to walk away without fighting for what they'd had, what they'd been before all the doctor's appointments and hormone shots.

A pain in her chest grew as her throat tightened. The dreams they'd had for themselves, their family, were gone. Duncan loved children, and he wanted a family so much she could see the desperation in his eyes when he talked to her about adoption. He didn't understand that she didn't want to adopt. She wanted children of her own, their own. He told her that was crazy, and maybe it was. But it was how she felt, she couldn't help it, the longing to carry a child rose from deep within like a lava bubbling from a volcano.

She should let him go, let him remarry and find someone he could have a family with. A sob worked its way up her throat.

"Reeda?" a voice called her name.

She glanced up to see Lorenzo making his way through the throng of customers. Reeda drew a deep breath and pushed a smile onto her face.

"Reeda, there you are," he said with a broad grin. "I am going back to Rome and wondered if you want to come with me?"

He sat opposite her at the table, his kind eyes fixed on hers. She wanted to go with him. Wanted to return to Rome and live a few more weeks as a carefree tourist, but the open map on the table had piqued her curiosity. What if Charlie had followed the trail marked out by Rosa's pencil line? She was here, it seemed wrong to give up if there was a chance she could learn what'd happened to him. She was driven by an insatiable desire to discover the truth. Her curiosity had been awakened.

"No, I'm not returning to Rome. But thank you for the offer, Lorenzo. I really appreciate all you've done to help me."

His eyes narrowed. "What will you do?"

"I'm going to Pacentro. I think my grandfather might

have been there. At any rate, I'd like to visit and see if I can find out."

He pulled an envelope from the inside pocket of his jacket and handed it to her.

"This came for you. It was forwarded on from Rome, I believe."

She took it, her brow furrowed. Who would send her a letter when a phone call would do just as well? She'd kept Kate and Bindi updated on her whereabouts, since travelling alone had its risks. If they didn't know where she was, she could disappear, and no one would be any the wiser. Still, she hadn't expected to receive a letter.

Lorenzo waved goodbye and disappeared down the footpath. She watched him go, then turned her attention to the letter. It was from Kate.

DEAR REEDA,

I HOPE THIS LETTER FINDS YOU WELL AND YOU'RE UNCOVERING the answers you've been looking for. I thought you might like this. I found it pushed between two floorboards in the attic, as though it'd fallen free of the box it was in. Since we didn't renovate the attic, I'm going through it now, when I get a few spare minutes, one box at a time. There is a lot of dust and old crap in that big, lofty space, let me tell you.

Anyway, enjoy the letter. It is quite the eye opener. And have fun. We miss you!

LOVE KATE xo

. . .

It was another letter written by Charlie to Nan, Reeda knew it in the pit of her gut even before she read the cursive scrawl. Again, it wasn't dated, but her heart beat faster at the thought of what it might contain. Kate wouldn't send it on to her in Italy if it didn't reveal something of value. She inhaled a deep breath, her eyes squeezed shut, then began to read.

❧ 29 ❧

SEPTEMBER 1943

CAMPO 78

The door to the hut was opened earlier than usual. When Charlie woke, sunlight already streamed through the wide opening. Some of the men had wandered out into the daylight, others lay still in their bunks. He groaned and rolled onto his back. His hips and shoulders ached, and his stomach had formed a painful knot that never seemed to unravel. His clothes fit loosely on his body and the cool of an autumn morning sent a shiver through him.

Henry's feet swung down from the bunk overhead, then Henry followed, landing with a grunt.

"Why is the door already open?" he asked, rubbing his eyes and yawning.

Charlie sat up, shrugged and blinked. "Don't know."

Outside, the air was colder still. The chill warned of coming winter. Charlie shivered and hugged himself. He should get his flight jacket, although the day would warm up quickly enough and he wasn't likely to need it for long. How would they manage to get through a winter in these uninsulated, concrete buildings with no blankets or warm clothing? He shook his head, rubbed bleary eyes, and scanned the yard.

Men wandered about as usual. Some found a warm place in the sun to sit, others huddled in groups to talk.

"What I wouldn't give for a hot cup of tea," murmured Henry beside him.

Charlie chuckled. "Or some porridge."

Birds trilled as they dived and sailed around the yard, filling the morning with their song. The sun climbed higher in the sky, thawing out the cold warning of winter ahead.

"Indeed." Henry tented a hand over his eyes. "Where's old Cabbage Hat? I want to stay out of his way today."

Charlie looked for the guard but didn't see him. Perhaps they'd get lucky today and their tormentor would be assigned elsewhere. Or even better, maybe he'd been transferred.

"I don't know. Come to think of it, I can't see any of them."

Charlie's brow furrowed and he studied the fence line, then the watch towers. No telltale sign of a rifle or machine gun. No movement, no shadows. He strode forward. A few other men were trotting up the incline towards them. Behind the men, Charlie saw it for the first time: the front gate stood open.

"What's going on?" he called.

One of the men yelled as he ran past. "The gate's open and the guards are gone. We're getting out of here."

The bedlam that followed gradually grew in intensity as word spread throughout the compounds. Every door and gate in the place was open. Henry rushed off. Charlie watched him go, his thoughts in a whirl. There wasn't a guard in sight. Men rushed around the yard, checking for signs of their captors, and planning their escape.

Charlie faced the back of the prison, hands pressed to his hips, eyes squinting against the morning sunlight.

"What are you thinking, old pal?" asked Henry, puffing as he jogged back to stand beside Charlie.

Charlie shook his head. "Those cliffs are pretty steep. But they might be our best shot of getting out of here."

"I was in the officer's compound. Some of the lads said they're staying. Said the guards told them the order was to stay put. That the Wehrmacht is on its way."

"Why would we listen to orders from Hitler's stooges?" asked Charlie, anger burning in his gut.

"They think they've got a better chance of making it out of here if they stay."

"Their choice," replied Charlie. "Let's get our things. We don't know how much time we have before Fritz arrives."

Charlie ran to the officer's compound, dodging around men who were already on their way out. When he reached his bed, he dug beneath the mat for his flight jacket and scarf and threw them on. Then he shoved his hat onto his head. He wished he had a water bottle or canteen of some kind, but he'd been shot from the air with only the clothes on his back, so there wasn't anything else for him to take. He patted the pocket that held Edie's photograph.

"What will I pack?" asked Henry. "I have my jacket..."

"Weren't you hiding some of the supplies from your Red Cross packages in case things got worse?" asked Charlie. "We should take that food with us. We don't know when we'll find food once we leave here."

Henry nodded once, then began tugging food from a hole he'd ripped in his bed mat. He shoved it into a small rucksack he'd brought with him from the outside. It was worn, faded and the fabric was torn in places.

"Let's go," he said.

They stopped by the water tap for a last long draught of water. Then, headed for the gates. By now, there was a steady stream of prisoners striding for the opening and funnelling through like an army of ants leaving their hill. Hundreds of men, possibly thousands, poured through the narrow space, then dispersed to the right and left. Some men looked to be heading around the outside of the camp towards the cliffs, where Charlie planned to go. Others were marching towards *Fonte d'Amore*, no doubt hoping locals in the small hamlet would help them find a way back to the Allied forces, or at least give them some food.

Colin caught up to them, his boots slapping against the hard ground with each step. "Where are you headed?"

Charlie offered him a tight smile. "The mountains."

"Wouldn't it be easier to walk to town...?"

"That's the direction the Wehrmacht will be coming from," replied Charlie, still walking. He figured if they kept up a brisk pace, they'd cover plenty of ground. Brisk enough to put distance between them and Campo 78, but not so brisk they'd wear themselves out. Every one of them was hungry, some injured or sick. They had to conserve their energy.

"I don't like the look of those cliffs, old chap." Beside him, Henry's skinny legs struggled to keep pace with him.

"I know, I don't either. But we'd have no chance if we aim for the town. We'd be found in no time."

"I'm coming with you," replied Colin, his nostrils flaring already with the exertion.

"Fine. But I think we should keep it to the three of us," replied Charlie. "We'll follow the crowd for now, but at some point, I plan on splitting off. Too big a group will draw attention, and some of the men aren't up for a long trek—they'll probably hide in the foothills and be picked up by the Germans."

After they'd been climbing for an hour, all three of the men were blowing hard. Charlie found his head spun and his lungs screamed for air. He hadn't done any physical activity in months and the undernourishment during his time in Campo 78 had reduced his muscle mass. The mountain they scaled rose sharply behind the camp, directly upward, with slippery grasses, rocks and boulders pockmarking its steep face.

A hermitage was built into one particularly rocky section of the mountainside. It looked as though it'd melted into the rock itself, the rock walls protruding from the sheer cliff and disappearing into it. The hermitage had been visible from the camp but had seemed so far away as to be impossible to reach. Yet they were already level with it, about five hundred metres to the south of the structure. Charlie stopped to look at it, his hands pressed to his knees.

"I wonder if anyone lives there," mumbled Colin, between ragged breaths.

Charlie shook his head. "Can't imagine wanting to stay somewhere like that. I'm sure I'd get vertigo every time I looked out the window."

Men were dotted around the mountain. Some higher up than them, most lower. A few looked to be making their way towards the hermitage, possibly seeking shelter. Charlie intended to stay away from every recognisable structure in the area. Those were the places the Nazis would look first for the escaped prisoners. There was no way for them to know how close they were to the end of the war. If Italy had surrendered, perhaps Germany would too? Maybe they'd be safe if they stayed behind. But since they couldn't say that for certain, and the guards had told them the Germans were on their way, the only thing Charlie could think to do was to flee, as far and as fast as he could, from the camp and the approaching Wehrmacht.

The shepherd's trail they were following split a few

minutes later. Most of the men they were shadowing veered off to the left, on a path that looked as though it would take the travellers up and over the mountain ridge. Charlie stopped to study each path.

"What do you think?" asked Henry, hands pressed to his hips. He hadn't complained once about the rucksack on his back, but Charlie knew it must've made his climb more difficult.

He held out a hand. "I'll carry the bag for a while, if you like."

Henry handed it over with a nod. "Just a few minutes would do me. I'm afraid I'm not the rugged, handsome athlete I once was." He laughed, but it came out more like a wheeze.

"Should we follow the lads going up to the left?" asked Colin, eying the departing group of men.

"You can if you like, I'm not going to stop you, but I want to put some distance between me and the bigger group," Charlie said. "I think our best chance of escape is if we all divide into smaller teams. It'll make Fritz chase his tail, instead of scooping us all up in one big group."

Colin nodded. "Good thinking. I'm with you, carry on then, sir."

They walked for another thirty minutes and soon saw the distant town of Sulmona they'd passed through on their way to Fonte d'Amore the day they arrived by train in the Abruzzo region. Charlie studied the town while they walked. It sat in the centre of the valley. Other villages squatted here and there, hidden in the foothills of the surrounding mountain ranges. His breathing was not so laboured now, since they were no longer climbing, but traversing the side of the mountain range.

"There's Sulmona," he said.

The other men nodded. Colin grunted. "I'll be glad to put this valley behind us."

"Do either of you know what lies beyond it?" asked Charlie.

"Not really. If we find an opening, a way through the range, we could turn east and head towards the ocean. But I can't say what lies between here and there, or how far it might be. I wish I had my map with me, but they took all that stuff away when they arrested me. I remember a series of mountain ranges, but that's about all I can say." Henry shook his head. "Sorry chaps."

Charlie sighed. "Never mind. We'll find what we find."

They walked that way for the rest of the morning. Around noon, they decided to stop for lunch. They found a rock to sit behind as a kind of wind breaker. The farther they'd climbed up the mountain, the colder and more biting the wind had become. Henry pulled a can out of his rucksack, opened it with a makeshift can opener he'd fashioned during his time at the camp, and they took turns eating with a broken stick for a fork. They shared between them the can of lamb and green peas Henry said he'd swapped a tin of herrings for with a prisoner from New Zealand. It would've tasted better warm, but none of them had any complaints and made short work of the meal.

When he was finished, Charlie wiped his mouth with the back of his hand. "Henry, I can't tell you how much I appreciate you sharing this with us. It was a good idea to save some of the food, although I know it meant you missed out on eating it at the time. We should've all taken your advice."

Henry shrugged. "I hoped we'd get out of there one day. Glad I've got the two of you to keep me company."

Colin slapped Henry on the back with a smile. "Yeah, thanks Henry. You're a real mate."

Before they set off again, Charlie took a look around. He

doubled back a short way to see if they were being followed. Some of the prisoners had taken the same route as they had, and tipped their hats as they passed by, exchanging a few words of encouragement. All looked tired but determined. Other than that, he couldn't see any signs of a pursuit. The valley itself lay as still and quiet as it had earlier. He could no longer see the Fonte d'Amore village, so if the Germans had arrived there, he had no way of knowing it.

They set off again, continuing to follow the narrow shepherd's trail that traversed the side of the mountain range. It dipped here, climbed there, followed a gully down then back up the other side again. As the afternoon progressed, their pace slowed. All of them were tired, Charlie's legs ached, and the cold wind began to wear on them. Whereas before they'd been climbing through rock strewn grasses and small, squat shrubbery, now they were passing in and out of groves of fir trees that blocked the wind for a while, giving them a quiet respite from the pummelling and the whistling in their ears.

Before long, angry grey clouds rolled in from over the mountain peaks. They hid the summits above them and the other side of the valley from view, swirling and churning until they turned blacker and descended down the ragged mountain faces.

When the rain began to fall, it hit Charlie's face filled with sloppy ice. He pulled his scarf higher to protect his cheeks, ducked his head and walked faster, grateful for his leather jacket.

Within moments the rain hid everything. The mountain tops, the valley below, the path ahead of them and the rest of the men travelling around them. It was only Charlie, Colin, and Henry in this new bleak, wet world.

Rain trickled down Charlie's neck. It soaked his hat and through to his scalp. His pants were soon sodden, and his socks had begun to feel the cold damp of it, when he spotted a small opening in a pile of rocks. The rocks rose high in a dome, packed against the hillside, and smattered with patches of grass.

He ran to the circular hole, wondering what it might be. Any misgivings he had about poking his head into a dark hole, were overcome by the misery of the rain beating against their cold, tired bodies.

"What is it?" shouted Colin behind him, over the noise of the downpour.

He shook his head. "I don't know. Hold on."

Charlie pushed one hand through the opening, ducked his head and squeezed his way inside. It was a room. A small, circular room, like a cave but manmade. A shelter, maybe built by the same shepherds whose footsteps had fashioned the path they'd been following all afternoon. He peered out into the miserable darkening landscape with a smile.

"Come on in, fellas. It might be cold and dark, but at least it's dry."

✣ 30 ✣

JULY 1996

PACENTRO

The coach chugged away from the bus stop, leaving Reeda and her luggage standing on a mountainside with the hamlet of Pacentro in front of her. The village hugged the crest of a mountain, running along its spine, and looking out over a long, green valley.

She tugged a piece of paper from her jean pocket and read the instructions again. Estelle had booked her a room to stay in, with a friend of hers, and wrote the directions to the residence out for her. She'd cautioned Reeda the friend didn't speak English, but that her friend's daughter spoke it well. Reeda was sure they'd figure it out between them.

The letter she'd received from Kate had confirmed her suspicions, even as hope sparked in her chest. Charlie had escaped Campo 78 after all. He'd travelled with a small group of fellow prisoners and found his way into the mountains, perhaps they'd made it to a village like Pacentro, that'd taken them in and cared for them in spite of the enmity between their armies. Did he end his days with a rifle prodding his back, or did he make his way somewhere else only to succumb to illness? There were still so many questions she had no answers for.

She glanced up at the pale buildings in front of her. Several stories high, they appeared to be tall, thin residences. A street wound away beyond one of them, so narrow she wasn't sure how cars made it through.

"Can I help you, signora?" asked one of the other passengers, a man wearing a fedora and sporting a thin moustache.

"Oh yes, please. I'm looking for this..." she showed him the address. "I'm staying with Signora Rossi and her daughter."

"Ah, of course. Follow me. They live very close to my son."

She grabbed the handle on her roller bag and fell into step beside the man.

"I visit him so often these days to see the grandchildren, I feel as though it is my second home," he said with a smile.

The house was as tall and thin as all the other row houses she'd seen on her way. Signora Rossi welcomed her with an embrace, a kiss on each cheek, then proceeded to rattle off a monologue in rapid Italian. Reeda couldn't understand a word of it, but the woman seemed not to need any interaction other than a smile and occasional nod.

She followed Signora Rossi up two flights of stairs to a small but tidy bedroom, with a view out over the tops of row houses stacked together below, and the valley beyond them. It was spectacular. After her hostess left, she stood at the window, hands placed on the sill. Soaring peaks, rows of stucco housing clinging to the mountain ridge, snowy caps above. It was like nothing she'd ever seen before and it filled her with a sense of anticipation and excitement. For a moment she could almost forget the pain she'd left behind. Almost.

After she'd settled into her room and changed, Reeda ventured down the narrow, dark staircase. She found Signora Rossi on the ground floor in the kitchen. The woman stood at a stove top, stirring a pot of something. A black apron was tied around her waist over the top of the black dress she wore, with a white collar and cuffs. She glanced up at Reeda with a smile, then gestured to a chair.

Reeda sat. "Thank you. It smells delicious in here."

"My mother loves to cook," came a voice from behind a tall, open door. The door shut and a young woman stepped towards Reeda, hand outstretched. "Hi, I'm Angela Rossi."

Angela's long black hair reached almost to her tiny waist. Brown eyes fixed on Reeda, white teeth crossed over each other in front and dark eyebrows pressed upward and together between her eyes, giving her an endearing, quizzical look.

"Hi, I'm Reeda Summer. Pleased to meet you." They shook hands. "You speak English very well."

Angela laughed. "I studied in England. So, I supposed you could say I was thrown in the deep end."

"Wow, what did you study?"

"Teaching. I teach down at the *scuola primaria* in Sulmona. But now it's summer, so I stay with Mamma. It gives me a chance to catch up on all the gossip from home, and besides, she makes the best pasta." Angela chuckled and patted Signora Rossi on the shoulder. Her mother offered her a loving smile as she pushed her hands into a bowl on the bench and began to knead.

"Do you like it?" asked Reeda.

Angela handed her a small bowl of grapes. "Grape?"

"Yes, please."

"I love it. The children are a delight, most of the time.

And besides, I have none of my own yet, so they're a good substitute." She explained something to Signora Rossi in Italian, and the woman chuckled, rolled her eyes, and shook her head from side to side. "Mamma doesn't like me to suggest I'm getting too old to have children of my own, she thinks it's unlucky," Angela explained.

Reeda bit into a grape and the sweet flavour exploded over her tongue, filling her mouth with the delicious juice. "Wow, these are delicious."

"They're from Mamma's vineyard. We have some for eating, the rest for wine."

"You make your own wine?"

"But of course," replied Angela, as though it were the most natural thing in the world to do. "Our own olive oil as well from our olive trees, and Mamma's garden supplies many of the vegetables we eat throughout the year. Though, of course, when Mamma has guests coming and going, we often have to purchase supplies from her neighbours to make up the shortfall."

"That must be a lot of work," replied Reeda.

"Mamma enjoys it. It keeps her busy. And I help her during the summer months when most of the work is done."

The idea of it appealed to something in Reeda, the part of her that was tired, sick of the rat race, of climbing out of bed to rush to work in an office all day long, then rush home to collapse in front of the television set all alone until bedtime. She relished the concept of growing her own produce and making her own food, living a simple life away from the demands of the modern world in sync with her neighbours. Still, she wasn't sure she could manage it, or enjoy it, in practice.

"Do most people in Pacentro live that way?" Reeda asked.

"Some. Others commute to work. It's an old way of living that is dying out, I'm afraid."

"Yes, in Australia too."

Signora Rossi raised her hands from the bowl; they were covered in a batter of some kind. She gestured towards Reeda and said something to Angela.

"Would you like to help?" asked Angela.

"What are you making?"

"Gnocchi with marinara sauce."

Reeda's stomach growled and she clapped a hand to it. "I'd love to help."

Signora Rossi stepped aside and showed Reeda how to mix the gnocchi. She reached for a bunch of herbs on the bench, pulled off some of the leaves and tossed them into the bowl as Reeda mixed.

"Thyme," explained Angela as she poured freshly brewed espresso into three small cups and set them in front of each of the women, then took a seat on the other side of the bench to watch.

Signora Rossi coated a square cutting board with flour, then tipped the mixture onto the flour and showed Reeda how to knead it into a dough. Reeda took her turn as the other women sipped espresso.

"Have you been to Italy before?" asked Angela.

Reeda shook her head. "No, this is my first time."

"And you're travelling alone?"

Reeda chuckled. "Yes, I am."

"That's unusual. Good for you."

"I've always wanted to visit, and I thought this would be a good opportunity. Also, I'm looking for clues about what happened to my grandfather. He was a prisoner at Campo 78 during the second world war, and I suspect he might've escaped, though I can't be sure. That's why I'm here. He disappeared, at any rate."

Angela's eyes narrowed, her eyebrows pressed closer

together. "Really? You think he might've passed through Pacentro?"

"Possibly. I'm hoping someone here will know something about it, although given the amount of time that's passed, I suppose it's not likely."

Signora Rossi took the ball of mixture and cut it into two pieces. She began rolling one half of it into a long sausage, and indicated Reeda should do the same with her half. She took it between her hands and rolled it back and forth, watching it lengthen.

Angela explained their discussion to Signora Rossi, who stopped rolling for a moment, a frown creasing her already lined forehead. She responded, then returned to her rolling.

"Mamma says she remembers them."

"Remembers who?" Reeda's heart thudded.

"The foreign soldiers. They came through here when she was a child. Before the Germans showed up. Apparently, most of the townspeople were evacuated by the Germans just before Christmas."

"Were there any Australians?" asked Reeda.

Angela asked Signora Rossi the question. The woman shook her head as she responded. "Mamma says she isn't sure. They spoke English, that's all she remembers. The Allies were bombing villages all over this area, but Pacentro escaped harm because of our location. Still, the Germans forced them to leave. They'd occupied the town for several months at that point, so if there were any foreign soldiers still here, they were most likely arrested. I remember hearing the stories myself as a child, of that Christmas. After the war, the town never really recovered from the losses of crops, animals, and property from that evacuation. Many of the men had to move elsewhere to find jobs."

"Do you know who I could talk to - to find out more?

Someone who might remember the foreign soldiers, where they were from, names, anything?"

"Signor Ricci might know. Matteo Ricci. He lives a few doors down. Seems to remember everything that ever happened, at least he likes to brag about his memory." Angela chuckled. "Maybe it will finally be of use."

As Reeda sliced and formed the gnocchi into tiny pillows, Angela sliced tomatoes and mozzarella for caprese salad and Signora Rossi continued to stir the marinara sauce on the stovetop. Reeda and Angela talked about life, laughed over the funny shapes of the gnocchi, or the antics of pupils in Angela's class, and poured themselves another espresso.

They ate lunch outside on a small balcony overlooking the kitchen garden, olive trees, and sloping vineyard all packed into a rectangular fenced yard. The yards on either side looked much the same, no space wasted on a lawn, but every square metre utilised for a purpose.

The salad was fresh, the gnocchi delicious, the wine plentiful, and the conversation punctuated with laughter. As Reeda sipped the last of her wine, she stared out over the sloping line of row-houses, stucco, tiles, and hundreds of years of history crammed onto the ridge of a looming mountain, and sighed.

ॐ

THE SUN HAD SET BEYOND THE HORIZON. REEDA AND Angela sat on the balcony on mismatched, timber chairs. Angela rested her feet in the seat of another chair, a glass of Chianti raised in one hand.

Reeda stared out at the dark landscape beyond the twinkle of lights from surrounding homes. The mountainside loomed like a leviathan rising from the depths of the ocean in the darkness.

"How long will you be in my country?" asked Angela.

Reeda hesitated. She hadn't decided yet how much longer to extend her trip. Part of her wanted to stay on indefinitely, the other part longed to return home to her family. To see her sisters, to confront Duncan about their future whether together or apart. And at the same time, she didn't want to hear what he had to say. Hiding seemed like a good option.

"I'm not sure. Maybe a couple more weeks, perhaps longer..."

"Will you meet your husband?...I'm sorry, I don't mean to pry."

Unconsciously, Reeda fingered the empty space on her left ring finger. "No, he's not coming."

"I'm sorry again."

"I don't mind, you're not prying. We're...taking some time apart."

"Is that what you want?" Angela's voice was soft, soothing.

Reeda instinctively trusted the petite woman with the thick, dark hair.

"Yes, at least I think so. It's been good to have a break from all the bickering and tension. I'm enjoying myself more here than I have in years."

"I understand..."

"Do you?" questioned Reeda, leaning forward in her chair in an attempt to make out Angela's features in the dim light emitting from the nearby kitchen window.

"Yes." Angela sighed. "My husband left me five years ago."

"I'm so sorry."

"Thank you," replied Angela. "It was a difficult time for me. I thought we'd have a family by now, had so many plans for our future together. He decided he'd made the wrong choice, that he didn't want the responsibility of a wife, a family, after all."

"He's missing out," replied Reeda, resting one hand on Angela's arm.

Angela patted her hand. "Thank you, I like to think so." She chuckled. "It's hard to think of him now though. He married another woman. They live together in Rome with their baby."

Reeda grunted. "Wow. That's rough. I'm sorry again."

"Thank you. I've come to terms with it, though Mamma hasn't forgiven him. He grew up here, we were high school sweethearts, married young. Too young, I suppose. But we loved each other. I can't remember a time I didn't love him.

"University changed us. I went to England, he to Rome, and when we returned home after our studies, he wasn't the man I remembered. Still, we went through with our engagement. I think he was unsure, even then. I wish he'd called things off before the wedding, but he was scared, I suppose. So many people wanted us married..."

"Did you want to marry him?" asked Reeda.

"He was my dream come true," whispered Angela, taking a sip of wine.

Reeda didn't respond. What could she say? That kind of heartbreak couldn't be soothed away with words. Her throat tightened and she blinked back tears. She and Duncan loved each other that way once as well.

She coughed to clear her throat. "And what about your mother? Was she married once?"

Angela inhaled a sharp breath in the darkness. "Yes, my father. They were married twenty-five years when he left. We're a couple of hopeless cases, I'm afraid." She issued a hollow laugh. "At least my brother and I were fully grown when he left, we didn't have to live through the divorce. I was in England, my brother in Milan. He lives there still. Pappa ran off with a younger woman. He'd taken a job in Rome and only came home on weekends. You see, for so many years now there has been little employment in Pacentro. When he fell in love with his secretary, there was nothing Mamma could do. His lover was twenty years his junior, if you can believe it."

Angela shook her mane of black hair, eyes sparking in the dim light. "They have a baby and ask me and my brother to visit at Christmas as though we're all one big happy family. But of course, I refuse to leave Mamma on her own."

"You're a good daughter."

"I don't know...I worry about Mamma. But at least she has her friends. If she wasn't still living in Pacentro, I don't know what she would've done. She misses him but doesn't talk about it. I can tell, sometimes she gets a faraway look in her eyes. But she won't mention his name. It's not healthy. She should let go, forgive, move on. I've done that with my husband...ex-husband."

"Do you think letting him go was a good thing?" asked Reeda. She bit down on her lower lip and stared up at the sliver of moon overhead.

Angela sighed. "I should've fought harder, I suppose. But at the time I didn't know what to do. I wanted to punish him, make him miss me...The only problem was, he didn't."

❧ 31 ❧

JUNE 1948

BATHURST

The ding of the bell hanging over the dealership's front door caught Edie's ear. She stood up in her seat, leaned forward to look and confirmed her suspicions. There was no salesperson on the floor. She huffed with frustration and pulled the PA microphone towards her.

"Good morning shoppers, welcome to Summer Motors. We have a sale on all models this weekend. A salesperson will be with you shortly."

She reached up a hand and tapped knuckles on the frosted glass window behind her. A few moments later, Paul's head poked through the open door. "Yes, my love?"

She wheeled her chair back to the place in front of the typewriter where she was typing up invoices. "There's no one on the floor and we've got a customer."

Paul's eyes narrowed. "Where's Bill?"

"Probably having a smoke somewhere, as usual."

Bill was the newest member of their sales team and so far, they'd had no end of issues with him showing up for work late, back-talking to customers and disappearing for stretches of time when he was supposed to be manning the sales floor.

Paul pulled on his jacket with a frown. "I'll take care of it."

He strode out to meet the customer. Edie watched him with a smile. He was still so handsome, with that thick, dark hair and bright green eyes. Now that Keith had started attending the primary school in town, they drove together from the farm every morning in the car, dropped Keith at the school, and came to work at the dealership.

Paul had bought the car dealership with some of the money from his trust fund right before they were married. He thought it would be a good opportunity for him to put down roots and to support the family. He hadn't liked the idea of moving into the farmhouse with her parents, but she'd told him she couldn't take Keith away from them and it would give them a chance to save for their future lives together.

Finally, he'd agreed to give it a chance, and they'd both regretted it ever since. It was one thing to live with her parents as a single mother in need of help. It was entirely another to squeeze into that tiny bedroom with a tall, lanky husband and a growing boy. Juggling the family dynamics over the past two years had been exhausting.

When Paul returned to the office, he shrugged off his jacket and sat on Edie's desk. She stopped typing to give him her attention.

"I couldn't find Bill," he said.

She rolled her eyes. "Okay."

"I guess I'll have to find a new sales guy."

"Guess so," she agreed. "Sorry, my love."

He shrugged. "That's business."

He went to leave, hesitated, then sat again.

Hands poised over the typewriter, she glanced up at him with an arched eyebrow. "What's wrong?"

He sighed. "Are you happy with the way things are?"

She stood, moving closer to him until he could put his arms around her waist. She looped her hands over his shoulders, staring deep into his eyes. "What's wrong, my love? Are you unhappy?"

Paul shook his head. "No, of course not. I love you; I love Keith. I'm happy. It's just..."

"What is it?"

"Living with your parents..."

She grunted. "Don't start."

"I mean it. I don't think I can keep it up. Yesterday, your dad asked how much we made last month on the dealership and did I think I could really support a family with a business that ripped people off the way it does."

Edie's mouth fell open. "What?"

"And it's not the first time. Your mum is everywhere. She knows everything that's going on. I mean, she washes our clothes and puts them in our drawers for us."

"That's not something I'm going to complain about," replied Edie with a grin.

"You know what I mean. I feel like we're still the kids living at home. We're squashed into that tiny room. You know we can't keep living that way. Keith needs his space. I need mine too." He pulled her close and kissed the side of her neck, his breath hot on her skin.

She gasped, pushed away and straightened her hair. "Paul, what if a customer comes in?"

He growled. "I don't care. I never get time alone with my wife!"

Her throat tightened. She hated to think she might be undermining her marriage by insisting they live with her parents, but could feel him slowly pulling away from her, bit by bit, day by day.

"I'll talk to them."

"And it's not just that..." He sighed, ran his fingers through his hair, setting it on end. "It's trying to get pregnant as well."

Edie swallowed. She'd felt the pressure herself, though she'd hoped it wasn't getting to Paul the way it was to her. What could she do about it? No matter what they tried, they hadn't been able to fall pregnant in the two years since they were married. Both had agreed it was a good idea to give Keith a sibling, and yet so far, she hadn't fallen. As easy as it'd been the first time, she'd never considered it might not happen the same way again.

"I know, I feel it too. It's been hard on both of us, the waiting, the hoping, the disappointment, month after month."

He inhaled a slow breath. "I think if we had a change of scenery, a place of our own...things might be different. It's not how I thought it would be, how I planned for it to be."

He was pulling away, further out of reach. What if he left and never came back? It'd happened before, though Charlie had a different reason to abandon her. He hadn't returned when she needed him, loved him, now Paul might leave as well.

She reached for his hand, squeezed it between her own. "We'll figure it out."

His tortured gaze met hers. "I know what I want us to do."

"What?" Her eyes widened.

"I've already got a buyer for the business. I think we should sell up, take our savings, and buy a bed and breakfast. I miss the ocean. In California, I went surfing all the time. It was warm, there was sunshine, sand, seafood...I miss it. I want to leave this cold, gloomy place and go somewhere we can really enjoy life. We only get one chance to live, and we've both seen enough of death to understand that...So, what do you say?"

"The beach?" she asked. She hadn't considered moving out of Bathurst. All her life she'd planned on staying in the town, raising her children there, perhaps even seeing her grandchildren grow and play on its streets.

"Yeah, the beach."

"And that would make you happy?" she asked.

He smiled. "I think it would make us all happy."

"Okay. Let's move to the beach." If he could be happy, then she could too. Fear gnawed at her gut—but what if it didn't make him happy? What then? She pushed it down, ignoring the twisting pain of it. They'd move to the beach, start again. And maybe they'd finally have another baby. Everything was going to work out, and they'd be happy as long as they were together.

WAVES LAPPED AT THE SHORE, THEN WITH A SIGH RUSHED into the ocean. The azure water sparkled beneath the sun's burning rays. It was hot. Hotter than anywhere she'd ever lived before. Edie wiped an arm over her brow, soaking up the sweat with her sleeve.

"This is the land you want us to buy?" she asked.

Paul smiled. "Yes. Don't you just love it?"

Edie nodded, but her brow furrowed with worry. Not only did Paul want them to move to the northern most part of the state, more than a full day's drive from Bathurst, but he wanted them to buy a vacant block of land in the middle of nowhere and build a bed and breakfast.

Panic settled in her chest.

"I love it," she said, forcing a smile onto her face.

LILLY MIRREN

It took six months for the sale to go through and for them to pack everything up in Bathurst for the move north. Father and Mother weren't thrilled about the idea, but Mother said she understood. Edie was sorry to say goodbye. For so many years of her childhood she'd been desperate to get out from under their strict parenting, but now that it was finally happening, she wasn't ready for it.

As the car pulled out of the driveway for the last time, she turned in her seat to look through the back window, waving her hand. Mother stood beside Father, waving back. Father had his hands plunged deep into his pants pockets. They both seemed small and old, and she wished for a moment they could turn back the clock and she could be a child again, safe in Father's arms.

Then, her parents were gone. And all that lay ahead of them was the road and a new adventure. As the miles passed beneath the tyres of their vehicle, Edie's excitement grew. She played *I Spy* with Keith, then they took turns spotting different types of trees or flowers. After a while, Keith fell asleep, his head pressed against her shoulder, his mouth ajar.

"How're you feeling?" asked Paul.

She smiled. "I'm a little sad, but mostly I'm nervous and excited. It's all kind of jumbled up inside of me so that I feel as if I could burst."

He laughed, looping an arm around her shoulders, Keith between them. "I know what you mean."

They were starting fresh. A new life, a new season for their marriage. Slowly her fear and sadness faded, and she began to think about what it would be like to live at the beach. How much Keith would love jumping over the waves and how she'd enjoying lying in the sand with the sunshine on her face.

Charlie had talked about it so often, the two of them one day moving somewhere hot, by the ocean to live out the rest of their lives together. Now he was gone, but she was going to follow through on the dreams they'd shared as teenagers. She would live the life he'd wanted. The life they'd both planned for before he was taken from them too soon. That she was doing it with Paul would've upset her once, but now it felt right. He was her husband, the man she loved. Charlie was her past, Paul her future.

It took them three days to drive all the way to Cabarita. Some of the roads weren't fully paved, and they didn't want to tire Keith out too much, so stopped whenever they could to rest. Finally they arrived at the location for their new bed and breakfast. She'd told Paul that calling it a boutique inn would make it more popular, and he said he didn't care what she called it, so long as it would be their home.

When they climbed from the car, travel weary and sore from sitting still so long, Keith stretched his little arms over his head and yawned.

"Hey, Mummy is this where we're gonna live?"

Edie's breath caught in her throat. It was the first time he'd called her that. He'd stopped calling his grandmother by the name a few months earlier, instead calling her Granny, but he still hadn't referred to Edie as his mother. Not until that moment; the moment he saw their new life through his big, blue eyes.

"Yes, this is where we'll live."

"But there's no house," he replied, his nose wrinkling.

She laughed. "We're going to build one."

"Oh. So, where will we live?"

Edie pushed her hands onto her hips and squinted against the glare of the sunshine. "We're going to rent a house nearby."

"Wow! I love it here already!"

She smiled as he ran off to explore the lot. It was overgrown with weeds and bushes. A few gum trees stood around the edges of a flat, smooth piece of land. Pandanus leaned over an embankment up ahead, and the roar of the ocean punctuated the quiet with its rhythm.

Paul was struggling with a bundle he'd pulled from the boot of the car. He bent over, pulled the bundle along, then straightened and caught her eye.

He smiled, offered a wink. "Want to help me with the tent?"

She laughed. "Not really, but I guess I can."

"We'll sleep in it tonight, then tomorrow we'll go house hunting."

"This is crazy. Isn't it?" she asked, as she helped him unpack their tent.

"It's an adventure," he replied.

"It's our adventure," she said, her heart swelling. "And as soon as we get our inn built, I'm going to dig a big garden and plant Mother's waratah seeds."

Paul shook his head with a chuckle. "Yes, ma'am."

"Mummy, Mummy, I found the beach!" shouted Keith. "Come on!"

With a laugh, Edie jogged after Keith as he disappeared down a winding, narrow trail. Paul strode after her. When she reached the place where Keith had leapt from sight, her breath caught in her throat. The small cove that stood before her was one of the main reasons she and Paul had agreed to buy the site, and its beauty still took her breath away.

The long stretch of white sand curved around to jagged black rocks on either end. A large black rock formation jutted out of the crystal blue waters. Perfectly round waves rolled to shore. Seagulls strutted along the sand. It was paradise.

32

JULY 1996

PACENTRO

The clatter of footsteps on the staircase woke Reeda from a deep sleep. She yawned and stretched her arms over her head, then rolled onto her side with her eyes still shut.

A door banged and her eyes blinked open.

She was in Pacentro.

A smile crossed her lips. She rose from the bed, stretched again, then tugged the shutters open. Sunlight streamed into the room, bringing with it the warmth of a new summer's day. Birds twittered as they dipped and dived in the air, snapping up insects. Sounds of the village coming awake echoed through the narrow streets and thin walls of the tall houses joined to the bed and breakfast on either side.

She dressed quickly, her stomach already craving food. In the bathroom, she splashed water on her face.

She'd washed her hair the night before and hadn't bothered to straighten it. The bathroom was small and cramped, and it didn't contain an outlet and looked as though it hadn't been updated in at least fifty years. Straightening her hair had seemed unimportant. It fluffed out around her face in waves, soft, brown, and unruly. She smiled at the sight of her makeup free face, ruddy cheeks, and fluffy hair. What did it matter? She had no one to impress.

Downstairs, Signora Rossi and Angela were in the kitchen speaking in animated voices, arms waving. Reeda had begun to recognise some words in Italian but couldn't piece together what they were talking about.

They stopped when she stepped through the doorway and welcomed her.

"Come, come have breakfast," said Angela, pulling out a stool beside her own for Reeda.

Reeda slid into it, smoothing her skirt down over her legs.

"You look beautiful today," said Angela, eyeing Reeda with curiosity. "Something has changed?"

Reeda shook her head. "I didn't straighten my hair."

"You look better with no makeup. Such a beautiful face, it suits you," said Angela.

"Thank you."

They ate fresh baked rolls with butter and jam and downed it all with steaming cups of café latte. Reeda preferred the latte to espresso, but found Italians seemed to enjoy the small, shots of coffee more often.

"Today is the festival, *Festa del Ritorno*," said Angela, between bites. "It is organised by the *Cooperativa Agricola Rivera Pacentro*, in honour of the people who emigrated away from the town."

"Really? That sounds fun. Are you going?" asked Reeda, setting her coffee on the bench and reaching for more jam.

"Yes, of course. Everyone will be there, including Signor Ricci. You can ask him about your grandfather."

REEDA, ANGELA, AND SIGNORA ROSSI STROLLED THROUGH the narrow, cobblestone streets of Pacentro side by side. Reeda and Angela each carried food—Angela a pot of linguine and Reeda a basket of fresh baked bread sticks, cut into slices and drizzled with olive oil.

Once, they had to press themselves up against the wall of a house to let a car drive by, but otherwise they had the road to themselves along with the other pedestrians making their way to the festival.

The street opened up into a square, with a small park at its centre. Timber benches lined one edge of the park and old men sat side by side on the benches, deep in conversation or throwing breadcrumbs to the birds that tip-tapped around their feet on the footpath.

Square booths were set up across from the park. White tents with white roofs, tables lined with eclectic products. Jam jars, jewellery, hats, honey, bottles of olive oil and more, all adorned the temporary tables erected beneath the white tents. Clothing hung from hangers around the top of the tents. Customers browsed, strolling from tent to tent, purchases stuffed into baskets or carry bags as they went.

They walked past a stone wall with a dripping tap fitted in the middle of it.

"*Ciao!*" A woman called to Signora Rossi and Angela.

"*Ciao.*"

The greeting came with regularity. Everyone seemed to know each other in the small hamlet. Several times, Signora Rossi or Angela stopped to speak more in depth with someone, to kiss cheeks, introduce Reeda, laugh together, then move on.

Whenever they were able, people tried out their halting English with Reeda. Some simply nodded in her direction before turning their attention back to Signora Rossi.

They walked through a small opening and into a small square lined with cobblestones, surrounded on four sides by tall, stucco buildings. The square was filled with rows of white collapsible tables, set up in lines. A stage at the front of the arrangement held black stacks of speakers on either side and a lone microphone stood in the centre of the stage. Behind the microphone a four-piece band played instrumental music. It bellowed from the speakers with a tinny ringing.

All around the outside of the square, tables were being filled with steaming pots, plates, and bowls of food by happy locals.

Children dodged between the tables, chasing each other with squeals of delight. The hum of conversation broke through the noise of the background music that variously crackled and crooned through the speakers.

"Wow, this is amazing," said Reeda, genuinely impressed with how much the town had crammed into the small space and how well everyone seemed to be working together to make the festival a success.

Signora Rossi indicated Angela and Reeda should follow her. They squeezed between tables, holding the pot and basket up. Angela was careful not to spill a drop of the steaming hot pasta dish. Then, they set the pot and basket of bread sticks on one of the tables. A buxom woman in a floral print dress beamed at them.

"*Ciao! Grazie bella signoras!*"

She kissed first Signora Rossi's cheeks, then Angela's.

"Signora Ricci, this is our friend and guest, Reeda Summer," Angela said.

"*Ciao* Signora Summer, what a pleasure to meet you," exclaimed the woman, grasping Reeda by both cheeks and pulling her in for a kiss on each.

"Thank you, it's a delight to meet you as well. Everything smells wonderful."

Signora Ricci's grin widened further still. "I hope it tastes as good as it smells, then."

"I'm sure it will." Reeda's foot tapped in time to the music and she watched as a group of children formed a circle in front of the stage and began to dance. Hand in hand they twirled in one direction, then the other, their feet slapping the ground in time to the beat.

"And what brings you to Pacentro?" asked Signora Ricci.

Reeda faced her with a warm smile. "I'm enjoying a hard-earned holiday. But also, looking for clues about what happened to my grandfather. He was a prisoner during the second world war down at Campo 78, and I have reason to believe he might have escaped and come through here."

Signora Ricci's eyes widened, and she clapped a hand to her heart. "Really? What an intrigue."

"We thought perhaps Signor Ricci might remember if Reeda's grandfather was in Pacentro, since he never forgets anything," interrupted Angela. "He is the man we were telling you about, Reeda. Signora Ricci's husband is the man to talk to about this matter. Isn't he, signora?"

Signora Ricci's chest puffed out. "*Sì*, that is very true. He will know, if anyone does, whether your grandfather passed through the village."

"Is he here?" asked Reeda.

"He is around here somewhere," replied Signora Ricci, still not taking her eyes off Reeda. She smiled. "And where is your husband tonight, signora?"

Reeda's cheeks flushed with warmth under the older woman's scrutiny. "He's back in Australia. We're...separated."

The signora's eyebrow arched high. "I am sorry to hear that."

"Thank you." Reeda didn't like to talk about it.

She wasn't sure that described their situation, not exactly. Since they hadn't discussed it—not with any finality. But it felt like a separation. When she returned to Sydney, it would surely be to pack up her things and move out. Where she'd go, she still had no idea. But if he didn't want her there, she wasn't about to stay. Even thinking about it made her chest ache.

"You know there are many handsome young men here tonight..." continued Signora Ricci. "Perhaps you will find someone, no?" She winked.

Reeda's stomach tightened into a knot. That was the last thing on her mind, finding someone else when she wasn't even sure where things stood between her and her husband.

"Let's get something to eat," said Angela, interrupting the awkward silence.

"Great idea," replied Reeda.

They found paper plates, napkins, and silverware on one table, then wandered between the food tables, piling spoonsful of whatever they fancied onto their plates. Reeda selected veal parmesan, linguine, osso buco, and crusty bread along with a salad of fresh greens and miniature sliced tomatoes.

She and Angela sat at a table already packed with other guests while Signora Ricci and Signora Rossi stood behind their table, serving out steaming spoonsful of delicious food to the festival goers now streaming into the square.

"I hope things will work out between you and your husband," said Angela, between bites.

"Thanks. It's complicated."

"Do you think you will get back together?"

Reeda shrugged, her heart heavy. "I don't know. It's been hard for a long time."

The food was delicious, rich, and hot. It slid into Reeda's stomach, warming her to the core.

"Maybe we won't be able to make it work, but this trip is helping me to see that I'll be all right. Even if I have to do life alone, I'll be okay. I can manage on my own, maybe even be more than okay."

Angela swallowed a mouthful of salad. "Of course you can."

The music stopped. A noise on the stage caught Reeda's attention and she spun to face it. A man in a white buttoned shirt, grey slacks and black suspenders tapped on the microphone, then cleared his throat. He said something in Italian, and everyone clapped. Then, he began a long monologue. People listened for a while, then returned to their eating and conversation while he droned on in the background.

"Mamma is calling you," said Angela.

Reeda wiped her mouth with a napkin and glanced up to see the signoras with an older gentleman, dressed in black pants and a blue buttoned shirt with tie.

"That is Signor Ricci," explained Angela.

Reeda set down her fork and hurried over to meet the man. He was the last lead she had, and her only hope of finding out what'd happened to Charlie. If he had no clues for her to follow, she wasn't sure where to turn to next. Angela trotted close behind her.

"Signora Summer, this is my husband, Signor Ricci," said Signora Ricci with a proud tilt of her chin.

Reeda reached out a hand and the man shook it with a solemn nod.

"Hello Signor Ricci, how lovely to meet you."

He smiled. "How can I help you?" He had a thick accent

and spoke slowly, but his words were clear. Thick glasses sat on the end of his nose, dark hair with streaks of silver was combed to one side and his full bottom lip jutted out a little farther than his top lip, giving him a fish-like appearance.

"I wanted to talk to you about the war," Reeda began.

He nodded for her to continue.

"My grandfather, Charlie Jackson, might have passed through here after he escaped from Campo 78. I can't be sure, but this is one of the villages prisoners fled to, I'm led to understand, and there's no record of what became of him... He was an Australian pilot."

"An Australian, you say?"

She nodded.

Signor Ricci frowned. "There were several Australian men here, before the Germans came. We gave them food and shelter, those of us who were able, and most of them left soon after. The ones who stayed were eventually discovered nearby by the Wehrmacht."

"Do you remember them by name?" Reeda asked, knowing it was probably too much to ask.

He stroked his chin, eyes narrowed. "I remember an Australian man. Blond, I think. Not like you. He had very blue eyes. So blue, my sister had a fondness for him." He chuckled. "He was here when the Germans came, I believe, but you see, I was a boy at the time. No one told me what became of the prisoners, they had to keep these things quiet you know. They didn't want the Wehrmacht to question us, to discover anything. We could be punished."

It could've been Charlie. He'd had blond hair and blue eyes, but it was hardly conclusive evidence. Still, it gave her hope.

"Where might he have gone, if the Germans didn't get him?" she asked.

Signor Ricci grunted. "Many different places. They scattered, the soldiers. But some went over the mountains to Casoli, I think."

"Casoli?"

"Away from the Germans. If he went in the direction of Rome, he would've been caught for certain. I have an older brother there, in Casoli. If your Australian was here, he would know."

REEDA SAT AT THE TABLE, WATCHING AS THE BAND PLAYED an up-tempo song. Couples tapped and spun around on a makeshift dance floor in front of the stage where the children had played earlier. She hummed, her chin resting in her hands, elbows pressed firmly to the table. The red cotton dress with white polka dots she wore fanned out around her legs. It had a lower neckline than she usually wore, but she'd found it in Rome and liked the way it made her feel young and carefree.

Angela was dancing with a young man with dark hair and a dimpled smile.

Signoras Ricci and Rossi were gossiping over glasses of Chianti behind their table, feet propped up on chairs in front of them.

"Good evening, signora," said a voice at her elbow.

She spun around to see Lorenzo's dark face beside her. He laughed at her surprise and pulled up a chair to sit close to her.

"Lorenzo," she exclaimed, throwing her arms around his neck before she caught herself and pulled them back to her sides. It'd been so nice to see a familiar face that she hadn't been able to help herself.

He laughed again, then leaned forward to kiss her cheek. His lips made her cheek tingle.

Her face flushed with heat as her gaze met his and held there. A tingle ran through her body. What was going on?

He shifted his chair closer still and took both her hands in his, kissing the back of each.

"Lorenzo..." she frowned.

He laughed, still not letting go. "I am glad to find you, signora. May I call you Reeda?"

She nodded. "Yes, of course. But...why are you here, in Pacentro?"

His face grew solemn. "Greta broke up with me, took my heart, and smashed it into pieces."

Reeda cocked her head to one side. He didn't seem broken-hearted, especially when he'd kissed her hands with full, soft lips. "Your girlfriend?"

He nodded.

"I'm sorry to hear that, Lorenzo. Still, that doesn't explain what you're doing here."

His smile returned, broadening until his tanned cheeks dimpled in a way that set her heart pitter-pattering. "I came to find you."

Lorenzo came to Pacentro to find her? Why? It didn't make any sense. She was married. He was broken-hearted, from a recent wounding, and he was younger than her. A lot younger. It was difficult to say how much, she was terrible at guessing people's ages, but still, he couldn't have been more than twenty-five, most likely younger.

"You came to find me?" she replied, her eyes wide.

He laughed. "Come, let's dance."

He tugged her hand until she stood and followed him to the dance floor. They wedged into the crowded space beside Angela and her dance partner. Angela eyed her with a hint of a smile. She didn't say anything; she didn't have to. It was obvious what she was thinking and Reeda's cheeks burned even hotter under Angela's knowing look.

The music followed a fast beat and Reeda did her best to keep up. Lorenzo threaded one arm around her waist, the other still cupping her hand, and led her around the dance floor until she was puffing, sweating, and laughing.

When the music slowed, Lorenzo pulled her close before she could object. He took her hands and wound them around his neck, then embraced her, his eyes fixed on hers with an intensity that stole the breath from her lungs.

"You are so beautiful," he whispered against her hair, breaking their shared gaze. His breath was hot on her skin and sent a wave of goosebumps down her back.

"Lorenzo, you know I'm married," she began.

He interrupted. "Yes, but you must be unhappy. I can see it in your eyes, and, where is he this husband of yours? Such a beautiful wife, left to travel alone throughout the land of romance. He is a fool, no?"

Reeda pushed Lorenzo's chest with the heel of her hand and stepped back. "Lorenzo...I can't."

He shrugged. "We can be friends. Okay?"

"Friends." Her eyes narrowed. "Just friends."

"Yes, just friends. Friends who dance together and laugh. Have some fun. No?"

She couldn't help smiling. "Okay."

◊✺◊

ALREADY REEDA WAS BEGINNING TO LOOK FORWARD TO her and Angela's nighttime ritual. Seated on the balcony looking out over a sleeping Pacentro, they sipped hot tea and talked about whatever was on their minds.

She felt a kinship with this woman who'd lost the love of her life, who'd experienced some of the same grief over dashed dreams that Reeda had.

"So, who is this Lorenzo?" asked Angela, a smirk in her voice.

Reeda chuckled. "I met him in Rome. He's a friend."

"A very good-looking and young friend, I think."

Reeda huffed. "Yes, very young."

"You are young, yourself. You know?"

"Not so young anymore," replied Reeda with a wry smile Angela couldn't see.

"How old?"

"Thirty-one."

"That is young," Angela said.

"And you?" asked Reeda.

"Twenty-eight years old. Though I feel forty some days." Angela chuckled.

Reeda lifted her mug and clinked it against the side of Angela's. "I know what you mean."

"So, your husband...are things so bad with him?" asked Angela, one eyebrow arched.

Reeda squeezed her eyes shut as a rush of pain surrounded her heart. "Yes. He's given up on us."

"Did he say that?"

Reeda's eyes flicked open. What had he said exactly? She'd barely heard him, focusing instead on his tone, body language. She scrubbed both hands over her eyes. "He wouldn't admit outright that it was over, but he said it was too hard to keep going; that he didn't think we'd make it."

"That does not sound so final to me. But I suppose it remains for you to decide what it is you want." Angela offered a warm smile and pressed one hand to Reeda's arm.

It wasn't so simple. How could it matter what she wanted if he wasn't willing to meet her there?

"Maybe you're right. I don't know. So much has happened between us...so many unkind words, so much pain..."

The back door opened, and Signora Rossi stepped outside

with her own mug of tea. She smiled and took a seat beside Reeda. Then she said something to Angela.

"Do you mind if I tell Mamma what we are talking about?" asked Angela.

Reeda nodded. "Fine with me."

After a brief discussion, Angela sighed. "Mamma wants me to tell you something."

Reeda straightened in her chair. "Yes?"

"She says..." Angela eyed her mother warily, then continued. "She says you should fight for a good man. If your husband is a good man who loves you, you can't let him go. She gave up too soon, I gave up too soon..." Angela sighed. "And we should've fought to keep what we had. We didn't let our husbands know what they meant to us. We were both stubborn, we took them for granted, we punished them by withdrawing our love, we were too full of pride to chase after them. And now we live without love." Angela's voice faltered over the last few words.

Signora Rossi watched Reeda while her daughter spoke, then gave a determined nod in Reeda's direction, her chin pressed forward. She raised her mug, clinked it to Reeda's, and swigged her tea.

Reeda studied the older woman's face. "But, we..." She choked on the words, coughed, and pressed on. "We can't have children. Will it be enough, just the two of us, for the rest of our lives? What if I'm not enough for him, or him for me? What if we grow to despise each other? What if he hates me for keeping him from having the family he so desperately wants?"

The words spilled out and her eyes welled with tears.

Angela's face warmed with compassion. She squeezed Reeda's shoulder, then translated for her mother. Signora Rossi shook her head and spoke in rapid Italian for a full minute.

"Mamma says, children don't make a marriage stronger, they test it for fault lines." Angela chuckled. "If there are any weaknesses in it, children will be the catalyst for finding them."

Reeda inhaled a sharp breath. Signora Rossi was right. If she and Duncan couldn't make it in their marriage now, without anyone else's needs to attend to, how could they survive raising a family? Maybe children weren't the answer to the issues in their relationship. Tears wound in trails down her cheeks. Signora Rossi spoke again. Angela waited to translate.

"Mamma also says, children grow up and make lives of their own. They aren't with you forever, only for a short time. After that, it's you and your husband—just the two of you. You think when you have babies that you'll never be lonely again. But you can't rely on them for your joy, since they aren't yours to keep. If you are blessed with a family, you only borrow them from God for a time, and then they fly off to live the life they choose for themselves. God willing, you will spend a season with your children, but your life will be with your husband."

Reeda cried softly as Angela spoke. She wiped tears from her face with the back of her hand and sniffled. She'd never thought of it that way before. She'd put all her hopes in having a family, never considering she should've been investing into her marriage just as heavily, or even more so. That it was the one relationship that would outlast all others. That Duncan was the one person she'd spend her days with when everyone else moved on to something else. Why had she neglected him, resented him? It wasn't his fault she couldn't get pregnant, yet for some reason she'd blamed him, targeted her anger and irritation in his direction. She wished she could take it all back, but it was too late.

❧ 33 ❧

DECEMBER 1953

CABARITA

"I want to put the angel on top of the tree," declared
Keith, hands pressed to his hips.

At ten years of age, he'd become the kind of boy
who knew exactly what he wanted and what he didn't in life.
What he usually wanted was the last sweet in the tin, or the
last slice of chocolate cake, what he didn't want was a
spoonful of brussel sprouts.

Edie smiled and handed him the angel. Usually she put it
on the highest part of the Christmas tree, but Keith was
almost as tall as she was. He could reach it this year. As he
stood on tiptoe to push the ornament into place, her heart
swelled with love.

Paul's arm snuck around her shoulders. She leaned into
him, finding the space beneath his arm that'd become familiar
to her.

"He's getting so tall," she murmured.

Paul chuckled. "I know. He'll be as tall as me before long."

"I don't know about that, but I'm definitely going to be the short one in the family."

Paul ruffled her hair with one hand. "Yes, you are. My cute little shortie."

The inn was no longer new. After almost five years of operation, it had a warm, lived-in look about it. Tinsel and ornaments hugged every available surface. Edie loved Christmas and decorating for it had become something of a passion, even if Paul complained that she overdid it. She didn't think it was possible to overdo Christmas. It was a special time of year, everything had to be just perfect.

And besides, the inn was always full at Christmas. They'd even gathered something of a regular crowd for the holidays. Several families from the first couple of years had continued to return, year after year, at the same time to celebrate Christmas at The Waratah Inn. It'd become their tradition and Edie couldn't be happier about it.

The inn had been Paul's idea, but she'd taken to it with gusto. With each month that passed after they arrived in the north, Edie had embraced a new aspect of their adventure. She'd worked with the architect they'd found in Brisbane to put together the best possible design. She'd selected every paint colour, each item of furniture, and the eclectic decorative items that were scattered over tables, buffets, mantles, and hung on walls. As it all came together, she'd embraced it, learned to love it in a way she hadn't imagined she could.

Keith loved it there as well. He spent much of each day traipsing through the sand to build sandcastles or cubbies. They'd bought him a book on botany and bird life for his last birthday, and she often found him sitting with it in his lap as he studied a bird or plant in front of him. He'd become a precocious, intelligent, and curious little boy, and being with him made her heart sing. Seeing their little family seated around the small dining table she'd set up in the kitchen, often brought a lump to her throat.

They'd done the impossible, created a life out of the remnants evil had left them. And they were happy.

Guests milled about behind them in the sitting room. The smell of apple cider filled the air. Paul had insisted she make it for the guests, though she'd assured him that a hot Australian Christmas didn't need apple cider, it required cold egg nog, or if he wanted to bring something of his own heritage to the inn, perhaps even a pitcher of ice cold tea.

He'd laughed and reminded her Australians drank hot tea all year round, so a little hot apple cider wouldn't hurt them. So, she'd made it, and the delicious scent permeated the inn as people wandered around or sat in the breakfast nook and games rooms, cradling cups of it between their hands. Edie reached for her cup of cider and took a sip. It really was delicious. Another thing to add to their list of Waratah Inn Christmas traditions.

Paul set a record in the record player, adjusted the needle to a starting point, and switched it on. Bing Crosby's croon filled the room, as he sang, "I'll be home for Christmas." It brought a lump to Edie's throat. She hadn't been home for Christmas since they left Bathurst. As much as they'd thrived in Cabarita, she still missed home. It was too far to go, and they were far too busy keeping the inn running. At least, that was what Paul always said. Of course, he couldn't go home either, a fact which didn't make her feel any better about missing her parents.

She missed Mima too, but they'd kept in touch with the occasional letter since Mima first moved to Newcastle. In the intervening years, her friend had travelled back to Sydney, and was sharing a house with a group of nurses. Mima had finished her nurse's training and was working at the Prince

Henry Hospital. She seemed happy, though it was hard for Edie to tell, since her letters rarely contained more than a few paragraphs about where she was, what she was doing and which celebrity her latest boyfriend most resembled.

"Mummy, have you been shopping for presents yet?" asked Keith, his small voice soft and his gaze fixed on her face.

"Presents? Are there supposed to be presents under this tree?" she asked, feigning shock.

He giggled. "Yes, there are. Where are they? You didn't forget, did you?"

She grabbed him and hugged him tight, then tickled his ribs. "Oh my goodness, I forgot all about it. I'll have to write it on that big to-do list I keep in the office. Buy presents. Good idea. I've got it now."

He shouted with delight then wriggled free of her grasp and ran to their bedroom. They all shared the master suite. Keith's small bedroom jutted off the side of their large one, with a doorway that could only be accessed from within their room. She liked them being close like that, and with guests coming and going, she also liked being able to lock the suite at night and know that Keith was sleeping soundly in his room while she tidied up or washed the dishes.

They really needed some help now that word had gotten out about the Waratah. It was all she and Paul could do to keep up with everything. Keith caught the bus each morning to the small Tweed Heads public school, which gave her a chance to catch up on her work in the kitchen and cleaning the empty rooms, but when he returned in the afternoon, she liked to spend that time with him. They'd visit the beach, take a swim, she'd even begun learning to surf, and he'd watch her from the shore. They'd collect seashells, chase gulls, or explore Castle Rock. Keith had christened it with that name after they'd perched on it to play *Kings and Queens* together one sunny afternoon.

Edie watched Keith leave with a smile, then folded her arms over her chest. Several of the guests had begun to slow-dance in front of the cold fireplace. Sweat shimmered on tanned skin. They laughed as they waltzed around the spacious room. Paul saw her and gave a wink. Then, he strode towards her and reached out a hand.

"Care to dance?" he asked.

She threw her head back and laughed. Then, nodded as she took his hand. When they spun around the floor, memories transported her back to that first day, on the lawn of the hospital when she'd danced with him for the first time. Her with a broken heart, him with a broken leg. Things were so very different now. She leaned into him, inhaling his scent, feeling his warmth. She was whole, loved, safe. He'd given her a second chance at life, at love. She never wanted to take that for granted.

After Edie put Keith to bed, most of the guests had retired to their rooms. Paul was fixing something on the verandah. She still had a few cups and saucers to wash, as well as the pot she'd heated the apple cider in. She carried it from the stove top to the sink and was about to rinse it beneath the cold tap when she heard a knock at the front door.

It was unusual to receive guests at night since the inn was so far from the main road. With a frown, she wiped her hands dry on her apron and went to open the door. When she saw Mima standing there beneath the dull glow of the verandah light, she gasped.

Mima smiled, bright red lips pulled tight over brilliant white teeth, and opened her arms wide. "Surprise!"

AFTER EDIE HAD REHEATED A CUP OF APPLE CIDER FOR both she and Mima, and Paul had taken Mima's suitcase to the one empty room left on the third floor of the inn, they sat outside together on the verandah.

Mima crossed her legs and Edie set her feet on a stool as they sipped their drinks. Edie had been overcome with emotion on seeing her friend but had dried her tears. Still, she felt the need to glance in her friend's direction every few seconds to make sure she was really there, that Mima wasn't a figment of her imagination.

"I can't believe you're here," said Edie, setting her cup down on a side table.

The crash of the waves in the distance punctuated her words.

"I can't believe it myself," replied Mima with a chuckle.

Mima hadn't changed much, but there were new lines around her eyes and her skin pulled tight in places over the bones in her neck and chest under the cotton dress she wore. Her arms were thin too, and her cheek bones protruded sharply, making her eyes look bigger than ever.

"How did you get here?"

"I caught the train to Murwillumbah, then a bus from there to Kingscliff. I found someone in Kingscliff who was willing to drive me out to the inn."

Edie shook her head. "I wish you'd written. I could've come and met you. Paul would've driven us."

"I didn't want to cause you any trouble. I know how hard the two of you work. From your letters, it sounds as though you've really done well with the place. It looks great." Mima's voice was low, almost as though it hid a well of tears. She could never hide anything from Edie for long though.

"What have you been doing with yourself lately?" asked Edie. "I haven't heard from you in a while."

Mima turned the cup around in her hands, staring at the cider within for several long moments. "I quit my job."

"Okay." Edie leaned forward to lay a hand on Mima's knee. "Why?"

"I couldn't take it anymore. I've been..." Her eyes filled with tears. "I'm not the kind of person I want to be. I don't know how I got to this place in my life."

The tears trickled down her cheeks as she met Edie's gaze. "I drink every day; I've done drugs. I...I don't know what's wrong with me. I've been with strangers, men I..." She sniffled, rubbed her hand over her nose. "Something is very wrong with me. And I'm so sad."

She moaned and began rocking back and forth in her chair as more tears poured from her eyes.

Edie knelt in front of her and wrapped her arms around Mima's thin body. "It's okay. Shhh. It's going to be fine. You'll see. You're here now, and we'll work it all out."

When Mima's tears finally subsided, Edie returned to her seat and the cup of cider. They sat in silence for what seemed like an age, as Mima sniffled and stared into the night.

"I like it here. It's peaceful," she said, breaking the silence.

"It is. How long will you stay?" asked Edie.

Mima shrugged. "I don't know. I hope you don't mind..."

"Stay as long as you like. Do you have any plans?"

Mima shook her head. "No. All I could think about was finding you. I haven't considered what comes next. I don't know. What should I do? I don't want to go back to Sydney..."

Edie's brow furrowed. "No, you should stay here. We'll give you a job. We need help with the inn, we were going to try to find some people to hire anyway. You're a great cook, you make the most delicious food."

Mima's glistening eyes fixed on Edie's. "Really? You'd do that for me?"

Edie smiled. "Of course. You can be the cook here at The Waratah Inn. It's perfect. I'll get more time to do the things

277

I've been wanting to do, like buy and train horses for the guests to ride and take care of Keith. And you'll have a job and a place to stay. What do you think?"

Mima laughed and swiped at the tears on her cheeks with a handkerchief. "Yes! I'd love to stay here and work for you."

❧ 34 ❧

JULY 1996

PACENTRO

Reeda yawned and rolled onto her side. She held Nan's journal in one hand as she read through the last paragraph on the page and then closed it gently, removed her glasses and rubbed her tired eyes.

Nan's journal entries were becoming more sporadic as the journal went on. She'd finished the first one and was almost through the second one. There were big time gaps between each entry, more and more as the years went on. No doubt the hectic world of raising a family and running a business caught up with Nan, and she didn't have the time to write down her thoughts the way she had in previous years. Life had a way of carrying one along, faster and faster as the years went by. Less time for introspection and smelling of roses, and more time spent on the mundanity of daily activities.

Still, Nan seemed happy enough. Her entries had echoed

with loneliness when they first moved to Cabarita, but since Mima joined them, the tone of her writing had lightened considerably.

It'd saddened her to think of all Nan and Pop had gone through. No wonder The Waratah Inn had meant so much to Nan. It was the thing that brought her family together, giving them a new start. A life that they could live freely, without worrying what anyone else thought of them, without anyone controlling their every move and thought. They were free to be themselves, to love Dad and raise him the way they thought best.

It must've been hard for Nan's mother as well, though, giving up the little boy she'd invested years of her life into raising.

The war had done a good job of tearing down the lives of everyone it touched.

If only she'd known all these things when she and her sisters had inherited the inn, she never would've suggested they sell it. Even thinking about that now sent a stab of panic through her chest. They couldn't sell the inn, it'd meant so much to Nan, Pop, and Dad. It was the thing that enabled them to be the family they became. A symbol of hope, freedom, and love.

Nan and Pop had their fair share of problems early on in the marriage, but it seemed moving away from her family and Bathurst had been a step in the right direction for them. They'd found a rhythm that suited them and Reeda was glad of it. It'd been hard for Nan to move on after losing her fiancé and her brother in a war that'd changed not only the course of history but rocked the faith of an entire generation in the previously assured inherent goodness of God and people. How could anyone recover from that kind of horror?

Everything she'd learned about Nan gave her a new yearning to go back in time and give her grandmother a hug.

To tell her she understood her better than she had before, that she loved her and was grateful for everything she'd done to raise them. Reading all Nan had been through helped her see how much Dad's death had taken from Nan, even more than she'd realised before. With the tragedy of her past, it was no wonder Nan was so consumed by the grief of losing her only son.

As a teenager, it'd been difficult for her to grasp why her grandmother wasn't there for her during those early months after the accident. She'd needed a shoulder to cry on, needed someone to tell her everything would be all right in the end. Nan hadn't done that, hadn't been able to face the world. Reeda had resented her for that, thought her selfish in a way, without forming the words in her head. Now she knew—Nan had already lost so much, Dad was her one link to Charlie, to the past, to the love she'd had to leave behind all those years earlier. He was her heart. And she'd lost him.

Reeda wondered now how Nan was able to come out of that dark place at all.

Downstairs, she found Angela and Signora Rossi in their usual place—the kitchen. Reeda had spent most of the morning in bed. She'd slept in, a delicious sensation. For months now, she hadn't slept well, but in fits and spurts. She'd woken early most days, gone to bed late, alone, and with an aching heart. But not last night.

After they'd talked until almost midnight on the balcony, she'd returned to her room feeling spent, but happy in a strange kind of way. Then, she'd slept like the dead until well after ten o'clock. When she woke, instead of coming right downstairs, she'd laid in bed a while longer, reading Nan's diary, then took a long shower, and dressed in a yellow print cotton dress. She wore her wet hair loose around her shoulders and barely glanced in the mirror.

One thing she did notice from a brief glimpse of her

reflection in the mirror, she'd gotten a tan under the Italian sun. Extra freckles sprinkled across her nose, her cheeks had plumped up with all the good food and she was fairly certain she'd need a larger bra size whenever she got the chance to go underwear shopping next.

"Good morning, Reeda," said Angela.

Signora Rossi smiled and nodded. She kneaded fresh bread dough on the bench, and flour coated her hands and apron.

Reeda grabbed an apron from the handrail tacked to the end of the bench and joined them.

They made ravioli with a creamy Alfredo sauce, along with fresh baked bread rolls and Reeda diced tomatoes for a marinara sauce simmering on the stovetop. Signora Rossi had a line of jars on the back of the bench ready to be filled with the sauce once it cooled. They'd add it to the underground pantry accessible by a small, dank staircase off the back of the kitchen and hidden by a whitewashed, old wooden door.

After a quick lunch of ravioli Alfredo with a fresh caprese salad, Reeda changed into hiking gear and headed out for a walk. Ever since she arrived in Pacentro she'd been dying to get out on the mountainside to explore.

It was time she burned some of the many calories she'd already consumed that day as well. If she wasn't careful, she'd outgrow every item of clothing in her luggage.

And for the first time in her life, she didn't care. She felt good. Happy, content, strong. She hadn't counted her calorie intake since she left Rome, and the usual panic about gaining a few kilograms hadn't taken hold of her. Her figure was growing rounder, fuller, and she liked it.

Still, it felt good to get out and push her muscles a little.

She strode up a path on the top of the mountain ridge, then followed a narrow trail down the side of it and back up again on the mountain's face.

She'd read a sign back in the village that said it was surrounded by the *Parco Nationale Marjella*. She stopped and spun about to face the valley below. The vista was stunning. She tented hands over her eyes and studied the distant highway, the cattle dotting green pastureland, the olive groves with gnarled branches hugging the mountainside.

By the time she returned to the village of Pacentro, she was bathed in sweat and every muscle in her body ached. It was growing dark. She stopped at a small general store, stocked with bottles of olive oil, milk, bread, magazines, and wide-brimmed hats. Somewhere in the eclectic collection of wares, she found a journal and bought it. So much time spent reading Nan's journals had given her the idea—she should write one of her own. Get some of her feelings down on paper. Maybe it would help her organise her thoughts and figure out what she wanted from life.

She'd already told Signora Rossi and Angela she would eat out for dinner, and Lorenzo had asked her to meet him the night before at the festival. She decided to stop in town and do just that, rather than heading home for a shower first. She was already late to meet him, and besides there was no need to dress up for Lorenzo, since they were just friends. She smoothed her flyaway hair back into a ponytail as she walked.

She found the restaurant perched on the edge of town with a magnificent view of the valley: *Anthony Jnr's Pizzeria and Ristorante*. The mountain range cast long shadows as the sun dipped towards the horizon. Lorenzo was already there, waiting for her. He sat at a table, reading a book. When she entered, he jumped up to kiss her cheeks, pulled out a chair for her and sat across from her with a wide smile.

"So nice to see you again, Reeda."

She smiled. "And you, Lorenzo."

"You have been walking?" he asked.

She nodded. "It was such a beautiful day. I spent hours on

the mountainside. I lay in the grass in one spot for at least an hour, staring out over the valley, thinking. It was just what I needed."

"I'm glad to hear it. Did you think of anything in particular?"

She knew what he wanted to hear, that she'd been thinking of him. He was young, full of confidence, hormones, and Italian bravado. In truth, she had thought of him. It was hard to ignore his interest in her, and if she were honest with herself, it was flattering. He was young, handsome, and kind. He'd make someone a wonderful husband someday, but it wouldn't be her.

Still, she could enjoy his company for a little longer. It boosted her confidence to see herself through his eyes, and she wasn't ready to give that up yet. Besides, it was nice to have the company.

They ate pizza, and vegetables marinated in olive oil, and drank wine. Then, a live band began to play, and they danced together until she could dance no more. Her feet ached, her legs felt like jelly and her head was light from the wine, laughter, and hours spent in the sunshine.

Reeda guzzled a few glasses of water, then announced it was time for her to head home to bed. Lorenzo wanted to walk her home, but she told him she'd be fine. He seemed disappointed, and even tried to kiss her on the lips when they parted, but she managed to dodge him well enough and skipped down the cobblestone road out of reach. After a few steps she turned, walking backwards, and waved her goodbye with a laugh when she saw the way he pouted after her.

He was adorable, like a doe-eyed puppy dog. But he was hurting, and instead of dealing with his pain was looking for her to dull it. She couldn't do that for him, not when all he wanted was a fling with a foreigner to help him get over the love he'd lost. He meant well, but it wasn't what either of them needed. The flirtation was fun, but she'd have to put a stop to it sooner rather than later, before he got hurt.

Back at home, the Rossi women were on the balcony with their mugs of tea. Reeda hurried to shower and change into her nightie and dressing gown, then joined them, her own steaming mug held between both hands to guard against the cool of the evening.

"Have you had a nice day?" asked Angela.

Reeda nodded. "Yes, thank you. I walked for hours in the national park, then ate and danced with Lorenzo."

Angela arched an eyebrow. "You like this Lorenzo?"

"I do, but not in a romantic way. In fact, you should spend some time with him, I think the two of you would hit it off. You're both kind, fun, and very beautiful." Reeda laughed as Angela's cheeks blushed red in the gloom.

In the kitchen, the tinny ring of the phone erupted, making all three women jump. It didn't ring often, since most of the neighbours simply dropped in to talk if they had something to say.

Angela hurried inside to answer it. Then returned a few moments later.

"Reeda, it's for you. It's Duncan."

Reeda's heart skipped a beat. She set down her tea and strode into the kitchen. She'd left the number for the bed and breakfast with Kate. Duncan must've called her sister for it.

"Hello?"

"Hi Reeda," said Duncan. His deep voice cut through the barrier she'd erected around her heart. She missed him. The thought surprised her, and a lump welled in her throat.

"How are you?"

"I'm fine. Busy with work. How are you? How's the trip going?"

"It's good. I'm having a wonderful time. I've been eating good food, sleeping until all hours of the morning...resting, relaxing, meeting interesting people. It's just what I needed."

"I'm glad," he replied. Then hesitated. "When will you be home?"

"I'm not sure. Probably a few weeks still."

He grunted. "Uh. Okay."

"You don't mind, do you? I thought you wanted some time apart."

"I'm not sure we can figure out a way forward with you on the other side of the world. I want to get things resolved between us. I hate being in this limbo-land."

"I'm sorry. I'll be back before too much longer, as I said, probably only a few weeks. I'm taking the time to think things through, to figure out what I want."

"What do you want?" he asked, his irritation clear in the brusque words.

"I'm not ready to talk about it yet, I haven't fully formed the thoughts in my mind. Something has changed, perhaps everything has changed. All the things I wanted in life... they're not working out the way I thought they would and instead of fighting it, perhaps it's time I accepted my reality and formed new dreams."

He inhaled a sharp breath. "New dreams...without me?"

"I'm not sure. Like I said, I'm not ready to talk about it yet. But I will be by the time I get home. Can you wait a little longer?"

"I suppose I don't have a choice. I..." He sighed. "I guess I'll see you when you get back."

When she hung up the phone, she realised his words hadn't shifted her sense of ease. Her contentment hung on, in spite of his frustration. Usually, the impatience ringing through in his words would cause her stress levels to spike, and she'd rush off to change her plans, to bend to his desires.

But she wasn't going to do that this time. She wouldn't let his emotions impact on her happiness.

She smiled, realising that for the first time in a long time she hadn't thought about babies, empty nurseries, or bought a pregnancy test in days. She hadn't obsessed about being pregnant since she left Rome. The ever-present anxiety of her previous life was gone. She was doing life alone, and she was happy. She felt strong, even if her muscles ached, was well-rested, content, and strangely at peace with her life. And with an amazed shake of her head, she wandered back to the balcony to join her new friends.

❧ 35 ❧

SEPTEMBER 1996

PACENTRO

Reeda leaned against the fence rail in front of her and peered into the hazy Italian light of a summer afternoon at the mountainside across from the village of Pacentro. Crowds lined the fence with her and followed the path down the mountain to the valley below. Beside her, Lorenzo reached for her hand, cupped it to his mouth and pressed his lips to her skin.

Her cheeks flushed and she laughed. "Lorenzo..."

He chuckled, eyes flashing. "You are too beautiful today to be angry with me."

She wasn't sure his words made sense, but it was still nice to hear him say it. She tugged her hand out of his grasp and pressed it back onto the fence railing. "I'm trying to focus."

He shrugged. "If only you would focus your attention on something truly important."

She laughed, shaking her head. "You're impossible."

Lorenzo had come back to Pacentro every chance he got since that first weekend. He'd pursued her with confidence and persistence that'd surprised her and made her a little uncomfortable. She wasn't used to the attention, but she couldn't say she didn't enjoy it. She'd made it clear to him repeatedly that she wasn't interested in a romantic relationship with him, but he'd replied that he wouldn't give up on love.

Angela squeezed through the crowd and sidled up to Reeda. "Phew, this is crazy. More people come to Pacentro every year for *La Corsa degli Zingari*."

"What does that mean, exactly?" asked Reeda, shadowing her face with a hand to better see the flapping Italian flags and clusters of young men gathered on the side of the mountain.

"The race of the gypsies," replied Angela. "It's an ancient initiation rite." She smiled at Lorenzo. "Hi, Lorenzo."

His cheeks grew red. "Good afternoon, signora."

Angela nodded. "And to you."

"You don't have to use English on my account," interrupted Reeda.

She grinned to herself. As much as Lorenzo acted the part of confident flirt with her, he was shy and respectful with Angela. Angela and Lorenzo exchanged a look before focusing their attention on the racers as well.

Fireworks shot into the afternoon sky, betrayed by colourful clouds of smoke that drifted on the wind. Reeda jumped and clapped a hand to her mouth as the loud cracks reverberated throughout the valley.

"Ah! Fireworks? But it's daylight," she complained, her heart hammering in her chest.

"Sorry, I forgot to warn you about those," replied Angela with a grin.

Just then, the church bells in the hamlet tolled, a clanging tinny sound that echoed through the town up and up the sloping mountain on which the village was perched. The small groups of runners set off down the hill, slipping, sliding, and running. They disappeared behind shrubs and trees, then emerged again farther down the mountain. Finally, one man emerged from the shrubbery and onto a narrow trail that ran down the length of the slope to the foot of the mountain. The crowds around Reeda sent up a chorus of congratulatory shouts. She glanced around at the happy faces in surprise.

Soon, there were several young men, all jogging down the winding trail. They made their way up into Pacentro, to the cheering of the crowd and the occasional clanging of the church bells. A camera man from Central Abruzzo News panned the crowd and followed the progress of the bare-footed runners as they headed into the village via the narrow, winding trail that'd brought them up the rise.

"Now what?" asked Reeda, as one by one, the sweaty, red-faced racers passed them and went on into the village.

"Now, they get their feet taken care of in the *Madonna di Loreto*, the church, and we wait for them to emerge, follow the winner to his home and then return to our own to eat and drink," replied Angela, pushing her way through the crowd.

"Sounds good to me," replied Reeda, following her.

The crowd around the church's entrance made it difficult to see. Reeda stood on tiptoe to peer down the footpath. A brass band played an upbeat melody at the church's front door with a breathtaking view of the valley behind them.

When the church doors opened, the crowd erupted into catcalls and applause, and Reeda was carried along with them to find the young man's home where a large crucifix was mounted to the front wall. His parents emerged with wine, and soon Angela, Reeda and Lorenzo were on their way back to the bed and breakfast.

Signora Rossi was there already, bustling around her cozy kitchen, wisps of disheveled hair curling around her lined face. The balcony was crowded with neighbours and friends, all drinking wine and eating plates of olives, cheeses, thinly sliced meats, marinated capsicum, fresh figs, and crostini.

Reeda immediately fetched her apron, tied it around her waist and got to work in the kitchen. She'd volunteered to make the pizzas. She'd decided on two flavours: simple *margherita*, with tomato sauce, mozzarella, and fresh basil, as well as *quattro stagioni* with tomato sauce, mozzarella, mushrooms, ham, artichokes, olives, and oregano. The crusts were already made, she only had to slice the toppings and slide them into the oven.

By the time she was done making the last pizza, the first ones had already been consumed by the crowd of guests. She untied her apron, wiped the sweat from her brow and made her way out onto the packed balcony with everyone else.

Angela was out there, crammed into a corner with Lorenzo. They looked very cosy, deep in conversation, and Reeda was glad to see it. She grinned, reached for a glass, and filled it with Chianti before taking a deep breath. The view was always amazing from here; she'd miss it when she was gone. She'd stayed in Pacentro longer than she'd planned to, but it'd been too hard to leave.

She'd spent her time walking on the rugged mountainside, cooking with Angela and Signora Rossi, and writing in her journal. Her forays into the national park left her amazed at the route the escaping prisoners of war must've taken all those years earlier, not certain of where it would lead them and in the early days of a cold winter.

Every now and then, she read another entry in Nan's journal, but mostly she'd taken a break from the past. Instead, she'd focused on working through her own thoughts. What did she want from life? Where was she headed? How had she gotten to this place in her life when the one thing she'd wanted for so long, wasn't going to happen and she didn't know how to move on from that?

It was well past bedtime when the last guest finally left. Reeda yawned, slumped into a kitchen chair, and set her feet up on another one. The kitchen was clean after she and Angela had spent what seemed like hours washing dirty dishes, plates, forks, and glasses, drying them and finally putting them away.

Signora Rossi sat down next to her and patted her shoulder with a smile.

"*Grazie* Reeda," she said with a sigh.

Angela set down the broom she was using to sweep up the remnants of pizza crumbs with and joined them. "My feet ache," she complained.

Reeda nodded. "I can't wait to go to bed. I haven't felt this tired in a long time." In truth, she hadn't felt tired at all in at least a month. She felt strong, capable, and healthy. Even though she'd been out walking every day, she no longer fit into any of the clothes she'd brought with her. Now all she wore were long, flowing dresses and matching cardigans she found at the local markets. She hadn't put on makeup once in that time either, and her natural curls had grown longer than ever, reaching halfway down her back.

Lorenzo leaned against the kitchen wall with his gaze fixed on Angela's face. Angela noticed him, her cheeks flushing red, then stood and followed him out the front door and into the street. Signora Rossi and Reeda exchanged a knowing look.

They'd be good for each other, Angela and Lorenzo. Both were looking for someone to love, each was as kind as the other, and they lived an easy drive apart. Reeda was grateful Lorenzo had so quickly changed the direction of his affection, especially since she was leaving Pacentro, and would soon be on her way back to Australia. She would feel much better about moving on, knowing both friends had someone to lean on without her there.

She pulled a long-distance telephone card from her pocket and dialled the number for The Waratah Inn.

"Hello Kate?" she said. "Just wanted to let you know, I'm going to Casoli tomorrow, then back to Rome and home to the Gold Coast. I'll be home in a few days."

❧ 36 ❧

SEPTEMBER 1943

PACENTRO

When Charlie saw the small, mountainside town the first time, adrenaline pumped through his veins and he ducked behind a tree to hide. Colin and Henry followed his lead, surveying the village from the safety of the tree line. Pale stucco buildings painted in white or sun-bleached pastels. Tiled roofs and two tall parapets jutted up against the skyline, with the wide valley stretched out below. The village clung to a mountain ridge, following its gentle slope downward and away from where they crouched.

A narrow, winding road led to the village. It was empty. They couldn't see any sign of life. What if the Germans were there? Though surely if they were, there'd be some sign to give them away: motorbikes zipping along the road, black staff cars sporting small Nazi flags parked out front, sentries on guard.

"What do you think?" asked Colin.

"No sign of Fritz," replied Henry, eyes narrowed.

"I could really use a drink of water," replied Charlie, licking his dry lips.

He'd woken early that morning with a crick in his neck and a sharp rock protruding into the space between his shoulder blades, uncertain of where he was. Once he'd regained his senses, he'd shaken the pain from his limbs and left the safety of their cave to explore. Sunshine had warmed the mountainside, drying most of the rain, leaving only droplets of it sitting on shaded patches of grass or in crevices and divots in the rocks. They'd tried sucking water from those places, but it hadn't been enough to quench their thirst.

They kept to the tree line and then the shadows as best they could. Inside the hamlet, villagers went about their daily lives. They shot the men a curious look, then continued on their way. Finally, they decided they'd have to approach someone. To put their trust in a stranger was a difficult thing to do, especially in enemy territory. But one thing they'd learned from their previous escape attempts, was that the locals were divided over their government's devotion to the German cause, and some of them supported the Allies. Something they could never openly do, but if this village had managed to stay out of the Nazi's reach so far, perhaps they'd find some kindness within its walls.

The village was a quaint, medieval looking structure. Narrow, cobblestone streets. Winding footpaths. Steps leading from one level to the next. The township was dotted with crucifixes and other signs of dedication to the Catholic faith. Charlie's heart thundered in his chest. Entering this town made them the most vulnerable they'd been since their escape. If they were going to be re-captured, it would be in this quaint, little village.

"Do either one of you speak Italian?" asked Charlie, as the three of them strode purposefully down a winding path between tall, stucco buildings.

"I speak a little," replied Henry.

Colin shook his head. "Nope." He wiped a trail of sweat from his brow with his sleeve. He looked as nervous as Charlie felt.

A young man, head down, eyes fixed to a newspaper stepped out of a nearby front door. He shut the door behind him without taking his eyes off the paper.

"*Scusami?*" Henry stepped forward.

The man glanced up, and fear crossed over his face then left as quickly as it had come. He offered a wan smile. "*Sì. Come posso aiutarla?*"

"*Lei parla inglese?*"

Charlie and Colin stayed back. Adrenaline pumped rapidly through Charlie's veins. He felt light-headed, licked his parched lips, and watched the exchange, his entire body poised for flight.

The man dipped his head. "Yes, a little."

Charlie released the breath he'd held captive in his lungs.

Henry smiled. "We were hoping you might be able to help us."

◈

THE RICCI'S ATTIC WAS SMALL, CRAMPED, AND THE CEILING wasn't high enough for Charlie to stand. But he wasn't about to complain. They'd eaten better since they arrived five days earlier in Pacentro and were taken in by the Ricci family than he had in months, possibly years. The fifteen-year-old Stefano Ricci constantly apologised that the food wasn't as good as it would've been before the war, but the three servicemen assured him that in their eyes, it was a delicious bounty. Charlie sat on a small bed mat on the floor, his legs crossed. It was warm inside the house, even the attic. Colin and Henry had already gone downstairs for breakfast. Stefano's mother, Signora Ricci, said they could come downstairs to eat at mealtimes, but otherwise they should stay in the attic in case someone came to the door. She didn't want even the neighbours to know they were there. The fewer people who knew about them, the better.

Charlie had asked her then if she trusted her neighbours. She waited for her son to interpret, then shook her head, waving a wooden spoon as she responded. Yes, she trusted them, but she didn't want to put them in a position to get in trouble with the Wehrmacht. It was better for them, and for him, if no one else knew their secret. He'd agreed they should stay hidden, but inside he wondered how long it would be before they'd be able to keep moving. Winter was coming, escape to the East would become far more difficult the longer they waited.

That'd made Signora Ricci, smile. Stefano's mother didn't speak a word of English, nor did his little brother Matteo, or his sister Sofia. According to Stefano, their father had gone off to war two years earlier. He was fighting somewhere in the north of the country, the last they knew. But they hadn't heard from him in months, so couldn't be certain he was still there.

Hearing their story stirred Charlie's heart. Little Sofia wasn't much older than Keith. She hadn't seen her father in two years. He'd never met Keith. Something inside of him itched to get moving, to keep walking out of Pacentro, head for the border and get back to his family in Australia as fast as he could. Still, he knew it wouldn't work. Even if he managed to get out of Italy, he'd only be returned to his squadron. Likely they were still somewhere in North Africa or the Middle East. Or maybe he'd be sent back to Asia to fight off the Japanese in the Pacific Theatre, like so many other Australian troops.

He sighed and stood slowly, careful not to knock his head on the low ceiling. He shrugged on his leather jacket and made his way down the narrow, winding staircase to the ground floor. He found the others in the kitchen with the Ricci family.

Stefano was speaking to his mother in Italian, hands flailing, his cheeks red. He spun to face Charlie, wild-eyed.

"They are coming. The Wehrmacht are coming," he said, his accent clipping the words and making it hard to understand.

Charlie's heart skipped a beat. "How long do we have?"

Henry and Colin were seated at the table eating donuts and drinking espresso. They stood and slipped on their jackets, faces grim.

"No time at all. You must leave now. Come. I will show you a way out."

Signora Ricci handed Charlie a small cup of espresso. He downed it in one gulp, patted her arm. "Thank you."

She nodded and smiled. Charlie grabbed a handful of the small donuts on the way out the door. Henry found his rucksack in the hall closet and slung it onto his back. They followed Stefano out the front door, waving a silent goodbye to the small boy and girl who stood hand-in-hand at the bottom of the staircase to watch them go, solemn brown eyes fixed on their faces.

The street was empty, unlike the usual lively place Charlie had seen from the attic window these past days. Word must've spread that the German army had arrived. How long before they searched the town, door to door?

The men broke into a run, with Stefano taking the lead. A

few curtains fell back into place as they passed. They couldn't escape without anyone seeing them. Charlie's only hope was that the townsfolk would keep what they'd seen to themselves. There wasn't anything he could do about that now.

Through the streets of Pacentro, the men hurried, boots clapping on the cobblestones. If only they could be quieter, draw less attention to themselves. Were the Germans on their heels? Charlie tried to listen for the sound of pursuers but could hear only his own gasps for air and his boots slapping the ground with each step he took.

"Down here!" Stefano ducked into a passageway that wound down a dark, dank staircase. It opened up into an alleyway that soon carried them out of town. When they reached the end of the alley, it opened up onto a wider path with nothing to hide their retreat. Charlie glanced back over his shoulder, the hairs on the back of his neck on end as he saw their vulnerability. They'd be out in the open for several minutes until they could reach clumps of bushes to duck behind on the mountainside.

As he looked back, he saw several other soldiers, all running in the same direction. It seemed other townsfolk had been hiding Allied soldiers as well.

"We've got company," he called ahead to Colin and Henry, in a low voice.

They each glanced back, still moving forward as quickly and quietly as they could manage. Colin waved a hand at the stragglers, who waved back. One called out a greeting. Charlie grimaced. He wanted to tell them to be quiet, keep it down, but didn't want to risk being overheard.

When Stefano heard the sound, he stopped, irritation written like thunder on his brow. "They are too loud. You must hurry, you don't have much time. The Germans may have heard your friend's shout."

They had reached the end of the path and found themselves in an olive grove. A small, narrow dirt trail climbed through the grove up the mountain.

"Go this way, follow the trail, it will take you over the ridge. You should go to Casoli. You will find it on the other side of the mountain range. I'm sorry I cannot help you more, but I must stay with my family."

"Of course, thank you," replied Charlie, shaking Stefano's hand.

He nodded, doubled back, and strode up the path, passing the British soldiers on their trail. Charlie ignored them and bounded up the path through the olive grove. The trees on either side of them provided some little shade but left them almost completely exposed to the village. Anyone looking their way would see their progress. There was nowhere nearby to hide. They couldn't stay where they were. Their only option was to keep moving and hope they made it over the ridge before the Nazis saw them.

The British soldiers on their trail soon caught up to them. One of the men, with short blond hair and freckles dotted across his nose and cheeks, grinned.

"Hello. Fancy meeting you chaps here."

Charlie was about to make a snide remark about them keeping it down, when he heard a shout. He looked back at the village. A group of Wehrmacht had spied them from the village walls. One of them looked to be setting up a machine gun, pointed in their direction.

"Run!" cried Charlie.

He set off at a loping pace. They were aiming directly up a steep, rocky incline. Moving as fast as he could still felt as though he was going at a snail's pace. Sweat beaded on his forehead then trickled down his temples. His breath came in ragged bursts. His heart felt as though it might burst as it pounded against his rib cage. The muscles in his legs tightened as he fought to keep going. Behind him, the other men puffed and strained to keep up.

The crack of the machine-gun fire spurred him on, adrenaline bursting through his body. Shouts behind him drew his attention. He stopped and dove for cover behind a thin olive tree. Colin followed him, grabbing at his leg as he landed on the ground beside Charlie.

"I'm hit," he groaned.

Charlie fell to his knees beside his friend, pressing his hands to Colin's wound as blood spurted. His heart fell.

Colin's face turned pale. He inhaled a sharp breath, moaning with the pain. "It's bad, isn't it? It's bad. I know it is. I'm not going to make it."

Charlie shook his head. "No, you stay strong. I'll get you some help. Hang in there, mate."

He crawled back to the olive tree and peered around it. Bullets rang out, ricocheting off nearby rocks and tree trunks. He could see Henry. He'd been hit and was down. He wasn't moving. Charlie couldn't get to him.

He swallowed, his heart thundering. This was it. He wasn't going to make it. They'd all die on this mountainside in Italy. He got down low and squirmed back to Colin's side.

"Henry's been hit too," he said.

Colin didn't respond.

"Colin?" He shook Colin by the shoulder. It was too late. Colin was gone too.

The British soldiers who'd followed them on the trail, snuck by, ducking from tree to tree, scurrying along low to the ground. Charlie drew a deep breath, said a quiet goodbye to his friends, his heart full of pain, then followed them.

He almost made it to the top of the ridge when he felt the sting of a bullet in his side. He grabbed his side and fell to the ground.

"Hey!" One of the men he was following stopped, ducked low, hurried back to him.

"You hit?" he asked, his freckled face bobbing in front of Charlie's vision.

Charlie nodded, biting down on his lower lip to hold in a cry of pain.

The man grabbed him beneath both arms and began to pull. "We've got to get you out of the line of fire," he mumbled.

The rocks beneath him on the trail clawed at his clothes as the soldier pulled him farther along the trail. They'd summited the mountain and were on their way across its narrow peak, still following the narrow, dusty trail from the village. Charlie's head swam. He stared up at the blue sky overhead. Fluffy white clouds sailed slowly across his vision. One morphed into an elephant, raising its trunk to trumpet over the mountain range. He smiled at the elephant cloud as the pain in his side faded. He'd never see his son, never get to squeeze his chubby cheeks, or throw him in the air and listen to his delighted squeals. It didn't seem fair, didn't seem right. He should've gotten a chance to kiss his little forehead once before he died. If only he could hold Edie one more time, feel her arms around him, hear her sweet voice. His head whacked against a hard rock and he cried out in pain. Then all the world faded away.

❧ 37 ❧

CASOLI

A s the bus pulled away from the bus stop, Reeda fingered the piece of paper in her hands. It contained the name of a man she was set to meet— Stefano Ricci. Matteo Ricci had assured her his older brother would know more than him about any escaped prisoners who may have passed through Pacentro, since he'd been a teenager during the war. Signor Ricci had given her his name and set up the meeting in the hopes he might be able to shed some light on the mystery of Charlie's disappearance.

The township of Casoli was perched on top of a green hill. She'd already checked into her hotel, located farther down the hillside. And now was meeting Stefano for lunch.

Flanked by impressive mountain peaks, the town was built in the same, medieval style as Pacentro, only larger. Tall buildings, painted in pastels with red and orange tiled roofs, were crammed side by side over the hill and down its slopes until they reached the valley below.

Reeda began to climb the footpath that led into the town. She stopped to ask an old lady with a shawl draped over her head for directions. The woman couldn't speak English but recognised the name of the restaurant written on Reeda's scrap of paper and pointed a single, bony finger up the same footpath with a nod. Ahead of Reeda, a wide stone staircase climbed the hillside and led to a narrow alleyway between tall, chipped stucco houses with shuttered windows.

Every building was higher than the one before, each climbing, up, up, up to the pinnacle of the village, the old stone church and watchtower. At each front door, pots of flowers and herbs lined the pavement. Washing hung from lines to dry. She glanced back over her shoulder; a patchwork of green hugged the rolling hills that surrounded the town. Squares of crops, pastureland, and all dotted with green, reaching trees.

She walked for what seemed like a long time, asking for directions again and again, until finally she came to a restaurant with a swinging timber sign that read, "Bella Casoli". Sweat beaded on her brow and she wiped it with the back of her hand as she studied the restaurant. How would she find Stefano?

After a few hesitant steps towards the restaurant's door, she noticed an old man waving in her direction. He sat at one of the establishment's outdoor tables, and wore a fedora pulled low on his head.

She waved back and strode in his direction, reaching out her hand to shake his. "Stefano Ricci?"

He smiled, stood to his feet, hands gripping the edge of the table, and leaned forward to kiss both her cheeks. "You must be Reeda Summer," he said. "I'm sorry, I need this *cosa fastidiosa* to lean on, I have injured my ankle climbing the

stairs. Old age is like a comb, everyone will pass through it."
He nodded his head in the direction of a walking stick, the
end of which was looped over the back of his chair.

She slid into a chair opposite him. "Of course. I understand, please sit. I hope you haven't been waiting long."

He followed her lead, his eyes sparkling. "No, no. Not
long. It's good to hear the Australian accent again. It has been
too long."

Her eyes narrowed. "So, you did meet Australian soldiers
during the war? Your brother said you had, but I wasn't sure
you'd remember."

"Of course I remember. I have so many memories, more
than I know what to do with. How to bring them to the
surface, if I wish to face them. It was the war that tore us all
apart, if it hadn't been for that..." He threw one hand in the
air, then waved it down as if to swat a fly. "Well, a lot of things
would've been different. For a lot of people."

She sighed. "So very true."

"I don't talk about it, you know. I don't like to say
anything about the war. No one does, and besides my children and grandchildren don't understand. They think the
world has always been this way—free, happy, safe, with plenty
to eat. They don't know any different, and they don't have the
patience to hear about it. I don't like to talk about it, they
don't like to hear about it, so..." He waved another hand and
made a "pfft" sound through pursed lips.

Reeda laughed. "I see how that works."

He grinned. "So, what is it you want to know? Matteo
called and told me you had some questions about Campo 78
and the soldiers who escaped to Pacentro."

"I do, I hope you don't mind if I pry a little bit."

He nodded. "That's fine, although it was a long time ago,
so some of it's a little fuzzy."

"I understand. Actually, I'm looking for someone. My

grandfather was a prisoner there. We've got a record of him being held at Campo 78 and letters he wrote confirm it. The problem is, he never came home after the war. I'm curious to find out what happened to him. I don't know if he made it to Pacentro, or if he went somewhere else. I was hoping you might be able to shed some light on that for me."

Stefano's eyes narrowed, he leaned forward in his chair. "Okay. We talk."

A waitress came then to take their order. Reeda ordered an antipasto platter, and Stefano went for the veal parmesan. They each ordered some sparkling water. Reeda took a sip, then returned to the subject of their meeting.

"So, it's possible my grandfather was sent to a German camp, but it's also possible he escaped."

Stefano nodded. "Yes, he might have. Hundreds fled the camp when the guards abandoned their posts—or so I heard. What was your grandfather's name? Perhaps I met him."

"Charles Jackson, he went by Charlie. He had blond hair, blue eyes and was a pilot in the RAAF."

"Charlie," repeated Stefano, his eyes brightening. "Hmmm...I recall that name. It was a long time ago, I was only a fifteen-year-old boy at the time, but I believe he was one of them...yes."

Reeda's pulse quickened. "You met him?"

"There was a blondish man, he went by the name Charlie if I remember right. He came to Pacentro, stayed with my family. I found him and two of his friends in the street one day. They asked if I could help, I took them home and my mother fed them. They stayed in the attic. Not for long, just a few nights."

After all this time she'd finally found some evidence of what'd happened to her grandfather. He'd escaped after all, made it to Pacentro.

"What happened to him? Where did he go?" she asked, perching on the edge of her seat.

Stefano rubbed his stubbled chin with one hand, his eyes peering off into the distance over her head. "He was shot."

His lips pulled into a thin line, and he turned the water glass around and around with his fingertips.

Reeda's heart fell. Had Charlie escaped the camp, found his way to Pacentro only to die alone and afraid?

"He was killed in Pacentro?" she asked.

Stefano inhaled a slow breath. "He escaped, made his way up the mountain, but the Wehrmacht gave chase. I heard the gunfire, but I didn't stay to see what happened. I believe they were all shot, although I cannot say for sure. I was in danger myself and had to hide inside an empty wine barrel until they left."

She nodded, her mind racing. "So, he might've been shot, but he might've survived?"

Stefano cocked his head to one side. "Perhaps. Yes. But if he lived, where is he?"

They finished eating and Stefano told her about life in Pacentro before the war. As fascinating as his stories were, she couldn't get past the fact that she'd uncovered a valuable clue about Charlie's fate. They might never uncover the reason why Charlie didn't return to Nan and her father after the war. But at least she knew this, he'd escaped the camp and sheltered in Pacentro. It wasn't final, or complete, but it was enough for now.

❧❧❧

Throughout the bus ride back to the hotel, Reeda sat staring out the window. Her eyes glazed at the beauty of Casoli. All she could think about was Charlie and whether he'd been shot and killed outside Pacentro. Whether he'd

LILLY MIRREN

died afraid and alone on a foreign mountain slope. Her throat tightened. Nan never knew what happened to him, and now she might not discover his fate either.

She missed Signora Rossi, Angela, and Lorenzo. Lorenzo and Angela had decided to try dating and she couldn't be happier for them. Still, it was hard to walk away from the new life she'd built for herself in Pacentro. A life without stress, worries or conflict. All she had to do was relax, explore, eat, and sleep. Unfortunately, that wasn't enough for her. She couldn't live that way forever. She had dreams, goals, and a family back in Australia. It might be easier not to have to face her husband, or to resolve things with her sisters, however that might look, but she had to do it sometime.

She climbed off the bus feeling resolved. She had to face the future and she was ready to do it.

The hotel was a small boutique inn. Sunlight glanced off the pale stucco, fresh red flowers bloomed in pots around the entrance. The glass doors slid open when she approached them, and a rush of air-conditioning swept out to greet her. It felt so good against her hot skin. She lifted the hair from the back of her neck with one hand as she made her way through the small lobby.

"Reeda!"

She spun on her heel with a frown. Duncan?

Her husband strode across the lobby towards her, his brow furrowed, a smile playing around the corners of his full mouth. He wore khaki shorts and a blue and white checked shirt. His golden curls were damp with sweat. Before she could stop herself, she rushed at him, throwing her arms around his neck with a cry.

"Duncan! What are you doing here?" Tears tightened her throat and spilled onto her cheeks, she sobbed into his shirt.

He laughed, pulled her away, and kissed her on the lips, a

soft but confident pressure of his lips on hers, his scent in her nostrils, his hands clenching tight to her arms.

She hadn't realised until that moment how much she'd missed him. The rush of emotion upon seeing him swept over her before she had a chance to push it down. She loved him more than anyone else in the world. Was it her lot to have her heart broken over and over by the one person she'd chosen to give it to?

Duncan kissed her forehead, her cheeks, the tip of her nose and then her lips all over again, and this time his lips were searching, seeking, urgent and in need of more.

She let herself be carried away in the emotion of the moment as tears streaked down her face, kissing him back with sporadic bursts of laughter and cries of delight.

"You're here. I wasn't expecting to see you."

He laughed and pulled her close, wrapping his arms around her. His musk was tinged with aftershave and soap. His strong arms held her against his firm body. His head bent down over hers, so she fit beneath his chin, her cheek pressed to his chest.

When they stepped apart, she wiped the tears from her eyes and drew a deep breath. "What are you doing here?" she asked again.

He grinned. "I came to surprise you. I missed you."

He threaded his fingers through hers.

"I missed you too. But I'm headed to the Gold Coast in a few days, and from there to Sydney. I would've been home soon." she said.

He shook his head. "I couldn't wait that long. Besides, I remembered how we used to talking about taking a trip to Italy together."

There was a pang of pain in her gut as she remembered all the things they'd dreamed of doing when they were younger that'd never come to pass. Nothing had changed. They were still them. They still had issues to resolve, problems to face. Just because they'd missed each other, didn't mean those same mountains that stood between them were gone.

She let go of his hand and stared at the ground. "We talked about doing a lot of things."

He sighed. "I know Reeda. But you're the one I love. We vowed to spend our lives together. I thought it was all getting too hard, but I was wrong. I want to fight for you, for us. I'm ready to do that now. I hated being apart, I couldn't imagine being away from you for the rest of our lives. I don't want that. Do you?"

She swallowed around the lump in her throat. "No. I don't."

"Then, let's work this thing out. Okay?"

"How did you find me?" she asked.

He smirked. "Kate told me you'd be here a few days ago, then I called her for an update when I landed, and she gave me the name of your hotel."

Reeda shook her head with a laugh. "Of course."

"I have my own room, I've been here for a few hours already. But would you go to dinner with me later?" he asked, taking her hand and kissing the back of it.

Her heart thudded inside her chest at his touch, the look in his eyes. She hadn't seen that look in years. It was as if the old Duncan she'd fallen in love with all those years ago was standing in front of her, with a few more lines around his eyes and mouth.

"Yes, dinner would be lovely," she said.

❧ 38 ❧

SEPTEMBER 1996

CASOLI

When Reeda met Duncan in the lobby again, he was dressed in a pair of slacks and a long-sleeved shirt. His hair was parted on one side and slicked back, accentuating the stubble on his square jaw. He'd left his glasses behind and his eyes gleamed in the dim lighting.

Reeda smoothed hands down the blue summer dress she'd bought at a market in Pacentro. Her curves were more prominent than they usually were and made her feel a little self-conscious in front of her husband as his eyes raked over her. She'd found her wedding and engagement rings in her luggage and pushed them back onto her finger before coming downstairs. Her finger had lost its paleness where the rings had been for so many years, an even tan covered the length of it now. The rings felt foreign, and yet familiar, comforting.

"Wow," he said with a grin. "You look amazing. You're glowing. I don't know what you've been doing, but it's obviously been good for you."

She smiled and took his offered hand. He glanced at the rings with a smile, kissed the back of her hand. They strolled along the footpath outside, selecting a *ristorante* with outdoor seating. Stars sparkled in the sky overhead like diamonds on a warm, black blanket.

They sat across from each other and Reeda crossed her ankles beneath the table. A candle glowed in the middle of the white tablecloth, and a single flower leaned to one side in a narrow vase.

They ordered their food, then sipped mineral water while they made small talk. Duncan told her about work, she filled him in on what she'd been up to for the past months in Italy.

She hadn't wanted to tell him about Charlie Jackson while she was in Australia. Thinking back to that time, it seemed like she'd been a different person. So morose, dark, mired in self-pity and rejection. She'd kept her grandfather's secret close to her chest, unwilling to let Duncan in to see her pain.

He listened with interest, interrupting every now and then with a thoughtful question.

"So, all this time, you've been looking for clues about what happened to your real grandfather?" he asked, leaning back in his chair, his mouth agape.

She nodded. "That's part of it. I wanted to come here anyway, but that gave me the final push to book the ticket."

He rubbed a hand over his chin. "And the trail has gone cold here in Casoli?"

She nodded again. "I'm afraid so."

He sighed. "Wow."

"Sorry I didn't tell you about it sooner. I was...struggling with everything that was going on between us. I didn't know how to talk to you. You were so angry..."

He arched an eyebrow. "I was. It wasn't your fault. I don't blame you for not wanting to talk to me about it. I snapped at everything you said. I'm ashamed to admit it now, but I was angry. About everything. The baby situation, the fact that I'm a doctor and couldn't do anything to help you with the one thing you most needed help with...I was frustrated..."

Reeda's brow furrowed. He'd felt guilty about her infertility? She had no idea. "How could you have done anything? You shouldn't take that burden on yourself. We both wanted a baby, a family together, but I was the one who couldn't give us our dreams. It was my fault."

He reached for her hand, lacing his fingers through hers. "It wasn't your fault, sweetheart. This thing we're doing, we're in it together, all the way. Whatever happens to one of us, happens to both. I'm finished with feeling guilty and blaming each other for everything that doesn't work out the way we'd hoped it would."

"Me too," she agreed. She'd had enough of blame, for herself, for Duncan and for her sisters.

When they strolled back to the hotel hand in hand, Reeda felt as though a weight had been lifted from her shoulders. Duncan was there with her, and they were in this together. Even though nothing between them had changed—they still didn't have a baby, he was still a workaholic, they hadn't resolved so many of the issues and fights they'd had over the years—she had hope for the first time that they would. That everything could be made new again, and that life could go on. It might look different than she'd planned so many years earlier when they first made vows to spend forever together, but it would be a good life. Their shared life.

THE NEXT FEW WEEKS WERE SPENT TRAVELLING AROUND

Italy with Duncan. Reeda called the travel agent first thing the next morning to extend the trip, and they rented a car. The first place they drove to was Florence, then up the coast to Venice where they rode in a gondola together and ate copious amounts of gelato. After that, they spent a week in Tuscany, with a day trip to *Cinque Terre*. Finally, they ended up back in Rome, ready to fly home to the Gold Coast.

It was the trip of a lifetime, and Reeda fairly hummed with contentment and joy by the time they climbed on board the plane, hands linked. Duncan had upgraded them to first class, and they snuggled together and watched movies, or slept in their pods, while the plane carried them back to the other side of the globe.

It was everything she'd hoped for. They'd shared a hotel room that first night after all, and every night since. They hadn't discussed the problems they'd faced over the past few years yet but had agreed to do it when they got back to their *real life*. What they needed, they'd both agreed, was to have a holiday, away from the pain and pressures of home. To enjoy each other the way they had when they were first married, and so that's what they did.

When they walked across the tarmac at the Gold Coast international airport, they found Bindi waiting for them by the small, baggage claim carousel. She grinned when she saw Duncan and arched a knowing eyebrow at Reeda.

Reeda laughed, gave Bindi a hug and whispered in her ear. "You and Kate are so busted."

Bindi chuckled. "I don't know what you mean."

Bindi's sandy blonde hair was longer than the last time Reeda had seen it and was pulled back into a bouncing ponytail. Bindi's freckles were darker as well, and she appeared thin beneath the light jacket.

"How are things at the inn?" asked Reeda, as they strode through the parking lot to find Bindi's car.

Bindi shrugged. "Good. We're busy all the time, so I suppose that's a good thing."

"Definitely," agreed Reeda, wondering what it was about Bindi that was bugging her.

She didn't have time to think much more about it though, since the drive home was dominated by conversation between Duncan and Bindi about their travels through Italy.

"I'm so jealous!" declared Bindi. "It sounds amazing. I'm glad you were able to meet up and spend that time together, it's very romantic."

Reeda exchanged a smile with Duncan over her shoulder. He reached forward and squeezed her shoulder with his fingertips. She laughed. He'd been so standoffish for the past few years, now it seemed he wanted to be touching her at all times.

Bindi pulled her Land Rover into the drive at The Waratah Inn. The pale-yellow paint gleamed in the winter sunlight. Mima's trespassing black cat with white socks rubbed against a fence post, tail wrapping lazily around the timber. A sense of peace and wellbeing flooded through Reeda at the sight of the Waratah. She was proud of what they'd done with the inn. It was beautiful.

"Wow," said Duncan beside her, leaning forward in his seat. "It looks amazing. You guys did a great job of fixing it up. I really like the yellow, much better than that dark pink. It looked like a spooky Barbie's dream house before, now it's very inviting."

Reeda laughed. "I've never heard it described that way, but you're right. And thank you. I'm pretty happy with it."

"We love it, and guests seem to as well," Bindi added.

"How is it going?" asked Duncan, as he helped Bindi get the luggage out of the boot.

"Busy, which is good. Kate's taken over in the kitchen, since Mima retired."

"How is Mima?" asked Reeda, feeling a stab of guilt over not calling Mima in months.

"She's great. She loves the retirement community. They have board games, outings, and adventures all the time. She and her friends have a real little gang going over there. Mima's at the centre of it all, of course."

"Of course," replied Reeda with a chuckle.

Inside the inn, guests lounged about in the sitting room playing board games, listening to music, or engaging in conversation. A fire crackled in the hearth, and the room smelled of pine.

Kate was in the kitchen, plaiting strands of fluffy bread dough together. She hugged Reeda, her hands covered in flour, then washed up to sit with them.

"Don't let us interrupt you," said Duncan.

Kate waved a hand as she sat across from them at the kitchen table. "No, it's fine. It has to rise again before I can bake it. I want to hear all about Italy."

Reeda reached for Duncan's hand and threaded her fingers through his, enjoying the warmth, the feeling of belonging to another person, belonging together.

"We had a wonderful time," replied Reeda.

"It looks that way." Kate's gaze slid from Reeda's face to Duncan's and back again, as a grin tickled her lips. "I'm glad. You needed some time to relax. How long has it been since the two of you had a real holiday?"

Reeda and Duncan exchanged a glance. He raised an eyebrow. "Uh, I don't know."

Reeda laughed. "It's been a long time. We got a chance to remember all the things we liked about each other. It was great." What she couldn't say was that they still hadn't resolved things between them. Those conversations were coming, though she hoped to avoid them for as long as possible since she was enjoying Duncan's closeness. Would it stay that way once they'd talked through all the things that'd driven them apart in recent years?

"You look wonderful, Reeda," continued Kate. "Italian life must agree with you."

Reeda's face flushed with warmth. "Thank you."

"No, really, you're so different. I almost wouldn't have recognised you."

"Maybe it's the food, I think I've gained about five kilograms," replied Reeda with a huff.

"You look great," replied Kate. "And I like your hair that way. It's natural and soft. It really suits you."

Reeda smiled. "I feel more like myself than I have in a long, long time. I had a chance to think through some things, and work through other things. It was good. I'll tell you all about it sometime over coffee."

"I'd love that." Kate studied her, still smiling. Reeda could tell what her sister was thinking. She was curious, wanted to know what was going on in her head. Kate never pushed, always waited for Reeda to open up. Often that meant that things remained unsaid between them for far too long.

Upstairs, Reeda and Duncan showered and changed. Duncan said he wanted to go for a walk in the cove, so Reeda stood at the back door and waved goodbye, then went back into the kitchen to help Kate. In truth, she wanted to show off the cooking skills she'd gained in Italy, and to talk to Kate about the inn.

She found Kate staring into the pantry, one hand resting on the door. "I was going to make Italian food tonight, but you're probably sick of that. So, I'm trying to figure out what to cook..."

Reeda looped an arm around Kate's waist and rested her head on Kate's shoulder. "It's good to be home."

Kate kissed her hair. "I'm glad you're back. We missed you."

"Hey, I'm happy to help you come up with an Italian meal tonight. I learned a few tricks while I was there."

Kate arched an eyebrow. "Do tell?"

Reeda chuckled. "Let's have a coffee first. My head is pounding like there's a tiny man with a hammer going to work on my skull."

Kate laughed as she got the coffee percolator out of the cupboard and switched on the kettle to boil.

"I will take you up on that. You can decide on the menu, then. And, we're using fresh vegetables from the garden."

Reeda's eyes widened. "Vegetables you grew?"

Kate nodded.

Reeda shook her head. "Very impressive."

Kate threw her head back and laughed. She seemed more relaxed than she'd been when Nan died the year before. Time spent at the inn had loosened the stiffness she'd carried around in her shoulders. Her eyes sparkled with humour and her skin glowed with a light tan. Kate was thriving at the inn, that much was clear. Likely Alex had a little something to do with it as well.

Bindi walked into the kitchen, her hair piled in a messy bun on top of her head, black rimmed glasses perched on her nose. "What's up?"

"We're having a coffee. Want one?" Reeda reached for the biscuit tin, and pulled out a half dozen Anzac biscuits, fanning them out on a small, white plate.

"Yes, please," replied Bindi. "Although, it'll be strange to not have Mima here to tell me it'll clog my arteries and stunt my growth." She laughed.

They took their mugs of coffee and a plate of Anzac biscuits out to the breakfast nook. Reeda was glad to find it empty. The guests seemed to have trundled off to the beach, the shops or theme parks for the day. The inn was quiet, but for the hum of a vacuum cleaner on the second floor.

Reeda sipped the coffee, leaned her head back against the chair and let her eyes drift shut. "Ah."

"Tired?" asked Bindi.

Reeda nodded. "We flew first class, so it wasn't too bad, but I'm jet lagged."

"How are things with you and Duncan?" asked Kate.

Reeda's eyes opened. She squinted at her sister. So much for not prying. "Good. I suppose. We have some issues to resolve. But we're working on it."

"I'm glad. I was worried about you two." Kate watched her, a frown creasing her forehead.

"Me too," murmured Bindi.

Reeda straightened, set down her coffee mug, and cleared her throat. It was time to tell them. She'd meant to do it months ago, but then Mima had fallen ill and it hadn't felt like the right time. Then, she'd gone to Italy, and she didn't like talking about important things over the phone.

"I never told the two of you what was bothering me last year during the renovation of the inn."

Kate's eyes narrowed. "No, you didn't. I figured you'd come out with it sometime, but you never did."

Reeda swallowed. It was harder than she'd thought. Telling her sisters about her fertility issues felt like admitting defeat. "Duncan and I have been trying to get pregnant for a long time. About five years, actually."

Bindi nodded, her eyes smiling an encouragement for Reeda to continue.

"Anyway, I've had a couple of miscarriages, but otherwise...nothing. It's been really hard on us. On our marriage. On me. On him. We didn't cope well with it. I've been getting hormone shots, and we've been sniping at each other. Well, if I'm honest, it's mostly been me sniping at him and him running away and hiding in his work." She hesitated, watching her sisters for a reaction.

Kate tipped her head to one side and reached out to lay a hand on Reeda's knee. "That must've been hard on you."

Reeda inhaled a quick breath. "It was. I kept hoping, believing it would happen. But every month, I'd buy the pregnancy tests, take them, and they'd always be negative."

She waited for the pain to steal her breath away, to fill her gut with a stone of sorrow that couldn't be shifted. But it didn't come. A vague sadness tinged her words, but it didn't lodge in her heart.

She pushed a smile onto her face. "When we were renovating this place, the reason I stayed on so long was because Duncan and I weren't doing well. We fought all the time; he worked late, I worked late. We hardly saw each other." The memory of that time washed over her. Things were so different now she hardly recognised the person she'd been then. "When I got back to Sydney, Duncan told me things couldn't keep going the way they were. I thought he wanted a divorce."

Kate covered her mouth with one hand.

Bindi gaped. "Really? I'm so sorry, Reeda."

Reeda swallowed down the painful memory. "Thanks. That's why I went to Italy. I needed to get away. Away from him, from the emptiness of my life, from the grief I felt over not having a baby."

Kate stood to embrace Reeda, then knelt beside her chair. "That must've been hard. I wish you'd talked to us about it."

"I couldn't," replied Reeda, wiping a stray tear from the corner of her eye. "It was too difficult, too painful. If I talked about it with anyone, it'd make it real. Some of my friends knew, of course. They knew I wanted to get pregnant and saw that I didn't, even as the months went by. Otherwise, I kept it to myself."

"You seem to be better than you were," said Bindi. "Better than last year."

Reeda nodded. "I am. I found peace about it all. I realised that I can have a life on my own, if I have to. I'd rather share it with Duncan, but if I needed to, I could live a full and satisfying life alone. Even though we'd love children, if we can't have them, we still have each other. It wasn't something I ever thought I'd come to terms with, but now I think I have. Finally." She smiled.

Kate's eyes glimmered with unshed tears. "Definitely, you guys are amazing. You'll have a wonderfully full life no matter what."

"Thanks," replied Reeda, squeezing Kate's hand.

"And how does Duncan feel about it all?" asked Bindi.

Reeda pursed her lips. She hadn't talked to him about it yet, so she didn't know for sure. But something inside him had changed as well. That much was true.

"We're still working through things. But he's changed his mind about the divorce. He wants us to stay together."

"That's good. Isn't it?" prompted Kate.

"It's great," admitted Reeda with a grin. "I was devastated, honestly. I tried to tell myself I could live without him. That he deserved better than I could give him. But the truth is, even though I can do it, I don't want to. He's my soulmate. The one I want to spend the rest of my days with. That hasn't changed."

Bindi's smile widened and she rubbed her eyes with her fingertips, her voice breaking. "Oh, that's beautiful."

Reeda laughed. "Yeah, it is."

"Speaking of beautiful." Kate pushed herself back to her feet and pulled the chair closer to Reeda. "I have something to tell you as well. I wanted to tell you before now, but you've been gallivanting all over the world. So..." Kate laughed.

Reeda rolled her eyes. "All over the world? Only to Italy. Though, who knows where we'll go next. I've got the bug."

"I have some good news. Alex proposed, and I said yes!"

Reeda jumped up and hugged Kate, her throat tight. "Congratulations! That's amazing. You two are perfect for each other."

"You're squeezing the life out of me!" said Kate in a muffled voice.

Reeda released Kate with a laugh. "Sorry."

"Just like Nan used to hug me," replied Kate, with a quick intake of breath.

All three sisters laughed at that.

"I wish she was here. She'd be so happy for you Kate," said Bindi softly.

Kate nodded. "I know. I miss her. But I'm glad I have the two of you with me."

Reeda's heart swelled. She'd missed so much of her sisters' lives because of grief and pain. Because she hadn't wanted to face the past, or a future without a family. She'd buried herself in work, buried the pain deep down inside her, and put up walls around her heart that'd kept everyone out, including her own husband and sisters.

"I'm glad as well. You two are so important to me."

Bindi looped an arm around Reeda. Reeda placed an arm around each of her sisters. The three of them hugged and laughed, as happy tears wet their cheeks.

"Let's see the ring then," demanded Reeda, reaching for Kate's left hand.

Kate waved her ring finger in front of Reeda's face. Reeda held it still with a smile. "It's beautiful."

"Thank you. And there's more," continued Kate, wiping

her cheeks with a sleeve. "Would you be my matron of honour?"

"Yes, of course!" cried Reeda, giving Kate another squeeze.

"I already asked Bindi to be a bridesmaid, and she's agreed. So it'll be the three of us up there. You can give me support and catch me if I faint," joked Kate.

Reeda laughed. "Absolutely. I'm stronger than I look."

❧ 39 ❧

APRIL 1981

CABARITA BEACH

The red of the waratah flowers stood out in stark contrast with the green of their leaves and the dark earth beneath them. Edie dug for a while around the base of the squat trees, loosening the sandy soil. She pushed back onto her haunches and then to her feet with a grunt.

"Getting too old for gardening, huh?" teased Mima from the lounge chair she'd pulled out next to the garden. She lay on her back in a high-cut one-piece swimsuit, sunglasses covering her eyes as the sun warmed her bronzed skin.

Edie chuckled. "Never too old for gardening. And if I was, I'd say you're too old for that swimsuit since you're the same age as me."

Mima laughed, her stomach jiggling beneath the lycra flowers on her suit. "Fair enough."

It'd been almost thirty years since Mima showed up on The Waratah Inn's front step. She'd lived there ever since and had become well known in the area for her famous lamb dishes and the tart flavour of her always delicious lemon meringue pie, using lemons from Edie's garden.

Edie brushed the dirt from her knees and rear end. Everything hurt. Sitting on the ground that way used to be easy, but not anymore. At fifty-six years of age she couldn't kneel for long, tending to her flowers or her vegetable patch, but had to do it in shifts, then take a break to walk around. A few years earlier, Paul had suggested she find something soft to kneel on, but she never had. When he died of a heart attack three years ago, a part of her had died as well.

She sighed, remembering the way he'd come out to visit her in the garden with a cup of tea for her and coffee for him. They'd sit in the rusted metal chairs by the fence and sip their drinks, looking out over their land, the horse paddock, and watching the sun as it dipped towards the horizon in a brilliant display of colours.

There wasn't a day that she didn't miss him. It'd hurt more at first, but now it was a dull ache that never quite faded but that sometimes she forgot about long enough to have a laugh. Having Mima there with her helped. Though, Keith had moved with his wife Mary and their three children to Sydney years earlier. She didn't see them as much as she'd like to, but when she did, it brought her back to life.

"Are you just going to stand there, or get us some tea?" asked Mima, shading her eyes with one hand.

Edie waved her off. "Hold your horses. I'll get to it. My legs are only now getting their feeling back."

Edie put her gardening things in the canvas bag she kept in the garden shed. She tugged off her gloves as she walked, put everything away in the shed, then headed for the inn. It was afternoon and most of the guests were resting or busy on the Gold Coast enjoying the beautiful autumn day. It wouldn't be long before she and Mima would have to head back inside to get started on tea and the evening rush of activities and chores. But for now, there was a lull in the hectic life of an innkeeper.

While the kettle boiled, Edie washed her hands and stared out the kitchen window. She could see Mima, still lying in the sun, swatting at a fly. She smiled to herself. What would she have done all these years without her friend?

Losing Paul had been difficult enough, but especially because she'd never told Keith the truth about his father. She'd meant to talk to him. All those years ago, she'd considered doing it, but Keith had been so small, only three years old. She hadn't thought he'd understand. Then, Paul showed up. Once they were married, she saw what a good father he was to Keith, and she was certain Keith would ask questions one day. But it seemed he'd forgotten that there was a time Paul wasn't in his life. He'd never once asked her anything about it.

Maybe she should broach the subject when he and the family next visited Cabarita.

She carried the two mugs of tea out to the garden and sat beside Mima on the lounge chair.

Mima sipped the tea, then sighed. "This is the good life."

"It sure is."

"Any regrets?" asked Mima.

Edie considered her question. There'd been so much pain in her early life, but those days were long behind her. And even with the way things had worked out, she wouldn't have dodged that pain even if she could've, since that would mean she didn't fall in love with Charlie, and that Keith would never have been born.

"No regrets," replied Edie. "I'm grateful for this inn, for you, for the years I had with my Paul. I love Keith, Mary, and the girls, though I wish they lived a little closer. There isn't anything I'd change. Except perhaps, I'd like to visit home a bit more often. I've only been back to Bathurst a few times over the years. Mum and Dad are so old now, I feel as though they missed out on most of Keith's childhood."

Mima nodded. "I know what you mean. Before Mum died, I'd held onto my resentment towards her for so long I'd forgotten what it was about. I really wish I'd told her how I felt about her, how much she meant to me. I can be stubborn sometimes."

"Stubborn? You're joking...not you?" Edie smirked and Mima slapped her arm.

"I know I'm stubborn, but you're the crazy woman who's put up with me all these years."

"That's very true." Edie leaned over to kiss Mima on the cheek. "And I have absolutely no regrets about that either."

Mima grinned.

"What about you? Any regrets Jemima Everest?"

Mima sighed. "I suppose not. I loved once, and I never could open my heart to love another again."

"Ollie was the one."

"Ollie was the one," agreed Mima. "I know it's crazy, because we didn't spend much time together. But he was the love of my life. I never got over losing him." Mima gulped another mouthful of tea.

Edie nodded and patted Mima's knee. Her mind still stuck on Keith and the truth she'd kept from her son all these years. "Do you think I should tell Keith about Charlie?"

Mima choked on a mouthful of tea, coughing and sputtering until Edie had to thump the middle of her back to help her breathe.

"What brought that on," rasped Mima, still fighting for breath. "You haven't spoken Charlie's name in years."

Edie shrugged. "Just thinking. I wanted to talk to Keith

about his father when I first told him I was his mother. But he was too young, and there was already enough confusion in his life. Then, Paul came along and before I knew it, we were married. He was such a good dad, he loved Keith like his own son. And we were never able to have other children, so I didn't want to take that from him. Keith seemed to accept him as his father, no questions asked, and it felt as though I'd be robbing Paul of the special relationship they shared if I brought Charlie into it."

"I understand." Mima rubbed her forehead with one hand.

"When Charlie's parents died so young, it made it easier to keep from telling Keith the truth."

"Are you saying you regret keeping it from him?" asked Mima.

Edie hesitated. Did she regret it? She wasn't sure she would do anything differently if she had her time over. "I don't think so. I was always grateful for Paul and the way he stepped in to help me raise Keith."

"I think so too. You did the right thing."

"But what about now?" asked Edie, facing her friend with a frown. "Should I tell Keith the truth now that Paul is gone?"

Mima pursed her lips. "I suppose you should ask yourself, why? What would be the purpose of telling him the father he knew wasn't actually his father?"

Edie's throat tightened. Could she get the words out? "Because it's the truth..." her voice faltered.

"I don't know...It seems like it might relieve your mind of some guilt, but would it benefit Keith and his family? What about the girls? They thought of Paul as their grandfather, loved him so much..."

Edie shook her head. "You're right. You're definitely right. I shouldn't do it. It wouldn't be fair on them."

"It's up to you, but if it were me, I wouldn't rock the boat."

Edie finished her tea and stood to her feet with a moan. The tightness in her muscles from the gardening and then ten minutes slumped on the lounge chair sent a twinge of pain up her spine.

"I won't say anything. It might help me feel better to get it off my chest, but it wouldn't do the same for Keith. No, you're right Mima."

"Can I get that in writing?" asked Mima, sliding back into repose on the chair.

Edie laughed. "Good idea. We should record it, since it doesn't happen often."

Mima lunged at her and Edie hopped out of the way laughing. "Thanks Mima, you're a good friend."

"And don't you forget it!"

40

CABARITA BEACH

The glow of sunset glanced off the surface of the lazy, curling waves. Long shadows pulled at the edge of the sand, the shapes of pandanus trees and spinifex grass morphing into long, thin fingers. A cool breeze lifted the hair on the back of Reeda's neck.

She shivered. "It's so beautiful here."

Beside her, Duncan bent at the waist to skip a smooth, round stone across the surface of a spent wave. White froth bubbled by his feet, then collapsed with a sigh as the water carrying it slid back into the ocean.

He smiled and took her hand in his, swinging it back and forth as they walked. The sand was cold beneath her feet.

"You're beautiful," he said.

She laughed.

"No, I mean it. I love your hair that way, with the natural

curls. And all your new curves. It reminds me of when we fell in love."

Reeda pursed her lips. "I'm happier, I guess. More content, with myself, life...I suppose it must show on my face, and in my eating." She laughed.

He kissed the back of her hand. "It does. And I'm glad you're happy. I am too. Happy that we're working things out, that perhaps I won't lose you after all. I was sure we couldn't make it for a long time. It just about killed me."

Reeda pulled Duncan to a stop, faced him with a solemn look. "We still have to talk about everything."

"I know," he said.

She sighed. "For me, things have changed."

"Oh?" He arched an eyebrow. "What's changed?"

"Trying for a baby exhausted me. It took every ounce of strength, energy, positivity...It was on my mind almost every moment of the day. And even though I was working hard, succeeding at my job, it was there in the back of my mind. When I was out with friends, they'd talk about their children, or have babies on the way, and my mind always drifted to my own sadness. I couldn't be happy for them, engage with them about things in their lives. I was consumed with jealousy, anger, spite. I don't want to live that way anymore."

"I agree. I know it wasn't as difficult for me, given that it wasn't my body going through the hormone treatments and the pregnancy tests, but I felt it too."

She traced a line down his cheek with a fingertip. "I know you did. But I didn't realise that at the time. I thought you were avoiding me, avoiding the pain I was going through. I thought you didn't care." A sob caught in her throat. It hurt to let the words out, to admit she'd believed that about him.

He pressed his lips together in a hard line and swallowed. "No. I cared; I just couldn't deal with the sadness. My job...I have a lot of sadness and people's emotions to contend with at work all day long. When I come home, it's hard to take on more of it. I know that's not fair, I didn't do right by you, but sometimes...sometimes I couldn't be there for you. It went on for so long, was so constant."

"I'm sorry," she whispered, her heart tearing at the edges. "Sorry for all of it."

He cupped her cheeks with his hands and kissed her lips softly. "It's not your fault."

"But taking it out on you was my fault. And I'm sorry I did that."

He smiled, kissed her again. "I'm sorry I couldn't handle it, that I wasn't strong enough."

He looped an arm around her shoulders, and they set off again, walking towards the sunset. She glanced at her husband. The glow of the sinking sun gave him an angelic look. A few grey hairs around his temples reminded her they were getting older, time had passed. She'd regretted so much of their years together, the grief, the way she'd behaved, their fights. She didn't want to live with any more regrets.

"I don't want to try any longer," she said.

He studied her as they walked.

"I mean, I don't want to try to get pregnant. I spent a lot of time thinking about it while I was in Italy, and I've decided to let it go. If it happens, it happens, if it doesn't...we have a pretty great life together. Don't we? At least we could...I think."

He squeezed her closer, his arm around her shoulders, and kissed the top of her head. "We could. I really think we could."

"I can be happy without a child. I never thought I'd be able to say that, but there it is. I can live a full and happy life without children. Do you think you can?" As the words left her mouth, she kept her eyes on the horizon, hoping.

He chuckled. "If you're with me, I'm happy. We don't

need kids for that. I would've loved to have children, but if that's not going to happen for us, I can accept it. Life is going to throw us a few curve balls, I want us to get better at dealing with those things, without turning against each other."

Tears blurred her vision. "Yes, me too. I want to be for you, not against you."

"Absolutely."

"I don't want to always be striving for something I don't have. There's so much joy to be found in the simple things, in love." She faced him. "That goes for my career as well. Every part of my life. I want to appreciate what I have instead of always wanting more. It's made me miserable."

He cupped her chin with one hand and leaned forward until his lips hovered over hers, his eyes fixed on hers, full of depth, intensity, love.

He kissed her. "You're amazing. I love you, Reeda."

"I love you too."

🦋 41 🦋

SEPTEMBER 1996

CABARITA BEACH

Reeda rolled over in bed, stretching her arms over her head. She'd overslept. The other side of the bed was empty, she patted at it with one hand, her vision still blurred. The space beside her was no longer warm, which meant Duncan had been up for a while. She yawned again, pushed back the covers, shivered, thought better of it, and pulled them beneath her chin again. With a smile she rolled onto her side, eyes squeezed shut.

Wellbeing and a sense of peace rushed to fill her soul.

Kookaburras laughed in the distance, along with the soft roar of waves as they crashed rhythmically to shore and the chirp of willy wagtails as they ducked and dived between the eaves and the nearest tree.

The door to the room squeaked open. "Are you awake yet, sleepy head?" asked Duncan.

Reeda's eyes popped open and she rubbed them with her fingertips. "Just."

"I got us breakfast," he replied.

He carried a tray into the room, opened the legs on the bottom of the tray and set it on her lap. She sat up, careful not to overturn the tray, and smiled. Scrambled eggs, fruit toast, and a cup of coffee. Her stomach grumbled and mouth watered.

"Where's yours?" she asked.

He laughed. "I'm going to get it from the kitchen now. I thought we could eat breakfast in bed together."

He disappeared through the open door, his footsteps thudding down the staircase. Reeda smiled, her heart full, the scent of coffee in her nostrils. She scanned the room, proud of the way the decor pulled together the historical legacy of the regal old building, and the modern look and feel of a stylish boutique inn. Subtle yellow and grey stripes wallpapered one end of the room, coupled with a matching yellow paint for the rest of the room. The hardwood floors held a lush, wool rug in a pale shade of grey. The light timber furniture was accented in yellows, greys and whites as well. The entire thing pulled together by an antique chandelier that hung over the centre of the bed.

Duncan soon returned with his own tray, shut their door, and sidled into bed next to Reeda. She pushed up against him, so their legs were touching as they ate.

"I've been thinking," he began.

She arched an eyebrow, chewing on a mouthful of eggs. "Hmmm?"

"I don't want us to go back to our old life in Sydney."

Reeda swallowed. "Okay. What does that mean?"

"This is the happiest we've been...well, at least it's the happiest I've been...in five years. The idea of going back to that house...my job...it makes my stomach churn."

Reeda took a swig of coffee, immediately burned her tongue, then set the cup back on the tray with a grimace. "Ouch. Hot."

He chuckled. "You always do that."

"Do not," she objected.

"Yes, you do. The coffee's hot and you burn your tongue." His eyes twinkled.

She couldn't help laughing. "Oh yeah? Well you...you always trip over the threshold."

"What?" His brow furrowed.

"You do. Wherever we go, you're always carrying too many things in your arms, and you're not thinking about what you're doing, and you trip on the threshold." A laugh bubbled up inside Reeda.

Duncan's frown evaporated and he laughed along with her. "You're right. I do, don't I?"

She nodded, still giggling. "Anyway, what's this about wanting to quit your job?"

His eyes narrowed. "I didn't say I wanted to quit my job... although now that you mention it, maybe I do. I never thought about it that way, but the idea of leaving is pretty enticing."

Reeda gaped. She'd been joking about him quitting his job. She'd never in a million years have guessed he'd go for the idea. She'd thought about it time and time again herself, but he loved his job, was so committed to it. It brought him fulfilment and satisfaction. She didn't think he'd ever be willing to give that up.

"Are you serious?" she asked.

He nodded. "Very serious. While we were in Italy, I spent some time thinking about our lives, about us, what we're doing, where we're going...I realised something—it's been a long time since I sat down and thought about the direction I want my life to take. I've been letting life carry me along like I'm a leaf in a stream. I don't want that anymore."

Reeda took another sip of coffee, mulling over his words. "I think you're right. We don't live the life we want, we let things happen, but we don't make them happen. I'm not expressing it very well, but I think I know what you're talking about."

He grinned. "No, you've got it. If we both sit down together and think about what we want our lives to look like, will we come up with the life we've got? Or something completely different?"

Reeda took a bite of fruit toast, chewing slowly as she stared at the wall. She'd pushed herself to start a business soon after university. She'd yearned for success, and she'd achieved it. But after success, what came next?

"What would we do? Where would we go?" she asked.

He shrugged. "Anything we want, and anywhere we like."

A bubble of excitement welled in her gut. They could do anything, what was stopping them? If Duncan was willing to try something new, she was too, and there was nothing holding them back.

"What about here?" she asked.

"What, Cabarita?" He faced her, setting down a forkful of eggs.

"Yes, we could live nearby. I could help out at the inn and build up my own small decorating business. There's a hospital in Tweed Heads, and others on the Gold Coast where you could work...We both love it here. There's really nothing keeping us in Sydney, and I feel as though I have my sisters back. Besides, Kate's getting married...I don't want to miss out on all the important parts of their lives anymore." Her throat tightened as the words poured out. She hadn't realised the longing deep down inside her to return to the place she'd called home for such a short part of her life, but that'd somehow taken hold of her heart.

Duncan rested a hand on her cheek, then leaned forward to kiss the top of her nose, followed by her lips. "That sounds amazing."

"Really? You'd consider moving here?"

He nodded, returning his attention to the eggs. "Yes, why not? It's beautiful, I love the beach, I've always wanted to learn to surf, but haven't had the time. Besides, I've been thinking about spending some time volunteering for Doctors Without Borders. I could work at one of the nearby hospitals part-time and volunteer as well. I don't want to keep working as though it's the only thing in my life. I want more than that."

Reeda felt as though her heart might burst. She let out a cry, pushed aside the tray, and reached for her husband. As their lips met, all the fears, the grief, the dreams quashed and the conflict between them was washed away by the hope for a new future. A future built on love, family, and the kind of life she'd previously only dreamed of.

She could sell her business easily enough—she'd had plenty of offers over the years. It didn't hold the same appeal to her that it used to, and she'd barely set foot in the place during the past year. Karen ran it as though it were her own, and perhaps she'd want to buy it from Reeda. She was surprised how little turmoil the idea of selling it prompted within her. She and Duncan could move to Cabarita Beach. They'd buy a place overlooking the ocean, she could visit the inn whenever she liked and be part of Kate and Bindi's lives.

"Let's do it," she said.

EPILOGUE

CABARITA BEACH

A clock on the wall ticked loudly as each hand inched around the circular, white face. The dark bricks behind it contrasted with the white furniture in the room, and the white tiled floor. Bindi Summer slid her Reeboks over the slick surface and the rubber bottoms squeaked on the tiles.

She inhaled a long, slow breath in an attempt to calm her breathing.

The door opened and a man in a long, white coat stepped through the opening, leaving it ajar behind him.

"Sorry about that, Bindi," he said.

"No worries, Doctor Ash." She sat on her hands to keep from fidgeting.

The doctor sat behind his desk and adjusted the half-moon glasses perched on the end of his long, bony nose. "Let's see." He flicked through some papers on his desk. "I've

343

been looking over your symptoms, and I don't think we can pinpoint the issue yet. Are you still feeling tired and short of breath?"

She nodded, wrapping her arms around her waist.

"And I see from your chart you've lost a bit of weight. Are you dieting?"

Bindi pursed her lips. "I'm not dieting."

"Okay, well that helps us..." He smiled at her, his eyes meeting hers over the top of his glasses. "Don't worry, we'll figure this thing out. I'd like you to get some blood tests. Okay?"

She nodded again.

"And then, we'll call you when the results come in to make another appointment. We'll decide on next steps when we know more."

When she walked out of the doctor's surgery, Bindi's legs trembled beneath her. She had to sit on a public bench with peeling brown paint and black graffiti lettering that read, "HM". Whatever that meant. It gave her something to focus on though, something to distract her spinning mind.

She leaned forward, pressing her elbows to her knees, and staring at the ground while she took measured breaths. What was happening to her? She didn't feel good but looked fine. The doctor couldn't figure it out and now she had to get blood tests. She was young and strong though, only twenty-eight years old. Surely it couldn't be anything serious.

As soon as she could breathe again without getting dizzy, she stood to her feet and wandered across the car park. The Land Rover was parked at the other end. She wished for a moment she'd parked closer to the surgery door. It was just a panic attack; she could handle it. She'd certainly handled worse before now.

She reached the car, climbed in, and steadied her nerves before turning the key in the ignition. The drive home was soothing. She flicked on the radio and found a station playing The Cranberries. The lead singer's voice enveloped her like honey. The long, narrow highway slid by beneath the SUV's tyres, and to her left, pandanus, spinifex and rolling sand dunes blocked her view of the long, golden beach she knew was there. She spotted it every now and then through gaps in the foliage and it brought a smile to her face.

She'd moved to Cabarita from Melbourne when Nan died, and she'd never considered going back. She loved it there, always had. Even when she was a girl, it'd been her favourite place to visit. After they lost their parents, she'd spent some time running from the place and the memories it held, but now it was her home and she had no intention of leaving it.

When she pulled into the drive, she saw Jack touching up the paint on a verandah railing. He waved the paint brush in her direction, then returned to his work. She pulled the vehicle around the side of the house to the newly renovated garage. When she switched off the engine, the garage was plunged into silence. One thing you couldn't argue about the Waratah, it had to be one of the most peaceful places on earth. At least on the outside.

Inside, kitchen staff raced about, and waiters hurried plates of food to the dining room. It was lunchtime at The Waratah Inn, and the scent of freshly cooked meats, salad dressings, and fresh fruit drifted out to greet her. Bindi's stomach grumbled and clenched, reminding her she hadn't eaten breakfast that morning.

"There you are!" called Kate above the din. "Where have you been?" Kate wiped down the edge of a plate of sliced tropical fruits and handed it to a waiter.

"I had a few things to do in town. Did you need me for something?"

"I was trying to get into my email earlier and couldn't get

online. It's probably user error, but I thought you might give it a try?" Kate smiled, arching an eyebrow.

Bindi chuckled. "Fine, I'll try. But you probably forgot to connect to the internet or something."

Kate clicked her fingers. "You know, that's it. I didn't do the whole dial-up thingy."

Bindi rolled her eyes as she walked through the kitchen to the office beyond it. "What would you do without me?"

"I wouldn't make it past Tuesday!" shouted Kate to her retreating back. Bindi laughed.

She sat at the desk, flicked on the computer, and waited while it booted up. She never could've imagined how much she'd enjoy working with her sister. And now that Reeda and Duncan had decided to move north as well, she was happier than she'd been in years. Her family, what was left of it, was finally coming back together. She'd longed for it, talked to Nan about it, hoped it would happen, but never believed in her heart that it would.

The computer screen blinked to life and she double-clicked the icon to get the dial-up modem to connect to the internet. It buzzed, hummed a melody, then connected. Bindi opened the email program and browsed through the inbox. There were a few emails from friends in Melbourne, some for Kate, since they shared an email address.

One email stood out and her heart fell. It was from Brendan. Her ex-boyfriend who'd dumped her after six years because he needed time to think about his life.

She leaned back in the chair and linked her hands behind her head to stare at the screen. She didn't want to open the message. Or she did. She wasn't sure which. Her heart raced. What could he have to say to her? The last time she'd spoken to him on the phone, he'd told her he'd met someone else, they were in love, and were getting married. This, after telling her repeatedly for six long years that he wasn't the marrying kind.

After a full minute, Bindi relented and clicked the mouse to open the message.

Hey Bindi,

I wanted to check in with you and see how things are going up north. I bet it's warmer than it is here. Haha! It's freezing. But you know all about that.

The last time we spoke, it didn't end well. I know I hurt you, and I'm sorry about that. I want to come up there and visit you. To say the things I should've said in person before you left.

Would that be okay with you?

Let me know. I hope you'll say yes, because I need to see you.

With love, Brendan xo

Bindi wrinkled her nose. He wanted to come to the inn? To see her, after he'd told her he proposed to someone else? That didn't make sense. Why would he travel all this way to rub it in? Or maybe he truly did want to make it up to her, perhaps even tell her he was sorry for wasting so many years of her life when he didn't love her. She wasn't sure a confession like that would really help her like him better or forgive him for what he'd done.

She stood to her feet and paced across the narrow room, stopping below a big map of the world that was pinned to the wall. What should she say? She had no reason to stop him from coming. He was a free person and could do what he liked. And maybe he had something to say to her, something that would help her move past his treatment of her. She was stronger than he'd ever given her credit for. If he needed closure, she wouldn't stand in his way.

She sat at the keyboard to type her response. If Brendan

was coming to the Waratah, she'd welcome him as a friend. After all, they'd spent six years in a relationship, she could be his friend.

The rest of the afternoon she spent on paperwork in the office. She managed to snag a plate of lunch and a cup of tea, but otherwise kept mostly to herself. After dinner she watched a movie alone in her room, then padded down the stairs looking for a bit of light supper once the inn had fallen quiet.

She found some Anzac biscuits in the biscuit tin, grabbed a couple of them with a glass of milk and headed out to the verandah. The noise of laughter and conversation drew her around the corner where she found Kate and Alex seated in two rocking chairs.

Cocoa the possum sat on Kate's shoulder and Kate was fussing about the possum's long nails digging into her skin. Every time Alex tried to dislodge the creature, it seemed to dig in deeper still, sending Kate into a fit of giggles with Alex laughing just as hard at her reaction.

"Hi," said Bindi.

Mid-laugh, Kate looked up with tears of laughter in her eyes. "Bindi, please help me. Cocoa is refusing to budge, and I think it's because she doesn't like Alex."

"Hey, that possum loves me. All animals love me," objected Alex, pretending to pout.

Bindi chuckled and reached for Cocoa, who immediately relented and climbed Bindi's shirt to sit on Bindi's shoulder. Since she was wearing a light jacket, she didn't mind the nails as much. She wondered where the baby was, and soon saw the smaller possum perched on a verandah rail nearby. It still wasn't sure about being petted but had edged closer to them lately.

"How did you do that?" asked Alex, his eyes wide. "That possum hates me."

"I told you," replied Kate with a laugh.

Alex lunged for her, tickling her ribs until she begged him to stop. Bindi watched them both with a smile. It was good to see Kate so happy. Alex was just the right kind of man for her sister. If only she could find someone as suited to her, someone who would love her the way Alex loved Kate.

She sighed and faced the ocean, pressing her hands to the verandah railing. The moment she did, Cocoa jumped lightly down and walked along the railing, her tail curled behind her.

"Did you have a good day?" asked Kate.

Bindi turned to face her, leaning against the railing. "It was fine. How about you?"

"Great. I had a go at sketching out my ideas for The Waratah Restaurant. I'll show you tomorrow."

"Wonderful." Kate wanted to open the Waratah's restaurant to the public. They still had a little money left over after the renovation and all three sisters had agreed that a restaurant was exactly the right kind of thing to add to their offerings, especially given that Kate was a well-known chef and had already generated some buzz for the inn with her delicious menu.

"You seem a bit low today, love," replied Kate, her eyes full of concern.

Bindi smiled. "I guess I am. But I'll be fine, it's nothing. I got an email from Brendan, that's all." She didn't want to say anything about her trip to the doctor. So far, she didn't know for sure that anything was wrong, and there was no need to alarm her family over a maybe.

"What did he want?" asked Alex.

Bindi shrugged. "He's coming to visit."

"Oh. That's good...I guess. Is that good?" Kate's brow furrowed.

"It's fine. He's engaged to someone else. I probably didn't tell you that."

Kate's eyes widened. "Really? I'm sorry Bindi."

Bindi hugged herself. "It's fine. We've been broken up for ages, so I'm happy for him." She wasn't sure that was true, but she wanted it to be.

"Good for you," replied Alex with a warm smile.

"So, why is he coming to visit then?" asked Kate.

Bindi shrugged. "I'm not sure. I guess I'll find out when he gets here."

THE END

ALSO BY LILLY MIRREN

The Waratah Inn

Wrested back to Cabarita Beach by her grandmother's sudden death, Kate Summer discovers a mystery buried in the past that changes everything.

One Summer in Italy

Reeda leaves the Waratah Inn and returns to Sydney, her husband, and her thriving interior design business, only to find her marriage in tatters. She's lost sight of what she wants in life and can't recognise the person she's become.

The Summer Sisters

Set against the golden sands and crystal clear waters of Cabarita Beach three sisters inherit an inn and discover a mystery about their grandmother's past that changes everything they thought they knew about their family...

Christmas at The Waratah Inn

Liz Cranwell is divorced and alone at Christmas. When

her friends convince her to holiday at The Waratah Inn, she's dreading her first Christmas on her own. Instead she discovers that strangers can be the balm to heal the wounds of a lonely heart in this heartwarming Christmas story.

GLOSSARY OF TERMS

Dear reader,

Since this book is set in Australia there may be some terms you're not familiar with. I've included them below to help you out! I hope they didn't trip you up too much.

Cheers, Lilly xo

༄༅

Terms

Beanie - a warm, knitted hat

Billy - a tin can used for boiling tea

Boot - car trunk

Brickie - a brick layer

Chook - another term for chicken (the bird, not the food)

A cuppa - a cup of hot tea or coffee

Eisteddfod - competition or festival of literature, music and performance

Fritz or *Jerry* - colloquialism used by Australian and British soldiers in the second world war for Germans

Lift - elevator

Loo - toilet

'Love' - a term of endearment for anyone from your spouse to a perfect stranger

Lurgy - a germ, cold or flu

Penny - pet name for the Kittyhawk fighter jet

Post - mail

Postbox - mailbox

Ringtail possum - adorable, furry marsupial with a curling tail, grey-brown coat, big eyes and small pink nose

Rugged-up - covered in warm clothing

Smoko - taking a break, to have something to eat and drink, or to smoke a cigarette

Tea - used to describe either a hot beverage made from leaves, or the evening meal

Wowser - an insult, meaning puritanical or teetotaller

DISCUSSION GUIDE

Book Club Questions

1. Did Reeda misunderstand Duncan?

2. What were some of the things Reeda was struggling with in her life?

3. When was the moment Reeda knew she loved her husband and wanted a second chance?

4. Should Reeda have gone to Italy the way she did?

5. Why did Reeda leave her business behind without seeming concerned about it?

6. How did Mima cope with the loss of her fiancé?

7. Did Edie do the right thing in moving away from Keith, to be a nurse in Sydney?

8. Did Edie have a right to go back to Bathurst and want to be Keith's mother?

9. Why does Reeda so strongly feel the need to find out about what happened to Charlie Jackson?

10. Did Reeda and Duncan make the right decision in moving to Cabarita?

ABOUT THE AUTHOR

Lilly Mirren lives in Brisbane, Australia with her husband and three children.

Lilly always dreamed of being a writer and is now living that dream. She is a graduate of both the University of Queensland, where she studied International Relations and Griffith University, where she completed a degree in Information Technology.

When she's not writing, she's chasing her children, doing housework or spending time with friends.

Lilly is also a bestselling romance author under the pen name *Vivi Holt*.

Sign up for her newsletter and stay up on all the latest Lilly book news.

And follow her on:

Website: lillymirren.com
Facebook: https://www.facebook.com/authorlillymirren/
Twitter: https://twitter.com/lilly_mirren
BookBub: https://www.bookbub.com/authors/lilly-mirren

CPSIA information can be obtained
at www.ICGtesting.com
Printed in the USA
LVHW011206221219
641390LV00004B/223